Runaway Train
The Dominion Falls Series 5

Sarah Cass

Historical Romance
Romantic Suspense
Historical Western Romance

A Divine Roses Ink Book
Historical Romance
Romantic Suspense
Historical Western Romance

PUBLISHER
Divine Roses Ink
http://www.divinerosesink.com

　　　　　　　　　　　　　　　　　　Sarah Cass

Other Books in
The Dominion Falls Series

Independent Brake
Changing Tracks
Derailed
Dark Territory
Green Eye
Home Signal
Red Zone

Coming Soon in
The Dominion Falls Series

Dust Raiser
Chase the Red
Blizzard Lights
Dead Man's Switch
Bird Cage
A Highball Arrangement
Douse the Glim
Blood
Grave Digger
Bad Order

Books by Sarah Cass
The Tribe Series
The Tribe
The Wolf
The Chief
The Raven
The Lake Point Series
Santa, Maybe
Deep-Fried Sweethearts
Stalled Independence
Witch Way
A Thorough Thanksgiving
Eve's New Year
Heartstrings & Hockey Pucks
Luck of the Cowgirl
Stars, Stripes & Motorbikes
Free Falling
Love for Hire
Haunted Hearts
Stand Alone Novels
Masked Hearts
Leap

Dedication

To Dad.
I love you. I miss you.

Table of Contents

Every heart sings a song, incomplete, until another heart whispers back. Those who wish to sing always find a song. At the touch of a lover, everyone becomes a poet.
—Plato

"I'm sorry." Al hovered at the door rather than enter the room.

"You should be." The words erupted with unnecessary harsh bitterness, but the pounding of Jane's head didn't leave her in a good enough temperament to care as she should. She stared in the mirror to assess the damage done while she could tolerate standing.

Al straightened, his worried features dissolving in a flash of hurt. "It was wrong of me—"

"Please, stop." Jane cut him off. She'd been kept awake all night. Mike refused to leave the room, which meant she hadn't been able to check on Cole. She brushed her fingers along her stitches with the lightest touch she could. "I know you didn't intend for any of this. You meant the greatest kindness, but your good heart put me in a terrible bind."

"I merely wanted to give you a choice, where maybe you thought you had none."

"I know. I appreciate the thought, if not the gesture." She turned from the mirror to face him. "My biggest struggle is always to balance logic and my heart. Your proposal stuck me right in the middle of that constant battle. Logically, to help Lizzie as much as I want to, it made perfect sense."

He bowed his head to stare at the floor. The muscles in his cheek worked as he flexed his jaw. Only a hint of emotion betrayed the thoughts behind his next words. "You want more."

"More than a marriage of convenience?"

"That's all it would have been to you?"

"Yes." Another wave of pressure hit her behind the eyes with a threat to make the room spin again. She pressed her fingers to the bridge of her nose until it passed. Despite the lingering muddy movement of her thoughts, she pressed forward. "You have always been a good friend, Al. I won't deny that. We may have even flirted at more once, but I have never loved you."

"Don't need love for a marriage."

"Al." She leaned on the back of a nearby chair. "I do not wish to be asked for logic's sake. Nor with the hope that one day I *may* love the man I marry. That would not be fair to me, or my husband. It certainly would not be fair to Lizzie. She was raised in a home filled with love; she doesn't need to be dropped into a family of convenience."

He kept his head bowed, the smallest of nods his only acknowledgment she'd spoken.

She took a deep, shaky breath in his lingering silence. "You are a good man, and you have a good heart. You deserve better, too. You deserve to find a woman you can propose to knowing she loves you, and only you, rather than an infuriatingly stupid man."

"It was never a real choice, then."

"Not for me."

Al lifted his head finally, a weak attempt at a smile creasing his features. "Even before I asked, I had a thought you wouldn't say yes."

"I appreciate your attempt to give me the option, even if it had disastrous consequences for us all." She crossed to the door so she could take his hands in hers. "Go home, Al. Find a life for yourself. Find someone that loves you the way—"

"You love Cole."

"The way you deserve to be loved. You know it wasn't me."

"Always did."

She gave him the briefest of hugs before she stepped back several feet. "I will miss you, but for the sake of your face, it might be best if you leave sooner rather than later."

"What about you?" The sadness he'd carried darkened into concern.

"I'll be fine." She touched her forehead. "I always am. We'll find Lizzie a good home, and I shall be content with that."

"That isn't what I meant." Apparently she hadn't pulled far enough away, for he was able to capture her wrist in a gentle grasp. "About Cole."

"No need to worry. Cole and I always work things out. Don't worry." She smiled but tugged her hand free again. "If you hadn't interrupted, it's a good chance the whole town would have seen how fast things get resolved between us."

"Jane."

"Really." She huffed her frustration and the incessant questions. "We fight. Often that means we yell at each other before we can talk. Over the past couple of years we've learned to not do so in such a public forum. This was an extreme case. We are hot heads. Everything we do is passionate."

"He grabbed you." Al frowned. "Held you in place."

"Oh. That? Really?" Realization dawned to replace her confusion, if not all of her annoyance. Despite her headache, she laughed. "That wasn't anything. Cole would never hurt me intentionally. The 'grabbing' you saw was barely a touch. I stayed because I was willing to see it out, not because he was hurting me or using any sort of force."

One brow rose. Al folded his arms across his chest. "Jane."

"Oh, honestly." She unbuttoned her sleeve to her elbow, annoyed at the amount of time it took to get him off the subject. The sleeve finally loose enough, she yanked it up to reveal the length of her arm. The skin remained smooth, unmarred by even the smallest of bruises. "See? No bruising. He did not hold me in a vice grip, and he never would. He doesn't hit women, least of all me. We both yell, quite a lot sometimes. Then we stop."

His frown remained, the doubt creasing his forehead clung like molasses.

"If he was hurting me on a regular basis, don't you think those Young boys would have dropped him off a cliff a long time ago? He's occasionally stupid, blind, ignorant—well, in short, he's a man. You'd understand what that's like." She smirked at her own joke, even if Al didn't follow suit. "But he gets a good strong dose of my own stupidity as well."

He eyed her arm the whole time she took to replace her sleeve. "I suppose I'm going to have to take you at your word, aren't I?"

"I don't lie, Al. At least, I try very hard not to. Trust that my brothers know how to protect me, and there's a big enough lot of them around. Go home. Write letters to tell me about the life you find there. That is what I need from you. That is *all* I need from you."

"Do you promise to take care of yourself?"

"As well as I always do."

"I'd truly prefer you say better than you always do."

She grinned. The action made the stitches throb, but she kept it in place. "I just said I don't lie. You're asking an awful lot of me to agree to such a thing. Best I can offer is that I will try."

This time he dared to cross the threshold. He enveloped her in a warm hug. "I never meant to hurt you."

"I know. I hold no hard feelings, I can't say the same of others, though." She fought the urge to kiss him on the cheek as she might have done days ago, blissfully unaware of how accurate Cole's suspicions would have panned out. Rather than linger, she stepped out of the hug. "Now go home. Send a telegraph when you arrive safe."

He tipped his hat to her, then turned to leave. She closed the door on his retreating footsteps. A sigh of relief at having one mess cleared up slipped free. She leaned against the door to let the latest flash of dizziness pass.

Another mess remained. The one she hadn't seen since the day before, and by all accounts had not come into the clinic to have his wounds checked. Jane could only imagine what state Cole might be in after all that had happened.

As the man hadn't come by at all during the night-long struggle to keep her awake, she could only imagine two scenarios. Either he blamed her, which was to be expected. Or he hated himself for what he'd done. Quite possibly, it could be both.

It wouldn't do.

They needed to talk. No amount of Daisy's orders to stay put for 'observation' would make her remain when things were so askew and unresolved with Cole. She had to, at the very least, see him. To talk to him, explain what had happened and clear the air would be the only thing to resolve her restless worry.

Once she had that done, she'd return promptly and let them keep fussing if needed.

If everything went well, she could even be back before she was missed.

Jane moved across the room quiet as could be until she reached the balcony doors. The distant whistle of the train signaled its approach. If Al had been quick enough, he could be leaving on that very train.

She pulled open the doors, taking a deep breath of air. Below her the street bustled with activity, shouts echoed from the next street over. Horses whinnied; the faint stench of their droppings carried under the smell of cooking from the nearby café. Now that the town had more store fronts than carts, voices of vendors bellowed through the town. They all sought to be rediscovered in their proper shops rather than the thoroughfare they'd once crowded.

The normality of the day around her soothed the chaos in her own mind. The tension in her shoulders eased. Some days the comfort of home was all she needed. She crossed to the stairs in a rush only to be forced to pause. The view down the steps made her head swim once again. She gripped the railing to ease her unsteady gait.

After a few breaths she felt steady enough to begin her descent, although she kept her gaze fixed on the railing the whole way down. Once on the secure surface of the packed dirt of the alley, she allowed herself to move quicker. She bolted across the street to the Inn which stood kitty-corner from the clinic.

Within seconds of crossing the threshold, about ten hands pointed toward the room she shared with Cole upstairs. She hadn't even had to ask. After a smile of gratitude, she crossed the saloon to climb the stairs.

"Just where do you think you're going?" Tommy's boots blocked her way.

She frowned at them before she risked tilting her head back to meet his gaze. Thankfully the room didn't spin too bad from the action. "Where do you think?"

"Janey."

"You already took it upon yourself to deal with it, didn't you? He didn't want to hit me, and you know it."

A smile tugged the corner of his mouth, but he kept it in check. He descended two steps to make it easier for her to see him, or so she thought. He tucked his finger under her chin. Once he tilted her head one way, then the other, his gaze set on her stitches, he shrugged. A wicked smirk brightened his expression. "Aren't you supposed to be under observation?"

"I slipped out."

"Daisy'll have your head."

"Then I suppose I'll need you to distract her so that Cole and I can talk."

"Talk?" He pursed his lips, but the wicked gleam remained in his bright blue eyes.

"What has he been doing?"

"Nothing." His expression darkened. With a sigh, he cast a glance across the building toward where her room sat. "At least nothing that I know of."

"Did you tell him I wanted to see him?"

"I did. Told him he'd regret it if he didn't. He said he had enough regrets for a lifetime. Kicked me out. No one has heard a peep since."

"Then talking is exactly what we'll be doing. May I pass?"

He stepped to the side, not without a begrudging sigh, though. When she playfully rubbed his round belly, he glowered. "Quiet."

"I think your girlfriend is angry. You should go get her some more food."

"You want another concussion?"

She grinned, but ascended the steps rather than risk him not helping distract Daisy. Nerves kicked in with every step closer to her room, unsure what she'd find on the other side. After a shaky breath, she slipped her key free from her reticule to unlock the door she was sure he'd locked against any intrusion as if anyone would dare enter his room. She slipped in fast, not checking the room before she leaned against the door with a small sigh.

Silence lingered long enough she thought he might be asleep. When she passed the wall that blocked all view from the door into the room, she found him sitting on their bed, hands clasped between his knees. One eye was bruised over, almost swollen shut. His lower lip had a gash that had scabbed. Bruises lined his knuckles as he rubbed them gently.

She couldn't have stopped her gasp of worry if she'd tried. Tears slipped down her eyes when he jerked away from her touch. "Cole."

"Ya better go. Get on out of here."

"No. I am not leaving right now. Not until we've talked. Look at me."

"I know what I done to ya." Bitterness seeped from every inch of him. His muscles tense, gaze averted so she could see another deep bruise blossoming on his jaw.

"Cole. Please, look at me." She cupped his cheek. Though he didn't jerk away this time, she needed to use some effort to drag his gaze to hers.

His clear eye echoed with pain she hadn't seen in a while. Though she wanted to reassure him, she couldn't help but peruse every wound on his flesh.

Gently, she brushed her fingers along the bruises. Regret surged to join the pained tears she couldn't stop. "Oh, Cole."

"I hit ya. You shouldn't." His voice caught; regret pierced his brow. As if he couldn't help himself, he bowed his head forward until it came to rest on her stomach.

She ran her fingers through his hair with a gentle touch. Her lip trembled, and for a few minutes words failed her. To cover the silence, she rubbed her hands along his back. After a few moments to regain her senses, she took a ragged breath. "You'd never hurt me on purpose. You've never hurt me before, and what happened, it wasn't your fault. I'm the one that jumped into the middle of that fight. I should have known better."

"Don't make it right."

She closed her eyes. "You didn't mean to. You wouldn't ever."

"I hurt ya."

"Yes." She wasn't sure now if he was speaking of her physical injuries. Closing her eyes, she prayed for an answer this time as she whispered, "Where did you go?"

"What did you say?"

"Al is leaving. I told him to go home, to find his own life. I told him his offer was kind, but I didn't want a proposal, or a marriage, for that reason. I certainly didn't want a marriage of convenience. I didn't want to be asked so I could selfishly give a child a home that was mine, for my own wishes. It wouldn't be fair to any of us…and most of all; he is not the man I love. I could never love him. I love you."

"But you considered it, didn't you?" He straightened to meet her gaze, though his hands lingered on her hips. "Because ya thought he could give you something I couldn't."

"No." She dropped to her knees, positioned between his legs. "I considered it for the slightest moment, but only for Lizzie. I did not entertain the idea for any fool reason like you might be any less than I have ever wanted you to be."

"Was he right? Did you wanna be asked?"

"I…" She paused, surprised by the answer she had been about to give. She had to be honest, as she'd always tried to be with him. As much as admitting the truth worried her, as he'd scared so easily before, she still had to tell him. "I suppose part of me did. However, even if you'd gone against what you wanted to do and asked me, I probably would have said no."

"You so sure it's against what I wanted?"

She grew still while his words sank in. Never had she considered he might want to get married again. They'd both sworn they hadn't wanted to be married again, but even if she'd had an inkling of a change of heart, she hadn't imagined he might as well. Quietly, she met his gaze. Her heart fluttered at the intensity of his stare and all of her sureness that he hadn't changed his mind flew away. "No. I guess not."

"If it wasn't? If I wanted to ask?"

"Knowing the thought crossed your mind is all I need. Anything else right now wouldn't be what I wanted. I meant what I told Al. Perhaps I wanted to be asked, but I don't want to be asked for Lizzie, and I certainly don't want to be asked because of this mess that has come of it." She set her hands on his shoulders. "Our lives are not as such that it's logical right now. Not for us."

"That so?" A dark frown appeared, accompanied by a disappointed flicker of his brow that caught her attention. Just what had he been doing when he disappeared?

"Once I give Graham the money to buy the place, we are essentially broke. We've got someone trying to make this place worthless. We can't do anything to expand or improve without a loan or investors—both of which are going to be hard come by after the silver crisis."

He pressed his fingers to her lips. "That's all business."

She nodded her reply. Obediently, she remained silent until he removed his finger. "I love you. You're a bull and a fool, but I love you."

"I thought about it. A lot."

"That's all I want to know right now."

His jaw flexed. He turned away again, but not before she saw the way his eyes tightened. "Damn it. I hit you."

The smile she'd found faltered. She dragged his face back toward hers, but only pressed her forehead to his. "It's a simple concussion. A couple of stitches. You didn't do this on purpose. I know this. You'd never hurt me on purpose, not ever."

His eye closed when she kissed his bruised cheek. Long fingers threaded into her hair, clutching. His voice broke when he spoke. "I didn't wanna hurt you. I ain't so sure I can forgive myself."

"I'm far angrier you disappeared on me, then I am over this," she whispered. "This was an accident. You didn't mean to do it. I'm the one that thought I could jump into the middle of that mess and emerge unscathed. I just didn't want you to kill him."

He tilted his head until his gaze locked with hers again. She could detect a faint shimmer of tears she knew he didn't want seen. "I still—"

"It was an accident." She hushed him. With her hands on his knees, she pushed herself up until she could slip in his lap. She ran her fingers through his hair quietly. As his shoulders began to relax, she placed a gentle kiss to his temple. "I love you."

Slowly, deliberately, she took care to kiss each bruise with a feather-light touch. Each kiss was punctuated with another declaration. His face turned slowly toward hers until she could give him a kiss so gentle he couldn't protest. Their foreheads pressed together again, a slow breath leaked from him, one last shudder of his shoulders hopefully edged the last of his protest away.

After a long minute of silence, his arms tightened around her waist. His lips set on hers in a slow, searching kiss.

They pulled apart, each wiping the dampness of their sorrow from the other's cheeks. He gently touched her wound and shook his head. "I'm sorry. I shouldn't have left you alone. I was just so angry—too mad to face you at first."

"I'm sorry I didn't trust your suspicions of Al. I truly thought we were past all of that, I never dreamed it would happen. When it did…" Her voice trailed off when the lump formed in her throat again. She forced it away. "I'm just so used to facing everything with you now. I felt so lost, and then I had to take Lizzie to Katherine's and see the beautiful room they set up for her. I came home and you were gone. I didn't know what to do, or why you'd even left."

"Didn't think of a note." He shook his head. "I came back expecting a row, but I didn't expect you to be that mad."

"I was hurt. When you disappeared, especially once I knew you knew what happened. Then you assumed I said yes. I'd never say yes blindly like that. Not to any other man. I don't know how to get you to understand that."

"I'm sorry."

"So am I." She managed a smile. "That is to say, I'm sorry Tommy messed you up so bad."

"Ain't sorry for yelling at me?"

"No. You deserved that."

He leaned back, one gorgeous eyebrow quirked. Her favorite cocky smile returned and he chuckled. "I do love ya."

"I know."

"Didn't like you even entertaining the idea. No matter the reason."

"I didn't for long. I knew I couldn't live without you."

"Sure you could."

"Fine. I wouldn't want to." She leaned close until her forehead touched his. A smile as bright as she dared with her headache formed. "Remember? You're not that easy to shake. I've tried."

A knock interrupted his reply. Tommy's voice echoed into the room. "Incoming doctor. She's not happy, Jane."

Jane sighed heavily and shrugged. "I left without telling her, or permission for that matter. Guess she thinks I need to be monitored."

"You do."

"I know."

Cole stood with her still in his arms and strode to the door. "Open up, Tom."

Tommy pushed open the door and stepped out of the way to let them pass. Jane heard him close the door behind them and lock it.

Daisy strode down the hall toward them. "Jane."

"Sorry." Jane smiled when Daisy stopped short at the apology. "I know I needed to stay, but I had to see him."

"You should have asked one of us to come get him." Daisy set her hands on her hips.

Jane scoffed. "Of course. That would have worked so well."

"You didn't try." Cole muttered near her ear.

"Just get her back to the clinic." Tommy squeezed her shoulder. "Take care of her, and I'll handle things here."

"I can walk, you know." Jane poked Cole in the chest.

"Don't care. I'm carrying you." Cole nodded to Daisy and walked past her and down the stairs. He didn't even wait for her to catch up, just kept walking through the saloon. Once they were outside, he frowned. "What did ya tell the girls?"

"They're to do more than offer their company." Jane sighed and nestled into his shoulder. The temptation to give into her bodies need for sleep got stronger every second. "Why?"

"They're all gussied up and serving drinks. Iris is running a poker table."

"Good."

Daisy had caught up to them at some point and looked between them both in confusion. "What?"

"Jane's trying to class up the place." Cole shrugged with one shoulder, so Jane's head remained safely un-jostled. "Seems to think we can get by with a little less business in the business."

"Is that so?" Daisy's brows rose and she nodded. "I'm surprised you're agreeing. What do you really think, Cole?"

"She ain't steered me wrong yet." He followed Daisy into the clinic and into an exam room. Once Jane was set on the exam table, he moved to her other side to give Daisy room to work. "What are her orders?"

"After her little side trip, I want to look her over, and then I'd like for her to stay here another night." Daisy chuckled at Jane's groan. "I'd still like to keep an eye on this injury over the next few days to make sure she remains coherent. Well, as coherent as she ever is."

Jane pursed her lips. "Just because I left doesn't mean I'm not coherent."

"Nah. Just means you're stubborn." Cole smirked.

"I learned from the best." Jane snapped.

Daisy sighed. "Are you going to give me any more trouble, Jane? I would be happy to send for David to make sure you stay put this time."

Laughing, Jane shook her head. "No. No shackles needed. I promise to behave now. Cole and I still have some talking to do—if it's all right that he stays?"

"Just talking." Daisy's brows knit in a stern glare at Cole.

"I promise." Jane tried to reassure her. On her other side, Cole pouted.

"Cole." Daisy pointed her reflex hammer at him.

"Are you sure it's medically necessary?" Cole frowned, but his lips kept twitching in an effort to hide a smile.

"Yes."

"Damn."

*In the love of a brave and faithful man
there is always a strain of maternal tenderness.
-George Eliot*

Daisy held a finger aloft in front of Jane. The light of the candle in her hand became near blinding with the slice of metal behind it. "Follow my finger with your eyes."

Jane's attempt to do as Daisy requested resulted in little more than a churning stomach. Still, she pushed on to the right, then the left, but on the trip back right, the turmoil became too great to bear. She gasped aloud. "Oh—heavens. I think I might be ill."

Daisy moved quick to grab the basin behind her. Just in time it landed in Jane's lap. Daisy rubbed Jane's back as she got sick.

"I apologize." Jane dabbed her mouth with the towel Daisy offered. She tried to not wrinkle her nose at the result of her stomach's upset sitting in her lap. "I've been feeling rather ill since early this morning."

"A concussion can do that to a person." Daisy relieved Jane of the basin in her lap, thankfully. After she'd deposited it on the side table, she poured a glass of water. "The nausea should clear on its own in a few days. You'll have to take it easy. Cole hit you pretty hard."

Jane touched her fingers to the side of the wound. The slightest pressure made the wound smart, followed by a shot of pain through her head. Daisy's harsh words aside, all had been forgiven when it came to Cole, for herself at least. However, it would be some time before the pain and lingering side effect allowed either of them to truly forget. "How long are you going to make me remain here?"

"You're coherent enough. I'll release you today."

Jane shoved aside the quick rush of excitement at the words. She wasn't fool enough to believe Daisy would let her off so easy. "But?"

Daisy did not disappoint. She cast a stern look Jane's way. "You need to take it easy the next few days. You're likely to feel tired, so rest when you need to. No strenuous activity—of any kind. I mean it."

Subtle as the woman might have tried to be, Jane didn't miss her meaning. Jane merely nodded, though unable to fully contain her amusement. "You'd prefer Cole and I wait to have our joyous reunion, then."

"I sure can't stop you. A charging bull couldn't stop the pair of you when you get a mind to something, but I must ask you to be careful." Daisy raised a brow. "Beyond that, if at any time Cole has trouble waking you, or you start to have problems being coherent, you need to return."

"I will keep that in mind. I have no doubt Cole will make quite certain everyone knows to bring me here at the first sign of idiocy." Jane's laughter cut itself short with another wave of nausea. This time a few deep breaths managed to rein in the upset. "Goodness, I do hope that symptom goes away soon. I could live without it quite happily."

"You tend to recover quickly from your maladies. I'm sure it won't be long." A low chuckle broke Daisy's stern stature. "I should say I believe you tend to heal quickly. I've never been entirely sure if you have actually recovered, or you're just far too stubborn to follow my care instructions."

"A little of both, I believe."

A brief spat of knocks was their only warning before Charlie stepped into the room without waiting permission.

"Charles. What if I'd been indecent?" Jane held her kerchief her to mouth to hide the smile that would bely her scolding.

"You're always indecent." Charlie's eyes narrowed as he leaned in closer. "Mike told me what happened. At least this time you caused a stir on my day off."

"I planned it that way." Her sarcasm could not be hidden, so she didn't bother to try. So much for the hope that she could skip seeing her brother before she was set free. "I certainly did not wish to be doctored by the likes of you again. I am quite tired of you."

Charlie curled his lip. "Pleased to see you are as charming as ever. As I said, always indecent. Good to know not even a concussion can dull your razor wit. How are you feeling otherwise?"

"Like I could throw up all over you if you keep that tone." Jane slipped off the table, taking care to step on his foot when she passed.

Daisy laughed from where she stood cleaning the mess. "She's feeling better. Some side effects are lingering. Nausea, a little dizziness, nothing surprising or concerning. Her orders are to take it easy for the next few days until the symptoms subside. I've told her I'll release her as long as she follows orders."

"That would mean she's staying, right?" Charlie stepped in front of Jane before she could escape. "I mean, she is no good at following orders."

"Ha ha. Now let me pass." Jane tried to move around him, but his fingers pressed to the bruised area. She stopped quick at the flash of pain. "Ow. Damn you."

"He got you good."

"He was aiming for a target much larger than myself." Jane shoved his hand away. "Daisy is my doctor in this case. Keep your hands off, and your opinions to yourself."

"All right, all right. I heard Tommy got him good anyhow." Charlie held his hands up in surrender when she lunged toward him. "Easy. I saw Cole outside. Looks like he got what he deserved in the end."

"I told you—opinions to yourself." Jane fought the urge to spin away too fast, knowing it would make her dizzy and likely stuck right where she was. "May I go, Daisy? I'm rather tired of his lip."

Daisy nodded. "You may, but I think you're just still tired of him after being cooped up in here for several weeks."

"Of course I am. He's a child who enjoys the sound of his own voice far too much." Jane elbowed him when he approached to lean close. Despite her harsh words, and the truth behind them, she still held affection for the overbearing brute.

"So are you." Charlie set his hand at her elbow. "After all, 'It is the ignorant and childish part of man that is the fighting part'. Emerson."

"'Of all the griefs that harass the distress'd, sure the most bitter is a scornful jest'." Jane stepped out of his grasp. "Samuel Johnson. Good day."

"Jane." Charlie followed her to the waiting room. He caught her arm again enough to turn her to face him. "Jane."

She huffed her flash of anger, trying to see reason behind his pestering. Brotherly concern was the only logical explanation. For that alone she paused. "What?"

"Tell me straight. Are you truly all right? Michael said that even by the standards you and Cole have established, that was one hell of a fight."

"I'm quite certain. The misunderstanding was rather tremendous, made worse by subsequent misunderstandings. We usually save that much anger and yelling for when we are alone. The argument itself might have been over in short order if David and Al had not seen fit to interrupt. From there things became quite complicated—and painful."

"Clearly."

"This is why we try to carry out most of our fights in private. They never end in bloodshed or punches thrown there. We find other ways to resolve things."

"Sometimes I truly believe most of your public fights are just for show."

Jane would never dare to admit how true Charlie's statement was. They lived to spawn gossip, only because so many saw fit to spread it no matter how they behaved. "That is neither here nor there. The truth is, I am quite well. Cole is worse off than I am because of his guilt over hitting me."

"Thought he didn't mean to."

"He didn't. That does nothing to lessen his guilt."

"Which shows despite the physical evidence before me, he's a decent man." Charlie squeezed her hand. "You'll follow doctor's orders?"

"Cole will leave me with no choice in the matter. The orders will be followed."

"That's sufficient for me." He kissed her forehead. "Please listen to Daisy. Rest for a few days, for once in your life."

"I will do my best. I already promised her."

"Good." Charlie pulled open the door. He guided her to Cole's side. "She's ready to go. Daisy and my orders are to take it easy—in every way, Cole."

"You got it, doc." Cole held out one arm, still a hint of hesitation about him.

Jane stepped into Cole's embrace. She held tight, only loosening when his arm went around her waist as well. Her body relaxed in his hold, even more so when the door to the clinic closed behind her. "I need to apologize to Maude, and visit with Lizzie."

"Thought you were supposed to take it easy." He led her across the street, heading toward the Inn rather than either of the locations she suggested.

She stuck her lip out. "I don't want to be cooped up in our room if I cannot enjoy it properly. Besides, I have things to do. I'll be careful. Really. I promise."

"Nope. Today you're resting. Tomorrow you can start worrying about getting out."

Her protest cut off in a gasp, her feet flew out from under her so fast. She found herself held aloft in his arms, knowing any bit of fight would result in nausea. "Cole. That's not fair."

"Don't much care." He carried her into the saloon without another word. Rather than carry her to the stairs, he took her behind the bar. He plopped her onto a stool.

"I don't understand, what is going on?"

Cole leaned on the bar, a sly grin making his eyes twinkle. "Wouldn't keep ya locked up in bed, but you gotta take it easy. I figured you'd wanna be social."

She could do little but stare at him. There could be little doubt she was impressed with his caring and ingenuity in the matter. She grabbed his tie to tug him close for a kiss. "Just what I needed. Thank you."

Iris interrupted, slamming several books on the bar. "In case we get slow and all."

"Thank you, Iris." Jane smiled at the woman.

For a moment, Iris didn't smile back, her eyes dark. The moment passed so fast, and the dark looked was replaced with a bright smile. "Ain't nothing."

"How is it at the tables?" Jane brushed off the moment as concern from the woman.

"I like it. Been fun doing somethin' different. Cole says I can keep on unless I'm needed elsewhere." Iris adjusted her exposed corset as if Jane wouldn't know what she meant.

"Good to hear. Seems Cole can be smart on occasion." Jane grinned at the sharp poke to her side from the man himself.

"Not too often, though." Tommy interjected. A wicked grin lit his features as he leaned on the bar. "Well, you look like hell, Janey, but you're a damn sight better looking than he is."

"Thomas." Jane tried to put a warning edge to her tone, but laughter won over any exasperation. "Did you at least act like a man and apologize?"

"He didn't need to. I deserved it," Cole stated. "Now let's stop dawdling. There's customers and guests—get to work."

The two scattered to go about their business. Jane soaked in the currently quiet atmosphere of the saloon. Right then it felt more like a real hotel than a brothel.

Cole moved to greet a new customer. As he leaned forward, Jane caught sight of a figure at the end of the bar.

She slid off the stool. Cole turned to protest, but she waved off his concern. "I only require a second. I'll be right back."

Cole followed her gaze. He nodded briefly. "All right." He gave a quick kiss to her temple before resuming his conversation with the customer.

She poured a beer to take along. Once it was full as it could be, she carried it the length of the bar to set before the older man before her. "Mr. Hamm."

Hammy lifted his head. A sad smile creased his friendly features. "Miss Spencer."

"I apologize from the bottom of my heart for yelling at you, Mr. Hamm. You meant no harm." Before he could protest, she squeezed his hands. "The timing was very poor, and I was upset but you could not have known such a thing. Once again I took my frustration out on you, and you didn't deserve it. I am more sorry that I've ever been, Mr. Hamm."

Ruddy hues seeped into Hammy's cheeks. He shrugged. "Ain't no big deal. I know ya didn't mean no harm, Lady Jane."

"I did not, but that is a poor excuse for my actions." Jane scooted around the bar to give him a kiss on the cheek. "I promise to never do that again if you would find it in your heart to forgive me."

"All's forgiven." He took a big sip of beer.

The grin she gained from the exchange must have been contagious, for Cole met her with one of his own. He kissed her neck the moment she sat. "Softy."

"I know." She patted the hand he'd set on her shoulder. The tension she'd still been carrying eased even further.

The rest of the day passed rather quickly from her perch behind the bar. It was difficult for her to agree to go to bed early, even if her body was ready to cave from exhaustion. Cole wouldn't accept any argument, though, so she found herself carried upstairs before she truly wanted.

Rather than fight the inevitable, she wrapped her arms around his neck and let it happen.

"Feeling better?"

"Yes, I am. Thank you for thinking of that." She snuggled closer even though they approached the room. "It was nice to be able to still do what I enjoy—even if it wasn't in the same way."

He set her on her feet only long enough to unlock the door. The moment the door swung open, he gathered her in his arms, kicking the door shut once inside.

At the bed, he got her settled on her feet. He unbuttoned her bodice, then slid it off her shoulders. Unlike the usual heated rush and wanton glances that came with undressing her, concern creased his brow. His touches were gentle, and almost timid.

Though she could undress herself, she broached not one word of protest as removed every layer to her corset. Gentle pressure on her shoulders led her to sit.

He knelt before her to undo the buttons of her shoe. Every action held such care, every touch such comfort, she found herself captivated. With her shoe off, he slid his hand leisurely up her leg until he found the edge of her stocking. Slow as molasses he slid it down her leg, the tips of his fingers teasing her flesh.

Her soft sigh brought a smile to his tense features. He switched legs, once again taking his time to remove her shoe, then her stocking. When the second stocking slid over her knee, he placed a soft kiss on her flesh.

He rose high enough to place another kiss between her breasts. She ran her fingers through his hair in response. His kisses drifted higher, and she tilted her head to the side to be sure he had full access. He paused below her ear, lingering there with soft-as-a-breath kisses until another soft sigh slipped free from her lips. He moved to capture her in a slow, lingering kiss.

He pulled back far too soon for her liking. Gently, he pressed her back onto the bed.

She shifted to make room for him while he stripped down to nothing. "No fair," she muttered at the sight of him.

He chuckled low as he slipped into the bed beside her. "I ain't got nothing like a corset to keep on."

She didn't fight his move to pull her close. "As if a corset would really stop you."

"Nah. It's just a reminder. Makes me less likely to misbehave 'cause I know why you got it on."

"Cheater."

"Sometimes you just gotta."

She curled closer, letting loose a sigh of resignation. No reason to fight the truth. If she were honest, she didn't feel up to much of anything anyhow. She traced lazy circles on his chest. "We really must be more careful, you know."

"I know. Fighting ain't supposed to be public."

"Spats are acceptable, they keep gossip flowing."

"Have we moved the line yet?"

Laughter bubbled, but she kept it contained. "No. The acceptable volume of our spats will remain the same."

"But you're half deaf."

"And you're half dumb."

He pinched her hip. "Careful, Jane."

His chuckle relaxed the last bit of tension from her body. She let her hand slip along his chest toward his side. With practiced skill she found the one spot on him she'd discovered to be ticklish. When he twisted and jerked under her ministrations, she giggled. "Careful now. You don't want to jostle me."

"Jane."

"What?" Despite her mock protest, she withdrew her hand. He gripped it tight in his own, not that he needed to. She didn't try to pull away. "You're just mad because with my corset on you are unable to tickle me back."

"The more ya torture me now, the more I'll be paying you back when doc says you're better."

"I'm well aware. That's what makes it so fun."

He rolled until she lay on her back. Propped on his elbows, he met her gaze. "You are evil."

"I prefer the term 'wicked'."

"That so?"

"'For good and evil in our actions meet, wicked is not much worse than indiscreet'."

"Donne," Cole supplied.

"You remembered." She resisted the strong urge to pull him close. "You shouldn't impress me with your acquired knowledge when I'm restricted."

His thumb brushed along her cheek. "'Each moment of a happy lover's hour is worth an age of dull and common life'."

"Oh, Cole." She laughed soft and low. "I believe I am beginning to influence you. You've just cited Behn."

"Ya say it all the time."

"Not that often."

"Sure you do." He dropped lower at her gentle tug. "You even say it in your sleep."

Content to have him close, she sighed. "I'm so glad Tommy didn't hurt you badly."

"I'm glad you weren't hurt worse. I could have—"

"Don't. You've been trying to make it up to me all day, and there is no need. You're here with me—that's all I need. All I want."

"You sure?"

"'In the confusion we stay together, happy to be together, speaking without saying a word'. Whitman." She ran her fingers along his arm, not enough to tease, just enough to feel him. "There is nothing more I need than you here, always. I don't care how mad you are, don't leave again. We can ignore each other all night if needed, but I want you here with me."

"I'll remind you of that the next time you kick me out and tell me to sleep in Tom's room."

"You'd better." A new wave of nausea hit her fast. She closed her eyes against the influx. Cole's forehead pressed into hers, a welcome focus for her attention. Still, the distraction didn't help. She took a ragged breath. "Cole."

"Hmmm?"

"Move."

"What?"

"Oh heavens. *Move*." She shoved him aside hard as she could so she could fly from the bed. The basin sat across the room, far enough that she barely made it in time before her stomach forced its contents free. Her knees buckled, but Cole's strong arms were there to catch her and hold her steady.

"Jane?" He rubbed her back. "Do ya need to go to the clinic?"

"I don't think so." Her voice sounded weak, but held steady. Behind her Cole moved around, though his arm stayed wrapped tight around her waist.

A cool, wet towel pressed to her neck. Right then it was the best feeling in the world. The world spun again so she had to grip the dresser.

"You all right to lay down again? You don't look too steady."

"I think so." She had no qualms using him for support to get back to the bed.

"I'm gonna go get Daisy."

"She said I could expect this." Jane laid down under his urging. He set the cool cloth on her forehead, so she pulled it low over her eyes. "Because of the concussion. I don't think you need to get her."

"I'm gonna anyway. I'll get Pansy to take care of that mess while I'm gone." He squeezed her hand. "I know you don't want a fuss."

"But you're going to anyway."

"Damn straight."

"I love you too."

Half a truth is often a great lie.
–Benjamin Franklin

Every time Jane tried to focus on the book in front of her, Cole made another pass in front of her desk. His nervous energy made her already taut nerves ready to snap. She slammed her hand down on the wood desk. "Cole!"

"What?"

"Would you stop? I am trying to focus, and your constant pacing is driving me up a wall. I swear, you are acting as if I'm unearthing the world's darkest secrets in this ledger." She leaned forward, her gaze locked with his. "Do you want to be business partners or not?"

"Sure." Cole sat across from her but didn't remain still even there. His hands fidgeted in his lap. Due to her having to be at the library, she'd asked him to meet her there with the ledger. They'd put it off long enough what with her illness.

"You're jumpier than a cat in a room full of rocking chairs. What difference should this make? You said you keep good books; I'm only looking to see where the money is going. What the profit margin looks like."

"Graham never cared about the books."

"I think we know I am in no way like Graham."

"Yeah." He diverted his gaze to the nearby book spines rather than meet her gaze.

All her glaring at him did was make her near-constant headache more pronounced, so she relaxed her brow. She turned her attention back to the ledger on her desk.

Of all the things in Cole's life he might be carefree about, the ledger was the exact opposite. Neat as a pin, every column in place. He hadn't been lying when he said he knew numbers. The records he kept were shockingly impeccable.

Unable to contain her surprise, she muttered, "I do love it when you surprise me."

"Hmm? What's that?"

"You said you knew numbers. I confess I still did not expect your ledger to be so perfect."

"Always was good with numbers. Don't know why."

"Like myself with words. Numbers? Now those I actually have to think about. Not bad with them, I just have to focus." She finished the page she was on, then flipped to the next. She might have wondered at the words held within the ledger, but he'd already told her that he put in the numbers, then told someone what to write. Again she flipped to the next page, and a third time led her to detect an odd pattern. "Cole?"

He grew still as a statue for the first time since he'd stepped into the library. Like perhaps all along he'd been expecting this.

"What are all of these entries labeled 'Denver'?" She ran her fingers down the line of entries, then onto the next page. "They are each for two hundred dollars a month, except for May wherein you list a full thousand dollars. That is an almost obscene amount of money."

Throughout her question, Cole remained motionless. The man's tanned features had paled, his gaze locked on his own hands. He stirred enough to rub his hands on his thighs.

"Cole?"

He cleared his throat. The fidgeting returned, which she let happen for several minutes. Then he let out a long sigh. "Guess you wouldn't buy that it's my regular trips there?"

"Perhaps if you didn't have separate entries for those, including finders' fees for whores and repayment when you didn't use all of the money, I just might. Sometimes those trips overlap these entries, but not always." Despite his bad case of nerves, hers were not on edge. Her curiosity was piqued, without a doubt, but she wasn't truly worried about what he might be hiding.

"There's something I ain't told you."

"Clearly."

"It's about my family."

Jane closed the ledger to grant him her full attention. One area of Cole's life that he struggled to talk about, and one she never pushed him on, was his family.

All she knew for certain was that he hated his pa, and that his ma and siblings had died in a fire just two years after he'd arrived in Dominion Falls. Tragedy seemed to fall into nearly every story about his family, so she didn't blame him for wanting to leave the matters in the past.

"I mean, sort of."

There was no need to fight off a smart retort his evasiveness might have brought about in any other conversation. The few times he'd confided in her about his family had been private moments, quietly revealed in the seclusion of their room. This was confrontational, in a public forum such as the library, even if no one else currently stood in the building. Revelations at this point would not be easy for him.

"Damn it."

"Cole, it's all right. Stop being so worried. You don't have to tell me yet. I know you will in time."

"I want to, it's just hard."

"I'm aware how difficult it is for you to speak of your family. You aren't ready yet, and that is perfectly acceptable."

He dropped his head to his hands, his fingers buried deep in the short locks. "I ain't trying to hide."

"I do not recall claiming you were." She pushed to her feet. The moment she reached her full height, she had to pause to accommodate for the brief dizzy spell that took over. Soon as the room stopped spinning, she moved toward Cole. The moment she was close enough, he leaned his head against her stomach. She slipped her fingers through his hair. "I understand. I promise. You will tell me when you're ready."

"It'll be easier to show ya."

If not for his tone, she might have suspected a turn of subject toward a naughty direction. Her brow furrowed, but the action pulled her stitches and sent another wave of vertigo through her. She clung to his hair until the movement steadied. The moment she felt steady, she relaxed her grip. "Show me?"

"Yeah."

"Well, then, if that is what it will take. When you're ready, you will show me. All I ask is that you answer me two questions."

"What?"

"Is it important?"

He nodded against her waist. "Yeah."

"Is it a flexible expense?"

"No."

"All right. That's all I need to know."

He lifted his head so fast, she had to fight the urge to take a step back in surprise. His gaze locked with hers. "That's all?"

"I trust you, Cole. If you say this is important, that's all that matters to me." She cupped his cheeks. "This is business, but it's also about trust. I know you will tell me when you're able. I can live with that."

"You—"

A soft, timid voice interrupted whatever he was about to say. "Excuse me, Miss Jane?"

Jane had to admit being reluctant to pull her gaze from the renewed affection in Cole's, but she did anyhow. The sight that greeted her elicited a surprised gasp for in the doorway stood none other than Graham's former paramour, Linh Moon. What was more, the young woman held an infant cuddled close to her chest. Jane fought for words, only succeeding with a simple exclamation. "My heavens, Linh!"

Cole's head whipped around so fast; she was surprised it didn't fly right off his shoulders. Inch by inch he rose from his seat, still half turned toward the door. "I'll be damned."

"I'm so sorry. I did not know where to go." Linh ducked her head. She pulled the baby closer, her cheek pressed to his forehead.

"No, don't apologize. I'm the one who is sorry. You startled me. I didn't expect to see you." Jane managed to gather her wits and find speech again, thankfully. Last thing they needed was for Cole to handle this conversation. Jane drew closer to Linh. "Why don't you come in?"

"Mr. Carrington. He told my family to never come back, but they sent me away because I brought shame to our family." Tears slipped down Linh's cheeks. She didn't fight Jane's guiding hand. When Cole scrambled away from the chair, she sat under Jane's gentle nudging. "My brother took pity on me. He let me stay there until my son was born."

Jane set her hand on the baby's forehead when Linh turned him to reveal his face. "He is a handsome babe. Does he have a name?"

"His father—he should give him a name," Linh whispered. "I have been calling him zhǎngzǐ, it means first son."

"Your English has greatly improved, Linh." When Linh turned her gaze upward, Jane smiled in hopes of easing her worries. "His father? Is it Graham?"

"Yes." Linh bowed her head at a fresh wave of tears. "He is married. His wife wants me gone. I know this. But he has a son."

A muttered curse erupted from Cole's direction, but Jane kept her smile firm in place. They didn't need to panic the girl any further. "We will deal with that in short order. First things first, we need to get you somewhere to stay."

"My boss, he will let me stay with him. He is very nice. My brother, he found me the job through a friend. They knew I wanted to return here." Linh ran a trembling hand along the baby's back. "My boss does not have a home yet, but I did his cleaning in Cheyenne. He let me come with him."

"That was very kind of him." Jane sat on the edge of her desk. "I will see what I can do to set up a meeting with you and Graham. I think he'll be happy to see you."

"He is married." Linh cuddled her son closer, tears still flowing free.

A short, lean gentleman stepped into the library. He was young, but something about him seemed oddly familiar. "Miss Moon? Oh yes, here you are."

"Good afternoon." Jane stepped around Linh's chair to give the young woman time to gather herself. The well-dressed man smiled in greeting, so Jane extended her hand. "Am I to assume you are the employer Linh spoke of?"

"I am that, indeed. I am Parker Krenshaw." His eyebrow rose when Jane's hand dropped before he'd clasped it, and Cole let out a loud curse. "I gather the pair of you knew my uncle, Jackson Krenshaw."

"You could say that." Jane took a step back, none of her decorum able to overcome the flash of fear brought by the man's presence.

"Then I must apologize retroactively for whatever he might have done." Parker nodded first to her, then to Cole. "I am rather aware that my uncle was no decent man. In full honesty, I was not expecting a warm reception in your town."

"You got that damn right," Cole snapped.

"What brings you to Dominion Falls, if you knew you were unlikely to be well received?" Jane clasped her hands behind her back. Suspicions over his timing battled for dominance of her mind.

"My uncle still owned a mine here which, upon his death, was left to me. As was his home. Surprisingly, after his considerable debts were all paid, the mine itself is still in my name, as is the home." Parker smiled. Though far warmer than his uncle's smiles, Jane still didn't know if she could trust him. "I'm going to oversee the mine until I decide if I want to sell it and move on or keep it and remain here."

"Well, then." Jane didn't trust herself to say anything further on the matter, for it would not be polite and might influence his decision. Instead, she changed the subject. "Then I suppose I should thank you for returning Linh to our midst."

"I was happy to. When I heard of her plight through my butler, I immediately offered my assistance." Parker cast a smile in Linh's direction. For all of her wishes that he would be a clean-cut letch like his uncle, the smile seemed rather genuine. "I've employed her people for quite a few years now, ever since I worked the railroad alongside many Chinamen. I only hope this gesture will bring her peace."

"We'll be doing what we can to assist her," Jane interjected. As yet, she didn't trust Parker so far as she could throw him, and thus her best efforts didn't keep the biting tone from her voice. "I am glad she's here, as I had someone looking for her."

"You did?" Linh turned a wide-eyed gaze on Jane. "Why?"

"Several reasons we will discuss soon." Jane turned back to her employer. "Mr. Krenshaw, will we be able to communicate with Linh where you are staying?"

"Of course. I had no desire to take up residence in my uncle's former home, so I rented some rooms at the boarding house. As we're staying there, Linh's services won't be needed as much. Linh has free rein to do as she wishes until I locate a home to stay in, wherein I may retain her services again and she'll have a schedule." Parker nodded. "Feel free to call on her anytime."

"Thank you." Jane moved close to Linh again.

"Of course. I do hope that in my time here, you'll come to see I am nothing like my uncle." Parker bowed. "Now, if you'll excuse me, I must visit the mine. Would you be so kind as to see Linh finds her room at the boarding house?"

"Of course." Jane turned her back on Parker without another word. She met Cole's gaze and held it firm.

Cole's jaw twitched in his silence for several long minutes. When he moved to speak, she assumed Parker had left. His words confirmed it. "I don't trust him."

"Neither do I." Jane set her hands on Linh's shoulders. "Cole, perhaps it would be prudent to go let Thomas know of Dominion Falls newest citizen. I'll see that Linh gets to the boarding house."

Cole nodded, leaving without another word.

Jane forced her shoulders to relax, smiling down at Linh. "Shall we?"

"Why do you not trust Mr. Parker?"

"Long story. I don't want you to worry about him. You have a son to care for."

All happiness or unhappiness solely depends upon the quality of the object to which we are attached by love.
-Baruch Spinoza

Jane smoothed her hands over the unruly curls making escape attempts from their pins. Unfortunately, she had no time to fix the issue properly; there was something more important to be done. She had to tell Graham about Linh before he heard some other way.

After Cole had left the library, Jane had locked up early and secreted Linh off to the boarding house. Without a doubt the young woman had been seen, but hopefully anyone that had seen her had not noticed her face, or even come close to recognizing her. Most people in town were unlikely to see beyond race, anyhow.

Once Linh was set up with the baby, Jane returned to the inn. Unsurprisingly, she'd found Cole and Tommy deep in conversation over Parker Krenshaw's arrival in town. Though she had plenty of thoughts on the matter, she avoided the conversation. She stopped long enough to tell them not to say a word to Graham, that she should do it. She ignored their protests in favor of heading upstairs to freshen up for the task.

Instead of any bit of refreshing, she'd ended up sound asleep for approximately two hours. While she felt rejuvenated after sleeping, she had far too much to do to be wasting time in sleep. The concussion would surely be the death of her before she healed from it.

She huffed her frustration out in a long, loud breath. There'd been enough dawdling; it was time to get moving. She grabbed two of the high-quality cigars she'd bought Cole from the box on the desk before she headed out.

In the two hours since she'd gone upstairs, the saloon had picked up business, but Cole and Tommy weren't inside. They were on the porch, laughing raucously at something unknown or unseen by her. Despite her mood borne of nothing but frustration at herself, she cracked a smile at the sight of Tommy and Cole joking back and forth as she'd learned her whole family liked to do on regular occasion.

"Gentlemen." Jane kept her hands behind her back as she breached the threshold. "How could you allow me to sleep so long? You knew I had somewhere to be."

"Sorry, Janey." Cole rarely called her that, but he was in such a good mood, she didn't reproach him further. "Doc said you'd be tired. Figured I'd let you sleep now."

"I don't see why; it isn't as though you are allowed to keep me up later." She pushed her lower lip out in her best pout. "For once in your life you're following Daisy's orders to behave."

"I always follow orders when they're for you. Can't have ya getting hurt worse." Cole winked. He beckoned her close, wherein he placed a kiss to her temple.

"He's got a point. He still doesn't listen to what anyone else tells him anyhow." Tommy chuckled. "We've behaved just as you told us. We didn't step a foot near Graham's place. You sure you're the one to do this, Jane?"

"Yes. His behavior the in the past few weeks has been much different. I believe he's remembered how to be human again. Has he talked to you at all, Thomas?" Jane tapped her fingers on the hidden cigars. She turned her attention away from Cole's handsome, playfully grinning visage to meet Tommy's answer.

"Asked me if I knew a good lawyer, since he doesn't have the money to compete with the likes of Carrington. I told him I more than knew one, I was related to one." Tommy grinned. "Nick's poker face comes in real handy in a court of law. Yes, I already sent the telegram."

"Good. A man trying to get a divorce is usually as easy as a two-bit whore, but he's going up against Brooks Carrington, he'll need the backup." Jane had to admit, she was rather pleased with the course this was taking. "I'm glad he took that step. The rest is just details now. However, telling him about Linh and the baby require a bit more finesse than you two galoots can handle."

"Hey now. I got plenty of finesse." Cole tugged the ends of his mildly frayed vest. "You tell me all the time in bed."

"That doesn't count in this situation, you boor." Jane pulled the cigars from behind her back. The distraction worked well enough for them both to focus on them. "You two enjoy these. I'm going to have a conversation with the undertaker."

"Ooh, you brought out the good cigars. You really do want us to stay away from the conversation." Tommy snatched the cigar from her hand as if she'd change her mind. "You should have started with these. You know, asking nicely first and all."

Cole withdrew his own cigar with more, dare she say, *finesse*. He tugged her close. "Go take care of business with the bastard. Just know, I'll be keeping an eye down the road."

"I never doubted it." She tilted her head back to receive the kiss he leaned in for. "Good thing you're so tall. The thoroughfare is busy today."

"We might be heading to Cora's for a bite," Cole admitted. Sitting kitty-corner to Graham's undertaker office, they would have a better view from there, without a doubt.

"Ah. Well, don't follow too close, you'll only annoy me." She stepped free of his embrace to head down the street toward Graham's. With a final wave over her shoulder, she stepped off the saloon porch onto the boardwalk.

Along the way she found herself stopped no less than three times for a quick chat with friendly neighbors. Each interruption took long enough that it was almost a full half hour later when she finally made it to Graham's door. Worse, she could see Cole and Tommy camped out on the mercantiles' porch, smoking their cigars without a care.

Nearly two years after her hanging, the idea of entering Graham's undertaking office still gave her a chill. She shook it off to push open the door where several sealed coffins waited for burial. After her own hanging, she'd been nailed inside a casket in this very room, where Graham had found her pounding on the lid in the middle of the night.

She shuddered off the memory before it could send her into a nervous fit. The door to the back room, which had once been Graham's living quarters sat partially open. Though he'd expanded his workspace since his marriage, Cole claimed the back room still had a bed and living space. She wondered how often he used it thanks to his lovely marriage.

"Graham?" Jane knocked on the door and pushed it open. "Are you in here?"

"Right here, Janey." Graham's back was to the door. On the table he stood over lay old Mr. Moore. An odd contraption she recognized as an embalmer from some articles she'd read to familiarize herself with the war sat on the table.

She herself had clearly not been embalmed, in fact it was a new practice of Graham's. Mostly for the wealthier in town. He didn't usually bother with it for the miners. Graham's arms and shoulders worked. "Need something?"

The smell of death hit her like a locomotive. Her stomach churned at the intrusion, her brain spun at the vivid images and reminders. The room tilted on its axis so fast she had to grip the wall to keep steady. Images and wavy lines of color swam across her vision when her knees gave out beneath her.

"Janey." Graham's voice sounded muffled and distant, but his hand felt solid enough on her back.

She didn't know where the bucket came from, but she clung to it with gratitude as she heaved. Any bit of relief from her nap flew away with each painful lurch of her stomach until she could heave no longer. Cold sweat broke across her flesh. She clung to the bucket like a lifeline while she tried to regain her bearings.

"You all right, there? Never seen you react like that in here before. You had to have come in here lots since your own death. Leastwise at least a few." Graham dabbed her forehead with a towel. "Should I get Daisy?"

"No." She didn't know how she'd managed to find her voice, but there it was. "I believe I'm still out of sorts after my concussion."

"Come on." Graham hauled her to her feet. He practically carried her across the room to the back door. He yanked it open and set her on a chair outside.

In the shade of the building, a cool breeze helped dispel some of the heat from her body's upheaval. When Graham returned with a cold mug of water, she took it with gratitude.

"I put some ginger in it. Should help your stomach." Graham plopped into the chair next to her. "Any better?"

"Yes. I apologize. You're right, this is not how I usually react, although I still don't like being in there. No offense."

"Don't know anyone that does." He wiped his bald head with his towel. "You don't need to be apologizing to me, anyhow. I've never apologized to you."

"Tommy tells me you've asked about a lawyer. Is that when you decided to start being nice to me again?"

He chuckled. "No. That ain't it."

"It isn't?"

"Nah. When you told me the Moon's are in Laramie is what did it. When I heard where she was, something changed. Can't rightly explain, I don't think."

"You do love her, don't you?" Jane knew it was true, though if he'd admit it was another story. She turned to face him. "Because if you don't, you have to know you're going to go through a lot of hell just to end up unhappy once again."

"I kept telling myself I don't. No, that I shouldn't. She isn't the right kind of person. Nobody would understand."

"You do love Linh."

"I guess I do."

She set her hand on his arm. "What if I told you she wasn't in Laramie with her family?"

"She's not?" He twisted the towel in his hands tight into his fists. "Then I'd still have to go, I guess. I've got to find out where she is."

"Or you could stay right here and find her again."

"Brooks ran them outta town last year. She can't be here."

"But she is."

He flew to his feet. "Where?"

"Sit down, please. There's more I have to tell you before you go running off half-cocked. You always get yourself in trouble when you do that." She kept her hand firm on his forearm, unwilling to remove it until he sat.

"What is she doing here?" Graham sank into the chair, his features pale. "Where is she?"

"She came back here to find you. Somehow she found employment with a gentleman on his way to Dominion Falls. Her family made her go away from bringing shame to them."

"Shame? Linh? No."

Jane squeezed his arm to regain his full attention. "Graham. There is a baby. A son."

Silence filled the space between them before his shoulders drooped. His hands ran along his smooth head, wrinkling the skin with the pressure. The tension lessened until he shook his head back and forth, then his shoulders shook. A low chuckle grew into outright laughter until he threw his head back in his amusement. His arms wrapped around his generous stomach as the laughter kept rolling out.

She sat still as could be. All she could do was stare, confounded by the reaction. The laughter could mean anything from disbelief to—well, she had no idea. "Graham?"

"Sor—sorry." He slapped his knee with another guffaw. In a moment he managed to tame his laughter into chuckles. "Becky kept saying I'm not a man because we haven't had a baby. Yet, here is Linh with a child. It's mine, right?"

"That's what she told me, and he does bear some resemblance." She allowed herself to smile, relieved he wasn't angry. One thing was a sure bet, she liked Graham much better when he wasn't a drunk and angry bastard. "You're starting to remind me of the man that saved my life two years ago."

"That mean you'll tell me where Linh is?"

"She's staying at the boarding house, but don't go rushing off. You have to be careful. Brooks will be none too happy with this turn of events. You must tread lightly until Nick can make everything final for you."

"I just wanna see her. I wanna see *him*." He turned to face her. "I'll talk to Nick tomorrow. Although I'm half-tempted to take Becky to an asylum and leave her there. It'd be my right."

"I understand that urge, believe me. I doubt it'll get you anything but a furious Brooks Carrington running you out of town, though."

"Let him try."

*A baby is an inestimable blessing,
and bother.
-Mark Twain*

Kat sipped water from her cup, her gaze across the field. After a few minutes of quiet, she set the cup down on the blanket. "I still can't get over it. Graham is really a pa?"

Jane gently chided, "Keep your voice down please."

"There's no one here but us three, the children are caught up in their game."

"Either way, I don't think Linh has dared to venture out of the boarding house for days. Graham is doing his best to keep things quiet until Nick gets all the paperwork in order." Jane set aside her half-eaten biscuit. She had no idea how her stomach could still be so queasy five full days after her concussion. At least she was seeing Daisy later that day. Perhaps she'd get some answers to the annoyance of the lingering symptom.

"I think he's been sneaking her to his office." Cole snatched up the biscuit she'd discarded and finished it off. Their impromptu picnic in the middle of the week had been a success. Cole had scarfed down an impressive amount of food. It appeared that being unable to satisfy one appetite had left him overcompensating with another.

"He well could be. Either way, he's happier than I've seen him in a while. I believe if word gets out before he's ready for the divorce, he might drop Becky off at the nearest asylum if for no other reason than to buy himself some time." Jane had a sneaking suspicion Graham had only been half kidding at the suggestion.

"Really?" Kat's eyes gleamed with the new hint of gossip. "Oh, what a stir that would cause. I almost wish he would just to see the show that would follow."

"You're terrible." Jane laughed despite her scolding. She turned her attention to the antics of the children, enjoying their laughter as much as the conversation. "The final paperwork for the sale of Graham's share should go through any day now. Then we can turn our attention to what we plan to do with the Hangman's Inn."

"Speaking of which, I'm dying of curiosity." Kat bumped her shoulder into Jane's to regain her attention. "How did you know Iris would be able to handle a table?"

Jane tore her gaze from where Lizzie, Cindy and Jesse played in the meadow to focus on Katherine. "What? Well, how on earth did you think Iris and Mel got together?"

Cole froze, his cup halfway to his mouth. "What?"

Jane was tickled by Cole's surprise. The man could be blisteringly dense, sometimes. "Well, what do you expect? While you and Graham lamented the lack of customers, and refused to get a piano, Mel decided to help curb Iris' boredom by teaching her first how to play, and then how to deal. Poker, Blackjack, Faro."

"He was teaching her to be a sharp?" Cole's eyes narrowed. "That could've been useful to know, you know."

"Guess you need to be more observant," Kat chided. "In the end, it did prove useful."

Cole finished his drink. "How many other secrets you keeping about the hotel?"

"No secrets. I learned my lesson." Jane laughed low, nudging his knee with the toe of her boot. "It is far from my fault that you're painfully unobservant when it comes to anyone other than me."

Kat shoved another drink into Cole's hand to stop his leer at Jane. "You've been patient for five days—you can wait a few more hours, especially noting there are children present."

"Don't mean I gotta like it. Been almost a week now." He took a swig of his drink. No matter what Kat had put in the cup, his heated gaze remained on Jane.

Kat threw a biscuit at him. Her laughter turned into a yelp when he returned the favor with a chicken leg.

Jane sighed. "Would you two stop? The children will get ideas."

Cole ducked behind Jane to hide from the spoon of jam Kat held aloft in a threatening manner. "You wouldn't get Jane, would ya?"

"Don't count on it." Kat moved the spoon around, like trying to find the best way to get most of it on Cole.

"Katherine!" Jane held up her finger in warning. "If you do that, know the children are watching and all bets are off. Remember how Norman reacted when Cindy came home all muddy last year? Imagine what he'll think if all three of you come home covered in food."

It was enough to make Kat hesitate before she lowered the spoon. She pursed her lips. "That was an unfair tactic,

Jane. Using my supplication to keep me from giving Cole what he deserves."

"Cole always gets what he deserves." Jane grinned. "Don't you worry about that."

"Wait." Cole settled in close beside Jane, his head practically in her lap. "What's this about supplication? That ain't Kat. What in blazes are you talking about?"

Jane took the spoon of jam Kat had been prepping for a weapon and spread it on a biscuit. Her smile grew at Kat's happy humming. "She's appealing to Norman for them to let Lizzie stay on with them—permanently."

"Ain't he a bit old to be taking on two kids?"

"Katherine." Jane scooted away from Cole quickly. "The jam."

A jam-laden biscuit made contact with Cole's cheek.

Jane darted across the meadow toward the children before any food could reach her, laughter trailing behind her. Soon as she reached the children, they spotted what happened at the blanket. Jane hopped out of the way when they raced to join.

If it had been any other day, Jane might have been abashed to see food go to such waste, but she was hardly hungry. The headache and dizziness had finally subsided, her thoughts no longer felt quite so muddled. The nausea lingered, though.

Her appointment with Daisy loomed ahead that afternoon, and Jane really hoped for a clean bill of health. She only feared the lingering nausea would prevent her chance to enjoy spending the rest of the day with Cole.

She sighed, turning back to the blanket only to find Cole had turned his focus on her. Though he remained yards away, she backed up a few steps. "Oh no."

When he rose to his feet, she backed up even more. Her retreat hit a solid wall. She yelped at the unexpected interruption.

"Lou." How the lumbering and large form of Tommy had managed to sneak up on her, she had no idea. "We gotta talk."

Jane couldn't help but worry at his dark tone. "All right. Sound serious."

"It is." Tommy led her to the edge of the meadow. He dug into his pocket, withdrawing a letter. "I figured out why Warren sounded familiar. It took some doing, and I had to call in a few favors to make sure this was right."

She read the letter once, twice, a third time. The blood drained from her head until the world spun. She gripped Tommy's arm. "But why?"

"What in blazes is going on?" Cole jogged up, jam still on his cheek. His hand went to the small of her back, anchoring her in the present again.

"A Pink. He's a Pinkerton." She kept a tight grip of Tommy's arm, despite Cole's presence.

"Was, Lou. He isn't any longer." Tommy spoke softly, but forcefully pried her fingers from his arm. "Joe's trying to figure out who he's working for now."

"Who?" Cole frowned when her gaze turned toward him. "Warren?"

She nodded. The letter in her hand trembled, an unacceptable sign of weakness. She shoved it back toward Tommy. "He was a Pinkerton until a few years back."

"Joe is still a Pink. He's working to figure out where our friend is getting his orders these days." Tommy squeezed her hand. "We'll get this taken care of, Lou."

"If he's truly out to ruin us, it wouldn't take much of a hard look at me and my past to make it happen." Jane folded her arms across her stomach as if it would stem this wave of nausea she knew came from pure fear. "If they're out for blood, Warren's been around the girls and enough alcohol-loosened tongues already. He may have what we needs once I've officially bought Graham's portion."

"Nobody thinks of that no more." Cole wrapped his arm tight around her waist. "Been years. I'm sure it ain't a problem."

"We certainly can hope." Tommy frowned. "Tomorrow's the day you sign the paperwork, yes?"

"Yeah." Cole rubbed his cheek, grimacing at the jam he met. "Between making sure Brooks don't see the real contract and sneaking it to Graham, we ain't been able to do it sooner."

"Would it be better to wait?" Jane's heart pounded in her ears. She'd thought she was done with this sort of terror. The fear that her past could once again ruin this new vision of a future ripped open wounds she'd thought long closed. "I don't want to make the Hangman's Inn more susceptible than it already is. We can't look for new investors if whoever this is discovers my dirty little secret and uses it against us."

"No. Change nothing. I'll send Joe another telegram. We'll keep going on like we know nothing." Tommy's frown deepened. "One more thing."

"What?" Cole's hand clenched on her waist. The tension was riling them all up, and not in a good way.

"Where'd you dig up Pansy?"

Jane startled at the question, brought out of her miserable reverie. "What? Why?"

"As the biggest trouble-maker you got, we need to cover all the possibilities. You said yourself that she got the opium, but never used it." Tommy reached for her when she swayed, even with Cole right there. "Easy. These are just questions."

"Graham found her when he went to visit that investor in St. Louis. What's his name—right, Cutler." Cole kept her steady on his feet, even as he answered the question. "You'd have to ask him how he came about finding her and bringing her here."

"I will. Don't worry, Janey. I got this." Tommy grinned, probably trying to ease her rising panic. "I can handle things. Don't you have an appointment to get to? One your man is awful anxious for?"

Jane nodded, trying to wrap her head around all the revelations. "Yes. Of course."

Cole gave her a small shake. "Jane."

The swirling thoughts stilled enough for her to pay attention again. "Sorry. I'm going. Cole—you need to get changed and cleaned up before you go anywhere. You've got jam everywhere, you're going to need a bath."

"Daisy damn well better say you're healthy." Cole offered a wicked grin. "Only way I'm getting a bath tonight."

That managed to return the cheer to her mood. "I don't know. I rather like you impatient. You're far more attentive."

Tommy groaned. "Enough. Separate now. I'll take Jane to her appointment while you get changed, Cole. I don't think Daisy, or anyone really, cares to see you like you are. You've got a piece of chicken in your pocket."

Cole's brows rose as he studied the pocket of his shirt. He freed the chicken, laughing at the find. "Lunch."

Jane shook her head when he popped the chicken leg in his mouth. "Boor."

"Proud of it, too." Cole kissed her cheek. "Be good for Daisy."

"I'll do my best." She laughed willingly, but with every step he took toward town, her laughter faded. The churning of her stomach rose again until she knew she couldn't stop the inevitable. She darted into the nearby bushes, vomiting what little she'd eaten that day.

Tommy's hand settled on her back. A handkerchief was shoved into her hand. "Jane?"

"Sorry," she muttered. She dabbed at her mouth with the kerchief, attempting to regain her composure.

"You shouldn't still be getting sick."

"I'm sure it's just the shock. It has to be. The thought of having everything I've built up ripped away again." She took a bracing breath. "Having it constantly in the back of my mind is one thing. To have it dragged out from hiding is quite another."

"It won't happen. I won't let it." Tommy laced her arm through his. The grip he used allowed her to lean most of her weight into him while she still appeared to walk upright. "You do know why I know Joe, and why Gus Warren sounded familiar to me, don't you?"

"No." Come to think of it, there was still much from Tommy's past she didn't know. He had a special skill at avoiding the topic of himself and managing to turn it on anyone else. She recalled making casual inquiries now and then only to be redirected quickly.

"Charlie and Nick signed up and went to war. I became a Pink. I was one of the group that guarded the President, may he rest in peace."

"You what?" She stopped short, eying him quietly. "Are you serious?"

"Dead serious."

"You couldn't have mentioned that sooner?"

"You didn't ask."

"I've tried to ask plenty in the past year, you keep changing the subject."

"I seem to remember a stubborn woman that cut off Mike every damn time he suggested calling me. He tried to tell you himself until you wore him out. Why would I bother telling?" Tommy urged her to walk again. "If you'd asked me why my marriage ended, that would have been part of the story. Of all the things you've asked me, that hasn't been part of it."

"I didn't know I'd have to be so specific."

"We're not all as candid about our past as you are."

"Good point." She squeezed his hand. "I would like to talk with you some more later. Now that I know the sort of question to ask about your mysterious past, maybe I'll learn more."

He winked. "See. And you thought you had the lock on mysterious pasts. 'Whenever nature leaves a hole in a person's mind, she generally plasters it over with a thick coat of self-conceit'. Longfellow."

"Oh, now that one is essentially ridiculous." She kissed him on the cheek as a way of dismissal when they reached the clinic. "Now off with you. I have an appointment to keep, and you have a telegram to send. Just bear in mind that if Daisy deems me healthy, you aren't likely to see me until tomorrow."

He scrunched his nose. "I wouldn't expect any less."

She waved and shut the door on him. "Daisy?"

Daisy popped her head out of the nearest exam room. "Jane. You're early. Come on in, I was just putting away our latest shipment of medicine."

Jane knew if she waited, she might second guess telling Daisy the truth. She followed her into the room and spoke without further address. "How long did you say the nausea should last?"

Halfway to the open crate across the room, Daisy paused. "I'm sorry?"

"The nausea. You said a few days but weren't more specific. How long would you deem appropriate?" Jane lifted herself onto the exam table.

"Goodness, you're diving right in today. I fully expected your usual delays and misdirection." Daisy abandoned her trek to the crate to return to the table. "I guess by that how-do-you-do, you're still feeling poorly?"

"The headache is gone. I still get a little dizzy, though not like I was. My thoughts feel clear again. It's the nausea— I can hardly eat sometimes." Jane's mind raced over the puzzle so she hardly noticed Daisy testing her reflexes.

Daisy held up a finger for Jane to follow. "Anything else?"

"I'm still rather tired, which has been beneficial toward your recommendation to take it easy." Jane sighed when Daisy lowered her hand. Listing the symptoms made her mind spin with the possibilities. A nervous shiver ran down her spine. "I can still function in a normal day; I just feel like I could nap several times during a day."

"Why don't you lie down?" Daisy moved the instrument tray toward Jane's feet. "I think a full exam is in order."

Jane tried to ignore the obvious reason for Daisy's suggestion. Pregnancy seemed patently out of the question. She was always exceedingly careful, and after the last time she imagined it to not be a viable possibility. "This is ridiculous."

"Is it?" Daisy cleaned her hands, not doing a good job of hiding her amusement. "You have no further symptoms of a concussion. Based on what you've told me, I think the further examination may be necessary."

"Daisy…" Jane's voice trailed off with the unasked question.

"You don't have to ask. I know you're smart enough. Weren't you thinking about the possibility yourself?"

"Honestly? No. Not until you suggested the exam," Jane admitted. "I'm very careful about my cycles, even if it makes Cole grumpy that I am. Plus, we also take great care with our precautions and I keep us as well supplied as the whores."

"I know. I help supply you." Daisy kept talking as she began the exam. "Don't forget you were also rather ill recently, which can alter our patterns. Not to mention that even the greatest of care doesn't always erase all chance of it happening."

"But I always wear a veil. Just because I was sick and—oh!"

Daisy paused, perhaps afraid she'd caused pain. "Oh?"

"I just remembered. When I was recuperating, when we were still in here, I didn't have my veil and Cole didn't have…"

"I thought Cole raided Charlie's office. The man was grumbling for days."

"He did." Jane tried to hide her smile, entirely unsuccessfully. "But that was after the first time. Once we both had our wits about us again, we realized our error."

"That's quite an error for someone usually so careful I can hardly keep my supplies in." Daisy stood, the exam over. "But I suppose being ill and missing each other can do that. Plus, I think you are well aware already that even your veil isn't always sufficient to stop a pregnancy."

"Far too aware." Her last pregnancy had happened despite every precaution. She again thought that, for certain, she wasn't meant to have children. "I just can't believe it could happen again. Even with our slip up."

"You're going to have to believe it." Daisy squeezed her knee. "You may sit up, or remain lying down while you let yourself take it in. You are pregnant."

Jane stared at the ceiling, trying to absorb the words. She heard the water splash while the doctor washed her hands, but Jane couldn't move. Her hands clenched tight. Fear clawed its way into her heart.

"Jane? Are you all right?" Daisy helped Jane sit. "It's not often I see you at a loss for words. A little assistance as to whether you're happy or if I need to get some help would be lovely."

Pregnant. The last time she'd been pregnant Cole had left, she'd lost the baby, her whole world fell apart. Without a doubt, she would be happy to have Cole's baby given their new status. However, the past being what it was, she feared the worst. "Are you quite certain?"

Daisy laughed softly. "Yes. Quite."

A smile tugged her lips despite her fears. She quashed it quickly. "Please. I do hate to ask, but do not tell Cole."

Daisy's smile faded immediately. "Jane. I'm not at liberty to share, but you aren't going to keep it from him again, are you? After what happened before?"

"Oh heavens, no. I won't keep it from him, not for long anyway. I need time to process this information. I also need to find a good time to tell him." A rueful chuckle slipped free. "Because, as always, the timing of this revelation is horrendously bad."

"The timing may be bad, but are you happy?"

"I am. I'm also overwhelmed. It honestly didn't even cross my mind. I have no idea when or how to tell Cole—but I suppose I'll know when it's right." The rush of joy turned to panic again in a heartbeat. Would she have time to tell him?

The fear must have shown on her face, for Daisy gripped her hand. "Jane?"

"I had a miscarriage last time. You didn't know why." Jane grasped Daisy's hand. "What if it happens again? I don't know if I could bear it."

"I'll do whatever I can to ensure that doesn't happen. Will you do as I ask?"

"Anything." For once, Jane meant it with all her being.

"Then the first instruction I'm going to give you is simple."

Jane's whole body vibrated with fear.

"Relax."

A knock on the door caused Jane to yelp and jump.

"Jane?" Cole's voice echoed concern. "You all right in there?"

"Cole," Jane whispered. She closed her eyes and took a deep breath. "He'll want to know if I'm able to—relax—how we usually do."

"Why am I not surprised that's how you relax?" Daisy's droll tone matched her expression.

"Are you telling me it isn't relaxing?"

"Quite true." Daisy laughed, then raised her voice. "Come on in, Cole."

"How's she look, Daisy?" Cole wrapped his arm around Jane's waist as soon as he got close. "If ya say she's all good, we got some plans."

Jane turned to Daisy wide-eyed, unable to contain her fear and hope.

Daisy nodded. "I think you're going to need to take it easy—Jane still appears to have some lingering dizziness from the blow to the head. However, I think it's all right to…relax."

Relief flooded Jane. She reached out to squeeze Daisy's hand. "It's been a while since we talked, Daisy. Would you mind if I stopped by tomorrow? We could have some tea."

"You're welcome any time, Jane."

Jane smiled, but further conversation got cut off. Cole scooped her up so fast, she gasped in surprise. "Cole!"

"I got jam in my hair. Ain't got time for chit-chat."

Jane laughed, tossing a wave over his shoulder to Daisy. She mouthed 'thank you' before he got her out of the door. When she turned her attention back to Cole, she wrinkled her nose. "Oh, you weren't kidding. You do have jam in your hair. Yuck."

"Guess we'll have to take our time in the tub."
"I guess so."
"Such a shame, wastin' all that time in water."
"Mmmm. It won't be wasted."

The minute I heard my first love story, I started looking for you, not knowing how blind that was. Lovers don't finally meet somewhere. They're in each other all along.
—Jalal al-Din

Jane's dreams filled with images of the extra-long bath they'd shared. Once she'd made certain his hair was cleaned of all jam, she'd made good on her promise that their time in the tub would not be wasted—not for Cole. By the time she'd finished, she was rather certain he knew she forgave him, several times over.

As the tub drained, he threw on trousers, but left her wrapped in nothing more than a blanket. Over her protests, he'd carried her to their room only to leave to get food since they'd missed meals. It was then that she'd pulled his pillow close, leaving the sheets thrown to the bottom of the bed to stave off the heat of the evening.

A cool wisp of air on the small of her back shocked every nerve awake. She sighed his name, her body stirred as it woke.

"Sorry I took so long, had to talk to Tom."

"For someone that beat the stuffing out of you a few days ago, you're certainly sharing plenty of secrets with him." Sleep teased her back toward it with the same veracity as his trailing fingers tugged her toward pleasures only her waking body could enjoy. Either way she followed was tempting, although Cole would always be the most appealing temptation.

"Not secrets. Surprises."

"Surprises?" That caught her attention. A flick of his tongue followed by another cool breath of air wiped the curiosity clean out of her. A shockwave of heat filled her until she squirmed under his hands.

His fingers danced along her thigh. Small whimpers poured from her lips as he continued to tease her without granting any release. He nipped the small circle of sensitive flesh at the small of her back again.

He had her so thoroughly pinned, any attempt to move was thwarted. She groaned her frustration. Every small, teasing caress built the fire inside without giving her the satisfaction of the intensity of touch.

His hold loosened enough to allow her to roll on her back before he was on the move again. Warm lips grazed along her stomach. His fingers dragged along her inner thigh until they reached her center where he gave into her quiet begging.

A shudder ran through her body, her back bowed off the bed. Her cries attested to her pleasure, while pleading for more. She clawed at his shoulders to drag him closer until he gave her the gratification of his mouth on hers where his tongue slid across her lips before plunging in as enthusiastically as his fingers dove through her heat.

She arched toward him, a grunt of dissatisfaction escaping when her flesh touched the rough texture of fabric between them. The blinding pleasure of his touch left her gasping for air. She dropped back to meet his intense gaze.

A noise not unlike a growl rumbled low in his chest. Rather than wait for him to accommodate her, she yanked on his shirt hard enough to pull buttons free. She'd barely had the pleasure of touching his flesh before the driving force of his fingers won out, and she cried out with release.

Her fingers buried in his hair and yanked him into an intense kiss.

Still trembling when he pulled back from the kiss, she pushed him until they were both sitting. Wordlessly she removed his shirt and threw it aside.

He chuckled when she rushed to help him remove the rest of his clothes. "Impatient?"

After she'd pushed him back onto the bed, she crawled up along his body. She hovered above him. She swiped her tongue across her bruised lips and felt his cock jerk against her belly. "Impatient? No. Are you?"

"Damn straight."

A squeal escaped when he grabbed her around the waist and spun, his lips crushing to hers as they joined together. Playful teasing was forgotten as they moved together, reveling in reconnecting.

Speaking without a word, they used every moment to share, regret and apologies giving way to love. As they reached the pinnacle, they were wrapped up in each other so tight it wasn't clear where one began and the other ended.

They remained locked in the embrace long after the fire had been quenched, no words passed between them. When they slowly untangled, they immediately resumed their closeness as he pulled her back toward him and curled his body flush against hers.

Sighing, she laced her fingers with his and shifted back against him even closer. She smiled when he nuzzled the back of her neck. "Imagine if you hadn't left."

"Then I wouldn't have been able to wake you up."

A quiet hum was her agreement. "That certainly was a benefit."

"But I think our food got cold."

"Don't much care right now."

He chuckled and kissed the back of her neck. "So do ya think I followed orders all right? Daisy said to take it easy."

Jane shifted to look up at him. A giggle fluttered up from her belly. "I don't think you know how to take it easy, Cole. But yes. For you, that was taking it easy."

"Good. Wouldn't want you to get in trouble."

"I wouldn't be me if I wasn't in some sort of trouble."

"True."

She held his gaze for several long minutes, willing him to spill the beans. Finally she pursed her lips. "Are you really going to make me ask?"

"Ask what?"

"Did you really think your distractions made me forget what you said?"

"If they didn't, I could come up with more distractions."

His wandering fingers threatened to distract her again. She bit her lip to remain present, focused on her curiosity over her libido. "No. You said something about surprises."

"It ain't a surprise if I tell you."

"Cole."

The teasing stopped. He propped himself on his elbow. Though he held her gaze for a long, anticipatory moment, in the end all he gave her was a shrug. A gentle kiss landed on her shoulder before he dropped back to the bed.

"You are not nice."

"Never claimed to be."

Frustration welled until only a childish response could take root. She slipped her hand along his side to tickle him. "Devil."

"Harlot."

She yelped at his return tickling. It took some maneuvering before she could scramble away. "Fine. You don't want to tell me." She threw on her robe, yanking the ties harder than necessary to close it. Her frustrated libido and curiosity left her with little to attain satisfaction except her mildly rumbling stomach. She reached for the tray of food he'd brought back.

"Thought you weren't hungry."

"Apparently, I've worked up quite the appetite. I'm starving." For the moment the thought of food didn't turn her stomach. It was a welcome relief, though it meant that in a matter of hours she'd gone from nausea to starvation. She knew better than to not take advantage while she could.

He threw on his trousers before he joined her at the table. One big stretch made his long body seem even more so. His feet settled on her lap when he'd finished. Her small glare of response was met with little more than a wink. "Most I seen ya eat in days. Guess you did work up an appetite."

"You tend to do that to me." She cast him a sideways glance before she grabbed another biscuit from the tray. "I'm always hungrier when we aren't under restrictions."

"You gotta stop getting put on restriction. We can't have you losing that appetite."

"Which appetite might you speak of? There is one appetite I find to never be satisfied."

His eyes lit with barely contained fire. "Already?"

"Not until I'm done eating."

"Damn."

She giggled. Each bite of meatloaf tasted so good; she fairly shoveled each bite into her mouth like she had no decorum whatsoever. Disappointed, she took the last bite wishing she'd savored it more. With a pout, she dug into the vegetables.

"Were you serious earlier?"

"Hm? Serious? About what?"

"About Kathy. You said she'd be taking in the girl—permanent."

"Yes." The turn of conversation caught her attention enough to slow her eating. She wiped her mouth. "She's been thinking about it much like I had. The first step was getting Norman to agree to let her stay on for a few days. Before he ever agreed, Kat was cleaning the room."

"She was working him over."

"No. She was hopeful."

"Uh-huh."

"Norman had his doubts, of course. Two young girls, and he's no spring chicken. He was the one that took turning that room into a girl's room a step further. Kat only wanted to make sure it was cleaned, but Norman painted and got it set up for her. I believe the whole situation is going to work out rather nicely."

"Good." That was it. The subject dropped as fast as it had started.

She tried to figure it out for a few minutes until a rumble from her stomach drew her attention back to her plate. She finished it off fast. When Cole offered her his plate, she took it gratefully. Halfway through eating, Cole's intense stare became evermore distracting. The hair on the back of her neck rose, concern shivered along her skin. Something had to be up, and his avoidance of whatever it might be enflamed her nerves. "What?"

"Nothing."

"Then why are you staring at me like that?"

"I always stare at you."

"Not like that." She threw her napkin on the table. Across her steepled fingers, she narrowed her eyes to study him. As familiar as she'd become with the man across from her, she couldn't read him. "I don't think I know what the look you're wearing means. It's certainly not hunger—and that's the look I'm most used to getting."

His feet slipped from her lap. He took her hand in his and used it to tug her toward him. Once she'd settled on his lap, the perplexing stare melted into his familiar smirk. "So I ain't allowed to look at you?"

"No. I mean, yes. Of course you are. I am simply curious as to what is going through your head right now?"

"How'd you like to go to Denver?"

"Um…" Confusion won over her vast vocabulary. His behavior had her completely flummoxed. "What? Why?"

"The girl is taken care of."

"Yes. We just established that."

"The business side is being handled."

"Right..."

"Nothing else is standing in the way."

"Cole." Her head spun, a whimper slipping free at her inability to grasp onto anything solid he could mean. "You're giving me a headache."

"You said you wanna be asked..."

The blood drained from her face. Her fingers grew ice cold. He couldn't be saying what it sounded like. She slipped off his lap. After several steps back to study him, she leaned on the table to steady herself. Was this the brute's way of proposing? Would he propose? He said never. She'd not once doubted he'd meant it when he'd said it. Then again, so had she.

"I told you I ain't so opposed to it no more." The man oozed romance when he wanted.

That aside, the shock of the situation made her wonder if her legs weren't about to give out on her. After all this time, all of the fighting he did about their commitment. He blurt it out? Like this? Because another man had asked? Or did he really want this? She had no idea what to say. Honestly, she was becoming tired at being constantly at a loss for words these days.

"You gonna say anything?"

"Why? Why now?"

Warm hands rested on her shoulders. "You said you wanna be asked—but not for logic, not for the girl. Well, I ain't much for logic anyway, and there's no reason. I wanna ask, just because."

The room swayed. She leaned harder on the table. Had he truly said he *wanted* to ask? "No logic. No reason."

"Just you. Only you."

"Just us."

"Yeah."

"I thought you didn't want to get married again—ever."

He chuckled, the warmth in the rich tone steadying her shock and nerves. "I remember you saying the same."

"I suppose I did. I'm just so surprised. After the past couple of years, it didn't seem we were meant for such a fate."

"Maybe that's why."

Well, that did make sense. They'd been fighting commitment as much as each other. She turned to face him. "Are you certain you want this?"

"Yeah."

"I don't—I'm—"

"What are we?"

She furrowed her brow. "What?"

"You heard me."

"We don't have to make it legal." She cupped his cheek. "Not for anyone."

"Wouldn't change nothing. You already got my name. My real one."

"It would end the scandal."

"Well, see—now ya went and made it no fun."

A laugh escaped. She threw her arms around his neck and gave him a bold kiss. Pulling back, she searched his eyes. Despite all the talk recently of marriage, she'd never expected this to happen. Now that it was here, she knew it was too special to let go of. For this she wanted to be selfish. "I don't want anyone to know."

"Is that a yes?"

"If we do this, it has to be about us, not about them. Not about the reasons why it should be done. Not about—"

A bold kiss was all it took to shut her up. His arms circled her waist and held her close. It wasn't until he'd drawn a deep moan from her that he released her. "You don't gotta use so many words."

"Just us."

"Exactly. Except for one thing."

She took a step back and narrowed her eyes.

"Tom knows." He sighed and shrugged. "When I was gone those days I was in Pueblo. Tom helped me get everything set up, made sure I talked to the right people. And Nick knows. Already got the paperwork drawn up for whatever legal stuff we need."

"So that's what that bastard was hiding from me. I knew he was lying about something." She sat down hard in the chair. "Just how long have you been thinking about this? How long have you been planning it?"

He knelt in front of her and leaned on the arms of the chair until they were nose to nose. "You really thought I got that mad 'cause that bastard asked ya?"

"Well…yes."

"It was reason enough, but I was also chuffed he did it before I'd got everything worked out. Before I'd been able to find out if ya really wanted it."

"So…"

"I love ya. Ain't no one made me even think of it before. I figured if you'd manage to spin me 'round enough to be considering it—you might just be worth trying it."

"Romantic to the end." She twisted her lips to hide her amusement.

He chuckled. One brow rose. "So are we going to Denver?"

"It would be a shame to waste the tickets since you already bought them."

"One more thing."

"Oh, dear. I'm not sure I can handle anything else."

He rose so fast her chair wobbled. As she steadied herself, he began to rifle through a drawer. A string of curses started to flow from his mouth until she giggled. He cut her a glare. "Hush."

"Consider me hushed." She pinched her lips together tight in an attempt to stifle.

"Damn it. I thought I put it in here."

"Cole." Tommy's voice called over the pounding on the door.

Jane rushed toward the door.

"You idiot. You forgot you gave it to me to hide. Said Jane knew every corner of your room. If you're busy, make a quick end of—oh, hello." Tommy's fist still hung in mid-air.

Jane's eyebrow rose. With one hand set on her hip, she narrowed her eyes.

"Did I catch you in the middle of something? You both look so grumpy."

"Your voice is as romantic as a beheading. Even if we had been in the middle of something, our enthusiasm would have been depleted by your mere presence." Jane smirked. "Go on. You had something to tell Cole?"

"Well." Tommy cleared his throat.

Cole waved him into the room. "Come on in. We were just talking."

"Oh." Tommy's shoulders sagged in relief. He looked between them and his eyes grew wide. "*Oh.*"

Jane shut the door behind him. As she passed him on her way back to the table, she smacked him upside the head. "Helping Cole keep secrets from me, are you?"

"Not secrets." Tommy chuckled. "Surprises."

"It's becoming a secret now." Jane folded her arms across her chest. "Not even Michael or Kat is going to know."

"What?" Nothing caught Tommy off guard, it was fun to watch. "You're serious?"

"This is about us." She grinned. "Period."

Cole's arms circled her from behind and she felt him nod against her head. "We got reputations to maintain, after all."

Tommy threw his head back in laughter. "That is perfect. You're damn right I'll keep the secret. If the two of you went public with this, it would cause all sorts of chaos. No one would know what to think if you started acting responsible and proper."

"Why is it you're here again?" Jane's amusement died into a frown. "We were still discussing things."

"Oh, right." He dug into his pocket and pulled out a small bag. Tommy grinned. "I'll get out of your hair. Got a saloon to keep an eye on, after all. Since the owners are all busy and such."

Cole caught the bag, a low laugh warming her ear. "See ya tomorrow."

Jane waved and waited for the door to shut. The moment it did she piped up. "He's insane. Are you sure he can be trusted?"

"Your whole damn family is insane."

"Good point."

"Here."

"Hmm?" Jane grunted at his small nudge and looked down. A gasp escaped. "Cole, that's not a—"

"It ain't a wedding ring." He interrupted. "Or an engagement ring. You can wear it instead of the one you're already wearing."

"But, how? Where did it come from?"

"Was your grandmothers'."

"What?"

"Tom had it. I bet if we told him to, he'd tell anyone that asked that he gave it to ya 'cause he had no use for it."

"Is there anything you didn't think of?" Jane couldn't stop her grin. It was almost too good to be true, but she knew it wasn't. Because the proposal had been true to Cole. Short, to the point, infuriating, and quietly, unobtrusively romantic.

"I had Tom helping."

"So, no then?" She handed him the ring back.

"What are you doing?"

"You'll need something to put on my hand when we're married." She wrinkled her nose and scoffed. "Did I really just say that?"

"Sure sounded like ya did."

"Just us."

"That's all we need."

Three may keep a secret, if two of them are dead.
-Benjamin Franklin

Kat practically squealed. "Oh my heavens. Are you serious?"

Jane hushed Kat. Across the restaurant, Cole leaned on a chair talking to Norman, Graham, and Tom. Thankfully he appeared wrapped enough in the conversation he hadn't noticed Kat's squeal. Or figured it was normal. "Cole does not know yet. I had to tell someone, or I might just burst."

Kat nudged her none-too-gently when she continued staring across the room. "Jane."

"Hm?" Jane dragged her gaze back to her friend. "What?"

"I'm guessing this time you're a bit more openly happy about it? And perhaps you won't hide it from him so long?"

"Oh goodness, for certain. I'm definitely not going to keep it from him. I have every intention of telling him."

"When?"

Jane took in Cole's tall frame again. A pleasant heat flooded her cheeks when she realized this time he was staring just as hard at her as she was at him. Memories of the night before, and their plans for the days ahead took over every thought.

"*Jane.*"

"Ow." Jane rubbed her arm where Kat's hard poke had stung. "I'm sorry. What?"

"I asked when you're going to tell him." Kat sipped her tea. "I swear. As much as I appreciate your happiness—you both can be quite impossible to deal with when you are so disturbingly happy."

Jane stuck her tongue out at her friend. She sipped her own tea, contemplating the question. Honestly, she'd struggled with the idea since he'd proposed on the basis that nothing was *making* them get married. Her pregnancy could well disrupt that very idea. "I suppose I'll tell him this weekend when we are in Denver."

"Denver?" Kat straightened. "You're going to Denver?"

"Yes. We leave on this afternoon's train."

"When did this happen?"

Jane bit her lip, daring to turn her attention from Kat again. Cole's stare remained fixed on her, though he appeared to be doing a better job keeping conversation flowing than she was. "Cole surprised me with the idea. It is to be a celebration of us becoming partners." She couldn't stop her grin at her own twist on the words to tell the truth while avoiding it.

"You're terrible at keeping secrets. If you continue grinning like that, he'll suspect you're up to something." Kat smacked her hand.

"Oh no. He's fully aware what I'm grinning about."

"You are hopeless. Do you know how you'll tell him?"

"I will probably open my mouth and form the words." Jane widened her eyes in an attempt to appear innocent.

Kat's pitiful efforts to glare at Jane only managed to make the situation worse. Within moments they both dissolved in laughter. Shaking her head, Kat took Jane's hand in her own. "I'm happy for you. When do you sign the papers?"

"One o'clock. The train leaves at two."

"Jane?" Daisy dropped into the seat beside Kat. A frown tugged her full lips when her gaze swept through the restaurant. "Are you sure we should talk here?"

"Don't worry, Daisy. Cole should leave us alone for a little while. It's best we meet here, anyhow. If I went to the clinic he might get suspicious."

"From the grin she's wearing." Daisy jerked her thumb at Kat. "I'm guessing you've already told her."

"She certainly did. In between longing glances at Cole, of course." Kat leaned closer. "Apparently they had a thoroughly relaxing night."

Jane chuckled under Daisy's exasperation. "I did get sleep, Daisy. A few hours here and there were enough."

"You need to be well rested," Daisy urged.

"I know." Jane rushed to placate the doctor. Last thing she needed today was a scolding. "Last night was a bit—different for us. I promise I sleep when my body demands. I have little choice in the matter."

"That's a good start." Daisy relaxed enough to indicate she was satisfied.

"We're going to Denver for a few days." Jane smiled down at her hands, her excitement exceedingly difficult to contain. She raised her head to find Cole's welcome grin again. "Cole planned it as a surprise for me."

"That sounds like a wonderful idea." Daisy scooted her chair closer. It was a nice gesture to keep things quiet, although the growing din of arriving customers did enough to cover their conversation without trying too hard.

Jane's smile faded. "I know you told me I need to relax."

Daisy raised a hand to cover her own laughter when Kat snorted. Once she had a handle on her own amusement, she spoke. "You should stay rested. Relaxed is important, but so is rested. Right now that, and eating when you feel up to it, are the best recommendations I can make. You need to take care of yourself is all."

"I will. How often do you need to see me?" Jane rearranged her napkin on her lap as if to cover the belly that had yet to form. She fought against the rising panic as the memories of her previous pregnancy rose yet again.

"All things considered; I'd like to keep a closer eye on you. It'll be easier once Cole knows, of course." Daisy set her hand on Jane's. "I'm not overly concerned at this time, but I'd still like to be cautious. We'll say every couple of weeks. If things go well and you're feeling well, we can slow down."

"I can manage that. Thank you." Jane exhaled the fear best she could, and even managed a smile. "I should be telling Cole this weekend. It'll be very good timing."

"I have to say, it's nice to see you in such a good mood." Daisy leaned on her hand. "I was concerned the news would be difficult—even with you and Cole currently getting along."

"It's still a shock," Jane admitted. "To be honest, I'm still not certain how Cole is going to react to the news."

"Oh, please. He's going to be thrilled." Kat scoffed. "He was just as torn up as you were the first go-round."

Daisy eyed Kat sideways, a frown marring her pretty features. For a moment Jane could have sworn she saw the old jealousy Daisy'd had over Jane and Cole rear its head. "You weren't even there."

"No, but Jane was wrapped up tight in the middle of the mess when I arrived in town. Even back then they were mad as March hare's—not because of anything but their own pain. It's one of their biggest flaws," Kat said. "Rather than admitting the hurt, they get all worked up and mad at each other."

"And then we get to make up," Jane chimed in. Her grin grew stronger again.

"Fine." Kat laughed. "It's also one of your biggest strengths."

"As I was saying." Jane dared another look toward Cole. Her stomach fluttered at his wink. With a deep sigh she dragged her attention back to her table. "Like I said yesterday, the timing of this little revelation is horrendously bad."

"Oh, I don't know. After everything that happened with Lizzie and Al." Kat shrugged. "It might just be the perfect time."

Jane rolled her eyes, but her smile just wouldn't leave her face. Not until the familiar stab of fear returned. "I'm also terrified of losing another child. It happened so suddenly; I had barely come to terms with it before it was gone."

"You were further along." Kat said quietly. "Which gives you more time to worry."

"I know. Last time I didn't have any symptoms, really. It was two months before I even thought it might be possible." Jane cleared her throat to remove the lump that had formed. "I'm just worried it could happen again. I'm worried about how in heavens we're going to raise a child with our lives as they are."

"You'll adjust." Kat shrugged. "You seem to have an enormous capacity for it."

"Will you move out of the saloon?" Daisy jumped when Jane cast a dark look her way. "I was just asking. You are going to have a child."

"The Hangman's Inn is our home. I can't imagine living in a house again. I wouldn't mind more room, but I thought that before I knew." Jane frowned and studied her cup of tea. "I'm sure we'll figure it out."

"I'm going to miss you." Kat called out unreasonably loud and shrill. She winked when Jane jumped at the yell. Without another word, Kat disappeared behind her teacup.

The smile shot back to her face when Jane spotted Cole sauntering over, and she rose to greet him. They met in a kiss to make up for all the longing glances. Her fingers buried in his hair, and she pressed into him eagerly. Only Daisy clearing her throat managed to pull back their burning desire.

When they separated, Cole's eyes burned with heat, but his wicked grin fell right into place. "So what have you been talking about?"

"I've been regaling Daisy and Kat with stories of our night together."

"Liar."

"You're just going to have to believe me." Jane chuckled. She stood on tiptoe and whispered. "Did Tommy find out anything?"

"Don't know." His thumb brushed along her side. He gave a nod to the table. "We got things to do."

Jane smiled and waved. "I'll give you a full report when we get back."

Cole pulled her toward the door without further ceremony. Once outside, he frowned. "Tom won't tell me nothing."

"Well why not? He needs to." Jane sped along the street with him.

"He says he don't want us to be distracted on our weekend." He slowed and pulled her toward the inn. "Tells me he's got everything handled."

"Maybe not knowing will keep me distracted."

Cole kept pulling her through the saloon portion of the inn. Straight back to the storeroom where he pressed her against the wall. "So you're gonna be thinking about business?"

"Maybe." She whispered breathlessly.

"Nothing I can do to—keep you focused?"

"Like what?" She squeaked when his lips assaulted her neck, teasing each nerve to life. Her nails dug into his arm and a moan escaped. "Cole…"

"Well, I could marry ya."

"That's not all you can do to me."

"It ain't all I got planned, neither."

Give all to love; obey thy heart.
-Ralph Waldo Emerson

Nearly half an hour later, Jane slipped outside. Her body still tingled in such delightful ways, she knew her grin had to show what a delightful half hour she'd spent. She smoothed down her skirts against wrinkles that might have emerged from the quick tryst.

A quick glance at the clock told her she had thirty minutes before they had to be at Lloyd's, so she set off to see that the library was set for the next few days.

"Lou."

Jane stopped short at Tommy's voice. Her bright smile didn't waver as she turned to find the source. She found him walking toward her from the jail. "Tommy!"

"Are you all set to go?" Tommy accepted her hug but placed a firm hand under her elbow. He guided her away from the library on a path through town instead.

"I am. Thank you for all of your assistance in this matter. I'm rather surprised—"

"'Cause I beat on him?"

"Not really. You were defending me, even though there was nothing to defend. I have seen you both over the past few days, it remains quite clear you hold no animosity, nor does he." She frowned. "Did you truly believe Cole would ever hit me on purpose?"

"To be honest, at that point thinking was not my strong suit. Never was when it came to the fools you got yourself involved with."

She gently freed her elbow to lace her arm through his. The simple action was meant to soothe the anger in his tone. Tommy alone knew the secrets Clara had long kept about the many men she let abuse her. "I am not her."

"I know." He cleared his throat, then shook off whatever emotion plagued him much as Jane herself tended to do. "Walk with me a bit, will you? I've got Edgar watching the saloon, Iris is running a table, and you've got half an hour before you need to sign the papers."

"All you had to do was ask. I didn't need reasoning." She smiled as they strode past the shops toward the outskirts of town. "Of course I'll walk with you, although you do look terribly serious at the moment."

"As the older of the two of us you're telling about your plans, I need to be."

"Is this where you become quite the overprotective bear of an older brother?"

"I always am."

"Fair point." She allowed him to lead her all the way out of town to the open field where the Army camp had once sat. In the relative quiet, she took a deep breath to brace herself. "Before you start—there's something else you should know so you might be properly bear-like."

He stopped their forward motion at her words. His suspicious gaze taking a measure of her. "Lou. That's not the way to start a thing."

"I'm pregnant." The way his face immediately flipped from suspicion to slack made her giddy. She tried to hide the burgeoning laughter, but the longer he stared, the more amusement she gleaned. "Thomas Eugene Young, wake the hell up."

Tommy blinked several times. "Sorry. I wasn't—wait. What did you call me?"

"Thomas Eugene."

"How'd you know my middle name?"

"I—heard it?" Even as she said the words, she knew they weren't right. Though she tried to place where she'd heard his middle name used before, no memory came to mind. She shrugged in resignation. "I have no idea. The words just came out. Such things happen sometimes, though it's unpredictable what or when. That is what you choose to comment on?"

"Cole didn't tell me anything about a baby."

"That would be because he doesn't know yet. I only learned myself yesterday." She bit her lip as her gaze slipped back toward town. A deep sigh welled. "I was overwhelmed by the whole idea, to be honest. After last time. Then last night Cole said…"

"He said he wanted it to be just about the two of you."

"Exactly, and this isn't just about us. I couldn't tell him then."

"When will you?"

"In Denver."

"I never would have agreed to help if I didn't think it was a good thing." Tommy draped an arm over her shoulder. "The marriage, I mean."

"But?"

"I want to know you're sure this is what you want."

"Marriage?"

"All of it. Marriage. The secrecy you're asking for."

"I love him. With everything that I am, I love him. I don't see marriage as a necessity, as something I 'need', and I never did. For us it will just be an extension of what we already are."

"It's a confirmation of what you already are, Mrs. Spencer."

A smile tugged at her lips, and she nodded. "Yes."

"And the secrecy?"

"'In your light I learn how to love, in your beauty, how to make poems. You dance inside my chest, where no one sees you'. Rumi."

"Problem with that is everyone does see."

"What Cole and I are to each other may be a matter of great public speculation and gossip—but the truth of us has always been between us and us alone. No one needs to know anything—for talk is only gossip, the heart is truth."

"I see."

"This marriage is about us, and us alone. We have been far more to each other than people realize or gossip about. Our public displays feed their suspicions and allow them to think we are merely unable to keep our hands off each other for long. They believe our relationship all passion and little true emotion. Even if they suspect something akin to love, they believe it more about possession than any true depth."

"And what of those that know different?"

"Those that do—such as you, Michael, or Katherine—are few." She took his hands in hers. "We are not doing this because we need to. We aren't doing this to make others happy, because such things are trivial. All we need is our own happiness."

"Then why do it at all?"

"Because we want to. For us, and us alone. To confirm to each other the commitment we know we share, what we are to each other. There is no need for anyone to know but us."

"I can't rightly figure if you're being logical or illogical about this."

"Both." She laughed, glad his joined hers. "Logic is only a part of why we're keeping it to ourselves. Why we're doing it is all about the heart, about us, and the love that we share. 'All are needed by each one; nothing is fair or good alone'. Emerson."

"The man is a damn fool for you." Tommy hugged her tight. When he released her from the embrace, he didn't let her far. His hands landed on her shoulders to hold tight. "For as long as you want the secret kept, I'll keep it. I just wanted to be sure you were clear on why you were doing it. You can be annoyingly illogical when it comes to someone you feel so strongly about."

"Do you not believe Cole is worth being completely illogical for?"

"Considering all you've put him though, and he's still hanging around? Yeah. I guess he might be a little worth it."

"No threats for if he hurts me?"

"I think you'd hurt him first—and I already made my threats."

"I'm not surprised."

*Whoever wishes to keep a secret must hide
the fact that he possesses one.
—Johann Wolfgang von Goethe*

Jane and Cole arrived in Denver so late in the afternoon, they wasted no time dawdling in the hotel. Once they'd secured their room and sent their luggage up, they headed for dinner.

Cole originally hinted that they might do the ceremony in the morning by pronouncing it an important day. Yet, as they strolled after dinner he backpedaled on such plans. She attributed it to a case of nerves at the idea of being married again. She worried telling him about the baby could make those nerves worse.

"I was thinking tomorrow I might show you what them marks in the ledger are. Ya know, the Denver ones." His grip on her hand grew immeasurably tighter, and the reason for his nerves found another explanation besides their upcoming nuptials.

Though surprised at this idea, she kept her face calm as it had been. She might have been curious, but she wouldn't force the issue. "All right. If you wish."

"Well…"

A feminine voice unfamiliar to Jane interrupted before he could finish whatever he hesitated to say. "Cole Mitchell, as I live and breathe."

Jane's mixture of concern and amusement grew when the already tense man beside her became even more locked up. Under normal circumstances a woman knowing his name had never caused him such turmoil.

She allowed a sideways glance his way, curious as to the hard set of his jaw and the way his gaze darted around as if for escape. Curiosity turned her attention back to the attractive young woman that approached.

If she were to guess, Jane would think she was perhaps a year or two younger than Kat. Her hair fell in flaxen waves rather than a proper restrained style. The clothes she wore with grace were elaborate, meant to draw attention, and they suited her well.

Without any semblance of propriety, the stranger embraced Cole and kissed him boldly on the cheek. "Well, well, aren't you all gussied up? Changing the image? Or are you deigning to visit Alma?"

Though the woman behaved in such a familiar way to her betrothed, Jane felt no threat. Even as Cole slipped his arm around Jane's waist and tugged her tight against his hip. Jane merely smiled at the stranger.

Cole finally spoke, his teeth gritted so the word was difficult to understand. "Leanne."

Leanne nodded to Jane, her gaze sweeping Cole's possessive hold on her. She grinned up at Cole. "What's this?"

"This is Jane Spencer, my—"

"Spencer!" Leanne gasped so loud several heads turned their way, but she never stopped smiling. "My goodness, you scallywag! Did you get married? How did she rope you?"

Cole's eye twitched, his jaw now firmly locked. Leanne's intense and joyous line of questioning was having quite the effect. Jane had no idea how Leanne knew his real name, but in light of his state of tension, she figured she might rescue him this once, if nothing else in hopes of assuaging her own curiosity on this new development.

"I'm his business partner," Jane interjected before Leanne could tease him further. She held out her hand. "I'm part owner of The Hangman's Inn. I bought out Graham Cooke for his portion of the business."

"Business partner? Really?" Leanna shook Jane's hand warmly, her brows almost disappearing under her elaborate hat." "I never thought Cole would be one to get a madam. Certainly not one so buttoned up."

"I am not a madam," Jane corrected, though not offended by the insinuation. Rather, she couldn't stop her chuckle at the idea.

"You're not?" Cole muttered under his breath, his familiar wicked smirk finally returning.

Jane offered him the tiniest of glares before returning her attention to Leanne. "You also must realize that some appearances can be deceiving, Miss…"

"Leanne DuBois. Please, call me Leanne. I'm an old friend of Cole's." Leanne nudged Cole, quite the wicked gleam of her own going to match his. "Actually, to be honest. I was under contract to him once, wasn't I? Ages ago, really."

Jane's stomach hurt from the laughter she held back at Cole's continuing discomfort. "Now isn't that interesting? Cole?"

"She left to start her own business." Cole didn't meet her gaze, or Leanne's. He stared down the street, offering little more than a shrug. "She was too demanding, so I let her out of her contract."

This time Jane let her laughter free, but the look Cole cut her forced her to rein it in. Though the whole situation was amusing and piqued her curiosity beyond belief, she didn't want to upset him too badly. However, such a statement couldn't be ignored. "Too demanding? Really?"

"And her name weren't DuBois when she was one of my girls." Cole's tone didn't sound quite upset, Jane could detect a hint of amusement. "It was Potts."

"Which is not very conducive to creating a high-class establishment." Leanne tossed her waves over her shoulder. "So I changed it."

"A high-class whorehouse, then?" Jane couldn't hide her intrigue, to leave Cole's to create such a place took some gumption. "Sounds intriguing. I guess you've done well for yourself."

"If Cole had listened to me, he might've done as well." Leanne shrugged. "No matter now, I suppose. Why don't you both come by? I bet we could find someone to your taste, Cole."

"Why don't we?" Jane tilted her head to meet Cole's gaze. She held no animosity, nor any fear he would take the bait Leanne offered. Maybe that's why tension seeped from his shoulders. "We could go see what you missed out on."

"I didn't miss out on nothing." Somehow Cole's fingers found a way to pinch her through her layers of skirts. "And I already got something to my taste, Leanne."

Leanne didn't hide her surprise. "Is that so? Well then, Miss Spencer."

"It's Jane," she corrected.

"Jane. You must also be more than appearances lead one to believe." Leanne took another step closer. "I feel we might be great friends."

"I am more than I appear. Very much so." Jane squeezed Cole's hand to stop his fingers nervous cadence against her corset. "You may be right. Why don't we go, Cole? I would not mind seeing Leanne's establishment."

"I dunno," Cole hedged.

"Oh you must." Leanne reached out to squeeze Jane's hand. "Come to the Bonne Nuit. Tonight. I would love for you to see it."

"We were gonna take a walk and head back to the hotel." Cole interrupted Jane's attempt at reply. "We got visiting to do tomorrow."

"Cole." Jane elbowed him. "I don't mind. I'm now more intrigued to see this place as she calls it 'The Good Night'."

Leanne gave a gleeful clap. "Impressive."

"That's what it means?" Cole couldn't stop his chuckle. "You never told me that."

"You never asked," Leanne corrected him. "Talk him into it, Jane. It's not far. You do remember where it is, don't you Cole?"

"I remember." Cole still avoided the woman's gaze.

"We'll be by shortly," Jane reassured the young woman, who remained nonplussed by Cole's rudeness. No matter,

Jane couldn't resist the chance to see the Bonne Nuit in person.

"Wonderful. I'll see you soon. I'll be sure to let the girls know to expect company beyond our usual fare." Leanne waved to Jane and dared to peck Cole on the cheek again as she passed.

Jane waited for the young woman to round a corner before she nudged Cole. "Yes?"

"I was hoping we could go visiting before we saw Leanne." He rubbed a hand over his face. For a moment, he looked older than normal, but shook his head and returned to his normal self in a moment. "This ain't gonna end well."

Jane couldn't match his level of foreboding. "Why? Do you expect me to get jealous?"

"Not exactly."

"She seems very nice. I'm not in the least bit jealous. I know what I have, and what she doesn't. I think tonight could be rather fun."

"She was a pain."

"So you said. Demanding is how you put it. Goodness knows how you hate a demanding woman."

"When they ain't you, I do."

The sentiment warmed another laugh free. "Good to know."

"Sure you want to do this?"

"I am. Are you?"

"Not a bit."

Our duty is to preserve what the past has had to say for itself, and to say for ourselves what shall be true for the future.
-John Ruskin

The building they stopped in front of could have been any home along the street. Elegant and large as though it belonged to one of the wealthier denizens, there was nothing garish, nothing that screamed whorehouse about it. It almost appeared more like a boarding house or hotel based on its size than a whorehouse.

In fact, only its proximity to the heart of the city and nearby entertainment establishments would have made Jane think to put such a place there. "This is it?"

"Back entrance down the alley for men pretending they ain't got business inside. Most men don't care. Leanne's got a reputation, after all."

"Does she now?" Jane eyed the building again, now spotting the simple shingle above the ringer with elegant writing on it which said, 'Le Bonne Nuit'. "How'd she afford such a place with what you pay the whores?"

"Don't matter, does it?"

"Would you quit fidgeting?"

Cole shrugged. "I think we'd have a better time if we went back to the hotel. Going here ain't worth our time."

"Relax." She loosened his tie and unbuttoned his top button. "It will be fine. This is just a whorehouse. It isn't like I'm not used to it."

His hands rested on her shoulders. "Just don't care to be spending time around Leanne and her lot if I got better things to be doing."

"You've always got better things to be doing." With a wink, she stepped back. Before he could waylay her, she hopped up the steps to ring the bell. Moments later he stood behind her, his warm breath lingered near her right her. She thought he might be speaking, but as he was at her bad ear, she hadn't the slightest clue what it could be.

Before Jane could demand to know what he'd said, the door swung open. Leanne stood there, her bright smile not covering her surprise. "Cole! I had begun to think you might have talked Jane out of coming. Get yourself on in here."

Over his protest, Cole got yanked through the door and plastered with another kiss on the cheek. He grimaced as he wiped the kiss off. Without a word, he dragged Jane in behind him.

"Jane, I'm so pleased you came along." Leanne clasped Jane's hands. "Cole is quite familiar with the place, so why don't I give you the grand tour?"

"Nah. She don't need a tour." Cole tried to grab Jane's arm, but Leanne was too quick for him. He all but pouted in reaction.

Jane chuckled low but remained at Leanne's side despite Cole's mood. "I would love a tour, actually. I appreciate whatever concern you're showing, but I don't need it. We both know my sensibilities are far from delicate. Besides, this place is beautiful and I would love to see more."

"I don't think it's you he's concerned about." Leanne didn't elaborate on the cryptic statement, but Cole's low grumble sounded like a bit of a warning. Leanne shook her head. "Uh-uh. Never you worry. I'll be good to your *business* partner. I'll only speak glowingly about you."

"That's what I'm afraid of," Cole muttered.

Jane tried to get a read on Cole after that statement, but Leanne whisked her away before she could make much sense of what was going on. They walked through a waiting area where several women dressed scantily, but at the same time not crudely, lounged.

"Help yourself to some whiskey," Leanne called over her shoulder. "It's a slow night so far. Be nice to the girls—they're bored."

Cole stalked over and pulled Jane close. He leaned down and nibbled at her neck, then spoke quietly into her right ear.

"Damn it, Cole. How many times do I have to tell you which ear?" She smacked his arm when he pulled back. Leanne still had a hold of her hand, so she lingered in limbo between the two of them, offering Cole a half-angry glare.

"Don't be so damn social." Cole grumbled into her good ear. "Just take the tour and we go. We got a lot to do. Behave yourself."

Jane pouted at the paternal sort of reprimand and reached out to grope him in retaliation. When he groaned she whispered, "Miss me," before scooting closer to Leanne.

"You truly are more than you appear." Leanne led her past the gilded bar to the carpeted stairs. "Aren't you?"

"Did you not believe me?" Jane followed without question, smiling at the note of awe she thought she detected in Leanne's voice. She let her hand glide along the well-polished banister and took note of the intricate carvings that bumped along her fingertips. At the top of the stairs, she paused to admire the stunning toile wallpaper.

"I have to admit," Leanne's warm voice interrupted Jane's admiration. "With how you appear, except for the bruises you carry on your visage, it is difficult to imagine."

"Is it now?"

"No offense, of course."

"Of course. However, you should know better than anyone that appearances can be deceiving. In this business I imagine you get all sorts, and none of them are usually as they appear to be."

"Quite true." Leanne peeked down the stairs before she moved closer. "To be honest, this isn't so much of a tour as it is my chance to get to know you. There isn't much to show. Downstairs, upstairs. Every girl has their own room. Mine is at the end of the hall. Then again, did you really want a tour of this place? Or did you perhaps just want to torture Cole?"

"A little of both," Jane admitted. "I don't know what has him so on edge, but it is rather fun to make him squirm."

"You two look awful cozy. How long have you known him?" Leanne led her down the hall toward the door Jane assumed to be her room.

"Goodness, over two years now. He quite literally saved my life."

Leanne stopped dead in her tracks. "No kidding?"

"No. I was nearly dead when I stumbled into his saloon. Graham tried to pronounce me as such, Cole sought to be certain. He got Daisy working on me and made her stay with me until I was well enough." The memory of her first lucid meeting with Cole brought a smile to her features. Then a shudder followed suit when she thought how she might have ended up in a pine box then as well came over her. She refocused on the conversation. "He was one of the few people in town I found tolerable at first, and we became friends."

"At first."

Jane laughed at the suspicious look in Leanne's eyes that tied with her smirk. She laced her arm with Leanne's and finished the walk to the madam's door. "However, I will not deny that I was completely attracted to him, and after some months we acted on the attraction. Since then, well it's been chaos. He's done a lot for me, though."

"What's life without a little chaos?"

"My life would be non-existent. I cannot seem to function without some level of chaos going on around me at all times."

Leanne unlocked her door for them but paused to fix her icy blue gaze on Jane. "So then you and Cole are together."

"Very much so."

"But you introduced yourself as business partners?"

"You assumed we were married, which we are not. Not to mention you did so based solely on my last name, which I find intriguing myself." Jane might have brushed off the event earlier to spare Cole some nerves, but that coupled with Leanne's familiarity with Cole had sparked many questions.

"Still. Business partners?" Leanne sidestepped the question.

"Quite honestly, it's simply the easiest explanation. We were screwing long before we came close to being anything like business partners. Now we live together, and as of earlier today I became part owner of The Hangman's Inn."

"I can't believe he named the—wait. Did you say you live together?" Leanne leaned against the door she had yet to open, her delicate skin paling further. "As in you and he, together, in the same room? Specifically, his room?"

"Yes."

"Wow. You must be different. No girl ever went into his room. Ever. He always used one of theirs. Nobody ever dared step into his room, not even his favorites."

"We aren't restricted to his room by any means, but as for every night, that is where we lie."

Leanne laughed outright. Whatever tension she'd carried dissipated as she pushed open the door. "Jane, I think I'm starting to like you."

"Only now beginning to? I had hoped my charm worked much faster." Jane followed her into the room, and politely closed the door behind them. When the lamp flickered to life, Jane stopped short. The room was not at all what she'd expected.

Rather than competing with the luxury of the rest of the whorehouse, as she'd expected for a madam's room, this room was rather small and plain, easily called comfortable. Wood walls that had been whitewashed, a single bed, a dresser, a small stove, and a table were all that occupied the space. A door beside the dresser intrigued Jane, but she wasn't so boldly nosy to go snooping about Leanne's room.

"This is my room. As this is my establishment, I don't serve our customers; I only make the matching with my girls. I like to be comfortable at the end of the night, and to me comfortable means simple." She gestured toward the door Jane had noted. "My closet is bigger than this room."

"You have a closet?" Jane couldn't contain her curiosity; relieved Leanne waved her on toward the door. Without further encouragement, she pulled it open. A large room, filled with an immense collection of clothes lining the walls, and shoes lining the floor greeted her. So many lovely colors and patterns to be found. "My goodness."

"This business is all about appearance. I have to keep a good supply of options." Leanne followed her into the room. One by one, she began to pull several items down. "I've got more than I need here. You know, Cole may get a kick out of the schoolmarm look, but you could stand to loosen up a little."

"No, I'm perfectly fine with—"

"I promise you'll still be perfectly respectable." Leanne shoved a pile of clothes in Jane's arms so high, she couldn't see over them. Then the clothes were pushed down until Leanne met her gaze. "You and Cole live together, are business partners, and he never once mentioned me?"

"Not that I'm aware of. What was your name when you were under contract?"

Leanne slipped by Jane, back into the bedroom. Her voice carried back so soft Jane hardly heard. "It was Leanne Potts."

Jane dropped the clothes in surprise. A whore without a floral name as Cole had adopted for every whore? Everything ran over in her mind. "You didn't have a whore's name? Not Lily, Bluebell, or Morning Glory?" She stepped over the pile of clothes into the room.

Leanne's back remained to her as she set a teapot on the stove. Her light brown hair swayed under the negative shake of her head. "No. Nothing like that. Just Leanne."

Cole's nerves. The eyes. The hair. "My heavens. You're family."

"Sort of."

Jane sank into a chair. Based on what she knew of Cole, this didn't fit. Then again, perhaps it did somehow. "I thought his family all died, save for his pa, whom he never speaks of."

"The family he counts sure is, save for our bastard pa." Leanne set the teapot on the table. "That being said, we share a pa. Our ma's aren't the same."

"And what of this Alma you mentioned?"

"Oh no. If I tell you that, he'll cut me off. Already he hardly speaks to me anymore." Leanne rubbed her hands on her skirts, her gaze distant. "Our pa, he married my ma too. After he'd been married to Cole's ma for a long time."

Jane poured them both some tea. She encouraged the young woman to hold onto the warm cup to stop her fidgeting.

"Cole, he didn't want nothing to do with us once he figured it all out. He hated us as much as he hated what his pa did. Until…" Leanne took a sip of tea to fill the quiet of her own dropped sentence. "Short of it is Pa was fixing to do something real bad, and it made Cole angrier than I've ever seen him. He gave Ma the money to take us away, far away, and she did. We went all the way to Indiana and stayed."

Jane set her hand on Leanne's arm the moment the woman set down her cup.

"We were rather content, and happier than we'd been in some time. Then Ma got sick, and went and died on us." Leanne's nail tapped the handle of her cup, her gaze far off. "Cole didn't have to do anything, really. He could have left us there alone."

Though she didn't miss the 'us' Leanne mentioned, she thought better than to speak of it. "But he didn't?"

"No. He brought me to Colorado. Claimed I was under contract. I never was a whore, but he made a good show of it, handing me off to those too drunk to do anything but pass out, or those on opium. I was only fourteen at the time."

Fourteen. Too young for any whore, though Jane knew many men didn't care. Despite his outward appearances, Cole would. Then again, he also pretended he didn't care about a lot of things he did. None of this surprised Jane in the least.

"Cole made me sign the contract, but I never once worked. I never serviced a man. When I got older and wise to what happened behind those closed doors, I got a mind to speak out. I guess it comes with being sixteen, but I sure gave Cole hell for a while."

"He usually deserves it when he's given hell by a woman." Jane smiled warmly to counter Leanne's more hesitant one. "But he said you were demanding?"

"I wanted in. I was young and stupid and had an idea to earn my keep as it were. Believe it or not, he protected me from all of that."

"I believe it."

"If the truth is to be known, it's all just like you said—appearances are deceiving. I run this joint—I don't actually use my talents under the guise of being madam. However, I never have used my talents. Not even once. Cole made certain of that."

Jane blinked fast to cover the surprise that dropped over her like a bucket. Then the amusement tickled the shock away. For a man that let this girl believe he despised her, he'd protected her from the sort of man that would have used her services in a mining camp. "Of course, he couldn't truly stop you now should you want to."

"No, I suppose not. What need do I have to do my own business now, though? I employ twenty lovely girls that get the job done very well. Cole helped me take over this place and get settled when I was seventeen. This building was falling apart and there were only six girls, but he kept helping for a while. I think that's why he got a partner, so he'd have a little more cash."

Answers to so many questions fell into place with this informative conversation. Then again, a hundred more cropped up to beg answers. Jane remained silent to them all. "With just a little help from Cole, you turned this place to what it is now? That is impressive."

"Not so much. Cole lent me a few of his girls so I wouldn't have to start from scratch. I got some carpenters to exchange business for business and got things fixed up in a year. Once it was decent and we started to turn a profit, it got much easier to do upkeep and put the gild on."

"And so, you've never had to service a man? Not ever?"

"No."

"And you've never perhaps wanted to?"

Leanne lifted her chin. The unease she'd been projecting now turned to amusement. "Not particularly. My girls don't know this—so don't tell. It's much easier to boss them around when they think I know more than just what I've learned by observation alone."

Jane couldn't keep the laughter from her voice. "Observation?"

"I was fifteen, of course I was curious. Then again, that's probably also part of why I have no desire to attempt on my own. Cole's clientele was not exactly appealing."

"True. Even now that it's the Hangman's Inn not all of the clientele are anything more than miners to this day."

"He hasn't been to visit me in a couple of years now. I guess I know why."

"We've been rather—it's been a crazy couple of years to say the least."

Leanne tilted her head now studying Jane intently. "Do tell how you ended up with the surname of Spencer."

"It's a rather long story." Jane took a sip of tea to balance her answer, for they could not cover her whole story in a short conversation, and she imagined Cole was already pacing the floor below. "Short version is that I have amnesia. I don't remember much of anything beyond the past two years."

"How horrible."

"Sometimes it is, but I have a full life. My family from before found me again in Colorado, and after some particularly awful events passed my life has been quite good. I didn't enjoy going by Jane Doe any longer, and I did not wish to use the name of the person I was before I lost my memory. In the end, I took the last name of Spencer."

Leanne leaned closer, her voice dropping to a conspiratorial hush. "You do know that's Cole's name, right? From before?"

Jane tried to keep her smile hidden away, but the corners of her lips tugged upward treacherously. "I do."

"Interesting."

"But that's neither here nor there." Already there'd been far too many revelations without Cole's knowledge. Jane wasn't upset with Cole for not telling her, not even a little, but she was intrigued even more. Not that she didn't have her own secret to reveal, she just needed to figure out when. "As it stands, Cole is probably a bundle of nerves."

"I'll sick one of the girls on him, it'll relax him."

"I'll break their fingers."

"Oooh, all right. I suppose I won't do that." Leanne laughed. "Of course, if we stay up here much longer he might just come up and bust in the door."

"I think we ought to have a little fun with him. After all, I'm sure this conversation is exactly why he didn't want me coming up here." Truth was, knowing what he did for Leanne made her admire the man more, but how he could be embarrassed about it, about telling her, was beyond her understanding.

"What sort of fun?" Leanne perked up, her eyes alit with amusement.

"We need to make him suffer." Jane smiled, a plan brewing quickly in her head. "We'll need to involve your girls, and some of your clothes, if you think everyone would be game."

"I'm certain it won't be an issue. I thought you didn't want the girls touching him?"

"For this, I will make an exception—sort of."

"What did you have in mind?"

"I'm going to drive him insane, and if all goes well he won't know for sure it's me."

"Oooh—how fun!"

Appearances are often deceiving.
—Aesop

Leanne walked around the bar cool as ice. She gave him a once-over, her lips pursed. "Would you relax?"

Cole's tension didn't ease at her words. A quick scan of the room showed she'd returned without Jane. He eyed the drink she poured him along with one for herself. "Where's Jane?"

"Making nice with my girls upstairs. Why? Afraid to let her out of your sight?"

"What did ya do up there for so long?" He had a sneaking suspicion he knew but tried to cover his own annoyance. He gripped the glass too tight, though.

"We had a lovely chat about what color the sky is."

"Leanne."

"It's blue, you know." Leanne didn't appear to notice the bite in his tone. Instead, she laughed. "After all of these years, you can't bring yourself to care two figs about me, can you? That man was a bastard, but he lied to us as much as he did to you."

"Did you tell her?"

"There's not a soul left to embarrass. Our mothers are both dead. He never gave a shit anyway. The only one with any embarrassment is you, because the story makes you out like a moderately decent person. Heaven forbid." She leaned toward him. "Why would you not tell your *business* partner who happens to carry your real name?"

"I was gonna tell her, on this trip actually. You went and did it for me anyway, didn't you?" He relaxed his grip so he didn't unintentionally shatter the glass off perfectly good whiskey. After a second he tossed it back, the last fear niggling his brain. "Did you tell her about Alma?"

"I'm not that stupid. Does she really live with you? In your room?" At his nod, her brows raised. "Then she must be awful special. How'd she come by the name Spencer anyhow?"

"What's it to ya?"

"Just curious. She's not at all your usual type. You've always like them vulnerable, and more importantly, owned by you. She's definitely not vulnerable, and it doesn't seem like you own her."

"No one could." Cole didn't deny the pride that seeped into his tone.

"So why her?"

"I don't gotta explain myself to you."

She gave him a dark look. "In the past half hour I've learned more about you and what you've been up to the past couple of years than you have ever bothered to tell me. When are you going to stop acting like I'm the one that created the problems? It was our pa, *not* me."

"You're the reason he married her too."

"You mean my mother? Sorry 'bout you, but you're wrong. They were married two years before I came along."

Cole pulled back like he'd been bitten. That wasn't how he'd heard it; then again he'd heard it from the lying bastard's mouth. He shook off the shock and tried to change the subject. "You're the one that stopped sending letters. Figured you finally gave up."

"You're hopeless. I don't know how Jane puts up with you. She's far too nice for a sad little man like you."

An unbridled smile graced his lips, and he downed the fresh whiskey she poured him. "She ain't so nice."

"I've noticed that too." With a chuckle, Leanne poured another drink for them both. "You're happy. It's disconcerting to see, but good. Don't you dare muck it up."

"Don't intend to."

A hand teased along Cole's side, wrapping around to dance across his thigh. A quick glance and the familiarity of the touch convinced him it was Jane's hand.

He quirked a brow and smirked before he grabbed the hand to still it. When he glanced over his shoulder to find a strange girl, the smirk was quickly replaced with a frown and he squeezed the hand tight. "What the hell do ya think you're doin'?"

Eyes wide, the girl flushed. "Weren't you here looking for some company?"

"No."

Leanne chuckled behind the bar. "Oh, let her go Cole. Jill was occupied when I gave word you were to be left alone."

Cole released the hand and turned his attention back to Leanne, ignoring the noise of the girl scrambling away. "Sure she was. What're you up to?"

"You are so suspicious."

"Really? So where did all the girls come from?" Cole turned back to the parlor where nearly fifteen girls now gathered, setting themselves into enticing positions. "They weren't down here when Jane and I got here."

"When you arrived, at least half of them were occupied. Now they aren't and down the street is a burlesque show that ends in about five minutes. I like to have a full parlor when that happens."

Cole pursed his lips and turned back to glare at Leanne. "So where's Jane?"

"I'm sure she's still upstairs talking to Kim—who doesn't appear to be down here." Leanne tossed back her whiskey and winked. "I've had an almost complete change of staff since you were here last. Take a look and tell me what you think. I do love getting your opinions on my establishment."

"Liar." Still, Cole turned back around to take a look. She wasn't lying, as only one of the women at first glance was familiar. After all, he still ran a brothel, it wouldn't hurt to look, and Jane wasn't the jealous kind. Much.

One by one he did a once-over of each of the girls. A blond with an elaborate get-up, a redhead in what appeared to be a wig. As done up and fancy as they all were, none of them caught his eye yet. Not when he had the real thing.

"See anything you like?" Leanne practically purred near him.

He was about to turn away when a brunette with her back to him captured his full attention. "Looks like you got a good group." He tried to turn away, but then the brunette bent over to whisper to the girl next to her. The top she wore was sheer and tucked into an elaborately embroidered corset that cinched her waist tight over the swell of her hips.

"A few of them are very new." Whiskey splashed into a glass and Leanne pushed it into the corner of his sight.

He blinked a few times to clear his vision, and once again tried to turn away, but then the brunette moved again. Her short, bustled skirt didn't cover much of her long legs, and when she set her foot on the leg of another girl to adjust her stockings he caught a flash of a garter.

With a dry throat, he narrowed his eyes and studied her intently. After all the hours he'd spent getting to know every single inch of Jane, he was certain he'd know her anywhere. He drew his gaze up the lean length of leg again and along her waist and shoulders, pausing at the dark brown, and very straight, hair. "Leanne."

"Yes?" When he turned around to face her, Leanne was chuckling as she wiped down a glass.

"Give me another damn whiskey." Before she could protest his full glass, he tossed it back and pushed it across the bar.

"You look miserable." The damn woman would not stop grinning. Every chuckle ramped his suspicions up further. "You usually enjoy watching my girls make their preparations. Are they not to your liking?"

"You're not—"

"Oh, excuse me. The first guests have arrived, and they have every intention of using the services of my girls."

Cole swiped the bottle from her hand before she could step away. He poured himself another very full glass of whiskey while she worked her magic.

He narrowed his eyes when one gentleman turned his attention to the brunette Cole had been eying and Leanne encouraged him in that direction. Cole worked the tension from his jaw and glanced at the stairs before looking back at the girls.

When the customer's arm circled the brunette's waist he caught Leanne's eye and shook his head. He'd bet the Hangman's Inn that the brunette was Jane; he was all too familiar with her assets.

Instead of paying him any attention, Leanne guided the pair toward the stairs.

Every inch of him wanted to protest, but he was numb with shock. His fingers were cold; his legs refused to obey his commands as the couple ascended the stairs. They stopped after two steps, and a flood of relief dampened his anger for just a second.

The 'girl' whispered to the gentleman and after a nod, he turned back to Leanne. Instead of revealing the trick, Leanne waved over a second girl, and the trio ascended the stairs together.

Cole saw red and managed to get to his feet. Jane wouldn't do that to him, no way no how, but he would have sworn it was her. The curve of her legs, the slope of her shoulders, it had to have been her.

He turned around and downed some more whiskey, replaying the whole scene in his head. Every instinct told him to go up there and haul Jane away, because it was her—but it couldn't be. Over and over he ran through the scene, the minutes clicking away on the clock across the bar. One, two, five. Devil, he had to stop it now before it went too far.

"What is your problem? You're disturbing my guests." Leanne leaned on the bar next to him.

"The jig is up. I know it was Jane."

"What jig? I told you, Jane is upstairs with Kim." She smirked and tilted the whiskey bottle to fill his empty glass. "Why? Did you see someone you liked? I can see about arranging something, perhaps Jane wouldn't mind."

"Ya think I don't know my woman when I see her?"

"Are you so sure that you do?" Leanne nodded toward the stairs.

Cole spun, and Jane stood right behind him with her own wicked grin in place. After a quick perusal of her body to see she was wearing exactly what she had been when they'd entered, he frowned. "How long have you been standing there?"

"I came down the stairs when you turned around, pouting like a five-year-old. Why? What's going on?" Jane quirked a brow. "And what's this about seeing something you liked? Should I be concerned?"

He narrowed his eyes and tried to decipher the burgeoning laughter in both women. "What are you up to?"

"Again, I say—you're so suspicious." Leanne nudged him.

Jane chuckled and leaned against Cole. Her fingers trailed teasing circles on his thigh as she spoke to Leanne. "Could I get some whiskey to take up to Kim? This could take a little while."

"What could?" Cole clamped his hand on hers and leveled his gaze at her. "We were supposed to visit and get back to the hotel. We'll go back now."

"You are so tense. All I'm doing is talking to Kim, she's having issues with one of her regular callers." Jane pulled her hand free and resumed her teasing. "She's afraid to talk to

Leanne, so I'm trying to help your friend. Why, are you enjoying the view too much? Worried about slipping?"

"No."

"Then let me finish. If you can be patient and wait until we get to the hotel, I'll make it up to you."

Leanne smirked and handed over a bottle. "If he's not patient enough I have a room you could use."

After glowering at them both, he downed another whiskey. "Ya don't play fair."

"I never do." Jane leaned up and nipped at his earlobe. With a wink to Leanne, she went back upstairs.

Cole didn't take his eyes off her all the way up the stairs until she was well out of sight. He narrowed his eyes and turned back to glare at Leanne. "I don't trust neither of ya."

"I don't know what you're talking about." Leanne wiped down the bar but kept her smug smile in place.

"Sure ya do."

Leanne stopped to stare him down. Once again, the time ticked by while she held his gaze. A grin rose. "I've never seen you smitten. It's almost cute. I didn't know you could be any inch of adorable, Cole."

"Shut your cock holster."

"Nice. Completely inaccurate, and crass, even for you."

"You've gone and made her mad at me for keeping secrets."

"Mad? I don't recall any anger. Surprise, maybe, but anger?"

That appeased him only the slightest bit. "Damn it. I still say it was her."

"I say you're losing your touch."

Cole was about to protest, but a voice piped up behind him.

"He let me get him all hot and bothered, but then went with Lulu." The tone was grumpy, and the girl leaned on the bar a few feet away.

"Of course he did, Ada." Leanne chuckled. "He's our most indecisive guest. Here you go."

Cole took a chance of a sideways glance and realized it was the brunette. Immediately, his gaze went down to the lace-clad legs, followed them up past her bustle to the tiny waist and up to her dark hair.

The way she stood, positioned her hair so it hung in a curtain covering her face. Her elegant fingers pulled the pouch Leanne tossed at her close to her chest and pushed the small bag into the top of her corset.

Leanne cleared her throat as she poured another drink for him. "Feel free to touch the merchandise."

He snapped his attention back to the drink in front of him. "You ain't funny."

"I think I'm hilarious."

"You would." A hand on his thigh ramped his tension right back up. He cut a glare toward Leanne.

She just laughed. "Leave him be, Ada. He's grumpy."

When he turned toward the brunette again, Ada was walking away with a shrug to join the other girls in the parlor. As she stretched out on the chaise, he studied every single inch of her body again. He knew it was Jane, there wasn't a doubt in his head, but the moment he went to stand up, Leanne interrupted him.

"Ada, Phyllis—would you go into the storeroom and get me more whiskey? Cole here is drinking me out and Mr. Tine will be down soon to have his share."

Cole frowned when the women rose and walked into a room off the parlor, under the stairs.

"Keep staring like that when Jane gets down here and she'll rip your eyes right out of your head." Leanne leaned on the bar. "Our talk was brief, but I get the feeling she's awful possessive of you."

"The feeling's mutual."

"Interesting." She giggled. "When I offered to help you bide your time she threatened to break my girls' fingers if they touched you."

"What game are you playing?"

"I'm not playing a game. Ah, thank you ladies." Leanne nodded toward the parlor. "Two boxes are perfect."

Cole rose and turned to face the women as they walked toward him, with their faces in clear view. When he realized the brunette was very much not Jane, he flopped back onto the stool and rubbed his hands over his face. He lifted his head again and shook it as she approached.

"Leanne told you that you could touch." Ada winked at him. "You sure look eager enough and I don't mind."

"Easy girl." Leanne chuckled. "He looks like he's going to jump out of his skin."

Cole glanced toward the stairs again, and then back at Ada, and once again into the parlor. He'd been sure as anything that had been Jane. "What the hell?"

"Cole. You look like you could use another drink." Leanne poured another cup, smiling when he turned around. "Are you all right?"

"Fine."

"Of course you are. Drink. It's always helped you before when you got in a snit."

He pushed the drink away and turned back to the parlor as the women got back in place. The brunette was not the same woman she'd been minutes ago. He knew it. After years of practice, he knew how to tell one woman from another, and one woman he knew better than any other was Jane. How was it now not her?

"You need to settle down. I can't imagine Jane got you going that much."

"She always gets me going," Cole muttered. He turned toward the bar and shifted uncomfortably. Over and over his mind went back to the brunette, when he'd been sure it was Jane. He'd never seen Jane dressed anything like that, and he had to admit he appreciated the effort.

"Hello again, Mr. Tine." Leanne interrupted Cole's musings to pour another drink and hand it to the man that sat next to him. "Here's your whiskey. I hope you enjoyed your evening."

"Always, Miss DuBois. Always." Mr. Tine sipped his whiskey and began to draw Leanne into a conversation.

Cole used the chance to peek into the parlor again to seek out the brunette. She'd left her place on the chaise and now stood by the window. One quick once-over and he was once again sure it was Jane.

Without another word, he hopped out of his chair and crossed the room. He strode up right behind her and set his hands on her hips. With a chuckle he leaned down to her right ear intentionally. She couldn't stand when he spoke into her nearly-deaf ear. Drove her batty. "This should make ya mad."

As expected, she tensed, and he knew he had her. Before he could do anything to prove his point, she pressed her ass back against him. His body reacted instantaneously, and he used his grip on her hips to tug her closer.

He groaned low as she rubbed against him and slipped his hands down her legs to tease her flesh under the top of her stockings. As she rubbed against his erection again, he switched ears to whisper, "Damn, woman."

"You like?"

"Hell yeah."

"Shall we take Leanne up on her offer of a room?"

"If we don't, I'll handle things right here."

*Perfect courage means doing unwitnessed
what we would be capable of
with the world looking on.
—Francois de La Rochefoucauld*

"Damn." Cole tugged Jane close. She let him lead her to the bed where they both collapsed, sated for the moment. A light sheen of sweat lingered on their flesh, their breathing heavy.

"Feel better?" She turned in his arms so she'd be able to face him.

He hummed a low agreement, his gaze roaming the room before settling on her. "Leanne might not appreciate the redecorating we did to the room."

Her low laughter matched his. "I guess I teased you a bit too much."

"No. Ya really didn't."

"You can thank the Virgin Madam for that little outfit."

His eyes flew open wide at her comment. The light of humor glinted in them, one corner of his lips lifted in a near-smirk. "What did you call her?"

"The Virgin Madam."

"She know you call her that?"

"Well, yes. I teased her with it while we were going over our plan to torture you." She smiled at his bark of laughter. "She appeared to appreciate the humor, too."

"Not in front of the girls?"

"Of course not. Then again, she has you to thank for that, doesn't she?"

Tension whipped through his body faster than a bolt of lightning. He rolled onto his back, releasing a gust of air. His eyes closed. "She did tell you everything."

"No, I'm sure she didn't. She told me some things, likely most of what related to her. That's what you were so nervous about, wasn't it?" She set her hand on his chest, glad his came to rest on her own.

"What did she tell you?"

"That she's your sister. Sort of."

"Yeah."

"She hates your pa as much as you do. Most importantly that she has you to thank for a great many things. I know it's tough to talk about your family, but I admire what you did for her." She touched her hand to his cheek to turn him toward her. "She's your sister. She's all the family you've got left."

"Nah. She ain't all." He sighed, turning to sit on the edge of the bed. His long fingers raked through his hair, shoulders slumped. "She didn't tell you about Alma?"

"No. I gathered she knew about her, but she left that story up to you." Jane moved to sit close to him. To make it easier, she remained behind him where he wouldn't have to look her in the eye. She wrapped her legs around his waist, and after a kiss to his shoulder, rested her cheek on his back. Her arms wrapped around him as well, until her hands rested on his chest.

He relaxed a miniscule amount, his hand rested on hers. "What did she tell you?"

She showed no annoyance at the repeated question, knowing he was searching for a place to begin. "She said you shared a pa. That you first helped her by helping her Ma get away from him because he was going to do something bad."

"She didn't tell you what?"

"No. She then said her ma got sick and died and that's when you took her in. You had her working at the saloon and signing a contract, but you protected her from servicing, even making it appear she did sometimes. You helped her buy this place and lent her whores. It was implied you continued to help until she started making a profit."

"Then she didn't tell you everything." His thumb ran along the back of her hand.

"No. I suppose not."

"Our pa, he married her ma, Margaret, when I was maybe eight. He had two babies by her, while still married to my ma. Kept both families."

She blinked at the admission of two children. Her brain slid the puzzle pieces together, until she couldn't help but whisper the words. "Two babies. Leanne, and Alma?"

"Yeah. Alma. She ain't right, mind you."

That could mean so many things, but she held her silence while he took a couple deep breaths.

"She came out backwards and ain't been right since. Leanne's ma said she wasn't breathing when the doc finally got Alma out, but whatever it was, she ain't right."

Jane rested her forehead on his shoulder. Through the tension cutting his body into harsh lines, she couldn't deny the hint of pain he tried to hide in his voice.

"Pa wasn't around enough to notice at first, but when he did he wanted to 'end her suffering'. Alma didn't eat right, she was so small you coulda broke her easy. She cried, all the time. Margaret, she had to carry her around all day, could hardly work. No one else could go near Alma, not without more screaming. Pa thought it better she were gone."

Jane lifted her head. She shifted to Cole's side to study him. Even years later, the memory tortured Cole. Harsh lines of stress cut across his forehead, his tone held a waver she didn't often hear. She never thought she'd see anything that had affected him as much as the loss of his first child many years ago, but Alma was clearly another deep pain for him.

Cole sighed deep, the lines in his forehead eased. "By then I knew all about Margaret and Leanne. Margaret told me all about the baby, and how Pa wanted her dead. So I helped them get away, took all my savings to do it, but they were gone. I hoped out of my life."

Jane didn't wince, even though he scrunched her hand tight in his own. "What you did was save her. All of them."

"Not enough." Hesitation lingered between them. His silence stretched, his tension not easing. She said nothing, knowing there was more to the story. "Margaret got sick. Real sick. Cancer, they said. Margaret asked me to come, and I did. Don't know why, but I did. She made me promise to care for Alma. She was worried pa would find the girl once she died."

Jane's fingers grew numb in his grip, but she didn't dare pull away. She barely dared to breathe while he continued.

"So I adopted her."

Shock sent the numbness of her fingers through her whole body. "You what?"

"She don't call me pa or nothing, I ain't her pa. I adopted her so I could make sure she was cared for. When Margaret died, I didn't know what to do. Alma was older then, but still different. Odd. I brought them both to Colorado, but I took Alma to Denver. I thought maybe an asylum would be best."

Jane bit down her protest, knowing he didn't need it. Asylums were terrible places to be, she knew all too well. She knew he did, too.

"When I got there, it wasn't right. I couldn't do it anymore than I could let Pa kill her as a babe." His grip on her hand loosened finally. "I found a school that would take her. She can play the piano like no one's business. She's real good, real good. The school liked that, even though she weren't right."

"The piano?" Her words brought the intensity of his stare onto her. She carefully schooled her surprise lest he think her angry. "That's why you were so opposed to one in the saloon."

"Don't like thinking about it none."

"But you did. All the time. Why would you not? Cole, you took care of them, even when you wanted to hate them because of what your pa did. They are your family and you've treated them as such despite yourself. I'm amazed at all you've done for them, but I always knew you were a good man."

"But I ain't."

"But you are." She ignored his further protest, choosing instead to slide over to straddle his lap. In his concerned gaze, she offered a smile. "I know you need to keep up appearances in town. I always understood that, but you need to see what you did here is not a bad thing. It is truly a beautiful gesture, all around."

"You forgive me for not telling?"

"Of course," she confirmed without hesitation. "Now will you forgive me for my secret?"

His brow furrowed. "That thing downstairs? Not a secret."

"No, not that. Something else."

"What secret?"

"Maybe not a secret, but a surprise."

"That so?" He slid her down his legs a short distance as if to see her more clearly. His lips puckered. "Tommy got anything to do with it?"

"Heavens, no. This all has to do with you, and me."

"Tell."

"I didn't plan for it to happen." Now that it was time to reveal, nerves rattled right through her. Her ramble couldn't be stopped, even though she tried. "I'm usually so careful, but then I got sick and everything got confused. We were so anxious after such a long illness to get convalescing that we weren't as careful as we usually are—"

"Jane!"

"I'm pregnant."

All color drained from his face. He grew eerily still.

She untangled himself from his embrace to scramble off the bed. He didn't follow or react at all even in her absence from his arms. She took a shaky breath. "You knocked me up again."

One slow blink was his only response.

Her own fears over everything slipped down her cheeks. If she would lose this baby as well, if he'd reject her and their marriage now. She'd thought he wouldn't, but he wouldn't say anything. Why wouldn't he speak? She slapped his shoulder. "You are *not* helping my nerves."

Cole flinched at her slap. "Ya sure?"

"Daisy told me at my appointment the other day. I didn't think I was, I had no inkling at all. I thought my symptoms were still from the concussion, but Daisy did a complete exam."

"You're just trying to make me sweat. Test me."

"No."

"You're really…" His mouth moved to form the word, but no sound escaped.

"The timing is terrible. Everything is in chaos." She turned her back on him, unable to take in his dumbstruck look any longer. She busied herself by crossing the room to get a glass of water. In the lingering silence, she took a long drink to try to settle her nerves. "Despite all of that, I am not upset. I'm happy, actually."

"I ain't either—upset, that is."

She exhaled a slow breath of pent up tension that had been winding her tight. "You aren't?"

"Surprised."

"Overwhelmed."

"Worried about you."

The words took her by such surprise, she spun to face him again.

His brow creased in a mix of amusement and deep concern. "After what happened last time, I know you gotta be scared."

"Terrified."

"Come here." He held out his hand, his fingers beckoning her over. She set down her drink without hesitation to rush back to the sanctuary of his arms. The moment she collapsed beside him, his fingers trailed soothingly along her spine. "Why'd you keep it from me?"

"I wasn't keeping it, really. Not in the way you mean. I was trying to figure out how to tell you. Then you surprised me with your proposal, and we agreed it was all supposed to just be—"

"About just us."

"That's what I wanted it to be. I think it still was. I was worried, though. Worried you'd be upset. When I found out, we'd only talked the once about marrying or kids in regards to Lizzie. We certainly hadn't discussed children of our own."

"Guess it was decided for us."

A tear slipped down her cheek. Though she wanted to, she could not bring herself to meet his gaze. "If it sticks this time."

"It will."

A sob welled, uncontrollable. It burst from her, so she buried her face in his shoulder. The tears she'd held back since she'd found out, of fear and worry, slipped free from the barrier she'd held them under. When he lay back down, she moved with him. Curled into his warmth, her tears eased at his gentle but firm hold. She swiped at the remnants on her cheeks. "What are we going to do?"

"Same thing we were gonna do before. Get the business stuff settled and find some new investors so we can build onto the hotel. We're gonna need that bigger room for sure now."

"Not to mention our own private bath."

"For sure." His fingers danced lightly along her arm. "You sure about getting investors? What about a loan? I ain't good at much, but I'm good at numbers. We can make it work."

"I don't trust banks, and the interest rates are ridiculous. Better to find smart men and businesses that have the good sense to avoid the upcoming economic fluctuations and are still willing to invest wisely."

"If ya say so. Sounds like a tough road."

"Toughest ones have always proven worth it to me."

"Don't mean you gotta take them every time."

She smiled at his exasperated tone. Warmth and humor dashed away the last of her fears, so she decided to return the teasing in kind. "I'm going to get fat."

He chuckled. "Ain't nothing to worry about."

"You might not find me so appealing."

"Doubt that."

She pursed her lips, unhappy her teasing had gotten little out of him. Then again, it hadn't been very strong. "Well, then. I'll be crazy emotional."

"That ain't no different than normal."

Though she'd expected some such comment, she smacked him in the chest. To catch him off guard, she reached toward his ticklish spot. He beat her to it and found hers first. A shriek of laughter slipped free while she tried to squirm free. "Cole!"

He pinned her to the bed, his laughter fading into a familiar intense gaze. The jokes were over, and he was ready to face her and their surprise situation head on. "It ain't nothing I'd been ready to think about."

"Marriage was tough enough, I know."

"That don't mean I'm upset. I'm…worried."

"I will do everything." Emotion threatened to choke off her words, but she held strong for him this time. "Everything Daisy tells me to, I promise. I'll do whatever it takes to make sure this baby is healthy. This one will stick. I promise."

"Ya can't promise."

"I promise to do everything in my power. Everything."

"What's Daisy telling you to do now?"

"Relax."

The tense lines of his forehead eased, a spark of humor returning to his eyes. "Relax, eh?"

She laughed outright when he waggled his brows. "Yes. It's best that I relax—I shouldn't be too tense."

"You seem real relaxed right now."

"You, sir, are an expert at relaxing me."

"What else?"

"To eat when I can and get plenty of rest."

"Rest?" He grinned at her giggle. "Does she want you to relax or rest?"

She wrapped her arms around his neck and tugged him into a deep kiss. When she pulled back, she sighed. "Both."

"Good."

As he started to nibble at her neck, she tilted her head back to accommodate him. "That's all she told me."

"But you ain't been eating much. Shouldn't you be eating more?"

"Unless you want me sick all day long, I wouldn't recommend it."

His paused his attentions and hovered just above her lips. "A baby."

"Yes—Pa."

He smirked and shook his head. "I still ain't used to knowing I'll be your husband soon."

"Barring any further catastrophes."

"You do seem to attract them."

She hummed agreement.

"Ain't gonna be able to keep this a secret."

"All the more reason to keep our marriage a secret. Imagine the terrible scandal now. Unwed, with a baby, living in the saloon—I'm a trifecta of sin."

"You're enjoying that far too much."

She shrugged and giggled. "I like giving them something to talk about. It saves them from switching to darker forms of gossip by adding in slander of people far less wicked than I.

"So you're doing it for them?"

"Of course." When he moved to kiss her again, she placed a finger on his lips. "I've been thinking."

"You always are." The words were muffled around her finger, but he didn't fight her attempt to keep him silent.

"Your sisters should be there."

He grew still, eyes narrowed.

"Two of my brothers know. Perhaps just Leanne since I've yet to meet Alma."

His shoulders sagged and his head dropped. "You'll meet her tomorrow. I'm taking you to the school, planned on it before Leanne blabbed."

"You didn't need to explain yourself, but I'll be happy to meet her. What do you think of my idea?"

"I dunno."

A knock on the door interrupted her reply. Leanne's voice sounded through the closed door. "Hey you two. I've locked up downstairs. You know where I am if you need anything."

"Come on in, Leanne." Jane sat up with a bright smile.

"Jane," Cole protested and drew the sheet up when the door opened.

Leanne chuckled as Cole fought with the twisted sheets. "Modesty was never your strong suit before, Cole. Glad to know Jane has had a positive effect on you."

Jane elbowed him in the ribs at the first hint of a curse, but kept a smile on Leanne. "Thank you for all your help tonight. I had fun."

"Ada's still laughing. It was worth it to see the look on his face when she came out of the storeroom. I thought he was going to get sick all over my brand new rug." Leanne giggled and leaned on the doorframe.

Jane sighed. "I wish I could have seen that part of it, but I was stuck in that damn storeroom."

"How did ya manage it?" Cole's gaze switched between them rapidly. "I knew it was Jane…but then…"

"I distracted you when the girls came downstairs, remember?" Leanne's smile broadened. "That first time you were groped was Jane, she was hiding behind Jill and you about ruined it when you grabbed her hand so hard."

Jane nodded. "Then I had to rush to get into place. Since you'd been distracted, Ada was already in the storeroom. Honestly, I didn't think you'd catch on so quickly, but the girls assured me that you were looking rather intently."

"Which was exactly what we'd hoped," Leanne interjected. "I must say, I picked a great little outfit for her, didn't I? She really did look stunning."

"Part of the reason she picked that little outfit was she had one almost identical to it." Jane set her hand on his now that he wasn't wound quite as tight by Leanne's presence. "The color of Ada's was different, but we were hoping you wouldn't notice."

Cole smirked. "It wasn't the color I was looking at."

"Exactly." Leanne laughed. "So I kept plying you with liquor and distracting you. The gentleman that took Jane upstairs was a well-established customer. We convinced him very easily to help out."

"How'd ya get changed so quick?" Cole squeezed her hand.

"Threw my skirts over that little bustle, popped the corset off and threw on my other bodice. There were girls at the top of the stairs helping me, not other customers. When I came back downstairs the second time, Ada was close to make the comment about getting him all hot and bothered."

"The two of you are evil." Cole pursed his lips tight, but a grin was still visible.

"We know." Jane chuckled and shoved at his shoulder. "But you deserved every last bit of it."

Leanne nodded. "She's right. You did. Plus, it was a hell of a lot of fun for me and the girls. Sometimes you just need something to break the monotony."

Jane nudged Cole. "Anything else?"

Cole's fingers fiddled with hers and he fixed his gaze on their hands for a minute. After a huge sigh, he lifted his head. "Sorry."

Leanne's wide-eyed shock competed with Jane's internal shock. She hadn't expected an apology, just an invite to the wedding. After she shook her head, Leanne stepped closer. "I'm sorry. What?"

"I shouldn't have blamed you." Cole dropped his gaze down. "Janey and I, we're getting married."

"Considering she already has your name, that's fitting." Leanne closed the door behind her. "Does she know?"

"He's taking me to meet Alma tomorrow." Jane nodded. "But our wedding is a secret back home. Only my brother Tommy knows."

"Oooh, you have a brother?" Leanne perked up.

"Actually I have six. One deceased, three married, two single." Jane laughed when Cole grumbled. "Sorry."

"You coming or not?" Cole turned back to Leanne.

"Oh. Oh. Ohhh." Leanne blinked fast like she was trying to hide tears, but she grinned and nodded. "Tell me when and where, I'll be there. Wouldn't miss it for nothing."

"We'll tell you everything in the morning." Jane smiled.

"It's still probably best no one back in Dominion Falls knows what you are. Ain't no one that'll let you live it down." Cole frowned. "But I won't ignore you no more. Not just 'cause Jane won't let me."

"Because I won't either. I'm going to pester you constantly, Cole." Leanne grinned. "If you're going to hate me now, you're going to hate me for me."

"Too late," Cole grumbled.

All three of them burst out laughing, and Jane smacked his arm. "Behave."

"He doesn't know how." Leanne snorted.

"Good point." Jane chuckled.

"You're both gonna give me a headache, aren't you?" Cole cut a glare at Jane that she knew had felled greater men than her.

"Probably." Jane just shrugged. The grin she'd just contained grew again.

Cole rested his forehead on his hand and shook his head. "Leanne. Don't ever come to Dominion Falls."

Leanne's brow furrowed. "What? Well, why not?"

"Because if Jane has both you and Kathy around to feed off, she won't be nothing I can live with." Cole's shoulders drooped dramatically.

Jane gasped and punched him in the arm. "Cole!"

Leanne laughed out loud. "Just for that, I may have to."

"Damn. I'm in trouble."

"You'd better believe it."

I do think that families are the most beautiful things in the world.
-Louisa May Alcott

Jane did her best to ignore the bundle of nerves Cole had turned into. They'd returned to the hotel to change earlier in the morning, and every moment since he'd gotten more tense. Over and over he'd repeated a speech showing how familiar he was with his youngest sister after all.

As if reading her thoughts, he began the speech again. "She don't like to be touched much, unless she says. She don't like when ya look her in the eye. She don't like change none, so she might not like you."

"Music soothes her," Jane continued on the speech she'd remembered the first time he'd rambled the words. "She likes books and being read to. She is good at math, but does not like tests. While you say she's 'different', she still has a heart and a soul. According to Leanne, Alma loves you."

"That's debatable." He tugged at his tie. Though he'd worn one their whole trip, suddenly he couldn't stop threatening to pull it right off. He took a deep breath at the base of the steps. "Are you sure?"

"With all of my heart. You clearly care deeply about this young woman as you do Leanne, even if you are afraid to admit either affection. You know all of these little details about her." She readjusted the tie he'd set askew. "We will take this one step at a time. There's no rush here. We have time, and you indicated she needed it."

In typical Cole fashion, he barreled up the stairs without another word. He rang the bell with unnecessary force. At his side, his hand clenched and released in a rapid pace.

Jane followed up the steps with more discretion. She arrived at the top at the same moment the door opened to reveal a mature woman with delicate spectacles, loose gray hair, and a few soft lines across her features.

The kind face of the woman broke into a warm smile. "Mr. Mitchell. It's been too long. We are pleased to see you, as is Alma, she's been mentioning you nonstop since we told her of your upcoming arrival. You must be Miss Spencer. Hello, I'm Mrs. Wellman."

Jane took the offered hand. "Good morning."

"Mr. Mitchell, I was hoping we might speak before you see Alma. I had a matter to discuss with you of some importance." Mrs. Wellman held open the door for them. "Miss Spencer, do you mind?"

"Not at all. I can wait." Jane nodded at Cole, who appeared as though he might lose his stomach all over the fine carpet. "Go on. I will be fine. I'm capable of entertaining myself."

"Library's right there." Cole nodded behind her, the words coming out mildly garbled through his tense jaw. With another moment's hesitation, he disappeared into the office on their left.

Jane smiled pleasantly at Mrs. Wellman in the moments before she also joined Cole in the office. Concern made the façade fade soon as the door shut behind them. Cole's tension had been off the charts just coming to the school. She hoped the line of conversation to be had didn't make it any worse. If what he'd told her of Alma was all true, the last thing he needed to be when they did meet with her was tense.

From what she gathered from their conversations that morning, Alma was more sensitive than Cole let himself believe. Jane imagined Alma didn't care for tests because of the pressure to perform. She didn't like change because it disrupted her sense of order in the world. She seemed more sensitive to the world rather than less, as Cole's words might lead one to believe. If she were honest, she suspected Cole felt the same, that's why he'd avoided so much. Too much emotion had always been difficult for him, after all.

With a deep sigh, Jane turned to enter the library as Cole had suggested. A few light notes from a piano made her pause. Even though she knew she ought to ignore it, she couldn't stop herself from following the sound down the hall.

On the back of the building there was a large sitting room full of windows to let the sunshine in. The windows lined both the outer wall and ceiling of the beautiful sunlit room. Bathed in the warmth sat groups of children of all ages. They ranged from what she guessed to be seven, and into their teen years. All of them sat in scattered groups of three or four, huddled together either working, reading, or playing games.

Jane smiled at the sight, glad to see Cole had found such a lovely place for Alma to have as a home. She perused the room until her gaze settled on a piano nestled in the corner. A young woman with hair the color of corn silk which fell in soft waves down her back played a complex piece Jane wished she could emulate.

A young teacher bent near the young woman, her brow furrowed in plea. "Miss Alma, it isn't time for piano. You haven't finished your work."

"It is noon," Alma said in a quiet, but firm voice. "Piano at noon. Piano at noon. Dine at one-thirty. Piano at noon."

"After you've finished your work," the teacher supplied, but found herself ignored. A small smile crossed her features. "You always ignore the second part of that."

Jane took the three small steps into the room, and crossed the short distance to the piano. "I'm sorry to interrupt."

"Oh. Hello." The teacher stood straight, and held her hand out. "Are you Miss Spencer? Mrs. Wellman said to expect Mr. Mitchell and you this morning."

"I am. Cole is in speaking with Mrs. Wellman. I believe Alma knew we were coming for a visit today?" Jane turned her attention to Alma's fingers as they flew over the keys. "She must be excited and nervous about the whole thing. Perhaps her work can wait until after she's seen Cole? I'd be happy to assist her if she'd allow me."

"She did know, and came to the piano soon as the clock struck noon when she'd usually finish her work." The teacher smiled warmly. "I'm sure her work can wait until her day has settled into something she's more accustomed to. I'm Miss Paterno, by the way."

"Pleasure to meet you. Might I reamin here and listen for a while?" Jane circled the piano so she might get a glimpse of Alma's features. Remembering Cole's words, she was careful to not meet Alma's occasional glance head on. "Would it be all right with you if I stayed here, Alma?"

Alma nodded, her attention and intensity of the music not wavering.

Miss Paterno touched Jane's shoulder. "Well done. I'll go assist the other students. If you need me, let me know."

"Thank you." Jane kept her attention on Alma's playing, until the song ended and another softer melody followed. "Do you mind if I talk to you while you play?"

The cadence slowed a little more, and after a moment Alma nodded.

"Cole told me you like reading, too."

"Books. L-l-like music." Alma's sweet voice held to an almost whisper. Though Jane knew her to be seventeen, she sounded younger in years.

"Yes, they can be almost like music if they're read right." Jane grinned at the simile, her mind racing over the best stories for such a likeness. "Although, I can read an entire library but cannot play a bit of music. My brother tried to teach me a scale and I could not do even that."

A smile peeked out at the edges of Alma's mouth. The song she'd been playing switched from a quiet melody to a run of scales up and down the piano before the melody returned.

Jane laughed softly. "Impressive. My fingers trip all over each other when I try."

"Y-you like books?"

"Oh, very much. I run the library back home, and I have read every book we have, and all that arrive to be put on the shelves." Jane's gaze lifted to find Cole watching them from the door. She tried to not react at the raw pain creasing his features into deep lines. Maybe it wasn't pain, but fear. Hard to tell for sure. She kept her voice steady. "I remember all of those books the way you remember music. I don't need them in front of me to remember what they say."

Cole walked toward them; the previous pain wiped into a stoic mask. "Alma."

Alma's fingers paused over the keys. She rocked back and forth, her fingers twitching in curls in the air above her beloved keys. A grin on her features kept Jane from worrying when a high-pitched keening filled the air. After a moment, the keening stopped for her squeal. "Cole."

Jane's grin at the reaction was unfettered and as broad as the warmth in her soul at Alma's excitement. Her heart lightened to see even Cole's trepidation disappeared into a smile. "I see you met Jane, who was supposed to wait in the library."

Jane shrugged. "I heard Alma's beautiful music and couldn't keep away. Besides, sometimes the anticipation of an event is worse than the event itself. Best to end it sooner rather than later."

"Cole, Cole, Cole." Alma turned, holding out her hands to him. Though she didn't look right at him, her eager smile and grasping hands were a sign of how much she did love him.

Cole knelt beside the piano bench to fold his sister into a hug. "Sorry I didn't come in June like before. Jane was sick."

The embrace broke off after mere seconds. Alma continued to rock slightly, though not as strong as before the hug. "I'll play."

"One more song, and then we'll have lunch." Cole rose and stood next to Jane. As the first notes of music filled the room again, he closed his eyes. A deep sigh sank him into a rare slouch.

Jane whispered close to his ear, under the music. "What's wrong?"

"They won't keep her no longer. She'll be eighteen soon." His cheek pressed to her temple. Another deep sigh brushed her ear. "I don't know what to do."

"You'll bring her home." Jane clasped his hand when he jerked away. She knew the expression on his features all too well. The stubborn refusal to let anyone know him, the real him. Alma could blow it all for him.

"No. I can't."

"You can't, but *we* can. We'll find a way."

Right actions in the future are the best apologies for bad actions in the past.
-Tryon Edwards

After they'd eaten, Alma's routine dictated she take a walk through the gardens. Cole had requested that Jane speak to Mrs. Wellman herself, so Jane urged him to walk with his sister. After those tasks, they planned to read together since books were something Alma and Jane could both share.

Jane couldn't have been more pleased at how well their lunch had gone. Alma had even granted her a hug before heading off on her walk with Cole. While they hadn't had much time to discuss the matter in depth, Cole seemed gratified Jane was so ready to take in his sister.

Now they only had to figure out how. Changes would need to be made, and fast.

She knocked on Mrs. Wellman's door, glad to receive a prompt beckoning response. Jane closed the door behind her. "I hope I'm not disturbing you, Mrs. Wellman. Cole suggested I speak with you directly over the matter of Alma's enrollment."

"Of course, Mr. Mitchell suggested he might send you to speak with me. Please, have a seat." Mrs. Wellman set aside the papers she'd been going through to give Jane her attention. "I truly regret having to make this decision. Alma is a delight to have with us. However, she is turning eighteen next spring, and our school is only so large."

"Of course. You have students that wish for a place here. I completely understand. I think it's wonderful you've kept her on so long."

"Most of our students leave us at sixteen, though a few stay on. I was glad to have her here, watching her grow has been a joy." Mr. Wellman sighed. "Now as for what happens next, I have a few suggestions prepared."

"Suggestions?"

"There's a nice home nearby that's for…"

"You aren't suggesting an asylum?"

Mrs. Wellman looked struck by Jane's sharp tone. "Oh, no. It isn't exactly an asylum."

"No matter." Jane shook her head, trying to soften her tone. "There will be no asylum or the like. We will be taking her home. To Dominion Falls."

"Oh." Relief flooded the older woman's features, relaxing the lines that had grown deeper in the tension. "That is wonderful to hear. I had suggestions, but they are so limited for a young woman such as Alma."

"I'm aware. However, we will start making plans immediately for where she'll stay. Rather, where we will all stay, once she leaves here. In the meantime, I know change is difficult for her. I was thinking that perhaps we might ease her into the change by having her visit and increase her visitations until it's time for her to remain permanently."

Mrs. Wellman's brows rose. "You've given this some thought."

"Not too much yet, we did decide shortly before lunch." Jane laughed as she sat straighter in the chair. "We would like to have her visit soon. Perhaps September? Then again for Christmas. I know she has school, but possibly after the new year we can increase those visits and make them longer?"

"We can certainly accommodate whatever schedule you come up with. Of course, I'd be remiss if I didn't suggest—"

"We have a piano, and there's one at the church which might be better for her to get some quiet," Jane interrupted, guessing what the suggestion was. "I also have a good supply of books, and I'm sure I have plenty at whatever her reading level might be."

"Very good."

"Also, I wondered if we might be able to take her on an outing tomorrow. I know Miss DuBois visits often, and she would be the one coming to get her."

"An outing is always welcome. The city often overwhelms Alma, but Miss DuBois is well aware of her limitations. I'm certain we can arrange it. Alma will be so pleased to spend more time with Mr. Mitchell. She looks forward to his visits."

"I can tell." Jane rose. "I'll take no more of your time today. If you think of anything else we can do to help Alma with this transition, please don't hesitate to let me know. You and your teachers know her best, after all."

"Please, do the same. It sounds like you've got a good grasp on this." Mrs. Wellman rose as well. "Most people that have met Alma aren't quite so understanding so fast."

"There's little to understand. She's a human being, and we all have our own peculiarities, we just tend to do better at hiding them. I have a feeling she wishes to be treated like any one of us." Jane moved toward the door. "I should probably return. Alma kept mentioning butterflies, and I would like to see them myself."

"Then they'll be in the garden near the fountain. Several of the flowers placed there attract the butterflies."

"Thank you." Jane followed the path she'd taken earlier to the solarium. This time she passed through it, out the door to the gardens. The warm air stole her breath, but she kept on toward the sound of the fountain and Alma saying 'butterflies'.

Cole stood when she approached. Concern continued to crease his brow, but his tension had dissipated somewhat. "You get what you need?"

"Yes. Mrs. Wellman is rather kind, and cares about Alma a good deal. We'll take this slow to let Alma adjust. Don't look so worried." Jane squeezed his hand in reassurance. She turned her attention to where Alma sat in the midst of the flowers, butterflies dancing around her to get their nectar.

"What about everyone back there? They ain't gonna be so accommodating. They're not like you, ya know."

"Heavens, do I. However, they'll learn. If they don't, then we'll deal with those events as they happen. She looks rather happy right now."

"She does this every time when weather's right. She'll miss the butterflies."

"Then we'll have to make a garden back home." Jane approached Alma but left the young woman in the circle of flowers and chose to sit on the nearest bench. "Alma, would you like if Cole had a garden like this you could visit?"

"Yes." Alma's head tilted toward the sky; her eyes closed. "Butterflies."

"Would you like to visit Cole and I in Dominion Falls soon?" Jane held out her hand to Cole and smiled. "Maybe in September?"

"A train goes there." Alma swayed side to side, humming under her breath.

"Yes it does." Cole squeezed Jane's hand. "We can come and get you, bring you back for a visit."

"Or Leanne can bring you and visit as well." Jane giggled when Cole's smile quickly turned into a glare. "And maybe you both can visit for Christmas too."

"The train is big. Loud. I remember." Alma set her hands over her ears. "Big train brought me here."

"They're also fast. It would take days and days on a horse." Jane said quietly.

"No horses."

"She's afraid of horses." Cole frowned.

"Well then a train is her best option." Jane nodded. "As far as horses go, we'll adjust. There's a lot of them everywhere, and you train them, so that's another challenge to face. We'll figure this out."

"Where's she gonna stay?" Cole eyed her, but then grinned. "One is on your head, Alma. Don't you move none."

Alma gasped and froze. She opened her eyes and turned them skyward. Her nose scrunched under her effort to see the butterfly. "Really?"

"Really." Cole chuckled. "Did you ask about tomorrow, Jane?"

"Of course. Mrs. Wellman said Alma is free to have an outing. I told her Leanne would pick her up and bring her." Jane laced her fingers with his. "We'll let Leanne know this evening before we retire to the hotel."

"Leanne is coming? It's not Sunday." Alma started to rock again, and the butterfly flew off her head. "Sunday is when Leanne comes."

"Cole and I wanted to see if you would like an outing. After we're done with the ceremony, we'll have a picnic at the park." Jane leaned against Cole. "We'll find a nice quiet spot, and all eat together. It will be a special day."

"Will we read books?"

"I'll have Cole read them." Jane smirked. "His voice is like music."

"Cole can't read." Alma got to her feet. "But he does talk music."

"I read now," Cole admitted. "I learned how."

"You'll read?"

"Yes." Cole sighed. "I'll read."

"I'll bring the book." Alma jumped and clapped. "You'll read."

Jane laughed. "She's more excited to hear you read than I am."

"Only because I ain't reading Whitman."

"Good point."

Gold is tried by fire, brave men by adversity.
-Seneca

If the past two years had taught Jane anything, it was how fleeting bliss could be. To that end, she was happy to revel in every moment of it she got. All too soon after the ceremony they'd boarded a train bound for home.

They sat side by side for the few hours journey, discussing plans for the arrival of Alma, Leanne visiting, and their own child. Cole's arm draped over her shoulder to hold her close while telegraph lines swooped past the window. Each dip brought them closer to home until they were only ten minutes from Dominion Falls.

She would return to the only home she remembered a married woman. After two years of struggling with her past, and Cole's resistance to love and commitment, it all seemed rather impossible at times.

Of course, not a soul would know she was married but Cole and two of her brothers, Tommy and Nick, which she was almost fine with. She worried over leaving Kat out of the mix. The woman was, after all, her best friend and closest confidante.

Cole touched her forehead where she hadn't realized a wrinkle had formed. "What is it?"

"Nothing."

"Bull."

"Pondering again if it's wrong to keep the truth from Kat."

"More people that know, more it's likely to get out."

"You just don't want her looking at you different."

"Maybe." He chuckled low at her smile of response. "She'll know soon enough about the kid, and Alma, don't wanna overwhelm her delicate constitution."

Jane offered the most unladylike snort in response to that ridiculous statement.

"It's up to you. Tell her, or don't."

"That's helpful."

"Wasn't trying to be."

"Boor." She leaned into his embrace despite her snide comment. In a few short months the town would be all abuzz over her pregnancy. Of course, she had enough to worry about alone with the pregnancy.

Both of them had fears over the baby, and they certainly were far from baseless. Jane's last pregnancy had ended so tragically halfway through and she never knew why. This time, though life was still chaotic and stressful, she and Cole were in a much better place.

She'd tell Kat, at some point. She didn't imagine she'd be able to keep the secret forever. She wasn't good at secrets.

"What's that grin for?"

"I've been married today and found a new family. I'm going to have a baby. In the next year we'll be taking in your little sister as a ward. While in Denver we set appointments with investors, *and* we are going home to spend our first marital night in our own bed. I believe I have more than enough reason to grin."

"You sure you're all right with bringing Alma home? It ain't gonna be easy. She don't like change, and people don't always understand. They'll be saying we should have put her in asylum or the like."

"Which would have been far too cruel. No, we will adapt and so will she." Despite the public location of the car, she made a bold move to straddle him in the seat. Her skirts puffed between them forming a barrier of silk and cotton to keep them from being too indecent. Then again, the cool brush of air across her ankles told her they'd made a wholly inappropriate appearance with her action. "Don't try to make me nervous simply because *you* are. I thought you didn't care what others thought about what you did?"

"That's when they thought I was being a rake."

A long, loud whistle from the train covered her giggle. "Oh, but you are a rake. Unfortunately for you, you're a rake with a good heart I refuse to ignore, which means others are bound to see it. I'm ruining your rotten reputation left and right."

"I'm getting used to it, I guess." His fingers danced along the exposed flesh of her shin. "Leastwise, I like my rewards for not complaining."

"As do I." She gave him a rushed, brutal kiss. The squeal of brakes prompted her to hop from his lap to stare out the window at the approaching platform.

"Who you expecting?"

"I'm not certain who will be there. We are arriving awful late in the day." They'd been married before noon and boarded the train after an all-too-brief picnic with Leanne and Alma. Even leaving at around one, they were arriving home near supper time. "I would assume at least Tommy, though."

"What about your boy?"

"I would hope so. David knows I'm returning tonight and hoped to be home in time to have supper with Jesse. That could mean possibly Kat, with Cindy and Lizzie might be there, too. I did miss Jesse and Lizzie terribly."

"We were gone three days and you decided to take in another stray in that time."

"Alma is no stray, she's family, even if no one knows that part." She tore her gaze from the window to cast him a glare. "Be nice."

"I'd like to be nice, but you want to see all these people. We just got married, so I wanna get real nice and friendly tonight." He leaned close, using the train's loud whistled interruption to capture her lips in a deep kiss.

She didn't offer a lick of protest and gave into the kiss easily. As soon as he tugged her close, she wrapped her arms around his neck. By the time he let her go and the brakes squealed, every inch of her skin tingled. "Oh, yes. We'll get friendly. Although we should probably stop saying we got married. It's supposed to be a secret."

"I'm good at keeping secrets."

"I know all too well." Jane pushed him back and quirked a brow. After all, he had recently revealed his two half-sisters still alive and well, and mostly through force of circumstance. "From me, even. If I was a lesser woman, I'd be worried."

"You ain't no lesser woman, so you got nothing to worry about." He held out his hand and offered a wink as he rose. "Let's get going so you can gossip with Kathy."

"And see Jesse, and Lizzie and you can see Cindy." She took the offered hand, her stomach still twisted into excited little knots over their adventure in Denver. "Good thing Kat is a patient woman. I can't wait to show her all the dresses I bought in Denver."

"Don't ya think you went overboard? We had to buy a new trunk." He grumped, even as he tugged her closer.

"Some of those items were free and a gift from Leanne, including an outfit I recall you being quite pleased with." Before he could reply, she bumped her hip against his and took the offered hand of the conductor. She was rather pleased that her reminder of the high-class whore's outfit she'd worn in Denver for an hour still made Cole so eager he leaped off the train and tugged her close again.

"You don't play fair."

"Neither do you, sir." After one last grin at him, she glanced around the platform. Some of her excitement waned when she realized there wasn't one familiar face beyond Norman's apprentice Byron. "Well, I'll be. I don't even see Norman."

"Wonder what's going on."

"I have no idea. At the very least Norman should be here, but it looks like Byron is handling things for him. I'd also expect Michael and Tommy, they should be drumming up business for the hotels. This makes no sense."

Cole's brow furrowed and he laced his fingers with hers. "Must be something going on. Let's go see if we can't find out. Think Byron will get your trunks sent on?"

"They have my name on them, I'm sure he will." Jane didn't bother to hesitate a moment longer, her curiosity led her right off the platform behind Cole. With a sigh, she leaned into him. "When do you think we should start talking about the baby? Or should we wait for it to be obvious?"

"Maybe we should wait. Just to be sure, and all."

Her smile faltered, but she nodded in agreement. Since the last time Jane had been pregnant the child had been lost midway through, it was probably safer to keep hush. "You're probably right, although a few already know."

"Kathy and Tom?"

"And Daisy, of course. Sorry, Dr. Pearson. Don't know that I'll ever get used to that."

"She's been a whore too long."

"She hasn't been a whore for over a year now." Jane sighed.

"Exactly. Once you're a whore, it's hard to go back to something else."

"So even a month a whore is too long."

"Yup."

"Quaint." She wrinkled her nose, laughing when he gave her a kiss in response.

"I do my best."

"Of course, if Dr. Pearson knows, then my annoying brother Charlie probably knows as well, he is her partner in the clinic." Jane frowned. Charlie was her brother and another doctor. After a recent bout of scarlet fever, she'd been trapped in the clinic with him as her doctor for a month. In that time, she'd gotten rather tired of him, and he of her.

"So we should probably tell Mike. Ain't fair you leave out one of your brothers if the rest of 'em know."

"All right. We tell my brothers, Kat, and Daisy. I probably should have told Leanne, but next time we see her I'll tell her."

"The alarm bell woke us all up middle of the night. I reckon pa was mad as a March hare thinking it was a false one again." A young man and his friends came around the corner behind Jane and Cole, huddled together. "He still ain't forgotten what we did on Halloween last year."

"The fire was huge, bet he saw it right off," said one of his friends.

Jane's stomach dropped to the ground, and she stopped short as the boys moved past them down the street. She cleared her throat. "Jacob?"

The first boy, a gangly fourteen-year-old with scruffy black hair and skin as pale as moonlight stopped short and turned toward them. His eyes grew wide, and he backed up a few steps. "Aw, geez."

When the whole group took off down the road at full tilt, Cole grew still next to her.

"Fire," Jane managed to whisper. "No. They couldn't mean…"

Cole took a few steps, but then stopped. "No. They woulda told us. Telegram or the like woulda come."

She couldn't ignore the deepening pit in her stomach and reached down to gather her skirts. Rather than wait for him to initiate, she took off running down the street, sticking close to the right side of the road so she'd have to wait longer to see what she dreaded she'd find.

Even staying close against the old boarding house, the Hangman's Inn came into view much too soon. A huge gaping black hole where the bar once had been, all the way up to where their bedroom had been on the second floor.

Shouting went back and forth, hammers banged on boards, people mingled outside the destroyed building.

Jane's fingers went numb, her whole body growing cold as she started to tremble and shake her head. She tried to speak, but words failed her for a full minute. Just as the first person took notice of her she managed to find her voice, only to let out a gut-wrenching scream. *"No!"*

Night brings our troubles to the light,
rather than banishes them.
-Seneca

Kat jolted awake in a flash of confusion. The darkness of night flickered at the edge of her vision as if she'd left the lamp lit on accident. An odd sense of panic kept her heart racing while she tried to get her bearings.

What had woken her?

Her mind scrambled for the answer.

A scream.

She'd heard a scream. Or had she? She nudged Norman. "Did you hear that?"

Norman's grunt of complaint indicated his continued slumber.

"Norman. Someone screamed. What is that?" Her brain now hooked on the odd flickering in the night. A quick scan of the room indicated no candle or lantern. In fact, the flickering appeared to be coming from the curtains. "Norman! Get up."

"Go back to sleep," he grumbled.

This time when a scream rented through the air again, it was followed shortly by a loud clanging bell. The bell was only used in emergencies. This time she shoved Norman so hard he fell right off the bed with a pained grunt. "Get up, you old codger."

"What in tarnation is your—what is that? What's going on?"

Kat threw on a pair of trousers. "An emergency. I told you I heard a scream. Get up." Soon as she grabbed her blouse, she rushed out of the room to the front door. The flickering grew brighter, orange through the front curtains.

"Kat!"

She threw open the door, a blast of heat knocking the wind from her lungs. "Balls."

Screams of 'fire' rented through the air. People not already in the street helping streamed out of homes and businesses. A line had already formed at the well. Kat took it all in quick as a wink but paused on the blaze burning so strong across the street.

The front of the saloon was alit in flame. In the chaos she looked for the whores, Graham, Tommy, any of them. She spotted a few whores, but little else. The buckets were moving along the line of helpers now, but Kat stood dumbstruck.

"Get moving." Norman shoved a quilt in her hands. "Fire's jumping."

On instinct alone, Kat moved ahead to shove the quilt into a trough to get it good and wet before she began beating it against bits of fire along the boardwalk, and the railing of the cooper's shop beside the saloon.

Her lungs grew dry and raspy, the heat was incredible, but she couldn't stop. She only hoped that they would be able to salvage something for Jane.

"Tommy. Where's Tommy?"

Kat paused at the renewed screaming and chaos. Calls went out for the man, and Kat looked around in surprise. The fire was hardly sated, and a blur of fabric rushed right past Kat into the blaze.

"Pansy, no." Michael's familiar voice cried out before he tried to race in behind her, only to be stopped by another flash of the fire. "Shit."

Kat stood slack while Jane's brother raced around the back of the building. A chunk of flame shot right past her face, startling her out of the stupor. She beat at it with her blanket until the bit of wood smoked ominously but burned no more.

After replenishing her quilt with water, she resumed the brutal pace of stopping the spread. She beat at the fires until her arms were weak, and her lungs raw. She finally collapsed around sunup, gladly accepting the water someone handed her.

Men still worked to put out the fire, which had finally settled into a low burn around what had been the bar. Kat surveyed the damage with burning eyes, unable to shed the tears that added pressure to her sore lungs. "Oh dear."

"Easy, Kat." Charlie handed her another glass of water. "Take it slow. Everyone's a bit out of sorts, some are more the worse for wear than others."

"Norman?"

"Resting in the clinic."

"Did they find Tommy?"

"Pansy did. Dragged him halfway across the balcony before Mike got to her. She's burned pretty bad, as is Tommy. I've got her in the clinic. Stubborn bastard is in there, though." He gestured dismissively toward the saloon.

"He was in there?" Panic seized her again, until she gasped for air.

"Easy. Slow down. No one died, thank heavens." Charlie rubbed his hands over his face, lending a layer of soot to the normally sparkling clean visage. "We couldn't save the bar, but we saved the people and part of the building.

Kat sipped the water again, for which her parched throat expressed its gratitude with a painful swallow. "I should get back to work."

"Take a rest. We're all taking shifts. The worst of it is out, shouldn't take long now."

He was wrong, of course. Hot spots flared up for several hours until they finally had no more flare ups for around an hour. Everyone continued to work, crawling around the place like ants to start clearing parts of it away.

Kat worked until she thought she might not be able to stand any longer. She vaguely heard the train whistle, but her focus remained on the cleanup.

That is until another scream rented the air. *"No!"*

Jane.

My heart burnt within me with idignation and grief; we could think of nothing else.
-Elizabeth Gaskill

Cole couldn't move, even as Jane's scream resonated in his ear. None of it was happening if he just didn't move. Jane's second scream when she crumpled beside him spurred him into enough action to catch her fall. He scooped her in his arms, but remained staring at the sight before him.

The saloon had been his one success. The one thing he'd made work for a long time without fail. Now this.

Three forms ran toward them, but he was blind to their faces, his sole focus on the blacked outline around the gaping hole in the front of his business. He snarled toward the nearest approaching form, "What in blazes happened?"

"We aren't sure how it happened, but the fire started in the middle of the night." Kathy's voice brought her concerned features into focus. She'd set a hand on Jane's sobbing back, her brows pursed as she studied her friend. "The alcohol made it really speed along so it got out of control right quick."

"We think it started outside." Mike's voice came from Cole's right. Cole ignored him in favor of surveying the damage further.

"Jane. We should get you to the clinic." Daisy's voice was so quiet, he'd barely heard. The suggestion spurred Jane to action.

Tears clung to her cheeks, but her sobs faded to hiccups. "No. No, not yet. I have to see it."

"I don't think that's such a good idea." Daisy held Jane's gaze with intensity. "This is stressful enough. You should rest and let them keep working. Perhaps later."

"It will kill me more to lie there not knowing the true depth of this." Jane lifted her head so she could meet Cole's gaze head on. Her chin had the stubborn set to it, her eyes belying the fierce strength the shock had knocked out of her. "Imagining will be far worse. I must see it, please put me down. I'll be all right now."

Cole hesitated a fraction of a second. She'd said she'd listen to doc's orders, but this was something different. He knew her mind worked fast and too much bad had happened to her for her to not imagine the worst. The moments debate over, he set her down.

Jane brushed down her skirts, but her hands shook as she did. The whole thing took too much of her focus. She was stalling.

"We don't gotta," he started.

"Yes. We do." She took his hand, her other hand lacing with Kat's before she lifted her gaze to the carnage. Her jaw clenched, but she held her ground.

"It took us hours," Kat whispered. "They saved as much as they could. Worked nonstop."

"Oh. Oh no. Tommy's room is half gone. Where's Tommy? *Tommy?*" Jane's hand clenched tight to Cole's for a fierce moment before she released it and took off. "Thomas Eugene! My stars, what happened?"

Cole walked up behind Jane, wondering at the panic in her voice, that is until he saw the subject of her attentions. His friend and brother-in-law had been in the fire by the looks of it. "Hell's bells, Tom."

Tommy's face was blistered and charred, more on his right than his left. The arms he'd wrapped around Jane showed evidence of the same. In Jane's tight embrace the brute of a man winced, but didn't try to squirm away. "I'm sorry. Don't know why I didn't wake up. Not even the fire woke me. Pansy had to drag my ass away from the fire. Took more than these burns to wake me up."

Jane stepped back from the embrace, her eyes wide, jaw slack. "Did you say Pansy dragged you away? Little tiny Pansy?"

"Sure did. Had me halfway down the hall before Mike found us to help her."

Cole blinked, not sure what to make of that. The young whore had been a bit of a troublemaker and had some sass, but Jane wasn't lying. The girl didn't seem to have enough meat on her to do her duties, much less haul Tommy anywhere. "I'll be damned."

Tommy shook his head. "Can't believe she ran back in there blazing like it was. Graham and Mike say she ran headlong into the fire when she found out I wasn't outside. She's at the clinic."

"Damn," Cole muttered.

"I'm sorry." Tommy's attention fixed on Cole now. His jaw worked in tense circles. Usually Cole couldn't get a good grip on the guys emotions, he'd spent so long as a Pink he hid everything real good. Now, tension worked his jaw in tight clenches. His brows turned down with something akin to regret. "I did wrong by you."

"Don't." Jane interrupted before either Tommy or Cole could say another word. "Don't you dare, Thomas. This isn't your fault."

Cole's mounting tension took a hit at Jane's words. Easy as it would be to pin it on Tom to direct his anger somewhere, anywhere, she was right. He nodded to the man. "She's right. This ain't your fault. We'll find out whose it is."

"On my word." The tension in Tommy rose again, his jaw getting the same stubborn set as Jane's when he meant something. Not that Cole doubted, Tom had always been good as his word. Tom hugged Jane again, leaning in close to her good ear. Whatever he said to her, she nodded in reply before kissing him on the less injured cheek.

"Go on. Get Daisy to take care of those burns." Jane set her hand on Tommy's cheek. "Please. I need as little to worry about as possible, and all of that is enough without worrying about a buffoon such as yourself. Go. No arguments."

"There's more cleanup," he protested anyway.

"From what I can see, over half the town is here working. You need to get yourself taken care of. Please. I'll be along soon, once I've seen what the place looks like inside." Jane's hand reached for Cole's before she'd taken a step away from her brother. "Don't keep punishing yourself by working like this. Let Daisy do her job, or I'll call Charlie to do it instead."

"Devil woman." Tommy managed a weak smile.

"Don't you forget it. Now go." Jane stood tall as ever when Cole wrapped a reassuring arm around her waist, but her hands still trembled on her way to her skirts. He had a feeling it was more for show for those around them casting pitying looks their way.

He didn't blame her. Last thing he wanted was to be pitied, her stubborn pride would hate it as much as his. He couldn't bear to add to that feeling for her, but knowing of the baby, he worried anyhow. If she were to lose that, too, he had a feeling he'd lose her like David had once lost Clara.

"Cole?"

Cole jolted out of his thoughts to give her a reassuring squeeze. "I'm right here. Are you sure you wanna do this? Now?"

"No. Not in the least." She turned to face him, a hint of humor under the tears eased his spirits until it disappeared as quick as it had shown up.

"Not much choice, though. Is there?"

"Not really. I have to do this." She stepped over a charred board in their path to the Inn.

Their path forward cleared as everyone stepped aside. Murmured condolences barely seeped through.

A familiar scruffy old man stepped out from the shadow of the porch. He pulled his rumpled hat from his head. Hammy twitched the hat between his fingers. "Real sorry, Lady Jane. We're gonna fix ya up real fast. No charge, I promise ya."

"Oh, Mr. Hamm." Jane embraced the old man tight. The kiss she pressed to his cheek brought a ruddy embarrassment to his face. "You are the kindest man that ever was."

"Ain't no such thing, Lady Jane. It just ain't right after all you done." Hammy shuffled his feet. "Best get back to work."

Cole squeezed Jane's hand after the man had departed. She still hadn't moved from the spot. "You sure?"

"Let's go before you have to ask a third time." She released his hand to brace the door frame so she could step over some fallen boards.

Two steps beyond the threshold, they both stopped dead. The charred frame of their bed stood vigil twisted and blackened on the remains of the bar. The mattress completely gone, and the metal frame so grotesquely melted, it barely resembled a bed any longer.

She moved closer to the center of destruction, skirting along the blackened rubble like a ghost. At the remains of their bed, she paused. Her gaze lifted to where the ceiling had once been.

Cole kept moving through the room toward the storeroom. Broken glass crunched under his boots, soot stirring up from the remains of chairs and tables. The gaping maw of what had been the doorway to the storeroom revealed only two shelves had survived complete destruction. While the shelves survived, the glassware on them sat half-melted. The cost to replace everything ratcheted up in his head.

A board clattered nearby, startling him from the mental calculations of destruction. He turned to discover Jane no longer where he'd left her. "Jane?"

Another board flew over the lump of rubble where the bar had stood. Her blond hair appeared for a moment before she disappeared behind it again.

"What are you doing?"

"Just…a…moment." She grunted the words, then toppled back enough to be seen. A soft 'oof' slipped from her lips, but she rose quick enough for him to know she wasn't hurt. With one hand, she dusted the soot off her bodice. From the other hung a blackened arc of metal. "Well, your so-called lucky horseshoe survived. That's about it back here. "Store room?"

"A few glasses at the most."

"Damn. All the liquor and the glassware. Half the tables, not that most of them were much more than the ramshackle ones Mr. Hamm built a while back."

"How high's your tally?"

"Probably not as high as yours. I need paper for numbers. You've proven you don't." She gathered her skirts to climb over a high pile of boards to reach his side. "Some of the boards are still warm."

"You ready to go upstairs?" He frowned toward the broad hole in the balcony that circled the bar area. "It's gonna be unsteady, and I don't know how much of our room we'll even be able to get to. We'll have to be careful."

"Thank you for the obvious observation, Mr. Mitchell." She gripped his hand tight enough to show her own panic. Despite that, she headed for the stairs. Instead of taking the customary right to their room, she turned left to take the long way around.

By taking this direction they could get close to their room. The other side, which held Tommy's room, was burned up the worst. Based on what he could see, Tommy's room was a goner, and it had been right next to theirs. From what he'd been able to tell from below, the room on their other side appeared mostly untouched, only the wall between it and their room had been lost to the blaze.

The balcony became unsteady the closer they got the edge. Fortunately, they were able to enter the room next to theirs a few feet from where the balcony disappeared completely. Though most everything in the room was blackened by soot, the furniture remained intact.

Cole grasped Jane's hand when she drew close to the edge of floor. "Stay back, Jane."

"Everything's gone." Her wide eyes didn't miss an inch of the wide gap where their room had been.

From where they stood he could see just bits of floor beyond the half-burned wall. Their desk leaned dangerously close to falling through. A single plank of wood seemed to have caught the corner to hold it in place.

"My books. Our clothes. Our picture. The, oh!"

Cole startled at her gasp. He clutched her hand tight as possible when she tried to tug away. "Jane. Stop. What is it?"

"Let go." She ripped her hand free of his grasp. Over his protest, she edged ever closer to the edge of the hole in the wall, toward the desk he'd noticed dangling so close to falling.

"Damn it Jane, don't."

"Stop. Your weight could change everything." She held her hand out toward him, but kept her gaze locked on the desk.

"Stop, please." He wanted to run and grab her, but she was right. The boards trembled with each of her cautious steps.

"I have to. Just wait."

"Don't you dare."

"It's not far. Hold on." She snaked her arm around the bit of wall remaining. When she came stumbling back, he caught her around the waist.

"What the hell were ya doing? Ya crazy?"

"I had to." She turned to face him. In her hands lay the wooden box he'd kept for years.

His heart sank into the floor. A few years back the box and its contents had bbeen his greatest secret. Jane had been the first, and remained the only, person he'd let see and know. Now the edges were darkened, but when she cracked the box open, he could see the booties, ring and picture remained untouched. "Damn."

"You wouldn't want just anyone finding this when they cleaned up." She set her hand on his arm. "It survived. They survived."

The remnants of his old life as Colton Spencer, his deceased wife and child, were reduced to the contents of the box. Where they'd been for long enough Cole had almost completely put them behind. No, he wouldn't want anyone else learning of it, but would it have crushed them if they'd burned as everything else had? He couldn't be sure, but one thing he did know. "I've moved on."

"But you can never lose your past. I think I've proved that."

"You sure did."

She turned away, staring toward where their room had been a few days ago. Without the outer walls, all he could see past her was the barber shop across the street, and the edge of the clinic next to it.

Cole closed the box so he would wrap an arm around her waist. He rested his chin on top of her head. "We've survived worse."

"I suppose we have."

"We'll survive this, too."

"We have to. I just haven't the faintest clue how yet."

A knock startled them both. Someone cleared their throat. "It ain't much," Iris' voice rasped raw.

Jane's hands brushed across her face before she turned to face the door. "Iris?"

"Me and the girls, we took up a collection." Iris held out the pouch. "It ain't much, really."

"You and the girls all right?" Cole set a hand on Jane's shoulder, not reaching for the pouch, though Iris held it toward him, not Jane.

"All 'cept for Pansy, we only got a few scrapes and burns." Iris brushed a finger over her own bruised check.

"Thank goodness." Jane sagged against Cole.

Cole eyed Iris. "I don't understand."

Iris took a step into the room, and pushed the pouch into his free hand. "We all talked about it. We ain't going nowhere. We got contracts anyhow, but it ain't right to take off 'cuz of this."

The weight of the bag startled Cole. A quick shift of his hand made the coins inside jangle. "We ain't taking your money, Iris."

Iris shrugged. "It's 'cause of Jane we got any. It's only right. Our room is still good. We're gonna stay there. Ain't like no one else would take us in. We got enough to get some grub for a couple weeks anyhow."

A deep sob erupted from Jane. She dropped her head into her hands.

Iris turned a wide-eyed gaze at Cole. "I didn't mean nothing by it."

"Don't worry Iris. She ain't mad at ya, just the opposite. Go on, now. We'll see ya tomorrow." Cole turned Jane toward him best as he could with his hands now full. She melted into him, her body shaking with sobs. Once Iris's footsteps faded, he kissed the top of Jane's head. "We'll fix it."

"Say it again. I need to believe it."

"We'll fix it."

*They tell us, sir, that we are weak,
unable to cope with so formidable an
adversary. But when shall we
be stronger?
-Patrick Henry*

Cole's strong hand ran along Jane's back. His smooth voice warmed her ear. "Easy, Jane. You got this"

"I certainly don't feel like I do," she managed to croak. Whether it was the pregnancy itself, or the added stress of the saloon fire, or all of the above—she'd been sick for hours that morning. After a heavy sigh, she rested her elbow on the edge of the bucket.

"Strongest woman I know."

"Flattery won't make my stomach stop." She rested her forehead on her hand, trying to take steady breaths. "You should eat. Just because I can't does not mean you shouldn't. You're going to be working at the Inn today. Eat."

"The sound of me eating makes you sick." Cole chuckled low. "Me eating would start ya all over again, and you just got a breather. Once you're feeling up to getting dressed, I'll get you sitting outside and then I'll eat."

If every inch of her didn't hurt at the moment, she might smack him just for his humorous attitude. "None of this is funny."

"No. It ain't."

Jane blew out a long breath of air. For the first time that morning, her stomach didn't turn over just because she dared to breath. Relief flooded her at that notion.

For the moment, the two of them were holed up in her old room in Kat's home, which had once been the boarding house. Over Jane's protest, Kat had insisted Lizzie and Cindy would enjoy sharing a room for a while. Still, Jane didn't feel right using the room.

She glanced around the room at the white-washed walls, all the way to the curtained doors leading to the balcony. After the past several hours of vomiting, fresh air seemed like a good idea.

"Better?"

"Moderately." A half-truth, but she did feel more in control of her faculties. The idea of getting into the fresh air also bolstered it toward the truth. With Cole's assistance, she rose to her feet. At the wash basin she washed her face and chest. By the time she finished, Cole already stood behind her with her bodice held out. Together they managed to get her dressed in a relatively quick fashion.

Cole patted her bustle. "Now hold your nose and get your ass downstairs. Kathy said something about books when she dropped off the tray."

"Books?" Jane eyed him in curiosity. "They were all destroyed in the fire, I thought?"

"Don't ask me, just tellin' you what she said."

Jane pursed her lips, contemplating. "Fine. If it means you'll eat, I'll see what Katherine has in store for me."

Cole tugged her close to kiss her forehead. "I'll be at the Inn if ya need anything."

"I know. Thank you." As ordered, she closed her fingers over her nose. He opened the door for her, and she leapt lightly over the tray sitting outside the door.

If only Katherine hadn't brought eggs, perhaps she would have been better sooner. The smell alone did her in.

Jane shuddered off the last of the nausea at the bottom of the steps. "Katherine?"

"Out here." Kat's voice was half-muffled, but her hand waved through the front window before disappearing. "This needed to be done in the open air."

"What on earth are you talking about?" Jane edged through the half-open front door. Kat knelt on the porch, her back to Jane. Before the woman sat a large pile of books in various stages of health. Jane dropped to her knees next to Kat. A soft gasp escaped as she reached for a moderately burned tome. "Oh my. But, how?"

"This is the last of them." Graham approached with an armful of books, which he dropped on top of the pile. "Janey."

"Graham? What?" Jane shook her head, stunned at all of it. The books themselves. Graham's state of helpfulness. "I don't understand. I thought they were all gone."

"I managed to get a few." Graham shrugged as if it meant nothing. He folded his arms across his chest, which drew Jane's attention to the bandages on his hands. "Knew the bar was done for no matter what. While they were throwing water, I hauled out what I could until I couldn't no more."

Gratitude almost choked off her words. Jane forced out a joke to try to hide her tears. "What you're saying is that once again instead of working to stop the damage, you did something else?"

Graham grinned. "You always tell me I'm good for nothing. Can't say any of them are good, the fire was already eating up one wall. I didn't know Tom was in there or I woulda got him first. Might've saved him some burns. Sorry, Janey."

Jane waved off the apology. "Stop. If you didn't know, you didn't know."

"Wish I had, is all I'm saying."

Kat's hand on her back helped stave off the tears Jane felt burning again. "I appreciate that. I appreciate this, Graham. More than I can say."

Graham knelt down next to her, his beefy hand clamped firm on her shoulder. "Your brother Nick's already working on my problem. I owed you one, and many more than that."

"Just don't go turning into a big idiot again." Jane patted his hand. "I actually like you when you're happy."

"Everyone does," Kat agreed. She held out the Whitman book to Jane as Graham stood to make his exit. "This one is in good shape. We'll go through and see what's salvageable, all right?"

"Sounds like a plan." Jane nodded to her, and glanced again at Graham. "Thank you both."

Kat smiled. "It's what friends are for. Now, let's get you to work. Busy is good and distracting, which you need."

"Very much so."

Neither fire nor wind, birth nor death,
can erase our good deeds.
—Buddha

Cole brought the mallet down hard on a charred board, not at all surprised when it gave way to drop into the ever-growing hole to land on the floor of the Inn. Along the roof to his right Tommy did the same with another board. To his left, Mike showed more success by pounding on a series of boards without dropping one.

Mike wiped at his forehead. "These are all clear. Looks like we're getting close, Cole."

"Don't matter much. We don't have any way to fix it up once we get rid of the damage." Cole slammed his mallet into the support beam, which resonated in response. Flakes of ash rained down into the empty bar area.

"Hey Mike!" Tommy called to his brother from behind Cole.

Cole ignored Mike's departure, choosing to focus on Jane across the street. On the porch of the old boarding house, she and Kat had been going through a pile of books. Once in a great while, Jane's laughter would filter up to his ears. Though it never lasted long, the sound was not only welcomed, he needed to hear it.

Heavy footsteps approached. Tommy plopped down beside him, a canteen in his hand.

Cole drank heartily from the canteen of ginger water. He set it aside, his attention back on the roof. He slammed the mallet into another board, which cracked easily under the impact. "This one's gotta go too. That's half the damned roof."

"You know, it's not your fault, either." Tom propped one foot up on the edge of the hole. His free leg hung down into the open air. He draped an arm over the raised knee. "She wanted to be your partner—in every way."

"I ain't in the mood."

"Fine. Be a bastard for all I care. The longer you sulk, the longer she struggles."

Cole's venom flew away at the mention of Jane struggling. He hated it when she suffered. His shoulders sagged under his frustration and grief. "All I had to give her was a room. Now I ain't even got that."

"She doesn't care about that." Tommy smirked at Cole's snorted response. "If the two of you had nothing but a care, you'd get along just fine. She may like pretty things and pleasures, but she doesn't need them. She does need you, however."

"Do you always gotta be right, Tom?"

"It's a family trait."

"It's a family trait to annoy the hell outta me."

"And we're damn good at it." Tommy nudged him. The laughter in his voice could have been contagious if not for the situation. "Lou's the best at it, too—so you're not allowed to complain too much. You're the one that married her."

Cole slugged the man hard in the shoulder, making him tip precariously over the edge. "If you keep holding that over my head, I might let you fall right off this roof."

"Lou would kill you. She has enough to panic about."

A shout from across the street drew Cole's gaze back to Kat's porch. Jane stood there arguing rather dramatically with both Charlie and Mike. Cole smirked at the sight. "That's not good."

"My fault."

Before Cole could ask for an explanation, Jane gripped Mike's arm as she swayed. Cole shot to his feet, but Jane didn't faint. Instead, she vomited all over the porch.

Tommy laughed so hard, he fell back onto the roof. He let out a loud whoop. "I told Mike to make sure she ate something. He doesn't know about why she don't want to early in the day."

Cole nudged Tommy in the ribs with his boot, but couldn't stop his own chuckle. "Problem is that's as mean to Jane as it is to Mikey. She'll kill you if she finds out you're behind that."

"Probably."

The yelling resumed across the street. "I should go rescue her."

"Or them, depending on how you look at it." Tommy guffawed when Jane punched Mike in the stomach. "I'll be down in a few. I want to check a few more boards."

"Thanks, Tom." Cole moved to the edge of the roof. He ignored the ladder to drop down onto the half of the porch roof that remained intact. Before he'd set a foot on the hitchng post to make it the rest of the way down, Jane's argument carried to him.

"Stop fussing. Let me clean this up and leave me be," Jane snapped.

By the time Cole turned around Jane had removed her skirt, flashing her petticoats for the world to see. Cole sighed when she knelt down to clean her own sick from the porch.

Mike tried to bend down to help, but Cole grabbed him to hold him back. He offered the man a brief shake of his head, and moved behind Jane. He picked her up by the elbows, ignoring her yelp of protest. "Go get yourself another skirt."

"Don't you tell me what to do, Mr. Mitchell. I am not one of your whores."

He smacked her ass at the protest. When she spun to smack him, he caught her wrist. He raised a brow. "You sure as hell ain't one of my whores, and I've never treated you like one."

"Ordering—,"

"You got three decent skirts left, and two fancies. You just went and ruined one of the only skirts you got left, with no money to buy new. Mikey'll get you a mop to clean this up proper when you get back."

He could see her fuming, wanting to blow. Her blue eyes grew darker with each of her sharp exhales. It seemed she couldn't find fault in his argument, though. For instead of yelling, she spun on her heel to storm inside. The door slammed behind her hard.

He sighed and rubbed his hand over his face. While he hated pissing her off, it had been necessary to make her stop mopping up her mess with her own skirt. The fire had her messed up as bad as him, and he couldn't yet see how they could make it right.

"I'll get the damn mop," Mike broke the silence. He disappeared inside Kat's far quieter than Jane, but still hollered for Kat when he entered.

Charlie bent to gather some of the destroyed books from the porch. "Will you help me straighten these books? At least we can get them off the ground."

"They're already ruined, but sure. So long as we don't touch that mess. She'd wring our necks." Cole bent with Charlie to gather the books. He stacked them haphazardly on the bench.

"Has she been eating enough?" Charlie wiped the soot from his hands onto a kerchief he'd pulled from a pocket. He handed it off to Cole. "With everything going on—I don't want her missing any because she thinks there are more important things to do."

"Are you kidding? Did you see her at supper last night? Once we managed to sit down that woman ate three times more than Tommy, and Tommy can really shovel it in."

Charlie snorted. "You've got a point. Kat says she doesn't eat much lunch or break the fast. I'm worried that she'll get enough food."

"When she eats before two..." Cole gestured back toward the skirt on the porch. "Well, you've seen what happens."

Jane's familiar scoff sounded behind him. "Thank you for that eloquent description of my condition, Cole. Remind me to have you write my epitaph, I'm certain it will be ever so profound." She glared heartily at him, a sheet held out in her hand. Before he could ask what it was for, she used it to gather up her soiled skirt.

As she tied it off to set aside, Mike appeared with the mop in hand. His brow furrowed as he looked between the men on the porch and Jane. "Did I miss something?"

"Give me the damn mop." Jane snatched it from his grasp. In fast, efficient swipes she cleaned up the mess quick as a wink. The moment she finished her task, she stormed back into the building. Without another glance back, she slammed the door again.

"I've got this one." Charlie clamped a hand on Cole's shoulder.

"You sure? She don't like you much when you play doctor."

"Luckily, I can also play the part of her brother. Don't worry. I'll talk her down, and we'll meet you at Cora's."

"Right." Cole let out a frustrated breath. He nodded to Mike, and the pair of them started down the street. Tommy joined them in seconds.

"She can't stay like this forever," Mike muttered. "She didn't even mope this long over you, Cole."

"Yes she did, you big exaggerator." Tommy reached behind him to shove Mike off balance. A few horses startled at the stumbling man. "Mind you, she's got every right to be upset, just like Cole does. This is their business, and their home."

"We were gonna have company in a few weeks," Cole realized miserably. He didn't now how Alma could visit now. He'd have to send Leanne a wire. At this rate, he didn't know if they could still take Alma in at all, or where they'd live with the baby. Not that he'd known that for sure before all of this. "Not sure it'll happen now."

Tommy hopped up the steps ahead of Cole. "There's other rooms. If Jane's up to moving back in, you should. I'm gonna take the room downstairs until we get something rebuilt."

"We. You going to become an investor now, Tommy?" Mike scoffed. He dropped into a seat next to his brother. He plucked his hat off of his head, but cringed when Tommy immediately ruffled his hair. "Bastard."

"I am the manager, even if I'm a lousy one. I'm allowed to say 'we'." Tommy's argument faded with the arrival of the waitress, for which Cole was grateful. Right then he didn't even want to think of money, or their scheduled plans to meet with investors they'd have to cancel now.

Cole dropped his face in his hands. The numbers ran through his head anyway, no matter his determination to not think about them. The damage to the saloon, what it would take to even get functioning again. Their clothes, the loss of rooms for entertainment. It seemed utterly and completely impossible to both fix it and find a way to expand like they'd planned.

A small, warm hand settled on his shoulder. Skirts rustled next to him. "Cole," she whispered.

"Play with us, Janey. You need a smile." Tommy's teasing tone interrupted whatever she was going to say. His booming voice carried in a way that both amused and annoyed Cole. "Tell-tale tit! Your tongue shall be slit."

"And all the dogs in town shall have a little bit," Jane finished. Her brow puckered in a glare toward Tommy. "Please. As I've told Charlie, I am not a parlor trick."

"Rowsty dowt, my fires all out—,"

"Enough with the nursery rhymes, Thomas." Charlie took a seat at the table, dropping his hat on the back of his chair. "Why not give her a true challenge. From the Earth to the Moon, chapter twenty, paragraph nineteen."

"No fair, that's a long one. I will humor you with a sentence or two." Jane took a sip of tea, a warm blush lighting her cheeks as though secretly flattered and pleased at the so-called game. "'Nobody knew him, and the president, uneasy as to the result of so free a discussion, watched his new friend with some anxiety'."

Mike tapped a finger on his cup. "All right, let's try this one. Les Miserables, Cosette, Book the fifth, chapter six, final paragraph."

"Ugh. Depressing." Jane's gaze focused on nothing, a small frown tweaking her lips downward. Still, she spoke anyway. "'All fell silent again. There was no longer anything in the street; there was nothing in the garden. That which had menaced, and that which had reassured him—all had vanished. The breeze swayed a few dry weeds on the crest of the wall, and they gave a faint, sweet, melancholy sound'."

Tommy slammed his hand on the table so hard everyone jumped, and tea sloshed onto saucers. "I've got it. I know what'll make you smile. Whitman! 'Hark close and still what I now whisper to you'."

"'I love you, O you entirely possess me, O that you and I escape from the rest and go utterly off, free and lawless'." Jane's eyes fell closed, the first real hint of a smile graced her lips. With every further word she spoke, her smile grew.

Charlie opened his mouth when she took a breath, but stopped at Tommy's gesture. Tommy gave Cole a wink before turning his attention back to Jane's recitation.

The familiar words of a poem she'd read to him more times than he could count spilled from her lips easy as anything. Her hand slipped onto his knee, so he closed his fingers over hers.

"'From what the divine husband knows, from the work of fatherhood'." She turned toward him, her eyes open. She gave a quick startle when she took note of the growing group of people listening to her recitation, but didn't stop. "'From one so unwilling to have me leave, and me just as unwilling to leave, yet a moment O tender waiter, and I will return'."

Tommy laughed, lifting his arms as if to conduct an orchestra. All three brothers chimed in at once to finish once Jane's voice had ceased. "'From the hour of shining stars and dropping dews, from the night a moment I emerging flitting out, celebrate you, act divine—and you children, prepare for—and you *stalwart loins*'."

Even Jane burst into laughter at the last words, shouted quite loud by all three of her brothers. Several women in the crowd gasped and scattered at such impropriety.

"Your whole damn family is crazy." Cole leaned in to kiss her cheek. "But I don't care none if it got you smiling."

"For now." She cupped his cheek and made to lean in for a real kiss. A hard bang on the table by Tommy startled her to distraction, damn him.

"I've got another." Despite the groans from Charlie and Mike, Tommy persisted. "'I am for those who believe in loose delights, I share in the midnight orgies—"

"Jane!" David's voice interrupted what promised to be another fun recitation.

Cole shrugged at Jane's confused look.

Jane stared over Cole's shoulder a moment before she rose. "David? What's wrong?"

"Come here. You too, Cole. Come on." David disappeared outside before Cole had turned in his seat.

Cole groaned, he'd much rather stay where he was. Jane tugged his arm anyway, so he rose. "Fine. I'm coming."

"Reverend!" Jane paused in surprise, then rushed down the steps. "What are you two doing out today?"

Reverend Green tipped his hat to Jane. "Seeing as you were understandably busy today, and Katherine was assisting you, I asked David to join me for my weekly ride out to the settlement."

Jane grasped his hand. "I apologize, I'd forgotten it was even Tuesday."

"There are no apologies necessary. You were where you needed to be."

"Still."

Cole set his hand on Jane's shoulder. "Janey. Don't go beating yourself up over this, too."

"He's right." The Reverend nodded to Cole. "What happened at the Inn needs to be dealt with. The families in the settlement are rather concerned about you."

"And look at this." David grinned, waving to the wagon bed.

Jane peeked over the edge of the wagon. Her gasp pulled Cole's curiosity to look in as well as David yanked back the blankets. Stacks of lumber piled on one side, on the other were crates, baskets, even a steamer trunk.

Cole stared in surprise, only barely noticing Jane climbing the wheel until she was up high enough to cause him concern. Instinctively, he braced a hand at her waist, but couldn't tear his eyes from the items in the wagon.

"What is all of this?" Jane set her hand on the smooth wood of the lumber pile closest.

"The Morris's asked that you take this in the same kindness that the wood you purchased for the Broder's home was meant." Reverend Green leaned over the back of the wagon seat.

"This is so much more than wood," Jane protested. She pointed toward the crates and trunk. "What about those?"

"Those are books there from Mrs. Dooley. She says she never reads them, and they have no children to pass them onto. In turn, she'd like you to have them." David grinned broadly. "She said you are too great a lover of books to have lost so many. There's lots of clothes, and they're a mixed lot—about every family that had clothes that might fit either of you put something in."

"Mrs. Webb apologized. She knows they aren't your usual taste, but she did hope you could use the dresses." The reverend tapped the trunk. "I assured her the style wouldn't matter so much in this time of need."

"I can't—I just can't. I don't—oh," Jane stammered.

"Jane," David chided. "This is a blessing."

"How can I take their things? They already have so little." Jane trembled in Cole's arms, sinking from her perch to the ground.

"'Thousands of candles can be lit from a single candle, and the life of the candle will not be shortened. Happiness never decreases by being shared'." Michael leaned on the wagon near the reverend. "Buddha."

Cole glanced back to see all three brothers had born witness to the gifts.

Jane wiped at her cheeks, sniffling until Tommy shoved a handkerchief in her hand. "They've already given me so much—much more important than tangible items. I don't know that I can accept any more from them."

Charlie set his bowler back on his head. "'To the generous mind the heaviest debt is that of gratitude, when it is not in your power to repay it'. Benjamin Franklin."

Cole smirked down at Jane. "Not good with the fancy words, but I'm guessing they're telling us to shut up and accept the gifts? Do I got that right?"

Jane laughed outright. A few last sniffles escaped through the chuckles. "Yes."

"No fancy words—just take it, Jane." Tommy squeezed her arm. "You've helped supply them with food and building materials all while tutoring their rotten kids. You and Kat found a place for Lizzie. Now you're the one in need, and you would deny them the chance to help?"

Jane took one last deep, ragged breath before facing the wagon again. She nodded. "All right. Thank you so much Reverend, David. I would like to return with you again next week as is my custom."

"So long as you don't try to thank them. They don't wish to be thanked any more than you wanted to be thanked for helping them." The reverend smiled down. "Just continue on as you always have, and that will be gratitude enough."

"I'll do my best." She leaned back against Cole's chest. "Would you both be kind enough to take the wagon over to the Inn? I'm certain Mr. Hamm will know what to do with the wood. I'll sort through the books and clothes later."

David hopped back into the wagon. "We'll take care of it."

Cole pulled Jane close to his side, leading her away from the huddle of her brothers. Rather than head straight down to Kathy's, he led her the long way back along Second Street. They strolled along past the new buildings and businesses still waiting to open, silent as Jane continued to gather herself.

He trailed his thumb along her arm, wondering over the wagon of goods himself. "I really don't know how ya do it."

"I didn't do this." Her voice was low, still husky with emotion. "They did."

"Because of you. You've been so good with them. Just like the girls. They didn't pitch in that money because of me."

Jane stopped short, turning to face him. Her face was a mix of surprise, amusement, and a smidge of anger. "Don't say that. They would. Now they would."

"Again, that's 'cause of you. You make me listen."

Once more a delicious, true smile graced her delicious lips in a way he hadn't seen since Denver. "'What is it to us what the rest do or think? What is all else to us? Only that we enjoy each other and exhaust each other if it must be so'."

Whitman again. She never stopped, but the words excited him nonetheless. He tugged her close, sealing his lips firm over hers. The moment she responded, her arms snaking around his neck, he traced his tongue over the seam of her lips until she opened to him. He tasted the familiar planes of her mouth until she moaned so deep he knew she'd forgotten the crowd around them.

Regret filled him as he withdrew from the kiss slow as molasses. "We're gonna fix this."

"I think I'm really starting to believe it."

"Good."

Perserverance is more prevailing than violence; and many things which cannot be overcome when they are together, yield themselves up when taken little by little.
—Plutarch

David shook his head. His coffee in front of him long cold as he surveyed the work happening in the opposite corner of the Inn from them. "Nobody saw a thing. At least no one around town. I tried asking the girls here even, but they don't like talking to me."

"Your goodness frightens them," Jane said with a note of humor.

"Funny." He set a hand on her arm. "You look tired."

"Thank you for that observation." She set her hand on his, grateful for the small comfort. The sudden change in fortune shouldn't have surprised her, not after the life she'd lived. "It was going too well. My life can't be that boring, I guess."

"Wait. What? Going well?"

"Yes."

"Jane. You got Scarlet Fever, lost hearing in one ear, then you can Cole got in a tremendous fight, and you suffered a concussion due to a misunderstanding. How is that going well, exactly?"

"I didn't have a maniac murderer after me. I wasn't hanged." The laughter bubbled up despite the headache pounding behind her eyes. She let it loose, happy when David joined her.

"That's true."

"Sorry. Sometimes you have to laugh." She sighed softly, staring over at the work being done again. "Worst part for me is knowing that whoever did this, truly wanted to hurt Thomas. The man may be a bear, but he's the most vigilant person I've ever met. I can't believe it was a coincidence that this was the one night he couldn't wake up for anything."

"Neither does he. We've talked about it."

"What about Gus Warren?"

"Gone. Disappeared into the night like he was never here before this ever happened. There was no sign of him in town while you were gone. If there was, I bet anything Tommy would have been even more vigilant than usual."

"You're right, of course." Jane rubbed her fingers across her forehead against the pounding in her head. Banging hammers and wheezing saws did little to aid the pain. Still, she felt like she needed to be there.

"It's not your fault either, you know."

"It feels like it is. I think there's something I overlooked. I was so busy focusing on Cole, Jesse, Lizzie and—"

"You mean you were busy living life instead of being suspicious of everything?"

"I pride myself on being observant. What have I missed, David? Who did I overlook?"

"I know this is hard for you to hear." He pulled his chair closer, bending to meet her gaze. "But you need to hear it. You can't know everything. No one expects you to."

"I expect me to." She leaned back in her chair, frustration adding tension to her aching body.

Three whores crossed the saloon in hushed conversation. As they slipped outside to lure in some customers, she saw an opportunity to change the subject.

"We have three rooms still suitable for servicing customers, so my least favorite part of the business is resuming today."

"You aren't serious?"

"I am." Jane sighed, wondering if the noise of construction would sour the prospect of business. "We sat down and fixed a bit of a schedule. I wish we had alcohol or glasses, but they won't be here until tomorrow's train. We have nowhere to store it, and a gaping hole in the building, but maybe we'll get some business in here even with the construction."

"Not even a fire keeps you down."

"Guess not." Jane forced a smile she didn't feel, knowing the words hadn't had the strength behind them they should have. If only it were true, maybe she wouldn't be ready to throw up her hands and leave. How she'd gone from such an extreme high to such a low so fast, she had no idea.

"Have you been to see Pansy yet?"

"No. I hope to tomorrow. Daisy told me she's still sleeping most of the day, and in bad pain during all of the in-betweens. If she's feeling better today, perhaps tomorrow she'll have some time when I can see her."

"I saw her yesterday to try to question her. She wasn't in any condition then." David leaned his chin on his hand. "You were complaining about how much of a troublemaker she was. Do you suspect she had a hand in this?"

"No." Jane frowned in surprise at how quick her response came. Though she'd even expected she would have given a different answer in recent weeks, her gut now told her different. "I honestly don't believe she had anything to do with it."

"Why not? I trust your instincts, but I'm curious after all the trouble you said she has been inciting among the girls."

"Pansy reminds me more of a surly child than a true wicked soul. Almost like she was egged into worse activity by Mr. Warren. The attentions of an attractive man that preferred her as his usual whore. She'd be easy to manipulate."

"A surly child?"

"I don't know why." She tapped her finger on table. "I suppose it's because when I've caught her in the act, she reminds me of Jesse when I've scolded him."

"How would you know? You hardly ever scold him."

She grinned a far more genuine smile than earlier. "That's why he loves me so much more. I leave the scolding to you."

"Ha ha."

She allowed a brief chuckle before sighing deeply. "Anyhow. Pansy risked her life to save Thomas, and now lies in the clinic suffering deeply for it. Hardly seems the actions of a girl that made sure he'd remain asleep before setting a fire."

"Well, someone sure did. If you'll ask the girls if they saw anything, I'd appreciate it. They might be more forthcoming with you than they were with me."

"I'll let Cole handle that. He's more intimidating."

"You underestimate your own powers of intimidation." David rose. He offered her his arm when she followed suit. "I've seen you stand nose to nose with Graham and win."

"I've also lost there plenty of times."

"Only because he's got brawn."

"True." She walked with him to the door. Outside, she paused alongside him. "I'll see what we can do, Sheriff."

"Thank you. Now I have one more favor to ask." He turned toward her, drawing her hands close to his chest. "Join us for supper this weekend. You can even bring Cole and I won't complain. Not even a little bit."

"I don't like being fussed over, David. Your fiancée is a fusser."

"Then do it for Jesse and suffer the fussing."

"You are a cruel man, using my son like that." Jane sighed deeply. The idea of keeping a façade for an entire evening seemed and exhausting prospect. She'd always been bad at turning down her ex-husband, though. "Fine. I'll speak to Cole about it."

"Ma!" Jesse's voice cut through their conversation. He raced down the road toward them, Cindy and Lizzie coming behind him nearly as fast.

Jane dropped down to meet his oncoming hug. He nearly tackled her to the ground in his inability to slow before he made contact. "Ooof. Goodness, Jesse. I missed you, too. Terribly."

"Did ya get me anything?" Jesse jumped back, his bright smile fading right after he'd asked. "Oh, sorry. I'm sorry about your home."

"I appreciate that. We'll fix it, though." Jane took a shaky breath, feeling tears burn again behind her eyes. "You'll see, everything will be fine."

Jesse hugged her tight again. He grunted when another small set of arms encircled Jane's neck, bumping Jesse in the process.

Jane laughed, extricating an arm to wrap around Lizzie as well. "Now I know what I've been missing all this time. Really good hugs."

When the children pulled back, Jane smiled at Lizzie and squeezed her hand. While she'd seen Lizzie and Cindy since she and Cole were staying in Lizzie's room, the girls had kept a wide berth the past day knowing how upset Jane was.

Cindy had her hand to her forehead, squinting up to the sky. "Where is he?"

"Who? Cole? He's back toward the middle of the roof. You can probably see him best from the balcony outside your window, but not from here." Jane stayed crouched low with one arm around Jesse. "Or, if you want to peek inside the door here, you should be able to see him."

Cindy hesitated, eying the Inn carefully. She'd probably not been allowed inside seeing as it was primarily saloon and brothel.

Jesse held out his hand. "It ain't a big deal. Come on, I'll show you."

Jane performed a cursory glance to ensure all three whores remained on the porch, so there'd be no servicing with the children inside. She gave Cindy a nod. "Go ahead and say hi."

The two disappeared inside, leaving a confused Lizzie tugging on Jane's skirt. Jane smiled and nodded, waving her to follow her friends.

David leaned close. "Cindy know yet?"

"I believe she suspects the truth. Over the past year Cole and her have spent some time together. He still isn't used to the idea of being a Pa." Jane kept her voice low despite the din of construction so the nearby whores wouldn't hear. "One of these days, they'll both figure it out. She's almost seven now. Jesse was seven when he knew who we were without being told."

"What does Kat think?"

"Now that she's seen him with her, and knows he's going to be a Pa again anyway, she's come around." She winced the moment the words slipped out of her mouth. In her distraction, she'd spilled all of the beans. She prayed David didn't catch her unintentional confession.

"I'm sure it does make a—" He turned toward her slow as molasses, his eyes wide. "Wait. I'm sorry, what?"

She cursed her addled brain. Stammering at first, she clasped his hands tight. "Don't ask, please. Please. Don't say a word. I wasn't supposed to tell anyone. We don't even know if it'll stick. I'm not thinking clear right now, I didn't mean—"

"Jane. Breathe." David extricated a hand to brush a stray curl behind her ear. "I'm as good as my word, you know that. I won't say anything."

"Please, don't."

He pulled her into a warm hug. "I won't. Are you all right?"

"No more all right than I was three minutes ago. Hush your mouth and let it be. I'm scared enough without you fussing and fretting and hi Jesse." Jane raised her voice as the children raced out of the Inn, Cole's tall form right behind them. "And hello to you, Mr. Mitchell."

Cole nodded to David, his hand on Cindy's shoulder. "Jane. Your boy keeps asking me to come to dinner. Says we're cheating by staying at Cindy's. She gets dinner with us all the time."

Jane shrugged. "David asked the same thing. I do believe they are plotting against us. They want us to be happy or something."

"Then give us a whole and complete hotel." Cole squeezed Cindy's shoulders. "You should go see your Ma. I got work to do, and I heard your Ma say something about chores for you and Lizzie this morning."

Cindy groaned. "Aww. We don't like changing the straw tick's. It makes Lizzie sneeze. I want to stay and help."

"So do I Cindy, but I have to go too. Cole doesn't like me getting my hands dirty." Jane leaned down to Cindy's level. "I'm supposed to go work at the library, but maybe I can ask Sheriff Schaffer's fiancée to stay a little longer so I might help you with those mattresses."

David smiled. "No need. I'll stop by and talk to her. Mike gave her the week off at the hotel, and I have to talk to a few more of your neighbors. I'm sure she won't mind sparing you a few more hours today."

"So long as you don't work too hard," Cole cautioned. His hand clasped around her wrist, but he didn't pull her close.

Jane slipped her arm up so her hand could squeeze his. She gave him a small nod. "Don't you worry."

"I'm gonna," he said low.

"I know." She turned her attention back to the girls. With hand-speak for Lizzie at the same time, she spoke aloud to Cindy. "Why don't you both head home and get started on your chores? I'll be there soon to help with the bedding. Tell your Ma I want to help."

"Okay, thanks!" Cindy hugged her tight before she darted across the street. Lizzie followed suit, both disappearing inside the home across the street in seconds.

Jane ruffled Jesse's hair. "Why don't you go with your Pa? Maybe you can stay and help Lee out at the library for a bit? Then perhaps we can all eat at Cora's together tonight?"

"You mean it?" Jesse stuck out his lower lip. "I ain't—"

"Jesse Michael."

Jesse huffed, starting his sentence again despite the unspoken protest. "I haven't seen you much since you got back."

"I know. I went out of town and came back to this, and it's taken all of my time. I promise, we'll spend more time together soon." Jane kissed his cheek. "Go with your Pa now."

"Yes ma'am." Jesse's shoulders sagged, but he still hugged her before he trudged to the other end of the porch.

"I think that's the first time he's ever been jealous of chores." David smiled, leaning in to kiss her cheek. "He'll be happy enough to see you at supper. We'll meet you at Cora's."

"See you then." Jane turned back to Cole, a frown set firm so he'd know she was serious. "You're going to make everyone suspicious if you keep hovering and fussing so much.”

“Excuse me for worrying.” Cole’s eyes narrowed. He took a step back, hands in the air. His lip curled. “Would you rather I walk away again?”

“Of course not! I—”

“Jane!” Charlie’s voice called over the sounds of the town. The rattle of a wagon moving at high speed drew close. “Look what we brought you.”

Jane huffed out her exasperation at yet another ill-timed interruption. She turned her back on Cole to greet her oncoming brother. Much to her surprise, she found not just Charlie in the wagon, but Daisy and another of her brothers, Nick. “Nick! My stars, what are you doing here?”

“I thought I would bring Graham’s paperwork to him in person. That way I could ensure everything was handled nice and quiet right under Mr. Carmichael’s nose.” Nick leaped out of the back of the wagon, his landing smooth despite the still moving wagon. As usual, his thick goatee covered his mouth, not seeming to move even when he spoke. Also, Jane cold have sworn he might have been smiling, but it was hard seeing as Nick was impossible to read.

“Well, I’m thrilled to see you. I didn’t know you’d be coming out yourself.” Jane threw her arms around him to hug him tight. Of all her brothers, Nick had been the one to struggle most with her memory loss. He’d been so furious with Clara for abandoning them, that even now their relationship was touch and go.

Still, Nick returned her hug just as tight. Even when the hug ended, he kept an arm around her shoulder. Whether because of the tragedy, or time and communication, it appeared he'd softened toward her. "I'm sorry to hear about your hotel. Rough way to start a business. I'd offer to help if I could."

"No. No, you're already silent partner for Mike. Don't worry. We'll make do. We always do, somehow." Jane wiped her tears before she pulled from the hug so they wouldn't be visible. "Isn't that right, Cole?"

"Guess so." Cole hadn't approached the group. He remained near the door, his eyes still dark and angry.

"Jane." Charlie chuckled. "Don't you want to see what we brought you?"

"What? I thought Nick was what you brought me." Jane smiled at her enigma of a brother. "And that is quite enough."

"Fine, I guess. I think you'll really want this, though. We found it when we finally started tearing out the old money cage." Charlie stepped over the wagon seat. They'd spent almost two years turning the old hotel, The Silver Saddle, into a medical clinic. They'd closed off the money cage to use for storage, but Charlie had been talking about making it more efficient.

"What on earth could you have found?" Jane stepped toward the wagon. She gripped the edge, unsure if she dared peek over the side. "I can't imagine what could be of interest to me that you found in an old, dusty room."

"A storage cellar hidden in the corner of the room." Charlie lifted the tarpaulin with a flourish. "Filled with glasses, an even some alcohol. Got gin, whiskey, and bourbon. No beer, I'm afraid. Hammy's out of luck until tomorrow's train, but still. We have no use for it. You, however, very much do."

"Are you serious?" Jane peered into the wagon. A handful of crates sat inside. The gleam of glass reflected between the hay in one half-opened crate. "My goodness. This is marvelous. Cole, come see."

Cole's warmth hovered close behind her. Without warning, he gripped her waist. He lifted her all the way up and over the edge of the wagon. "Check those glasses for me. Nick and I will get the booze inside. Charlie, Daisy, gotta thank you."

"Don't thank us. It was dumb luck, really." Daisy moved closer to the two crates Jane headed for. "I had no idea anything was down there, but Charlie thought the floor sound hollow, so we went looking. I figured we'd find money, not booze."

"If Guy had any money hidden on the premises, I'm not surprised it's gone." Jane dropped next to the half-open crate and picked through glasses. Daisy started on the crate beside hers. Jane held up a glass, checking for cracks. "Don't forget Jackson was Guy's partner. After Guy's death, before Mike bought the place, I'll bet Jackson raided it. Probably why he was not at the funeral, he was raiding the joint."

Daisy gasped. "I didn't even think about that. I just noticed it wasn't there. What a filthy creature Jackson was."

"Speak of the devil," Charlie muttered.

"That particular devil is dead, Charlie," Jane protested. She followed his gaze toward the carriage heading down the middle of Main Street. The carriage itself was an elaborate affair, the likes of which she'd not ever seen in Dominion Falls.

"But his progeny lives on. Although I have to say I'm glad Jackson himself never procreated," Daisy whispered. "What do you think about that one?"

"Parker?" Jane followed the carriages path, wrinkling her nose when Parker Krenshaw put both reins in one hand to tip his hat at them as he passed. "His arrival is suspicious, for certain. I don't trust him seeing as he does carry the Krenshaw name."

"So far he's done little to raise suspicion, I think." Charlie quirked a brow at the carriage that disappeared around the corner. "Although he does appear to like to flaunt wealth as his uncle did."

"That was Jack's carriage. He only drove it for a year, then never again. Bastard just bought it to spend money." Cole reached in to grab a crate of gin. "Here, Nick. Put these in Tommy's room. Without a storage room, he'll have to keep guard."

This time Jane was sure he heard a chuckle coming from Nick's direction. "He's going to love that."

Jane managed to smile, but then turned her attention back to the glasses. "These look good. There isn't a lot, and we'll need to wash them before we use them, but it will do for now. The train will be here tomorrow, and these two crates will about double what we were able to order."

"Still ain't enough, but we can't order more until we make some money again." Cole heaved the next crate of whiskey out of the wagon. "So what was the Nancy doing in Jack's old carriage?"

"Who knows? I don't care. So long as he stays far away from me and mine, he can do whatever he wishes." Jane pushed the crate of glasses across the wagon. "Before you ask, David told me he has an airtight alibi from none other than Linh herself. She was up for hours around the time of the fire because the baby was sick."

"Of course he does. Don't mean he can't buy help." Cole yanked the crate out of the wagon and stormed into the Inn.

Jane sank back onto her rump and groaned. "I didn't say I assumed his innocence, just that he wasn't here."

Daisy squeezed her shoulder. "David and Tommy are both doing what they can to figure this out. I'm sure it will happen."

"And meanwhile I feel as useless as Charlie most days." Jane grunted and dropped back to stare at the sky.

"Hey, now. This useless brother saved your life, so watch your tongue, sissy." Charlie nudged her with his boot.

"Sorry. Tempers are high today." Jane rubbed her hands over her face. "And I promised Cindy and Lizzie I'd help them change the straw in the mattresses and clean them, and that I'd meet Jesse for supper. I should get to it."

"I'd suggest you take Nick, but he'd scare the children." Charlie chuckled.

"Of course he would, he scares most adults with his disconcerting ability to talk without moving a muscle." Jane let Charlie help her sit, and then accepted Nick's help getting out of the wagon.

In the shade of his bowler hat, Jane was certain Nick's brow quirked. Perhaps that meant he was grinning as well. "I'll keep that in mind, Jane. I'll try to be more emotive for your sensitive nature."

"Oh heavens don't change for me. Besides, you'll need to keep that stoic appearance if you have to deal with Graham." She kissed his cheek. "Join us for supper, won't you? Perhaps after we can catch up over some popcorn back at Kat's."

"I'll be happy to join you." Nick tipped his hat. "For now I'm off to business. Have fun cleaning."

Jane laughed. "Fun and cleaning don't often go hand in hand, but with two little girls it will definitely be interesting."

Forget injuries;
never forget kindness.
-Confucius

Jane knocked on the door frame. "Daisy? How is Pansy doing?"

Daisy's head lifted from her notes. A warm smile graced her features. "Afternoon, Jane. She's doing well as can be expected."

"All I was told is that she pulled Tommy from the fire. I saw how he looked, but I don't know what her injuries were like. How bad was it?"

Daisy's smile faltered. "She has some severe burns to her face, chest, and hands. I thought she might not make it at first, her throat was so damaged."

"Oh dear." Jane's heart ached for the poor thing. Though she'd been a bit of a troublemaker, Jane didn't care for her to be injured as she was. Not to mention that she'd saved Thomas's life. "Will she recover?"

"There will be scarring, but she's been awake and talking, so she's out of the worst of it. Aside from the pain of course." Daisy rose. "I'll show you to her room."

Jane stepped aside to let the doctor pass. "She must be in a great deal of pain. I imagine Thomas is, though his stubborn ass likes to pretend otherwise."

"He's worse than you when it comes to getting treated by a doctor."

"That is bad," Jane acknowledged. She laughed softly at the humor of the thought. Jane certainly had ignored doctors orders quite a few times. After the moment of humor passed, she shook her head in sadness. "I always thought she acted much like a spoiled child, but I'd never wish such a thing on her, or any of the girls."

"Of course you wouldn't. You always treat them with a semblance of respect, even when you're leading with a firm hand." Daisy sighed as they crested the top of the steps. "She's worried about how bad she'll scar and what it'll mean for her contract."

"She has always been a stunning beauty. One of Cole's finest in recent years. I can imagine she's concerned, but the last thing she needs to fret about is her contract." Jane stopped outside of the room Daisy hovered near. "Is this it?"

"Yes. I can't guarantee she's awake. The morphine I give her for pain keeps her asleep most of the time."

"I understand. Thank you, Daisy." Jane turned to the door, not opening it immediately. Daisy excused herself quietly. By the time she'd reached the bottom step, Jane had only set her hand on the knob. After a bracing breath, she pushed open the door to the room.

Pansy lay on her side, facing the window. By all appearances, she appeared to be sleeping.

Jane rapped on the door lightly. "Pansy?"

"Jane?" Pansy scrambled to sit, gathering the sheets up to cover as much of herself as she could. The motion wasn't quick enough to hide the burns across the top of her chest.

Jane moved to a seat beside the bed, unable to stop her frown at the girls' protective measures. She tugged the blanket from Pansy's hands. Rather than stare blatantly, she smoothed she covers down along the girl's lap. "Daisy says you are doing well, but in pain. I hope the pain isn't too terrible for you."

"They're giving me somethin'."

"Morphine."

"Yeah. It makes me tired all the time, but I don't hurt as much." Pansy's eyes teared up, her hands flitting toward her face as if to cover the damage Daisy had left exposed to the air. "Won't get ya no money no more, anyway."

Jane waved off the last statement, "I'm not concerned about your contract right now. What I came here for was to thank you, from the bottom of my heart."

Pansy's motion stilled; her eyes wide as saucers. In her stunned silence, Jane could clearly see what she'd caught glimpses of in the past year. On the unburned side of her features, the cheek still slightly rounded. The unmade eyes losing many of the years she'd appeared to have under layers of powders and charcoal.

Of course, the pain she had to be in erased years from her as well. The hardness and strength the whores used to cover what they did, often used as a guard against feelings of any kind, had disappeared into the pain.

"What?" Pansy appeared to have found her voice again, no matter how hoarse it sounded. "I…what?"

"You saved Thomas. They told me how you ran back inside when you saw he wasn't in the water line. Right through the fire is what Michael told me. You risked your own life to save my brother, and I cannot thank you enough."

The moment Pansy burst into tears, Jane vacated her seat to sit on the edge of the bed. She smoothed her hand over the girls hair. "It's all right, Pansy."

"I'm sorry—so sorry."

"What on earth do you have to be sorry for?"

"For being so difficult. For ignoring my dates. For the opium For…for everything."

"Hush. Don't you worry a thing about any of that now." Jane pulled forward a curling lock of Pansy's hair. She brushed a tear from the girl's undamaged cheek. "I'd like to know something, if I may."

Pansy's eyes lowered to focus on her trembling hands. "What?"

"What is your real name?"

"I—um…don't remember."

"I doubt that."

"It's…" Pansy hesitated further, fiddling with the edge of the blanket. Finally whatever fight she might have been ready to put up faded into the pain-filled expression of her condition. "It's Sally."

"Sally." Jane smiled. Rather than grasp the wounded hands, she set her hand on Pansy's knee. "That suits you far better. I think it suits your real age, too. Now that you are without makeup, and your airs, I can see it so much clearer. I wish I'd seen it much sooner. You are not eighteen as you liked to tell me, are you? Not even close."

"No." She met Jane's eyes, not speaking further yet. Sally's eyes shimmered with unshed tears. Still, she didn't speak.

"It's all right. I won't yell. I promise. Not at you, at least. Maybe Graham, since he's the one that found you…or myself since I didn't see it sooner."

Pansy's gaze dropped, though the corner of her lip twitched in a hint of a smile.

"Please, Sally. Help me make this right. I can help if I know how old you truly are."

"I'll be fifteen in two months."

The sick feeling she'd had for days dropped like a boulder in the pit of her stomach. Thanks to Graham they had been whoring a child. "You were barely thirteen when you came to us."

"Yes."

"You'd run away, hadn't you? Left home and nowhere else to turn?"

Sally nodded, silent. The nervous twitch of her fingers along the edge of the blanket continued.

"Your Ma too overbearing? Is that why you fought me so much?"

"She was awful."

Jane sighed, her hand remaining on Sally's knee in what she hoped would be a reassuring gesture. "Well then, Sally. If we manage to get the Inn back up and running, you're done working. That's final."

"But—"

"I'm not going to kick you out on the street." Jane interrupted whatever protest Sally had been trying to make. "I would not do that to you. However, I will not knowingly prostitute a child."

Sally's chin jutted out in her first act of defiance and fire. "I'm not a child."

"You are." Jane would not budge on this. Now that she knew Sally's true age, she wouldn't do it. "Whether you think you're older after what you've been through or not, you are still far too young for a long life of that business."

"Iris did it," she mumbled.

"I didn't have Iris in my employ when she was thirteen, or fifteen. I wasn't even me when Iris was that age." Jane smiled when Sally chuckled despite her continued pout. "I want to help you."

"How? You ain't sending me back. I'll just run again."

"I didn't say I was going to. You'll have to work with me if you want to stay in Dominion Falls. You'll have to go to school. We'll have work for you at the Inn that will not involve prostituting yourself."

"Why? It's my choice. I'm almost fifteen."

"And you could very well run away again if you chose. Of course, there's a good chance you'll end up somewhere far worse than The Hangman's Inn." Jane lifted a brow at Sally's scoff. "You've had it easy here, relatively speaking, Sally. We don't allow men to beat you or worse. We have strict rules for clientele as well as the whores. Other places do not care, or offer special, and very dark, services."

Sally's lips pursed, but she offered no further protest.

Jane leaned one arm across Sally's hips to better meet her gaze. "You saved Tommy. You are welcome to stay with us as our ward—if, and only if, you follow the rules I set."

Another tear slipped down Sally's cheek. "I…"

"Think about it," Jane said quietly. She cupped Sally's healthy cheek. "I don't want you to decide anything right now. What you need to do is heal. Focus on that for now. We'll worry about the rest later."

Sally sank lower into the covers, her nod barely discernible in the movement. When Jane went to stand, Sally reached for her arm. A small whimper slipped from the girl's lips. "Can—would you stay until I fall asleep?"

"Of course. I know how quiet these rooms can get." Jane returned to the chair, but held Sally's bandaged hand in her own. While the girl drifted off to sleep, Jane maintained a quiet, steady stream of meaningless conversation until she was certain Sally slept.

Jane rose slow as she could to remain quiet. She straightened her skirts, eying Sally carefully. In her current state, the young age couldn't be more obvious. "Fool," she whispered to herself.

She closed the door silent as she could, then rested her forehead against it. Silent chastisement of her failure to see Sally's age sooner ran through her head, piling on top of all of her other woes, angers and fears.

"It wasn't her."

Jane jumped a mile, a yelp managing to escape her throat around her heart, which had lodged solidly in her throat at the fright. She spun, her hand clutched to her chest. "Thomas! You scared me half to death."

"She's just a kid."

"So I've learned. Graham was probably too stupid to see it when he got her. Or rather, he likely didn't care a lick how young she was. I'm furious with myself for not seeing it sooner. I'm supposed to be so damned observant."

"I didn't see it either." Thomas shook his head. "She looked older, even without the getup."

Jane leaned back against the wall, her heart finally returning to its normal rhythm. She buried her face in her hands. "Please tell me you came here with some good news for a change."

"No news. Lou." Tommy chucked a finger under her chin to tilt her head up. "Go spend time with your—"

"What the hell id that supposed to mean?"

"It means you haven't relaxed since you got back."

"Stay out of my business."

"Lou."

She shoved his hands away roughly. When he moved to grab her hand, she skirted around him fast to storm down the stairs. Unable to even look at The Hangman's Inn, she ran across the street through the alley, and took the long way to the library.

Once there she unlocked the door and burst inside. She slammed the door shut behind her, locking it firmly to keep everyone out.

The silence in the library rang in her ears like a thousand hammers against all the bells of a cathedral. It filled her ears, and pierced into her wounded heart until it started to bleed.

Her cursed memory reminded her of every last detail of each and every item lost in the fire as if she stood in the room again, in their home. Joining those grief-filled memories came a tidal wave of the events of the last few months; the troubles the Inn had, how long it had taken her to see it, Sally, all of it. The worst was realizing how long it had taken her to see it all.

She'd been so wrapped up in her own world.

Sally, Thomas—Thomas' burns that he was all but ignoring out of his own guilt. The generous gifts they'd been given that she felt horrible for even accepting.

Her body trembled with each passing thought. Wrong upon wrong upon wrong.

Then her ring caught a sliver of sunlight, distracting her from her incessant emotions for a startling moment. The moment she'd first seen the ring replayed in her mind, only to be covered in smoke and ash, dissolving into the sucking pit of despair.

Her hand fluttered to her stomach, a sob wrenching free as she thought of the baby, then Alma. They had no home now. They'd been married, and had rushed home to their marriage bed, but there'd been nothing.

Nothing.

A scream of frustration erupted from the dark depths. She pounded on the locked door trying to release even more. Tears slid down her cheeks as the scream faded back into the absolute silence she'd been faced with.

She backed away from the door. Her breathing wouldn't steady, the short gasps hardly enough to supply the sobs that eeked out at every inhale.

Her back thumped into the shelves at the same time the numbness overtook her legs. The room around her warped out of focus, save for two books across the room. Sweat broke out across her forehead, her hands clenched so tight her nails bit into her palms.

Still she didn't move, she couldn't. She could hardly breathe.

A solid pounding on the door barely cut through the ringing in her ears. Glass shattered, *"Jane!"*

Home is a place not only of strong affections, but of entire unreserved; it is life's undress rehearsal, its backroom, its dressing room, from which we go forth to more careful and guarded intercourse, leaving behind...cast-off and everyday clothing. –Harriet Beecher Stowe

Cole stood frozen in the door for what seemed like ages. Jane sat wide-eyed, her breath coming in rapid-fire gasping sobs. She didn't even seem to notice him, her focus directly across from her on the shelves of the library.

A quick glance assured him nothing at all was there. He rushed to her side almost afrid to touch her. "Jesus, Jane. What the hell are you doing?"

A deep rasping gasp croaked out of her when he touched her arm. Her whole body shivered. Sweat beaded on her forehead, but she turned her gaze on him. A heartbeat later, her arms surrounded him.

"Jane," he whispered. He tried to lift her, but she fought against him. Instead, he drew her into his lap until her fight ended. "Why didn't you come find me?"

She shook her head, her words muffled against his neck.

"Scared me half to death. Tom came, told me you'd run off like a scared rabbit. We've been looking for an hour."

They'd even checked the library, but finding it locked with the curtains drawn, they hadn't been able to see her. At that time, there'd been no sound from inside.

This time when he'd come by he'd heard…something. Now he knew it to be her panicked breathing. He sighed as her body shook with tears. She hadn't cried yet, not truly anyway.

He let her cry, sitting still on the floor until she calmed. Her breath grew steady with sleep. The state of her when he'd found her had left his own pain bleeding and raw. The mere weight of her in his arms was enough to soothe the savage beast for now, but not for long.

He remained there until a distant shout for Jane stirred him to move. Best to let her brothers know she'd been found, and to make sure she was all right.

He got to his feet, careful as he could so she wouldn't wake. Her sleep seemed too deep for disturbance, though. Not even an eyelid flickered at the jostling needed to get to his full height.

He had to get her back to their room at Kat's. They needed some time. Much as he needed to work on the Inn, Jane was his priority now.

The moment he strode outside with Jane in his arms, a shout went up from Charlie. Mike joined his brother in a dash toward them.

Cole glared at Mike soon as the man opened his mouth to speak. "No. She ain't all right. What the hell do you think?"

"Easy, Cole." Charlie kept following, even when Mike raised his hands in surrender and let them pass. "We were worried about her, too. Not to mention, I'm worried about the baby."

The last words were said in a whisper, right as they reached the door to Kat's. Cole stopped short, fear spiked through his heart.

Charlie opened the door for him. "Let me examine her."

"No. Get Daisy."

"Fair enough. So long as you allow it. Take her upstairs. I'll send Daisy over."

Cole didn't wait for any other questions or suggestions. He carried Jane up to their room. Once she was situated on the bed, he stripped off the sweat-soaked shirt he'd been working in. He tossed it in a ball in the corner and made a beeline for the water pitcher.

While he waited for Daisy, he filled the basin. He paused to glance at Jane, still sound asleep on the bed. Her delicate pink lips parted slightly, but none of the worry or fear creased her brow.

Footsteps outside drew Cole's focus and he buried every emotion deep as he could. Daisy stopped right outside the open door, toes on the threshold. Her old habit of not being allowed in his room seemed to have stuck, even when it wasn't actually his room. "Cole? Charlie sent me."

"Make sure she and the baby are good." He dropped the sponge into the basin, fighting his own ratcheting tension.

"What happened?"

"Dunno. Tom said she took off like a scared rabbit. We've been searching for an hour. I checked the library first thing but didn't hear nothing. Just checked again and heard…"

Daisy paused with her hand still on Jane's wrist. "Heard?"

"Not sure, just something. Found her breathing crazy, crying, staring, and…I don't know."

Daisy turned her attention back to Jane. Probably for the best, since he didn't know what else to tell her. "Last I saw her, she'd come to visit Pansy. Did she hurt herself?"

Cole carried the basin over while Daisy pulled open Jane's hand. "Don't think so. Fell asleep shortly after I found her."

Daisy tsked at the crescent shapes on Jane's palms. A few of them had broken skin, and dribbles of blood stretched to her wrist. "Her nails broke through a few places. Nothing major, just seems like she didn't let them heal over."

"Let them? She didn't—"

"Easy." Daisy held up her hands. "She probably wasn't aware. I'm thinking she had a fit of hysteria. Understandable, given everything you are going through."

"I suppose." He studied Jane while Daisy continued her exam. Jane didn't move for all of Daisy's poking and prodding. "Ain't like her to not be complaining we're fussing."

"She's probably exhausted," Daisy said quietly.

"She ain't slept much the past few days." He found it hard to believe that three days ago he'd been happier than he'd been in a long time. They'd been married. Yet they had yet to enjoy the pleasures of their own marriage. They'd rushed home to see to it, only to find the Inn half destroyed, their bed gone. "Not that I blame her. I haven't either."

"You've been working non-stop on the Inn. It's cleaning up real fast, I'm impressed." Daisy rose from where she'd been perched on the bed.

"The baby?"

"One minute, please. I like to focus on one patient at a time." Daisy began to dig through her bag for something.

Cole turned his back on her and paced the room. Thankfully, she took the hint and remained silent while she worked. He couldn't watch her work any longer, he couldn't worry with the blasted woman still there.

"Everything looks good, but she must relax. I know." Daisy held up a finger to stem his protest. "It seems impossible with everything gong on, but you and Jane have always managed to find ways to enjoy life even at its worst. You've survived her death, you can survive a fire."

"Thanks." He tried to mean it, or better yet add some sarcasm to his tone, but the word had come out weak. He was too numb to keep the front up any longer.

Daisy set a hand on his arm as if to say something comforting. For a moment, the look in her gaze was close to one she'd used often as his whore. A look of desperately wanting to please him. In a flash it was gone, and she was halfway to the door. The swish of her skirts was the last he heard until the door clicked shut.

The moment they were alone, Cole locked the door. He moved to Jane's side, half-wishing she'd wake, and half-relieved she finally slept.

Sweat left a sheen on her forehead and chest, something she wouldn't abide she were awake. He moved to her side to remove her clothing. Layer by layer he peeled them off in slow methodical movements to not disturb her sleep.

He inched off her skirt and petticoats, shoes and stockings. Her bodice unbuttoned easy enough, and she'd taken to wearing her corset loose enough he was unable to unhook the busks easy as anything. Getting the sleeves off and everything out from under her proved more challenging. He worked slow and careful, sighing in relief when he got all the layers off with little more than a quiet sigh from Jane. In just her chemise now, she appeared far more comfortable. Not that she could say as much.

Cole tossed all of her layers on a chair, then sat on the edge of the bed beside her. "It's a blasted mess, Jane. I don't know what ya need from me."

He rubbed his hands over his face to clear away the thoughts. Rather than try to talk to the unconscious woman, he grabbed the basin. He wrung water from the sponge and dabbed it across her forehead. Each swipe of the sponge along her flesh erased the heat of summer and exertion of her tears. From her palms he carefully removed the drops of blood from where she'd broken the skin.

With her cleaned, he set aside the basin and resumed his vigil. From outside the usual sounds of the town filtered in, the underlying bang and clatter of work across the street pounding on his attempts at calm restraint.

Cole pushed to his feet, his nerves ramping up again. He should be across the street working, but he needed to be here for her. At the doors to the balcony he paused to observe the work going on. He leaned an arm against the frame as he watched men crawling along the beams and porch roof.

Half the town worked on the Hangman's Inn. Most of the visible signs of the fire had been eliminated already. Every charred board had been removed, all the beams that could no longer support weight were gone.

Cole's frown deepened at the gaping hole where their room had been. What the loss was doing to Jane, and the fact that he had no way to resolve it—ate him up inside. Until she'd come along it had just been a room.

All she'd had to do was step inside, the first person ever to cross the threshold, and she'd had him pegged cold.

"You really don't live, do you?"

He leaned back against the door with a frown. He shouldn't have brought her in. She was too smart. Instinct made him bristle against her honest assessment. "What the hell do you mean? I live plenty."

"No." Her eyes fell on the empty shelves, the bare dresser, and the unadorned walls. "You don't. This isn't living. A hotel is more personal."

He couldn't deny the truth of her statement, even as he'd tried to shove away every word. No matter what he said, she saw through him. She'd seen him, and the box. Every inch of him had been in the box then, hidden from the world.

He deflected. He was good at that. She'd let it go soon enough and they could return to the plan at hand. If he let her open the box, he'd be letting her in. No one got in. Not even her.

"Of course it did." Disappointment seeped into every word. Her fingertips hovered on the box, one more little push and she'd drop it. That's all he needed to do, one more deflection. She made it easy. "If you didn't want to make this personal, we wouldn't be in here. Now do I open the box or do we go to Turner's and test that theory?"

Was it the tone of her voice or her refusal to meet his eyes for the first time he could remember that did it? No matter the reason, his resolve crumbled. He realized if he refused, she may return to his bed, but it wouldn't be the same. She'd be broken and he had broken enough women.

He wanted all of her, strong and unbroken.

Of course, he already knew everything about her. Just that morning she'd bared her fear over her nightmares. How could he hide his own past?

He didn't want to hide it any longer. Not from her. He wanted her to open the box, even as he feared her opening it. His throat thickened and he looked away. "Do what you want. I don't care."

"Yes, you do." Her voice cut through him. Fingers running along the edge of the box, she pulled her hand back. "I'll meet you at Turner's."

He gripped her arm before she could pass, meeting her eyes. The fire lingered, wounded but still burning and he wanted to make sure it didn't go out. Shaking his head, he released her. "Open it."

"Why?"

"Do it."

"Tell me why." Jane moved close. One touch to his cheek and she had him stuck. "If it's just to keep me from being grumpy, forget it."

"I want you to."

With the simple admission he'd let her in, and despite all his attempts to push her away, and her attempts to push him away, they always ended up in each other's arms. Where they belonged. He knew that now, he just wished it hadn't taken so long.

Maybe if he'd seen it sooner, she wouldn't have had to worm her way into his room slowly. The simple addition of her book, *Leaves of Grass*, had been all it took. The moment it was on his night stand the room had been hers as much as it had ever been his.

Over time she'd turned the once-empty room into a home. Their home.

He'd give anything to give that back to her.

Their hotel, whole and complete. A room she could turn into a home again. Promises he'd made that they'd fix it sounded hollow to his own ears now.

Sheets rustled on the bed, indicating Jane moving for the first time since he'd brought her back. His heart twisted, worried what he'd find when he turned.

"Cole," She whispered. Her voice cracked in the one syllable.

He turned to face her, relieved she was awake at least. Tears shimmered at the edges of her eyes, but her face wasn't twisted in grief as he'd seen just a little while before.

She pushed herself up, halfway to sitting. Her hand reached for him. "Cole."

He crossed the room in two strides, not about to force her to ask again. The moment he took her hand, she relaxed even more. He kissed her palm, then drew her hand to his chest. Now sitting fully, she used her free hand to cup his cheek.

Words weren't his strong suit, never had been, but they completely failed him now. He wouldn't have the slightest clue where to start, how to fix it. Nothing he could think to say felt like it would be nearly enough. Thankfully he didn't have to break the silence.

"I need you." Her words had gained strength. The moment he opened his mouth to speak, her thumb pressed to his lips to keep him quiet. He held silent as she'd wanted. In response, she trailed her thumb along the outline of his lips. "No words—just you."

Desire and hope will push us on
toward the future.
-Michel de Montaigne

Cole's fingers danced along her spine. A teasing, light touch; enough to be relaxing rather than stoke the fire. "Better?"

"My goodness, yes." Jane exhaled a contented sigh. The looming grief and worry still hovered in her periphery, but their afternoon had sufficiently relaxed the worst out of her for the moment. "How in heavens name have we managed to not do that since our wedding? For that matter, how did we manage to go over three days? Only time we do such nonsense is when we fight."

"I ain't sure. I know I didn't like it none. I missed you."

Jane lifted her head from his chest so she could meet his gaze. She offered a soft smile at the statement, touched. For all their tender moments, he really didn't excel at the words. Never had. "Let's never make this mistake again, shall we?"

"Wouldn't dream of it."

She shifted to prop herself up on an elbow. When he turned toward her to mirror her position, she didn't waiver in her hold on his gaze. "I only ever needed you. It's all I ever need. The rest will work itself out somehow. As long as you are there, that's enough for me."

"You sound sure." He touched her cheek with his fingertip, then her lips, then slipped his arm around her waist to pull her impossibly closer. "And strong. Haven't sounded like that since we got back."

"I guess I needed a reminder of all I do have instead of what I lost." She rolled with him until her head lay back on his chest. Her leg draped across his casually. The soft touch of his thumb along her spine resumed. The dull ache reminding her of what they'd lost lingered in her heart, subdued but not gone. "I cannot say I won't lose my grip again. It hurts—so much worse than I ever could have imagined—but you are here with me. Wherever you are is home."

"Wish I could make the pain stop for you. Fix it right up."

"'I'm a little wounded, but not slain; I will lay me down for to bleed a while, then rise to fight with you again'. Dryden."

He chuckled low. "Fight with me, eh?"

"It is one of the things I do best."

"You had me worried."

"I know. I'm sorry. I scared myself a little, too." She took a shaky breath to brace herself for the explanation. "Everything hit me all at once after I spoke with Pansy. You were working on the Inn and I couldn't bear to even see it, much less go in it to find you."

"Tommy came looking for you, said he wanted to apologize, that he'd upset you, that you'd actually snapped at him?" Her nodded confirmation seemed all he needed to continue. "He couldn't find you, so he came to get me. I swung by the library, heard nothing then."

She thought of what little she remembered from her time in the library. A scream of frustration and then—what? "I went right there. I don't remember much else."

"Well, I checked with Kathy and the kids, you weren't there. So I kept looking. When I got back to the library, that time I heard you." His thumb had stopped his easy rhythm along her spine, his gaze toward the windows. "Sounded like a wounded animal."

"I'm sorry. Everything hurt so much, I wasn't thinking right."

"Rarely do."

She gasped, rising to glare at him only to find him baring his teeth in a wicked grin. "You rotten, no good."

His tickling attack brought a shriek of laughter from her. They rolled and play-fought for several minutes before the came to a slightly breathless pause, Cole hovering inches above her. His lips were dangerously close to hers. "You really better?"

"Much. You were right there when I needed you." She slipped her hands along his shoulders to his back. "'Oh that it were possible after long grief and pain to fnd the arms of my true love around me once again'. Tennyson."

When she pulled him toward her, he met her lips with an intensity that jolted her right to the core. The closer he held her, the more she relaxed. By the time he pulled back he was grinning broadly. "Now it's back to the doc's orders."

She laughed at the naughty implication in his leer. "Let me guess. Lots of relaxation."

"Damn right."

"And rest."

"I s'pose she said something like that."

"I have no doubt you would prefer the relaxation first, then rest."

"Wouldn't you?"

"Oh, I do *always* enjoy a good afternoon of relaxation."

He brushed loose tendrils of hair from her cheek. "Think you're up to seeing the progress on the Inn now?"

Part of her wanted to jump at the proposal. After the day she'd had, her hesitation won out. "Not right now. Perhaps tomorrow."

"We're gonna start putting the walls backup tomorrow."

"Oh." Jane brightened despite her momentary hesitation. The idea of Cole hard at work on rebuilding the saloon sparked her imagination to life. "I want to watch."

"Really?" His brow quirked, a playful grin splitting his features. "Looking forward to seeing the Inn get patched up?"

"Oh heavens, yes. However, what I am really looking forward to is watching you work on it." She slipped her hands along his arms slow as molasses. Each finger trailed over the curves of his muscles with quiet eagerness. "That is—if it's very hot out as August tends to be, and you're forced to roll up your sleeves. Or, better yet, take your shirt completely off. I wouldn't mind the show one little bit—or letting anyone else see what I have."

His laughter boomed through the room, brighter than she'd heard since Denver. "The sun has been brutal, I can't lie."

"I've noticed."

"And…"

Music resonated into the room, drawing both their attentions from each other. Fast as the tinkling of the piano had started the notes faded away. A moment later they rose in volume again, only to be joined with several more instruments. They toned in and out, moving up and down the scale as if to tune to each other.

She furrowed her brow. Gaze on the window, she propped herself up as if she'd be able to see out the closed curtains. "What the devil is going on?"

"I dunno. I've been in here with you for the past…"

At his hesitation, she glanced at the clock. "Oh my goodness. Five hours. It's well past supper by now."

"That mean you're hungry?"

"Not at the moment."

The piano grew more boisterous. In short order a concertina fell into step. Then a banjo, and a mouth harp. Cole sat upright. "What are they doing out there?"

"Only one way to find out, I suppose." She hopped out of the bed. On her way to the window she grabbed her robe to slip on. She peeked out the window.

Out on the porch of the Inn sat the piano, a little the worse for wear, but clearly still playable and Edgar played it with aplomb. Beside it stood Graham with his banjo, plucking a lively tune in accompaniment to the piano. Nick turned out to be the culprit with the mouth harp. Archie, the blacksmith and mayor, worked the concertina with impressive skill.

Jane gasped at the sight. For not only were the four men playing music without reason, but the street was flooded with people dressed in their Sunday best.

Cole pushed the curtain aside above her head. "Well, hell. Look at the Inn."

Jane managed to tear her gaze from the dancing crowd to face the gaping hole she'd become all-too-familiar with, only to find it changed. Their room was still gone, but the saloon behind it was closed in with fresh boards. The girls traipsed out of the saloon in some of the finer clothes she'd given them to join the celebration in the streets.

The realization of how hard people had had to work to get all of this together took her breath away. The words she usually favored flew from her head, leaving her to mutter and most inelegant, "Oh."

"Think we'd best join them."

"Oh. My."

He pinched her hip hard enough to stir her out of her stunned ineloquence. "Mrs. Mitchell."

"What?"

"I said I think we'd best join them."

"I believe you're right. We'd best make a quick trick of it as well, or my brothers will come up here and drag us out." She raced across the room to the travel trunks. With a specific dress in mind, she dug through the mounds of fabric until she found the lavender silk dress.

Hurriedly, they threw on underthings and clothes, but she still took much longer due to her layers. Once she was finally dressed, she turned her attention toward her unruly cascade of curls.

He set his hand on hers, pulling them away from the locks. "Leave it down."

"What? But I never," she protested. While she was far from a proper woman in most respects, she couldn't recall a time she'd worn her hair down in public.

"Ya look beautiful."

"My hair is a fright. We've rather disturbed it with our vigorous relaxation."

"Then brush it, but leave it."

She pursed her lips, trying to come up with an argument, but a pounding at the door interrupted her objections.

Tommy bellowed through the door, "Get your hands of each other and get out here!"

Jane burst into laughter. She met Cole's gaze in the mirror. "I guess you win."

"I think Tom won." Cole grinned back. He handed her the brush. "Best be quick."

The door burst open, but neither of them flinched. Jane ran the brush through her hair quick as she could with the tangles while Cole addressed the elephant in the room, figuratively speaking.

"What in blazes is going on out there, Tom?"

"We figured out the piano still worked. The walls were up. So, we got a little celebratory." Tom grinned at them both. "I haven't been able to dance with the bride here—and we haven't been able to celebrate the news of the kid you've got coming."

Jane tied a ribbon around her head to keep her curly locks somewhat tamed, but left it down as Cole had asked. She quirked an eyebrow at her brother. "What bride?"

"Shut up and get out there." Tommy laughed. "We got the first floor all patched up, and I haven't even told you the best part yet."

Cole's brow wrinkled. "Best part?"

"The new bar is on its way. Should be on one of tomorrow's trains." Tommy tugged his vest. "It's a right-fancy one, too. So long as none of these ruffians mess it up, we should be able to use it in whatever fix-up you do at the Inn."

"What new bar?" Cole glanced at Jane, confusion clear in his features. "We ain't got the funds for none of that."

"It's my wedding gift to you." Tommy shrugged. "Let everyone else think it's because I feel right guilty over the fire."

"Thomas!" Jane gasped. "No, you didn't have to."

"Don't argue with me." Tommy pointed at her, stern as he could appear while still smiling. "I will win."

When Jane braced for the challenge, Cole stepped in between them. He held his hand out to her. "We appreciate it, Tom. It'll help us get back in business."

Tom grinned so broad the bandage on his cheek wrinkled. "Enough talk—let's dance!"

Jane yelped when Tommy grabbed her hand and dragged her from the room. By the time he got her down to the street, she was laughing outright.. He moved to swing her into the dance, but Cole once again stepped between them. He pushed his now-brother-in-law back with a grin.

"First dance is always mine." Cole spun Jane out into the crowd of dancers and into step.

"It always will be," she concurred.

Desire and hope will push us on toward the future.
-Michel de Montaigne

Cole managed to get two dances out of Jane before she rushed away from him to drag Hammy onto the street for a dance. Amused by the sight, he didn't mind one bit. He strolled to where her family gathered.

As he approached, he heard Mike's voice. "She does look better. We know what happened yet?"

"No." Tom shook his head. "Didn't ask—I was too busy making sure we got them out here."

Cole leaned on the hitching post beside them. "It all got too much for her, is all. She's strong, but everything was…everything."

"Fair enough," Charlie said. The music shifted to a boisterous polka, and a loud cheer from the crowd drew his attention. "Well, my word."

Cole turned toward the dancers to see what had Charlie stunned. He laughed as Jane and Hammy's antics cleared the area around them. The pair swung through the street, matching the mixed beat of the instruments and clapping crowd. Cole joined the clapping with the rest of the crowd. He nodded to the approaching woman. "Kathy."

"She looks better." Kat laughed at the sight herself. "Although Hammy might be partially to blame at the moment. She's not pushing it away again, is she?"

"Nah." Cole shook his head. "This ain't her pushing it away. We're working it out, we just needed time."

"You mean you needed to relax?" Kat laughed when Tommy snorted from his position next to Cole. "Like you always do?"

"Something like that." Cole gestured toward the Inn. "She's real happy to see all that got done today. How'd that happen?"

"Well, after they saw the state Jane was in earlier, this lot had a Young-ference." Kathy pointed to the three Young boys gathered near Cole. As she did, Tommy broke formation and swept Jane away from Hammy as the next dance started.

"A Young-ference?" Cole laughed. "Is that what you're calling it?"

"What? It was like a conference, but all the Young's got their heads together. They decided to work double time and try to get some sort of improvement to show the two of you." She leaned closer. "Hammy was more than eager to move things along. He'd do anything to help out Jane any way that he could."

"Of course he would. The old fogey's sweet on her."

"He sure is." Kath chuckled softly.

"Has been since he's known her."

"We all know it, too. Anyway, they all got to work right away." Kathy gestured toward the instruments. "Iris was cleaning up inside since it wasn't her turn to try to get business. She and Wills uncovered the piano."

Cole rubbed his hand over his face. He sighed softly. "In all the confusion I forgot about the damn thing."

"The piano was covered with some debris. It's a bit singed, so we weren't sure it would work. Iris tested a couple of keys, and it worked." Kat shrugged. "With the Young boys already on a roll, they decided we needed a celebration."

"We sure did."

"I agree. With the exception of your trip to Denver, there hasn't been a celebration for that baby that's coming. The fact that you're making progress on the Inn and maybe you can open again soon is another good reason."

Cole's gaze followed Jane as she spun around the street with Tommy before Charlie took his turn. Without a doubt, Mike would be next, although he wondered if the stoic Nick would join in the fun. "I'm glad to see her smiling for real again."

"So am I."

Cole held his hand out to her. "She shouldn't be the only one having fun."

Kat took his hand, laughing as he spun her out into the crowd. After a dance, they switched off. He took Lizzie from Tommy and spun her around a turn. Then Cindy, with whom he made sure to take an extra dance. He enjoyed her laughter when he lifted her in the air so she could see above the crowd.

After Cindy went to dance with Norman, Cole looked for Jane. He spotted Kathy dragging her away from the crowd for chat. Leaving the friends to their chat, he moved toward the Inn's porch where the musicians gathered and played.

For the first time that afternoon, he noticed that Linh Moon sat on a porch bench with her son. He offered her a nod, then walked over toward Graham. Graham paused his plucking to shake Cole's hand. Cole nodded toward the two on the bench. "That safe? Becky'll have your hide."

"Nope. She can't. I gotta give Jane's family credit. When they work, they mean business. Nick got my divorce, Becky and her pa, all taken care of this afternoon. I don't get none of her money, but I don't care a lick about that." Graham grinned broader than Cole had seen him grin in a long time. "That harpy's outta my life."

"Glad to hear it," Cole said without any malice. He definitely was pleased to see his friend happy, and not harping on Jane at every turn any more.

"Just wish I hadn't sold the place before I got some sense knocked into me." Graham touched his nose as if remembering Jane's punch. "Oh well, business is always good when you're an undertaker."

Cole clapped him on the shoulder. "You're a morbid devil, you know that?"

"I sure do." Graham grinned wickedly. In a moment, he'd sobered up just as fast. "Still sorry the fire happened. Sure isn't right. I'm beginning to think Jane wasn't so loopy when she suggested someone's trying to wreck the place."

"Sure seems that way." Cole shook off the dark thoughts best he could. "Don't matter. We're celebrating tonight, not worrying. You gonna dance with your woman or play all night?"

"Both, if we can get someone to watch Joshua. What do you say? Watch my boy for me? Won't be but a minute."

Cole held up his hands. "No way. Not on your life. That's your kid. Find a sappy woman for your troubles."

Graham waved him off, a deep chortle wobbling his banjo. "Get on outta here. I need to keep these idiots in tune."

Cole took his leave. He made his way toward where Jane and Kat stood huddled together still talking. Before she could even say one word to him, he grabbed Jane's wrist to spin her back out into the dancing crowd with him.

"Well, hello there." She smiled up at him, everything about her calm and relaxed for the first time in days. "Are you having fun, Mr. Mitchell?"

"I am." He pulled her way too close for propriety, and almost even for dancing. "Are you ready to go back to the room? We've celebrated like they wanted."

"No."

"The we'll—wait. No?" He stopped all motion so fast she stepped on his foot because she still followed the dance. "No?"

"No. I want to eat. Cora made fried chicken."

He continued to ignore those dancing around him, unable to believe what he as hearing. "You're turning me down for food?"

She threw her head back in laughter. "Oh, I most certainly am."

"But…"

"I'm starving."

"So am I."

"You are quite delicious in your own right, don't get me wrong. That appetite never ceases, but right now I need to eat real food if you expect me to assuage our other appetites later. For the first time all day I truly feel like eating. Doctor's orders are to eat when I feel up to it, after all."

"Damn."

"You did say I was to follow doctor's orders."

"I know, but I prefer the orders that tell you to relax." He grinned when she did, pleased to have her press close against them.

"So do I, but food first. Dessert later."

"Promise?"

"Promise." She dragged him toward the wagon that held all of Cora's food. "I've been thinking."

"That's always dangerous."

"Behave."

"Never."

She smacked him lightly in the chest. "Cole!"

"What've you been thinking?"

"I want to go home."

He slowed their pace until they stopped still. Her gaze turned up toward him, and he searched her eyes. "What?"

"It wouldn't be our room I know, but The Hangman's Inn is our home. We can take room three for now where the damage is minimal. It's smaller than our old room, but it will suit us just as well as the room at Kat's. As it stands, we wouldn't be taking in guests anyway, and we still have the rooms downstairs, plus two more upstairs for the girls to use to service customers."

He pressed his finger to her lips to stop her babbling arguments. "Are you sure? Today you didn't even want to look at it. You really want to live in it?"

"Yes. I am now." She guided him further from the crowd where they could talk without people bumping into them on the way to Cora's food wagon. "It isn't going to be easy, but we will be together, and that's all we need."

"I ain't going nowhere."

"You'd best not." She wrapped her arms around his neck to pull him close. Her whisper brushed his ear, "One divorce is all I ever intend to have."

"That wasn't you nohow, so how about we go for none?"

"Definitely."

"Mrs. Mitchell," Hammy muttered as he passed behind her and disappeared into the crowd again.

They both burst into laughter and fell into a deep kiss before he spun her into the crowd again.

*Your body is the church where
Nature asks to be reverenced.
—Marquis de Sade*

"Patrick said he would not step foot in this roughneck town until there was a proper burlesque," Kat lamented. "I swear, I even teased him with your presence and how much he would delight in meeting you."

"He would have delighted in me more when I first arrived with my amnesia and no ties. He might have wondered at the idea of corrupting such an innocent soul." Jane teased. "We'll convince him to come out one way or another. Even if we have to get a burlesque here to do it."

"I miss him terribly, is all." Kat carried the tray out through Cindy's room to the balcony. "I used to see him all the time, and now my life is such that I have not seen him in over a year. He is one of my very best friends."

"He'll come along." Jane set the pitcher of lemonade on the table beside the tray of glasses and treats. "I'm certain he misses you and Cindy as much as you do him."

"I'd thought so." Kat sighed, dropping into the rocking chair. Almost immediately her mood seemed to bounce back. "My goodness, Jane. You were right. This is the perfect spot."

Jane took the seat beside Kat, unable to block her own grin at the sight before them. Across the street they had a clear view of the men working on the roof of the Inn. "This is the perfect height and angle to see all the action. Downstairs on the porch we wouldn't have been able to see nearly as well."

Kat picked up her glass of lemonade, handing one to Jane. "I thought Cora was going to join us for lemonade and a show."

"And Lee. They'll be along eventually." This time when Jane looked across the road, she checked the progress as much as the view of Cole. For the past week all the work had been done inside the saloon portion of the Inn. The new bar had been installed, a new store room built, and tables and chairs as well until it was ready to open for business officially.

Now, even with the saloon open, there was still repair work being done on the icehouse—while work had begun outside to shore up the supports for the upper level and roof. She hated that they had so much repair work when she'd rather have taken the opportunity to start finding new investors. Financially they were taking a huge hit, even with all the assistance they'd received.

"Is there anyone else you invited to be terribly unseemly?" Kat's wicked question interrupted Jane's musings.

"I did invite Daisy, and Charlie's wife Millie, but apparently she has her limits. Gawking at men doing exactly what we love for them to do is one of them—at least out in public and clearly enjoying the show as we are."

"Well, here you are. I expected you to be downstairs." Daisy stepped out onto the balcony. "What are you doing up here?"

"Enjoying the view." Jane winked, gesturing across the way.

"Oh." Daisy eyed the roof across the street. "I see."

"So do we." Jane sipped her lemonade. "It's rather enjoyable, too."

"Well I don't know," Lee's voice reached them from inside. "I thought I saw Daisy come in here."

"Jane said to come in when we got here," Cora said after her. "Oh, here they are. Jane, Kat. Hello Daisy, I didn't know you were coming as well."

"Welcome to the women's burlesque." Jane gestured again across the street. "Or is it the men's burlesque? Should we refer to the audience or performers?"

"What?" Cora's eyes widened as she took in the working men across the street. A faint pink blush touched her cheeks. "Why, Jane Spencer, that's simply scandalous."

"Oh, come now." Kat smirked. "I've heard Jane say, and seen her do, far worse things in the middle of your store. We're in relative solitude up here."

"Besides." Jane leaned closer to Cora. She wagged her eyebrows. "I've heard tell that you and Kelly were rather a scandalous couple yourselves once upon a time. Rumors of your rather enthusiastic courtship and marriage linger to this day."

Cora blushed four shades of red. She gulped her lemonade to cover, but failed too cool down before the cup left her lips. After a sideways glance at Lee, then another at Kat, she cleared her throat. "What rumors?"

"It wasn't me." Lee held up her hands in defense. "I swear it."

"She is perfectly innocent in this. You forget Cora. I'm the reigning soiled dove according to the world at large. This gives them supposed carte blanche to share all sorts of scandalous tales with me. I've heard stories about yourself, Martha, and even Katherine." Jane squeezed Kat's hand. "Although those are usually told in an attempt to make me jealous of Kat's own scandalous affair with Cole. Never mind that it was over years ago and I have nothing to fear."

"Well." Cora chugged the last of her lemonade, at which point her blush had mostly dissipated. "I suppose expecting decorum with this lot would be too much to ask."

"Decorum certainly has its place, although I hardly think it should stand in a gathering of adult women, none of whom are unfamiliar with the pleasures of a man." Jane turned her attention back to the roof of the Inn. "Besides, what harm is there in enjoying what God has placed before us—men working as they were meant to."

"Amen," Daisy muttered under her breath. The comment sent a twitter of laughter through the group.

"I mean, honestly. Look at them." Jane gestured without shame toward the working men. "They're enjoying themselves quite immensely, why shouldn't I? Plus, I get to go home with that man who gives new meaning to Aurelius' statement 'The sexual embrace can only be compared with music and with prayer'."

"Those men are enjoying you enjoying yourself." Kat laughed heartily. "Even if your eyes are only going to one place."

"Not entirely. There are many fine specimens on the roof that should follow Cole's lead and take their shirts right off." Jane reached out to nudge Daisy's knee with the toe of her boot. "Don't you agree? Or maybe I should holler at Mike to take part in our enjoyment—well, not mine because he's my brother and ew."

Katherine spit her lemonade out in laughter. She pointed at Daisy. "Oh heavens! Daisy, you are so caught. Why don't the two of you get courting already?"

Daisy gulped, her eyes dropping to her skirts at the teasing as though they were more interesting than the view. "Lee? Cora? Care to help me out?"

"What in the world makes you think I can help?" Lee shook her head. "You came here willingly, and they're right. I'm curious myself."

"By the way, Lee. I must say, I'm beginning to see where my attraction to David came from when I was Clara. I never realized I'd been such a lucky woman—now you're the one who is lucky." Jane picked up a petit fours. "Bully for you."

Lee's attempt to hide her bright smile behind a sip of lemonade failed miserably. "I have to admit, I am not disheartened to have fallen for a man that is in such fine form."

Cora sighed. "You do enjoy stirring a hornet's nest, Jane."

"There is nothing wrong with admitting to pleasure." Jane wiped the corners of her mouth to erase the remains of sugar. "Or enjoying pleasure."

"She's going to cite again," Kat predicted without any malice.

Jane stuck her tongue out at Kat, but went forward with the quote anyway. "'The art of life lies in taking pleasures as they pass. And the keenest pleasures are not always intellectual, nor are they always moral'. Aristippus."

"I rather like that one." Lee nodded her head to Jane. "And it seems to define you rather well."

Jane winked, rising to cross to the railing. "I'm so tired of sitting. Tired of being forced to sit by and rest while everyone has been working on my home."

"Well, of course they're making you sit by and rest," Kat scolded.

"She isn't wrong," Daisy agreed heartily. "There is a very good reason every moment set firmly in rest is worth it."

Jane pursed her lips at the pair. "Hens."

"Cluck," Kat agreed.

They both chuckled over that. Jane shook her head. "The pair of you are as pitiful as my brothers at subtlety. I swear the whole town will know before it becomes obvious. Then again, I slipped up myself and admitted it to David the other day in my distraction."

Cora and Lee glanced at each other, then between the other three women. Finally Cora spoke, "What in heaven's name are you three talking about."

Jane set a hand on her abdomen. "Between Kat and my brother's making off-handed comments the whole town will soon suspect, but I will ease your curiosity. Cole and I are going to have a baby."

Lee's squeal escaped loud enough to draw the attention of the men on the roof.

Kat held up her glass toward Jane in toast. "Jane is ecstatic. Shockingly, Cole hasn't run screaming yet, so I'd say this is a celebration."

"Plus, the saloon is open for business again." Cora's lips twisted, her brows pursed. "Goodness, I never thought I'd see the day when I felt the saloon being open was cause of celebration; certainly not when it was to Cole's benefit."

Jane bit the corner of her lip to keep her smile too broad. "Oh, he's not so bad."

Lee's gaze travelled down to the street, her brow quirked. "I have to admit, he is not too shabby a specimen himself. And, he's heading this way."

"Oh, goody." Jane took a step away from the railing to give him room. She'd known him long enough to know by now he'd not bother with actually using the stairs.

As predicted, his hands appeared at the edge of the balcony moments later. He hefted himself up, then slung his long legs over the railing. Jane could not help her sigh of pleasure at the sight of him before her.

Cole offered a wicked grin to the gathered ladies. "Y'all enjoying the show?"

Jane didn't bother waiting for their answers. "I most certainly am. Lee and Katherine are, without a doubt. Cora has yet to give her opinion, and Daisy is pretending she isn't enjoying watching my brother even though I've seen her steal quite a few glances."

Cole smirked at Cora. "Ain't no man turning your head yet?"

"No man could compare with Kelly." Through a fierce blush, Cora met Cole's gaze unabashedly. "So, no."

Jane wrinkled her nose when Cole reached to grab her about the waist. "Don't you dare, Cole Mitchell. This is a brand new dress from our trip to Denver. I don't want you making it smell."

He yanked her against him over her protest. To still her squirming, he held her tight. "Then you shouldn't have worn it."

"Boor."

"Would hate to disappoint ya and act otherwise."

She hummed her attempt at disapproval. No matter what, her frown would not stick. With him so close, she couldn't help her natural reaction as her hands slid along his sweat-slicked arms.

"You got the canteens?"

"I do." Though she tried to move, he captured her lips before she got anywhere. She laughed, wrapping her arms around his neck. The chatter that popped up from the women had them both chuckling when they separated. "Let me get those for you."

Kat shook her head. "I swear the two of you are even worse since you got back from Denver. I had no idea that we hadn't hit the level of how bad you two could get."

Jane's reply got cut off by her yelp when Cole smacked her ass. She attempted to give him a stern glare as she went inside to gather the canteens. On her way back to him she said, "We are not any worse. If anything, we're less so because my mornings are so often spent over a bucket."

Cole's nose wrinkled at the reminder.

Lee snorted. "At least we know something stops the two of you."

Jane draped the canteens over his shoulder. "One for you, David, Mike, Nick, and Graham. A touch of ginger to keep you from getting sick, but you still need to take it easy."

"Yes ma'am."

"And get back to work." Jane's gaze flickered to his chest, then over to the roof. "I'd much rather be watching you work up there."

"You sure?" He snaked his arm around her waist to draw her close again.

"Oh, go on," Kat interrupted before their lips could touch. "Leave her be. Us hens were cackling as you and Norman are so fond of saying."

Jane fluttered her lashes innocently up at Cole before she stepped back from his embrace. Her escape was thwarted by him yanking her into another kiss. Her whole body felt flushed and tingly when he pulled away so that she pouted at his absence. "You were already not playing fair—that was just cruel."

He winked and threw a leg over the railing.

As he made his way down, Jane moved back to the railing to follow his progress across the street. She didn't waver in her attention as he climbed the ladder, the muscles in his legs and backside straining against his trousers.

"Jane."

She waved off the intrusion, to study every inch of him as he moved from the ladder to the roof. Once he was secure on top of the building, she turned. At the exasperation and amusement she encountered on the faces of her friends, she smiled. "What? It's almost better going than coming."

Even Kat's cheeks reddened this time. "Incorrigible."

Jane picked her lemonade back up to take a sip for her now parched throat. She sat, letting out a contented sigh. "'The greatest pleasure of life is love'. Euripides. And I have a great deal of both. There's nothing incorrigible about that."

"Then you are helpless." Kat poured herself another glass of lemonade.

"On the contrary. I am hopeful." Jane glanced back at the Inn. "As fast as they are working, Cole and I may be able to keep our appointments with investors."

"Why don't you try to seek out a loan instead?" Cora's brow furrowed, her sweet cake held inches from taking the bite she'd been about to. "That's what I did after Kelly passed. It was the only way to keep the store and restaurant. Thank heavens David was around since it was difficult for me, as a woman, to get one."

"Ridiculous rules," Kat spat in disgust.

A murmur of agreement went through the group at her comment.

"We considered a loan. On the one hand it would be easier, but there are several problems with getting a loan right now." Jane indicated to the Inn. "For one, we haven't got any collateral but the building and lot, so we'd never get the amount we need to do what I would love to do with the place."

"Grand plans," Kat agreed. "You do dream big, Jane."

"I have to. Our family is growing, and much faster than we'd expected. While we weren't the ones to adopt Lizzie, we'll most likely be taking in Sally as a ward, and a relative of Cole's will be coming to live with us, and of course our own little one."

"Wait, Cole has family?" Cora leaned forward, her sweet cake completely forgotten. "You aren't serious?"

Jane snorted. "You do know that most everyone has had family at some point. Whether they choose to forget, or accidentally forget like I did. Is it that hard to believe?"

"He's never, ever talked about family that I've heard of." Kat tilted her head. "I guess it's easier to imagine he was dropped to earth a full grown man."

"That usually only happens with Gods or demi-Gods. While I do agree that Cole could certainly qualify in many aspects, I'm afraid he is neither." Jane smiled. "But that's another story. We were talking about the Inn."

"Can we get back to this subject after?" Lee's brow rose. "I think it's safe to say we're all curious about all aspects of this growing family unit you're creating."

Jane chuckled. "Fair enough. As I was saying, a loan couldn't begin to cover what we hope to do with the Inn. Not just for our own lack of collateral, either."

"The Coinage Act really made things tight everywhere." Cora blew out a gust of frustration. "My own savings are almost gone. I'd hoped to send Arthur to college, and I don't see how I can now, short of selling the business. While I could survive with only a restaurant in a smaller place, Kelly built that business and I do hate to sell."

Jane set her hand on Cora's, smiling sadly at the mention of her deceased husband. "I can only imagine the struggle you're having with that decision. You are right, though. The economy, such as it is, is shaky. I have a bad feeling about what's coming. The market is leaning toward a loss, a big one. I can almost see it. I had some funds set aside, but I used them to purchase the Inn."

"Do you regret giving that money to the town now?" Kat leaned forward in curiosity. "It really could have helped you out."

"I only regret that the town has little to show for it a year later. The Council needs to stop arguing over what to use it for." Jane used a kerchief to dab at some sweat on her forehead. "I just don't trust the banks right now."

"Do you really think you can convince investors to give you the sort of backing you're looking for?" Daisy glanced at the Inn. "I know brothels are good business, but if Kat is right and your plans are grand, you're expecting a lot."

"They are, and they involve removing the brothel element completely if possible, which would actually make most investors more nervous because sex means money."

Cora gasped. "Jane!"

"It's true. The brothel has always been the most profitable part of Cole's business. In a town that remains approximately seventy-five percent men, it's going to be." Jane pursed her lips. "However, I have several plans laid out. All consist of the brothel element, and a mirror plan without. Each designed to turn a profit, as much of one as we can manage with or without whores."

"Either way, there will ways be whores here." Daisy shrugged, her shoulders drooped with the weight of her past. "If the Hangman's Inn doesn't have them, someone else will come in and bring them."

"I think I know someone who might, too." Jane took a long drink of her lemonade. She hadn't even mentioned to Cole that Leanne had bandied about the idea of returning to Dominion Falls more permanently. If she worked it right, they could have a piece of that business as well, and have income from dual sources.

"You do?" Kat leaned forward. "How?"

"You'll get to meet her soon enough, if you haven't already." Jane smiled into her cup of lemonade. "She was once contracted under Cole, after all."

"What? Who?" Daisy's eyes lit with a brief fury, that faded as quick. "She was? When? How did you meet her and why would we?"

Lee snicked. "You want to pick a question?"

"I think I can answer them all." Jane set down her empty glass. "When she was here, she went by the name Leanne Potts. These days she prefers Leanne DuBois. I met her in Denver when Cole and I bumped into her on the street. I found her delightful."

"Leanne Potts. I remember her." Cora's eyes widened. "She was the one whore that never got a flower name."

"Once you get one, they're hard to let go of," Daisy muttered. She shook off whatever plagued her, but her smile seemed less genuine now. "I remember her as well. Cole never let me near her to examine her, and I never understood why. I eventually passed it off as her being his favorite."

Jane coughed to cover her snort. She had to cover her mouth to hide her grin at the idea of Leanne being Cole's favorite. Of course, she was the only one that knew Leanne was his sister, and a virgin, but she couldn't spill the beans. "Sorry. While I adore Leanne, I can't ever see her being Cole's favorite."

"I don't believe I ever met her myself." Kat leaned back in her seat, eyes out of focus. "No. Not familiar. She must not have been here when Cole and I were screwing around. After that when I returned for visits, I spent most of my time with Norman so I didn't get to know any of the whores. However, if you like her, she must be something else."

"She really is." Jane nodded. "I'm glad she was kind enough to agree to escort Alma here and back for us. If the Inn hadn't been damaged, we might have been able to make the trip ourselves, but I wouldn't have been able to see Leanne again."

"Clearly this was your idea, not Cole's." Kat quirked a brow. "Is he happy about the imminent arrival of his former whore?"

"Oh, he's thrilled." Jane's dry tone portrayed her sarcasm perfectly. The whole idea of both his half-sisters being in town made Cole more nervous than a cat in a room full of rocking chairs. "Of course, I think he's more concerned with the idea of Leanne, Katherine, and I being in the same room together. It's a scary prospect."

A knock interrupted Kat's reply, startling them all to look toward the door leading inside. In the shadow of the doorway stood a familiar scruffy old man.

Jane rose with a bright smile. "Mr. Hamm."

"Mrs. Mitch—"

"Mr. Hamm," Jane scolded over the snickers on the balcony. Despite her chastising tone, she couldn't stop grinning. "Don't make me correct you again."

"Sorry, Lady Jane." Hammy's ruddy complexion deepened a few shades. He shuffled his feet reticently, but his own grin matched Janes. "Just wanted to let ya know we got the icehouse cleaned up. Replaced the bad straw and moved the good blocks to the other side so we could shore up the wall that got burned."

"Thank you." Jane cross the balcony to clasp his hand in a grateful handshake. "Did much of the ice survive?"

"Not too much. Ya got a good ten blocks, still." Hammy rubbed the back of his neck with is bandanna. "Leastwise until the lake freezes again."

"In this heat, that seems a long way off. Ten blocks is better than nothing, I suppose. We'll make do." Jane nodded. "Thank you for the update."

Kat giggled when he walked away. "He's certainly far less secretive about calling you Mrs. Mitchell. What does Cole think?"

Jane to keep her reaction minimal as she slipped back into her seat. "Cole knows Mr. Hamm does not mean any harm by it. And, to that matter, we are both very much in agreement about marriage—so it's not a problem."

"Even with a baby on the way?" Lee gasped at the bold statement. She clapped her hand over her mouth, red seeping into her cheeks. "My goodness, I'm sorry. I'm not judging, I just would think that might change how you view things."

"Don't apologize, I know you meant no harm." Jane squeezed her hand. "More important, I appreciate that you said it outright. Most of the old biddies in this town are going to have a field day whispering behind my back once I become great with child."

"And we all know how Jane enjoys causing a scandal." Daisy's lips twisted, but the laughter had returned to her eyes. "At least she's far better at handling it than most of us are."

"Who's that?" Cora's brow furrowed as she craned her head. "He doesn't look familiar, although he seems awfully interested in the Inn."

Jane spun in her seat to see the gentleman Cora spoke of. When she spotted him, she rose to her feet, concern gripping her stomach. "I've never seen him before either. He must have come on the train. I hope he isn't looking for a place to stay. Our one usable room is occupied right now. I'd rather not give him one of the rooms the whores have been using for business, we need that money."

"Go on, take care of business. Come back if you can. I would hate for you to miss too much of the show." Kat waved toward the Inn. "After all, this was your idea, and a damn good one, at that."

"I'll be back quick as a jack-rabbit if I can." Jane slipped out through Cindy's room and made her way downstairs. As she left Kat's home, the stranger circled the Inn, adjusting his glasses as he made his way toward the front.

Jane approached. "Good afternoon, Sir. Might I assist you with something?"

He turned in surprise. After a moment he tipped his hat politely. "Good afternoon."

"I'm Jane Spencer, one of the owners of this establishment you're showing so much interest in. Would you care to come inside and have a drink, or perhaps join one of the poker games?" Jane offered her hand, glad he took it in a handshake. "I'm afraid due to the recent fire we only have one available room, which is currently housing a guest."

"Miss Spencer, you say?" He adjusted his glasses. "Well, it's a pleasure to meet you. I'm T.R. Cutler. I invested in this establishment a few years back."

Jane's heart stopped at the name, and only extreme control and politeness kept her from shouting for Thomas and Cole to join her immediately. Somehow she managed to make her voice work out of pure propriety rather than clear thought. "I see. Mr. Cutler, we weren't expecting your visit. I believe we'd discussed Mr. Mitchell and I coming to St. Louis next month. I do wish you'd sent us notice, we would have ensured we had a room available for you."

"To be honest, I was not expecting to make this trip either. I received an interesting telegram last week, a day after we agreed to our meeting as a matter of fact."

"You did?"

"Yes. It was informing me that my investment was falling to ruins and closed for business." He turned his gaze back on the building. "It was suggested I come to check the security of my holding."

"I see." Jane fought her nerves. She was more eloquent than two word answers. A smile forced its way forward. "I'm afraid we did have to close for a few days due to the damage from the fire someone set. The damage was extensive and we feared it might have been a total loss. However, as you see we've made great progress on repairs in quick order. I expect to be back open in full operation within the week. At the very least, our saloon has re-opened and is quite busy despite the construction happening."

"I wouldn't mind seeing for myself."

"Of course. Please," Jane gestured toward the door, "Come in. Welcome to The Hangman's Inn."

*You have to have your heart in the business,
and the business in your heart.
–Thomas Jefferson*

"Thomas," Jane managed to say without a squeak, considering how right her throat had become.

Tommy set down the glass he'd been wiping. His keen eye must have detected something, because he tugged his vest straight over his round belly before he circled the bar. "Jane?"

"Thomas, I'd like you to meet Mr. T.R. Cutler." Jane smiled toward the gentleman on her left. "Mr. Cutler, this is our manager, Thomas Young."

After they shook hands, Tommy nodded to the newcomer. "What's your poison, Mr. Cutler?"

"Would you happen to have coffee on hand?" Mr. Cutler followed Jane to a table. "I never drink when I do business."

"Always do. We try not to drink while doing business ourselves." Tom bowed to them both. "I'll go bring out a pot for us all."

"Thank you, Thomas." Jane turned her seat to face Cutler head on. "As you can see, we're still very much in business. We focused on the saloon because as of yet it's still the most profitable aspect of the Inn."

"I would point out that it is difficult to make a profit running a hotel without a proper setup," Cutler said quietly.

"There is no reception desk. The saloon and brothel take up all of your main floor. This doesn't appeal to all patrons."

"It's a struggle we've had the past year, but we've done well by including meals at a local café and meeting them at the train."

"Interesting tactics."

"The decision to add on the hotel concept was a sudden move and progressing it forward has taken some work." Jane leaned forward. "As for your points, all are things I had hoped to address in any one of our plans."

"Plans. Plural." Cutler had managed to keep his face stoic this whole time, but now his brow rose in apparent intrigue.

"I have made several projected plans for the future of the Inn. I've had the carpenter create blueprints for all of them. From improving our current layout and footprint, up to my hopes for expansion in size and areas of business."

"Here we go." Tommy set a tray in the middle of the table. He handed everyone a mug before taking his seat. "What brings you to town, Mr. Cutler?"

"I received a telegram suggesting that my investment was floundering." Cutler's gaze drifted between them. Jane imagined that keen as his attentions were, he didn't miss the significant look Tommy cut her at the mention of the telegram. "And considering the hotel portion is down to one room, it wasn't entirely inaccurate."

"We are working fast as we can to correct that." Tommy leaned both forearms on the table. "Until the fire, business had really picked up—in fact the night of the fire the hotel was full with guests. We've been rebuilding constantly since then."

"You were injured in the fire, then." Cutler indicated to the bandage remaining on Tom's cheek.

"I was. Was fortunate to get saved. Hasn't stopped me working, though." Tom smiled Jane's way when she squeezed his arm where injuries also remained.

She knew his guilt kept him working far more than he probably should. Part of her wondered how bad the pain actually was. She fought back the lump in her throat to readdress Cutler. "The fire set us back in our timetable, but not as much as we'd initially feared."

Jane's statement had brought Cutler's attention back to her. "How could it not be?"

His question made her wonder if her tone had lacked any confidence. "We had scheduled our appointment with you for next month, but also with several other potential investors. The repairs have moved along at such a pace that we remain on schedule for those meetings. By that point the Inn will be back in full working order."

"Plans are well and good if they are well thought out and feasible." Cutler removed his glasses to clean them with a kerchief. "I'd be interested in seeing those plans and learn how you hope to initiate them."

Tommy tapped Jane's hand. "Why don't you go get the papers? I'll keep Mr. Cutler company as well as answer any questions he has about the current state of operations."

"Thank you, Thomas. Mr. Cutler, I'll be back in a few minutes." Jane rose, bowing her head respectfully when both men rose at her departure. Calm as she could, she climbed the stairs and turned to head to the room she and Cole were using. Before she went there, she stepped through the new door to their old room.

On the other side of the door remained an unlivable space as it was primarily a floor alone. The hole in the building and roof still gaped wide onto the town. She stepped forward to call through the hole in the roof. "Cole!"

In less than a minute his legs hung over the edge. He dropped to he floor with a grin. "Hey." No sooner had he spoke than his grin faded. "What's wrong?"

"Cutler is here." Jane rubbed her hands together, having just realized how numb they were. "He arrived to check on his investment. Apparently someone warned him the business could very well be floundering."

His eyes narrowed. "Someone warned him? Or did he already know?"

"Thomas is down there feeling him out right now."

"What's your take?"

She pursed her lips, then shook her head. "No. My first instinct is that he's honest. I'm certain we'll know soon enough."

"I'll get changed."

"No. Keep working. The sooner we get the hotel back in full working order, the better. Cutler appears to prefer a hotel over a saloon and brothel. I just wish we had something like Mike's waterfall to draw folks in."

"We got the best spot in town. That's all we need." Cole chucked her under the chin. "Sure you don't want me down there?"

"You'll meet him soon enough. Get the roof back on so we can finish these rooms." She leaned up to brush her lips across his. "I only came up to get the plans. Cutler wants to know what we have in mind—if it's any good or feasible."

"You've been working hard on them plans. He'll like 'em."

"One can hope."

"I'll get back on the roof. You're the one with the words."

"Words may not be enough. I need a bit of luck as well. If he's not here to destroy us, he truly could help us."

"If you can talk Graham into acting decent, and get me and Daisy acting civil to each other, you can talk just about anyone into anything."

"Thomas is better at this part of it, and I plan to abuse that." She winked before stealing another quick kiss. In a mad rush now, she scooted into their temporary living quarters. Tossing open the trunk, she pulled out the stack of papers.

The moment she got back to her feet strong arms wrapped around her waist.

She slapped Cole's arm, struggling to keep hold of her papers. "I do not need to smell like a sweaty man when I go downstairs."

"Too late." He spun her around so fast her papers went flying. Over her protest, his lips crushed into hers as he backed her against the wall. His low chuckle sounded into the kiss when she gave in despite her weak fight.

She moaned, her body coming alive under his insistence. With as much resolve as she could muster, she pushed him back. "That wasn't nice."

"You sure seemed to like it."

Exhaling as heat flooded her cheeks, she brushed a hand along her skirt. "I need a clear head to speak with Mr. Cutler, not a heightened libido."

"Men like to look at pretty women." He winked. "And you look even better when you're expecting something."

"Oh—you." She huffed, unable to truly yell over his flattery and her spiked libido. "Get on back to work."

He sauntered from the room without further argument. She couldn't stop the grin he'd managed to put on her face. After she shook off some of the excitement, she smoothed her hand over her hair. "All right. Focus, Jane."

She sprayed some perfume on, then gathered the papers to head back downstairs quick as she could. On her approach, she apologized for her absence. Both men rose to let her sit, and she eyed her brother. The confident smile he gave her in return soothed the last of her concerns over whether Cutler might be in on their troubles.

For the next two hours they went over each of the plans with a fine-toothed comb. Every possibility and unforeseen difficulty got touched on and examined by Cutler. The financial hurdles, and amount of investors they'd need versus what both she and Cutler thought would be feasible for them to acquire.

During the entire conversation she barely noticed anything else except the brief departure of Tom, and Norman stopping in half an hour later. She deflected all approaching questions toward Tommy, Iris, or Cuddy; choosing to focus wholly on Cutler and the papers before them until they'd gone through them all.

"All of your proposals are interesting," Cutler said in way of wrapping up their intense discussion. "I have to admit I'm curious how you went from promising enough to warrant these plans to how things stand right now."

"You and me both, Mr. Cutler. I'll tell you what we do know." Jane's attention was diverted by the tall man approaching the table. Cole had made a complete turnaround from his sweaty shirtless appearance of earlier to one of the finer suits she'd gotten for him. She rose, holding out her hand toward Cole. "Mr. Cutler, I'd like you to meet my partner, Mr. Cole Mitchell."

Cutler extended his hand, "Mr. Mitchell."

"I prefer Cole," he said, shaking Cutler's hand. He took the seat beside Jane. "Sorry I took so long. I was working on getting this place back together."

Jane focused on her lap to hide the intensity of her grin as she noted the exact precision Cole maintained in his speech. While over time his speech pattern had evolved from being in her presence, and therefore most of the time his speech didn't hold the crude vernacular it had upon her arrival, it still slipped in frequently enough. However, at this point he concentrated to keep it cool and collected as she'd taught when he'd pretended to be Charles Hodgkins.

"As I told Miss Spencer, it's best that you do. Business should always take precedence." Cutler scooted his chair closer to the table. Whatever he'd planned to say was interrupted by the arrival of Tommy with fresh coffee. After he'd thanked him, Cutler turned his attention back to Cole. "It is good to finally meet you, Mr. Mitchell. I only met your former partner, Mr. Cooke. I usually prefer to know everyone involved in my investments."

"Graham was always the one out looking while I stayed here to watch the place. We didn't have Tom back then." Cole glanced at Jane. "Now that Jane is partner, and we got a real manager to watch the place we're hoping to correct that."

"I must say, I was surprised when I got the letter from Mr. Young stating the name of your new partner." Cutler studied Jane. "It's not often a proper woman becomes involved in a business with such a strong brothel element."

Cole smirked, a familiar exasperation filtering into his next statement. "I'm sure she told you we're working on eliminating it."

"I've been debating with her on whether it is a wise business move. Based on the numbers during the past two years, that aspect has shown the most profit, in some cases the only profit. I'm pleased to see that Miss Spencer has included contingency plans to keep it in place if it's needed." Cutler settled back in his chair, hands folded in front of him. "I'm surprised at her business acumen, and now I understand better why you took her on. Most women are not as capable in business, no offense of course."

"None taken." Jane lifted her chin to display the defiance welling. "Because it is true. Many women are not capable in business, but on that note, neither are many men."

"Jane," Cole warned.

"No. It's all right." A hint of a smile tugged the edges of Cutler's mouth. Perhaps he enjoyed a bit of debate. "I'd like to hear what she has to say."

Jane resisted the urge to stick out her tongue at Cole. Focused on Cutler, she continued, "Many men are good at a trade; be it farming, coopering, or mining. That does not mean they have the faintest idea what good business is. Being a man does not automatically make you adept. Just as being a woman does not automatically make one an idiot. Although, I suspect many women do not attempt business because of such a mentality."

Cole shook his head. "Always gotta be honest."

"Yes I do," Jane concurred. She smiled at him. "Mr. Cutler does not seem to mind."

"I find your thoughts intriguing, Miss Spencer. You have made several valid points." Cutler straightened. "I'd like to remain in town for a few days. I'll have a chance to ponder over the proposals you've made, as well as keep an eye on the progress of rebuilding. Is there somewhere you can recommend for me to stay?"

"Of course." Jane nodded. "I do wish you could stay here but barring that there is a boarding house a few doors down. There is also another hotel outside of town."

"The boarding house will suffice." Cutler rose.

"Why don't I let you gentlemen talk? I'll go speak with Mrs. Rosenzweig about a room for you." Jane slipped from her seat. "It shouldn't take me but twenty minutes. As it is near suppertime, you are welcome to join us for a bite at Cora's. Cole can lead the way."

Cutler gave her a small bow. "I would be delighted. I appreciate your hospitality, Miss Spencer."

"Then I will see you at supper. Welcome to Dominion Falls." Jane squeezed Cole's hand in encouragement on her way to the door. On the balcony across the street all of the women except Cora remained. The three of them now sat rather close to the railing.

Jane waved at them, chuckling softly that her plans for the afternoon had gone so well for some of them. She headed down the street to the boarding house and made the arrangements for Cutler's stay.

Once that was set, she headed toward Cora's.

"Good afternoon, stranger." The familiar voice of her brother, Mike hit her from behind.

"My darling Mike." Jane laced her arm through his the second he caught up. "Done on the roof for today? I'll bet Daisy is disappointed, I'm surprised she's still taking part in the enjoyment with you gone."

"Jane," he admonished. A bit of red rushed into his cheeks.

"Fine, fine. I'll be nice. How are you this evening?"

"I'm faring well, dear lady. You are in quite the good mood. Good news?"

"I am feeling quite positive tonight. Our investor arrived on this morning's train." Jane shrugged. "Despite the ominous timing of his arrival, I believe things went rather well during my meeting with him. I've spent the past two hours showing him my ideas for the hotel. If I'm not mistaken, he was rather impressed."

"Wonderful news. How about the baby?"

"With the exception of despising Cole every morning for the depths of my violent illness, it's wonderful. Daisy has said everything is moving along well. Charles is behaving himself and allowing Daisy to be my doctor—although he still tries to give me advice."

"And the repairs are going swimmingly."

"Many thanks to all who have been working so hard, including you. It's moving ahead of schedule." Jane bumped him with her hip. "I do appreciate your assistance even though we are your competition."

"You are also family." He bumped her back.

"Mr. Hamm has been a work horse. It's all been a great relief to see things moving so quickly. With any luck our room will be done enough for us to use it once Alma arrives so she might use the room we're using now."

"Did I cover everything?"

"No."

Mike blinked in surprise. "No? What could I have missed?"

"That I miss my dear brother very much, and I am quite upset with him for being so incredibly busy that he cannot spend time with me." She squeezed his arm. "However, if that was his plan for supper this evening, he's terribly out of luck, for I am dining with Cole and our investor on this fine night."

"Then I shall expect you at lunch tomorrow. I refuse to take no for an answer."

"As long as you don't try to make me eat, or you'll be wearing my meal."

"I wouldn't dream of it. I've seen what happens when I try to force you." Mike kissed her cheek at the entrance to Cora's. "It appears Cole is waiting on you. I'll see you tomorrow."

Jane waved her farewell. She approached the table, her bright smile remaining in place. "You are all set, Mr. Cutler."

Cutler rose halfway out of his seat while Cole held out Jane's chair. Once she was settled, he sat back down. "Thank you."

"After supper you are more than welcome to have a nightcap at the saloon, and we'll see you find the boarding house at a decent hour." Relief warred with hunger when her plate was set before her almost immediately. All Jane had eaten that day had been the petit fours, due to her usual morning's illness. Now that her stomach would allow food, she swore she could have eaten three plates full if not for their company.

A strange voice called out across the restaurant. "TR!"

Cutler's head lifted. His brow pinched together in a flash of something akin to annoyance before he smiled and rose. "Daniel. What are you doing here?"

"I convinced myself to listen to you for a change. It's about time I learned what you do on these trips, so I got on the next train." A tall man with a stovepipe hat and a monocle strode over to shake hands with Cutler. Much like Jackson Krenshaw, everything about him—from his hat to his mutton chops, right down to the spats on his shoes—screamed false to Jane. He turned his attention to Jane and Cole. "Hello. The name's Daniel Underwood."

Pure propriety made Jane rise to shake the man's hand, even as her stomach roiled with unease. The simple introduction had shoved aside her days' worth of hunger into disquiet. Cutler's explanation of Daniel being a partner with a minor interest in all of Cutler's investments did little to ease the ache.

Jane force a smile forward and returned to her seat while Cole shook Daniel's hand. Attempting to maintain her calm politeness, she dug deep to speak with something more than propriety. "You have a part in the investments as well?"

"I handle the paperwork and legal details. TR is the one that always goes to check on our investments and gets to know the people behind the businesses we're investing in." Daniel took the seat next to Cutler, leaning on the table. "I've been wanting to get more involved and branch out. I figured your hotel was as good a place to start as any."

Cole opened his mouth to reply, but an intense, shrill whistle shot through town. His head snapped to the door. Jane frowned when she noted that across the restaurant Michael's did as well. Without hesitation or a farewell to the others at his table, Mike threw down his napkin. He rushed from the building like something chased him.

Jane nudged Cole for his lingering silence. He'd failed to answer the question Daniel had asked when Cole and Mike had begun to at oddly. She turned her attention back to Daniel. "Cole would be happy to give you a tour. I have to—"

Tommy rushed up behind her, interrupting her with a muttered excuse to the gentlemen. He leaned down and spoke low in Cole's ear. Being on Jane's right, and she imagined incredibly discreet, she didn't hear a word of it.

"Excuse me, we gotta run." Cole grabbed Jane's hand so tight she winced in surprise. Over her stammered surprise he dragged her to her feet. "I'll leave ya in Tom's care—he's got just as much smarts as Jane."

"Cole!" Jane finally managed to get out a solid protest, but he ignored her. She clenched her fist to stop from slapping him over the manhandling. "Not now."

"Yes. Now. It's a family emergency." Cole dragged her toward the back of the restaurant. He only succeeded because she didn't dare break out into a true fight in front of their investors. Rather than explain or even speak, he practically threw her out the back door of the building.

The second they were outside, she fought his grip hard as she could. "Colton James Spencer!"

"Hush."

She wrenched her arm free and spun to slap him. "Are you insane? Do you realize how utterly unprofessional—"

"Shut up."

"Excuse me?"

"We gotta get you outta here. Now."

She backed away from his grasping hands. Unfortunately, the wall stopped her progress before she could get far. She pressed her hands into his chest. "Don't you dare."

"Jane. I ain't kidding around. Let's go."

"Not until you tell me what the devil is going on!"

"Marshal Lewis."

The words poured over the heat of her anger like a bucket of ice water. She sagged into the wall. "Fuck."

"That whistle you heard was Charlie. Seems all your family does that in an emergency—gets all the Young boys on alert. He'd seen the Marshal arrive on that train and was warning us all. Now we gotta get you outta sight until we figure out what to do with you."

With every word, Jane's senses had returned to her. In her head she knew full well the logic of what they were doing but, "No."

"Jane!"

She pushed him further away. After all she'd been through and everything she'd had to fight for, she wouldn't crumble because of one man's arrival. "I am *not* afraid."

"Ya got more than yourself to worry about now. Maybe you should be."

"Clara Young is dead. She hanged until dead in 1871. I am not, nor have I ever been her. I can't spend my life in hiding. I won't live in fear. I did that once, I didn't like it."

“Jane, please.”
“We have a business to save. I don’t have time for fear.”

As courage imperils life,
fear protects it.
—Leonardo da Vinci

Charlie stormed through the restaurant, right past Jane to Cole's side. "What in hell does she think she's doing?"

Cole shook his head, unable to answer with the tension ratcheting through him. Halfway across the room Jane returned to her seat at the table. In moments she managed to get the two businessmen laughing. All the while Tommy glared daggers at her.

On the other side of the room David tried to keep the attention of Marshal Lewis.

Cole managed to unclench his jaw. "She said she ain't gonna live in fear."

"Is she insane?"

"Yeah."

Charlie looked sideways at Cole. "Are you all right?"

"If she gets through this damn fool action, I'm gonna kill her."

"Go get a drink. We'll keep an eye on her."

"I ain't going nowhere."

Charlie nodded his acceptance. His arms folded across his chest, nudging aside his coat enough to reveal his sidearm. Both men stood in silence as Jane carried on with the two gentlemen as if nothing had happened, eating heartily despite the large target on her back.

Cole knew that unbeknownst to Jane, Tommy had once interceded with vague threats to the marshal to keep him off her back. Even if Tommy managed to pull in a few favors this time around, that didn't mean Marshal Lewis wouldn't make Jane's life hell before that happened.

Across the room Mike had appeared by David's side, helping to keep the marshal well distracted. Everyone was making more of an effort than Jane likely understood to keep the situation under control. Then again, maybe she did know, and truly no longer cared.

Part of Cole couldn't blame her for being tired of living in fear. Her life had been pure hell for a long time, and their current state of affairs was hard enough. Worrying about one more thing did seem like way too much to take.

Jane finished her meal and rose. After she shook hands with the investors she turned toward the front door, only to have Tommy blocking her path. Cole had no clue what she said to her brother since her back was to him, but the anger and frustration creasing Tommy's features spoke volumes.

With an uneasy glance behind him, Tom stepped aside to let her pass. The tension shot through Cole when the bulky man headed toward them, giving Jane a clear path to the front doors. Her path would lead her right past the table filled with lawmen.

"Damn it," Cole muttered when Tommy reached them. "That damn woman is trying to get herself hanged again."

"You know I won't let that happen, Cole. Wouldn't have let it the first time if I'd been given the knowledge she still lived in time. Right now she's just mad as a March hare and crying to boot." Tom shook his head. "Said she's tired of hiding and if something was going to happen it might as well be now. She refuses to give up what scraps of her life she has every time Lewis comes to town."

Cole balled his hands into fists when Marshal Lewis stood seconds after Jane passed the table. While David and Mike tried to slow Lewis's progress, Cole spun on his heel to race out the back door he'd taken Jane out of earlier.

By the time he ran around the building and emerged onto the street, Lewis was already clamoring down the steps of Cora's.

Lewis strode after Jane, not paying attention to Cole if he'd even noticed him. "Miss Young."

Jane continued walking down the street, ignoring the name she'd only gone by once since he'd known her, and that was when she'd been found guilty and ordered to be hanged. A few people turned their heads at the marshal's call, but most went right back to their business.

"Miss Young! Excuse me." Lewis picked up his pace until he caught up to her. He grabbed her arm. "I said excuse me, Miss Young."

Jane turned, maneuvering her arm free. Her features creased with confusion as she stared at the marshal dead on. "I'm sorry?"

Cole kept his distance from the scene, lingering close enough to intercede if needed. To his right he noticed Tommy rush past down the middle of the street toward the Inn. On the steps of Turner's stood Mike, David, and Charlie. All three had their hands on their guns, tension lining their faces. Everyone was ready for a fight.

"I don't see many women get hanged, Miss Young." Lewis stuck close to her, not that she showed any signs of running away. "They tend to stick out in my mind. I know it's you."

"I do apologize. I haven't the foggiest idea what you mean." Jane's features remained stoic. No distress, no twinge over the near-lie. She'd have to toe a fine line indeed to avoid an outright lie, considering how much she hated them.

David brushed past Cole on his way to their side. "Marshal Lewis."

Lewis frowned at David. "Would you care to explain this?"

David looked between them, then shrugged. "What do you need me to explain?"

"This man apparently has me confused with someone else." Jane set her hands on her hips, her chin lifted in defiance. He couldn't tell from where he stood, but Cole guessed her eyes were deep grey in her anger. The woman wouldn't back down, even not knowing if her ex-husband would back her up on this one. "He keeps calling me Miss Young."

"Perhaps you'd prefer Mrs. Schaffer," Lewis suggested.

"I sincerely doubt she would." David shook his head, a low chuckle carrying through the air. "Considering my fiancée Lee has designs on the name. Marshal Lewis, might I introduce you to Jane Spencer."

Lewis frowned at Jane's extended hand. "Are you trying to tell me that you are not Clara Young, convicted murderer?"

Jane blinked at that, but then smiled so bright Cole knew at once it was fake. "I do apologize, but my name has been

Jane Spencer for as long as I can remember. Now, if you'll excuse me I have business to attend to."

Cole blinked in shock when Jane turned her back on the two men and strode to the saloon without another word. When the two lawmen began an intense discussion, Cole took off to the Inn as quick as he could.

Bursting into the saloon, he stopped short when he saw her behind the bar already handing Hammy a beer. He stalked toward her. "Jane."

"Not now. We're swamped." Jane poured another drink rather than even look at him.

Cole grabbed her arm, shouting at Rose to get behind the bar before he dragged Jane away. Despite her vibrant fight, he kept pulling her toward the stairs. He managed to drag her rather kicking and shrieking to their room.

Once he'd managed to force her through the door, he slammed it behind them. His back to the room, he leaned both hands against the door trying to calm his nerves before he really let her have it for her stupid bravery.

"How dare you manhandle me!"

"Are you *insane*?" Cole spun on her. "What in hell did you think you were doing back there? Do ya have that strong a hankering to get hanged again?"

"Yes, Cole," She spat in a sarcastic sneer. "That's at the top of my list of things to do with my life. I *enjoyed* the feeling of that rope around my neck so much I'm *dying* to feel it there again."

"This ain't funny."

"I know!"

"Do ya?"

When he grabbed her shoulders, tears sparked in her eyes. The pain of the hanging echoed out of her dark gaze as much as it twisted his own heart. Through it all, she managed to glare at him. "I am not an idiot. I just don't have time to be worried about the damn marshal."

"You've *always* gotta worry about it."

"I've been worried about it for well over a year. From the second I woke up in that coffin very *un*dead. I'm always worried about it." Tears flowed free down her cheeks as she yelled back at him. "Right now? Right now I have a hundred other things that I have to worry about and that's just one more thing. *I can't do it.*"

"Well, you gotta."

"How? When I can fit it in? Our entire lives went up in literal smoke. If we don't deal with this investor now, we could lose what little we have left. We have a child across the street we've been prostituting for over a year because I was too blind to see it. We have Alma coming in a few weeks. We have a baby on the way."

"*You* are what's important."

"This is me! You, this business, Alma and Jesse, all of it! I haven't room or time to disappear and cower and wait and hope that this time the marshal doesn't catch someone slipping up. Or to pray that this time my stupid brother doesn't have to use his mysterious powers of the Pink to keep me free and off the noose. I've done that twice this past year and I won't do it again. I absolutely refuse to keep hiding. I need to live."

"I need you to live."

"Then let me."

"I can't lose you again." He tugged her close. "You got that? I can't."

"You could live without me." Under her tears a weak smile formed.

"I don't want to."

"I can't go into hiding." She wrapped her arms around his neck and held his gaze firm. "I won't. I'm done with hiding. Our lives are too important."

"The bastard named ya for his death. The marshal could hang you for it."

"He also named Constance. There are no witnesses. Nick claimed responsibility. Most importantly, Alan is dead. There is nothing he can arrest me on."

"Fraud."

"He can't prove it." She pressed her forehead into his. "I haven't tried to get anything out of this place. There's been no deception for profit or unfair gain. I've lost almost as much as I've gained. I've been honest to a fault with this town—there's no fraud I can be accused of."

"Jane," he pleaded. If she was even a little wrong, he could lose her.

"I'm sorry. I can't," she whispered. She pulled out of his arms, leaving his aching worry to fend for itself. Across the room, she folded her arm across her chest. "It may be, to date, the dumbest thing I've ever done, but I'm not leaving. I'm not hiding. I'm staying here for my life. *My* life, Jane Spencer Mitchell. It's *mine*—not hers. I won't hide for someone else's mistakes for one more second."

"It's madness."

"'Though this be madness, there is yet method'. Shakespeare." Jane kept her back to him. Her ragged breath filled the room. "I wanted to live honestly. Hiding when one man comes to town is not doing that. I will be honest to my life here and now. I am not, nor have I ever been Clara Young. Jane Doe is merely a memory. I was given a chance to live again, and I am going to live."

"I can't lose ya."

"You won't."

"You don't know that!"

"Yes. I do. I told you, I'm fighting for my life. Do you think I would give up so easily? That I would allow myself to lie down and die after working so hard to become who I am now? That I would give up our life together—our family, our children?"

He took a few steps closer. "It ain't as easy as saying you're gonna fight."

"Yes it is."

"Jane."

She turned to meet his eyes. "When Clara hanged, I believed myself a horrible and wicked creature. As much as I loved you then, I couldn't admit it—because I believed I had to lie down and die for what she'd done. For crimes I couldn't remember committing."

"You'd accepted it, no matter how I fought you on it. Ya wouldn't even run with me."

"I made a lot of mistakes then."

"This could be one too."

"Maybe, but I'm not who I was. I will fight with resources I didn't use before." She cupped his cheek. "Now that I have you, our family, I am not giving up. If there is a fight to be fought toward that end, then I will fight until my very last breath. I have hope, I have a life, I have you, Alma, and this one I curse every morning right along with you for how it makes me ill."

"What if it ain't enough?"

"I have to believe it is. I have to have faith that God would not be so cruel as to rip us apart again. Not now after we fought so hard to get here."

He pulled her close against him. Her arms wrapped tight around him. He sighed, resting his cheek on top of her head. "Faith."

"'If you think you can win, you can. Faith is necessary to victory'. Hazlitt."

"You better be right."

She yanked back, looking askance at him. Mock surprise brought her hand to her chest. "What? Aren't I always right?"

"Not a chance."

"Are you done yelling at me now?"

"I'll never be done yelling at ya."

"I love you, too."

He bent as if to kiss her, but then shifted and scooped her into his arms instead. She leaned against him when he carried her to the bed, and he sat with her on his lap. He trailed his fingers up her spine and gave her a gentle kiss.

"I plan to spend years upon years making you regret every second that you thought marrying me was a good idea."

"You're doing a damn good job of it."

"So are you, you stubborn fool." She smiled and cupped his cheek. "We're going to fix this."

"I don't believe it."

"What a shame. I was ready to make up."

He frowned when she slipped from his lap and walked across the room. "Get your ass back here."

She didn't move from where she was, just stood staring out the window.

"All right. I ain't got the slightest clue how, but you're right."

"You don't have to know how. That's not what faith is." She sighed and leaned her forehead against the pane. "Look at what this town has done for us since the fire. Despite all that we do to cause scandal—they still came to our aide. Even Graham burned his hands to save as many of my books as he could. People with nothing gave us the clothes off their backs. They got that saloon back together in days. Did you ever think something like that would be done for us? For the saloon and brothel?"

"No."

"Anything is possible, Cole." She spun, the familiar and vibrant fire he loved returned to her eyes. "I don't believe anyone in this town that knows me would give me up. Those that don't know me, don't know about Clara. Marshal Lewis will hear the truth, I've been Jane Spencer for as long as I can remember. I have never been Clara Young. Even Michael and Nicholas now admit that I carry some traits, but I am not her."

She crossed the room and put her knees on either side of his hips to straddle him. He set his hands on her hips when she leaned close.

After a deep breath, the hardness of her stubbornness faded into the gentle, soft lines of a smile. "The only other name I care to know is Jane Mitchell. That's all there is to it."

"Ya done?"

"Are you?

"Yeah."

"Are you sure?"

He pressed his fingers into the small of her back, glad she followed his suggestion. Her lips fell to his in a slow kiss, and he let her tongue massage away all his lingering doubts as she pushed him back to the bed.

Pounding on the door interrupted the moment and Jane groaned. "Damn it. Go away!"

"Jane!" David's voice preceded another round of pounding. "Open up."

Cole met her gaze in silence when her features hardened into determination. Rather than let her take the lead this time, he pushed her aside and rose. Against her protest, he threw open the door. "David. Marshal."

Jane groaned toward the ceiling. "You've got a really vicious streak in you, God. You know that?"

Daring ideas are like chessman moved forward. They may be beaten, but they may start a winning game.
—Johann Wolfgang von Goethe

"Would you mind if we came in?" Marshal Lewis sounded far more polite than Jane believed him to be.

"Yes," Jane muttered from her position on the bed.

"It ain't the best time," Cole concurred. He hesitated, casting a glance her way before he continued, "But come on in."

Jane growled in frustration. She beat her fists on the mattress before she flew to her feat. By the time the two men were fully in the room, she had her hands on her hips glaring them down. Not even Cole returning to her side resolved the tension of both the current situation and her interrupted libido.

"Sorry," David started.

"You should be," Jane snapped her interruption. "We were occupied."

Lewis' eyebrows flew up as he studied them both, his gaze ending where Cole's hand sat on her waist. "Interesting. You stand here like this and yet dare say you're not Clara Young?"

Jane exhaled in frustration. The subterfuge was getting old, but she had a fine line to toe between truth and lies. "The God's honest truth is that I am not Clara Young. I do not know how many more ways I can say it. I am Jane Spencer."

"You're here with Mr. Mitchell. Considering his previous involvement with Clara this reeks of lies. Not to mention you exactly like Clara Young." Lewis might have a point, but so did she.

She glanced sideways at Cole, a sly smirk lifting the corner of her mouth. "Well, why in hell wouldn't I be with Cole? I've seen him with his shirt off—well, with everything off—and believe me, it's most definitely worth it."

"Jane," said David in warning.

"What?" Jane turned her dark look on him. "I'm being honest."

"Maybe a little less would be good." David pursed his lips in anger, but concern deepened his hazel eyes. "At least try to tone down the attitude."

"Excuse me? You are the one that interrupted us, and I am supposed to tone it down?" Jane scoffed. "I believe this entire town knows how much I hate to be interrupted."

"Miss Young," Lewis started.

"Spencer," Jane corrected the marshal. She lifted her chin, not willing to show a bit of fear over what this man could do if he was so inclined. "My name is Jane Spencer. That is who I am."

"I don't care for having the wool pulled over my eyes, or idle threats by men who think they have power." Lewis eyed her, calculating but not cruel. "I know what I see before me."

"What might that be?"

"The same person that I examined, and declared dead a year and a half ago."

"Then it would seem that you have a conundrum." Jane spun in a circle. "For as we can all see rather clearly, I am not dead. I'm quite alive and enjoying my life when it's not interrupted. If you declared this woman dead, how can you claim I am her?"

"Miss—"

"Why are you here?" Jane clasped her hands behind her, her back ramrod straight. "Have I committed a crime I'm unaware of? Or are you simply here to harass me?"

Lewis met her gaze evenly. "I'm here to determine how it is you are here."

"That hardly seems important in the scheme of things. It certainly is not a matter of life and death and law."

"Clara Young is supposed to be dead for crimes committed."

"You said yourself she was dead. You declared her dead yourself."

"Yet you are still here."

"I am not Clara." She wanted more than anything to ask him what brought him here this time, for she knew of know imminent trials. "I read the paper fresh off the press and I know of no crime awaiting trial here in town. Yet you are here, interrupting us for no reason than to harass me. Have I committed a crime?"

"Fraud, for one."

Jane tilted her head to study him. She knew he was frustrated, but she couldn't care about that. "No. I'm afraid fraud must have five proven elements, the key of which is injury to an alleged victim as a result of fraudulent activities.

I do not recall harming anyone beyond harsh words and one well-deserved broken nose. You may ask around if you wish. Not to mention—for fraud you would have to provide justifiable proof that I am deceiving this alleged victim."

Lewis' eyes grew wide over her rant. "You know the law?"

"I read a lot." Jane smiled when a miniscule snort came from David.

"And remembers everything," Cole muttered. "Everything."

"Everything except being Clara Young." Lewis frowned. "Clara claimed amnesia on the witness stand. Said she didn't remember committing any of the crimes she was accused of."

"Yes, and Clara Young was tried and sentenced on all charges—a sentencing you were witness to and as you said, you declared her dead yourself." Jane tapped her fingers on her bodice. "If I was her I could not be tried again. I'm not—but either way you would need to charge me with a crime I did commit. Have you one?"

"Murder." Lewis' dark tone seemed to jolt through the two men on her side.

Jane ignored Cole's step toward her. Without a waver in her stance, she eyed Lewis. "Murder? Oh, that is a charge, isn't it? Who am I to have murdered?"

"Alan Bingham."

Jane didn't budge an inch, continuing to stare him down.

Lewis cracked first. "He was in the jailhouse here awaiting trial. After he managed to escape when the deputies were distracted, he was shot in the stomach with a Derringer.

He died a slow, painful death, but lived long enough to name you, Clara, as his murder."

"He also named Constance," David supplied.

Jane's gratitude for David's assistance aside, she continued to stare down Lewis. Out of nowhere, she cracked a smile. "I'm sorry, did you say a Derringer?"

"I did," Lewis concurred.

She couldn't help it, she laughed so fast and hard she had to clamp her hand over her mouth.

"Jane," Cole snapped.

"What?" Jane giggled at the confusion on all their faces. "A Derringer? That puny little gun that Zeke tried to sell me for ages because it was a ladies gun?"

Lewis' brow furrowed. "I fail to see the humor."

"Why in the hell would I shoot a man with a tiny little weapon that he was likely to survive if I wasn't close enough? I despise those little things. I also wouldn't shoot them in the stomach." Jane scoffed. "If I wanted someone dead, I'd shoot to kill, not torture."

Lewis folded his arms across his chest. "He suffered before he died."

"And you said he was in jail—therefore a criminal." Jane glanced between the men's aghast stares. This was getting old. She turned back to the marshal. "Am I right?"

"Doesn't matter." Lewis sniffed, his stance remaining straight.

"Ah yes, of course. Well. Like I said—if I'd wanted the man dead, he would have died immediately." Jane stepped away from Cole's side to cross to the bedside table.

"Jane don't." Cole must've known her intention, his voice rose in panic. "Jane."

"This…" Jane ignored him. She withdrew the weapon from the drawer. Never once did she raise it in a threatening manner. Instead, she carried it over to Lewis and handed it to him. "This is my weapon of choice. She's done well by me."

"This is yours?" The disbelief in his tone carried into the downturn of his brows. He glancedat Cole, then back to her with suspicion. "It's a Remington."

"Remington 1858. It packs quite a punch, and I love it." Jane smirked at the continued suspicion in his gaze.

"Sure it's not his?" Lewis nodded to Cole, who himself looked like he might be sick.

"Cole's? Oh, heavens no." Jane grinned at Cole. She slid her fingers along his holster to the weapon at his side. "His preferred weapon is this beauty. A Walker Colt. I'm so jealous I could spit—but it's all his."

Despite the levels of fear he had to be feeling, a smirk creased Cole's features. He shook his head. "Hate to tell ya, but she's right. I don't like the Remington. I can't ever get the damn thing to aim straight for me."

Lewis turned the gun over in his hands. "Are you telling me you really believe you can handle this weapon?"

Jane heaved a heavy sigh. She returned to the marshal's side. Before he could argue, Jane took the weapon from his hands. "There's a knothole beside the window, Marshal Lewis."

"What?"

To prevent anyone from stopping her, she balanced the weapon in her left hand. Amidst several yells as they realized what she was doing, she fired toward the wall.

All three men stared at her in shock, hands over their ears.

Her lips twitched to cover her laughter. "Why don't you go check that knothole, Marshal?"

When he moved, Cole gripped her arm to yank her close. He snarled in her ear. "You're insane, woman!"

She smiled over his harsh words. "Perhaps, but you love me anyway."

"Jane."

Her reply got cut off by a pounding on the door. "Go ease Thomas' headache, would you?"

Cole went to the door and threw it open. "Jane was trying to prove a point."

"What the hell happened?" Tom stepped into the room, quickly taking in the scene. His gaze fell on the weapon still in her hand before he met Jane's gaze. "You're a damn crazy woman, you know that?"

"I most assuredly do."

"*Miss Spencer*," Lewis yelled from across the room.

Jane jumped at the yell, turning in surprise to the man in question. "I'm sorry, Marshal Lewis. What is it you needed?"

"Are you no longer answering to that name either? Are we changing it again? I've been calling you." Lewis' frown deepened impossibly further.

"You were on my right side, and that ear is deaf. With Mr. Young pounding on the door and yelling at me, my left ear was rather occupied." Jane shrugged. "I'm sorry I didn't hear you."

"Mr. Young, your timing is perfect." Lewis stepped closer to the group. "Quickly tell me. Your sister Clara, was she right handed? Or left?"

"Right," Tommy said without hesitation. Only Jane knew that Tommy had noted the distinct difference between herself and Clara long ago. Tom frowned. "What in blazes does that have to do with anything?"

Lewis pressed further without answering his question. "And how accurate was she with a pistol?"

"Couldn't shoot worth a damn. About took Pa's head off during her first lesson and he refused to teach her again." Tommy chuckled at the familiar story he'd shared on several occasions with anyone that would listen. "Then she ended up shooting Nick in the leg. None of us wanted to teach her after that."

Even David laughed at the story. "Makes me glad I never got around to teaching her, then. I might not be here today."

"Thank you, Mr. Young." Lewis all but dismissed Tommy.

Jane gave Tommy a nod. "I apologize for scaring you, Tom."

Tom shook his head. "Crazy woman." He was still laughing when he shut the door.

Cole snatched the weapon from her hand to set on the nightstand.

Jane turned to Lewis. "Do you have everything you need, Marshal Lewis? If you're done, I would very much like to get back to my business."

Lewis quirked a brow. "Your business?"

"I suppose not my business, technically. After all, that's downstairs and Thomas is handling that right now. I mean the business of screwing that man until he can't walk." She ignored the simultaneous groans of Cole and David. "That is, unless you have something to charge me with."

Lewis walked up to her. His gaze held hers evenly. "Would you knowingly commit murder and walk away like it never happened?"

Without a flinch, Jane held his gaze. "Is that not what you do? Every day in the name of justice?"

"Jane!" David stepped forward.

"No, wait." Jane tilted her head, not wavering. "You don't actually pull the lever yourself, do you? You leave that to men like Sheriff Schaffer. You simply watch and wait for death. That must get awful tiring, waiting for death, even in the name of so-called justice."

"If you committed this murder," Lewis threatened through gritted teeth.

"First off, I have been told you already had a confession, unless I've been told wrong. Plus, he was an escaped prisoner at the time, so was it really murder? I mean, you failed to go after Mr. Nicholas Young for murder when Mr. Bingham died."

A tic started below Lewis' eye.

"I would ask you something, Marshal Lewis."

"What would that be?"

"Before you go accusing me blindly of crimes you have no idea whether I've committed, go out there into the town." Jane gestured to the door. "Talk to every single person if you would like. Try to find an actual crime I may have committed, and you can prove. Find out who I am—my name is Jane Spencer, in case you've forgotten."

Lewis didn't move. "I want the truth."

"Then do what I have suggested. Talk to everyone in town if you must. Look for a crime. Read Clara's letters and see what crime she actually committed and if that is what you hanged her for. Then look at her life, her behavior—and then look at mine. I am not Clara Young. Now get out of my room."

"Jane." David launched forward. He froze when she pointed at him without ever taking her eyes off the marshal. "Damn it, Jane."

"I said get out. This is my land, and I fully intend to use it for my own pleasure. Unless you have designs on watching what is certain to be some very lewd acts, I do suggest you leave." Jane lowered her arm. She stepped back from Lewis. "If you wish to speak to me again, make it at a more convenient time."

Lewis tugged on his lapels. "Don't think I won't, Miss Young."

"It's Spencer, you yellow-bellied coc—"

"Jane," Cole snapped. "Don't."

Jane pulled her gaze away from the marshal. As the adrenaline wore off, her shoulders began to sag. Unwilling to show such weakness, she took several deep breaths to gather herself again.

"I'll see you tomorrow." Lewis took several steps closer to the door. "I expect you both to remain in town."

"Nowhere else to go. Have a business to save." Her wits gathered again, Jane lifted her head. "If I was committing fraud, Marshal, I'd have a hell of a lot more than I do right now. All I have is that man, and this business that is floundering under our feet. The only gain I have right now is a life filled with passion and friendship. There is no trickery, no deception for ill-gotten gains. I don't want such things. I want what I have—it may not be much when you look at the monetary side of it—but it's all I've ever wanted."

Lewis tipped his hat. "Miss Spencer."

David sighed as the man departed. "Jane. Cole."

"Get out," Cole grumbled. Not even when the door slammed shut did Cole move a muscle.

The echo of the door slamming faded. Silence blanketed the room. Jane kept her gaze on the ground as she tried to steady her crazy emotions. Many deep, ragged breaths later she got a hold of her center again. She lifted her gaze up the length of Cole's body on a reluctant path to his eyes.

"Damn crazy bitch."

"Domineering prick."

He took a step toward her, which she matched with a step of her own. "Ya trying to kill me?"

Initiating their movement another step closer, she felt the tug of a renewed smile. "Are you trying to ruin my mood?"

"What were you thinking?"

"That I wanted to spend my time with my husband, not some idiot lawmen. I had to get rid of them as fast as I could—and that meant being a rude, condescending, slightly off-kilter bitch."

"Nice thoughts."

"Nice gun—can I touch it?"

*All things are cause for either
laughter or weeping.
-Seneca*

Cole's finger trailed along her shoulder in small delicate circles. His gaze remained fixed on the ceiling. "Maybe we should go get Alma ourselves."

Confused, Jane propped her chin on his chest to study him quietly. "What?"

"Maybe we should go to Denver."

"We have agreed that isn't possible right now. Why would you say that?"

"When we get to Denver I can drop you at the asylum."

She pursed her lips to keep her grin at bay. Rather than argue, she slipped her hand down his chest. She allowed each finger to drift over his abs. As she inched her hand lower she asked, "Why would you do that?"

"Because you might just be crazy." His statement ended on a moan when she grasped the length of his cock in her hand.

With a giggle, she pressed her body against the hard planes of his. She kissed his chest. "'There is no genius free from some tincture of madness'," she whispered against his neck. "Seneca."

"Shut the hell up," He managed to murmur before he rolled her onto her back.

Their lips met in a passionate embrace, teasing, tasting; as their hands swept across flesh, searching, inviting the recently satiated need back. Tenderly they moved together, letting the hunger build slow and strong.

As his lips traveled along the delicate curves of her throat, the soft contours of her body molded to his until their flesh touched as much as possible. Her soft moans filled the room, pulling them both deeper into the depths of passion.

When their lips met again it was with an intensity that drove them into a frenzy. Tenderness flew away as pure rapture drove them toward their needed release—and nothing could block them from that goal.

Until a large crack filled the room. The world dropped out from under them with a thump, and they both dropped onto the mattress with a grunt.

Jane yelped, and they both grew still. Slowly they both turned their heads, and Jane noted they were several feet lower than they had been. She inhaled sharp against the laughter. "Oh my heavens."

"Did we …"

Their gazes locked and she started to giggle. "Oh…my…"

A loud pounding on the door startled them again. Tommy shouted through the door, "What the devil happened this time? Are you all right? Jane? Cole?"

She busted out laughing, her whole body shaking with laughter. Unable to answer Tommy, she could hardly breathe once Cole joined in the mirth.

Tommy beat on the door harder. "What the hell is going on?"

Jane wiped at her tears, unable to stop laughing, even though her stomach was starting to ache from the constant barrage. Cole buried his face in her shoulder, his own body quaking above hers. Her shriek of laughter rose even louder when Tommy nearly broke the door down to storm into the room.

"Aw, geez. Damn it, Lou!"

She began to struggle for air, and covered her face with her hand to try to compose herself.

"You broke the damn bed? Cover yourselves up, geez."

Jane shook her head, trying to say something, but gasping giggles was all she could manage. When Tommy covered them up, they slowly untangled, both still laughing too hard to talk.

"You're damn crazy, you realize this." Tommy chuckled.

Though she still had to wipe at her tears, Jane nodded. She sat up and held the blanket to cover herself. After she felt sure she could talk, she pointed at Tommy. "You—your face; the bed—oh…my…"

Cole cracked up and shook his head. "That ain't never happened to me before."

That set Jane off again and she collapsed back onto the bed.

Tommy snorted. "You stopped all action in the saloon with that racket. Scared the pants off of me. Again."

Cole nudged her when she began to giggle again. "Knock it off."

"He…we…HA!"

Tommy threw his head back, a loud laugh joining theirs. "You're insane! The both of you."

"I know." Jane couldn't seem to stop now that she'd started.

Cole could only shake his hand, pressing his thumbs against the bridge of his nose. "It's these damn beds Graham got for the hotel rooms."

Jane nodded. "We need solid oak."

Another booming guffaw from Tommy set them all off again, and even Tommy had to wipe tears from his eyes. "Going to need to have Hammy fix another door."

Jane exclaimed, "Why in hell didn't you use the damn master key?"

"I wasn't exactly thinking." Tommy gestured to the bed. "I had no idea *this* is what I'd find."

"Sorry." Jane snickered, doing her best to not lose control again.

"Yeah." Cole managed to rein himself in. "Sorry."

"That's twice tonight you've scared me, Janey." Tommy pointed at her. "Don't do it again."

Jane wiped at her tears with the heel of her hand and set her hand over her heart. "I promise. That's all tonight. Oh, my stomach. I have to stop."

Cole snorted when she lost it again. "Don't think this bed is going anywhere now."

When Jane squealed again, Tommy held up his hands. "I'm done. You two are too much for me. I'm going back to the saloon. Less crazy down there."

Jane managed a flimsy wave, another squeak escaping when Cole tickled her. She barely registered the slamming of the door as she tried to fight off Cole. "Stop."

Cole rolled with her, stopping when he hovered above her with a wicked grin. "You gonna stop laughing anytime soon?"

"I don't think I can."

He captured her lips, coaxing her into the kiss. When she laughed a few moments later, he pulled back and quirked his brow. "This could be a challenge."

"Good thing you like a challenge."

"I'd have to—to have put up with you this long." He leaned in and nibbled along her neck as his fingers danced along her flesh. Each touch slowed her laughter, although her breathing remained ragged. He nipped at her earlobe. "Better?"

She hummed her agreement. "A little."

His lips trailed lower, skimming along her chest.

Suddenly she burst into giggles again, and it grew into full blown laughter when he groaned in frustration. "I'm sorry. We—we broke the damn bed!"

Simultaneously they both lost it again, their merriment filling the room for a good half hour. Back and forth they teased each other until they were able to contain themselves.

Jane sighed at the release from the laughter, if not the joy. She snuggled closer to him, nestled in the familiar spot that seemed made just for her. The smile lingered as she ran her hand along his chest. "I needed that."

"Think we both did."

"Too much time spent in worry lately. I really do prefer laughter."

"Over everything else?"

"Well…not *everything*."

"Good." He chuckled and winked when she peeked up at him.

She smiled when his fingers laced with hers and relaxed against him. Everything settled down into calm, and for the first time all day she managed to release all the tension. If only for a moment.

Her stomach churned, bile hitting her throat. Jane tensed and swallowed against the sudden nausea. With a few deep breaths it seemed to settle.

Or maybe not.

She sat and clasped her hand over her mouth. Never before had the nausea hit her this hard at night. Perhaps it was the laughter. No matter the cause, the churning was getting worse fast.

"Jane?" Cole ran his hand along her back.

"Just…" She gasped in a deep breath, and closed her eyes. "A little…"

He sat next to her and brushed his hand along her hair, then down her back. "Are you feeling sick?"

She nodded, keeping her hand firm over her mouth. Every effort went into pushing back the sick that didn't want to be contained.

"Ain't ever happened at night before. What do you need?"

"Water," she whispered.

On his feet in an instant, he crossed the room and returned with her glass before she'd managed to situate herself at the edge of the mattress. Once she'd clasped her hands around the glass, he went to grab the bucket and set it before her.

When he sat beside her, she felt him drape her robe over her shoulders. Despite her shaky hands, she managed to take a sip of the water. "Sorry."

"Don't you dare apologize."

"Talk about ruining the mood."

"Think the bed managed that."

Unable to manage a laugh, she pushed forward a smile. She set her hand on her stomach when it churned again. "This is…"

When she didn't finish, he brushed her hair back over her shoulder. "What?"

"As bad as I usually wake up to."

"It'll pass." When she groaned and made good use of the bucket, he held her hair back. He soothed her until she'd finished.

She leaned back against him and tried to relax, but her stomach wouldn't quit. As bile rose again, she gasped and rushed toward the bucket again.

"Jane."

She only shook her head, unable to stop vomiting. The moment she was able to breathe again, she gasped. "Cole…"

No greater grief than to remember the days of gladness when sorrow is at hand.
—Friedrich von Schiller

"Thanks, Tom." Wills waved his way out of the Inn.

Tommy wiped down the bar at the man's departure to clean up any stray droplets of moisture. Every few seconds he scanned the room for signs of any issues. After the past few months of hell, he'd be damned if he'd see anything else happen on his watch.

"*Tom*," Cole bellowed from upstairs. His tone held something Tommy didn't immediately recognize, but it was concerning.

Tommy waved over Cuddy to watch the bar.

The door to Jane and Cole's room flew open. Cole burst out of the room, half-hanging off the railing by the time he stopped. This time Tommy couldn't deny the tone in his friend's voice, as the fear was written all over the man's face. "*Tom!*"

Tommy took the stairs two at a time, tearing down the hall until he and Cole practically tripped over each other on their way into the room. "Cole, what the hell?"

Jane hung over a bucket, her draping arm all that supported her. Her stomach heaved until she sagged into silence. For a moment she looked like death warmed over. Then she stirred, but little life returned to her features.

"Fuck."

"Get Charlie or Daisy—whoever the hell you can find. Get help, *now*." Cole rushed back to Jane's side.

Tom didn't wait for an explanation. He spun on his heel and ran back downstairs faster than he'd climbed them, leaping the last few steps. Outside, he tore across the street to pound on the darkened clinics door. Unsurprisingly there was no answer.

He grabbed a horse outside the saloon, and raced toward Charles' house as breakneck speed. Once there, he didn't bother to dismount.

"Charles!" Tommy turned the horse so its back was to the door. "It's Jane. Move!"

The moment he felt the impact of Charlie leaping onto the horse, he spurred the beast on toward town. He'd barely stopped when Charlie leaped off the back, and Tom followed suit, barely stopping to throw the reins back over the hitching post.

Tommy followed Charlie upstairs to the room, but stopped at the door to give Charlie room to work.

"She got real sick." Cole held Jane in his lap, her head drooped to the side. "She couldn't stop. She passed out."

Jane's head bobbed. "I'm…awake…"

"You got up because you threw up again," Cole snapped.

"But I'm—oh." Jane lurched forward before Charlie even had time to start the exam. She dry heaved into the bucket.

Charlie set his hand on the top of her head as Cole rubbed her back. When the heaving slowed, Charlie frowned. "I thought this was getting better."

"I did…too." She took a shaky breath. Her eyes fluttered closed.

Cole looked ready to jump out of his skin when Charlie began his exam. He couldn't seem to decide what to do with his hands as they intermittently reached for Jane and ran through his hair. "She always gets real sick in the morning, first thing. Like this, but she ain't ever passed out when it happened before."

"Jane. Jane, wake up. Look at me." Charlie braced her head between her hands. "Talk to me while I do this. It's easier if you're being a smartass."

She groaned at his vigorous shake. "I hate you."

"I know. Love you too." Charlie pressed on her abdomen. "Are you having pain with it this time?"

"I don't know…I—*ow*."

"Thank you. That's what I needed to know." Charlie propped each eye open, a candle in his hand as he did.

"I still hate you," She muttered again.

Cole set his hand on Jane's back, a cold glare leveled at Charlie. "What the hell are you doing?"

"Keeping her awake so I can figure out the problem." Charlie didn't flinch from Cole's wrath. "Jane. I need to—"

Another groan from Jane left her hanging back over the bucket. Cole held back her hair as she heaved. She gasped, her hand on her belly. "Oh."

"Get her to the clinic—now." Charlie threw his things back in his back. "We've got to stop the vomiting."

Jane sobbed when Cole picked her up, but only collapsed against his chest.

Tommy stepped out of the way to let them pass. He forced himself calm despite his internal panic. When Charlie got to the door, Tommy eyed him. "Charles."

"Get Dr. Pearson."

"I'm on it."

*Every tomorrow has two handles.
We can take hold of it with the handle of
anxiety or the handle of faith.
-Henry Ward Beecher*

Tommy barked, "Would you two knock it off?"

Cole stopped his pacing to glare at Tommy. He noticed Mike did the same just a few feet from himself

"What? The two of you are making me insane with all of that pacing. If Jane could see you, she'd smack you both and tell you to sit your asses down." Tommy glared right back at Cole.

Nick sat stoic as ever, his arms folded across his chest. "By all accounts even when she was a year old it made her nuts."

A bit of humor lit Tommy's features. "That's right. When Mikey was joining us, Clara was putting on a show to beat all shows. Song, dance, I think there was even puppets. Kept us all distracted the whole time Ma was getting that fat head into the world."

Mike kicked him in the leg. Nick leapt from the bench when Tommy retaliated. Nick moved to Cole's side as the two mock-battled in the middle of the waiting room. "I know, it's asinine—but it's what she'd want. She hates—"

"A fuss. Yeah, I know." Cole leaned against the wall, his gaze falling to the door Jane was behind. "She'd have us playing a game or doing anything to keep busy."

"Give!"

"Never!"

"What in heavens?" Kat's voice stilled all action. A second later, soon as Tommy and Mike had seen who it was, they went back to their fight.

Cole sighed. "They're distracting themselves so we don't fuss."

"Distracting themselves from what?" Kat followed Cole's gesture to the exam room door. "What happened? I heard a ruckus at the Inn which woke me. When I saw the lights on down here at the clinic I came straight away."

Cole tried to respond, but couldn't seem to form the words.

Nick took over in his continuing silence. "She became ill. Cole said she couldn't stop vomiting. Charles and Dr. Pearson are working on her now."

Kat stunned Cole by throwing her arms around him in a bracingly tight hug. When she pulled back, she took Cole's hand in hers, a surprisingly warm support to his cold, numb hands. "All right, then. The boys, while obnoxious, have the right idea. We need to be distracted."

"Hey! We're not—oof!"

Cole rolled his eyes when Mike got in a hit during Tommy's distraction. Despite the worries still twisting his heart, their antics and Kat's silent support bolstered him enough to draw a chuckle. Then his mind passed to the earlier incident and he released a sigh. "It might be best if the lot you distracted yourselves elsewhere. Ain't gonna help things with the marshal if he sees you here waiting on word."

"It's the middle of the night," Nick pointed out. "I doubt he'll be by."

"Jane ain't ever that lucky."

"Good point." Tommy straightened as the wrestling settled. "The saloon. Katherine, bring us word. Hate it, but Cole's right."

Kat nodded at the boys as they left. Once they were alone, Kat pulled Cole to a chair. She took the one beside him. "Are you all right?"

"Is she?"

"I'm certain she will be." She set a warm hand on his forearm. "Will you tell me what happened tonight? I saw Marshal Lewis head into the Inn. Talk to me."

"Don't wanna."

"Until Daisy or Charlie comes out of that room, there is nothing else to do. Distraction, remember? Now talk to me."

Cole took a shaky breath and leaned back against the wall. Much as he hated it, she had a point. "I thought she was gonna get herself arrested on her behavior alone. Crazy woman yelled at Lewis, called him a murderer, and fired off her gun."

"I would feign shock, but I'm not certain I can." She sighed. "What in heavens name is she thinking? Does she want to get arrested? Why didn't she lay low?"

"She's tired of hiding. Tired of being a afraid. I get that—but she could lose everything." He dropped forward to rest his forearms on his knees. "I could lose everything."

"It's utterly insane, but maybe it will work. With the exception of her brothers and David—all we've ever known is Jane. All she's ever known is Jane. Perhaps it is just crazy enough to work."

"Maybe."

Kathy let out a deep sigh. Her hand settled on his shoulder, but she said nothing further. They remained in silence as they waited on word.

Soon as the door opened, Cole flew to his feet. "How is she? The baby?"

"They're both fine for now," Daisy said quietly. "We finally got the nausea to subside a bit with some tea."

"What happened?"

"We're not sure." Daisy frowned. "Could be any number of things. Stress. Lack of sleep."

"She sleeps a lot. We ain't always making time, Daisy," Cole snapped. He was getting sick of the insinuation that they did nothing but screw around to the detriment of Jane's health.

"Cole." Kathy set her hand on his back. "Let Daisy finish. She wasn't blaming you."

"I shoulda made her get outta town when I heard about the marshal." Cole's stomach fell to the floor. There had be something he could've done, or could do. "It was too much, wasn't it? I tried to get her to leave, damn stubborn woman."

"It was too much before the marshal arrived." Daisy offered a sad smile. "But we always know Jane is always going—she always has. It could just be the baby. Some women have far worse illness than others for no reason at all. Jane has been violently ill every morning from early on. It could simply be getting worse now."

"But ya got it stopped," Cole said hopefully.

"For now," Daisy concurred in a less than confident tone. "I can't say for how long."

Cole ran his hands through his hair. It was taking everything in his power to not force his way into the room. "How bad is it?"

"The tea is helping, but not enough. She's managed to keep that down, but we can't even offer food without it turning her stomach."

Kat stepped forward. "How is she now? Can Cole see her now and get the details later? He might prefer that."

He could have kissed Kathy for that suggestion.

"Charlie took her up to a room the back way. She's finally resting, but you're welcome to go up, Cole." Daisy gestured to the stairs. "She's in room three. When she does wake, try to get her to drink some more tea. She's dehydrated and needs as much as she can tolerate."

Cole nodded. "I'll see to it."

"Charlie is experienced with a treatment used to aid cholera patients, but I'd prefer we get her eating and drinking on her own. It's much safer. Go on up and see her."

Cole hesitated long enough to glance at Kat. "The Young boys."

"I'll handle them," Kat said without hesitation. "Don't you worry about anything but Jane. Let her know I'll be by in the morning with Lizzie. For now, she needs rest."

"Thanks." Cole tore up the steps. The second he reached room three, though, he stopped in the doorway. Inside, Charlie adjusted the blankets and fiddled with a cup of tea. Cole cleared his throat. "She don't want no fussing."

"Too bad." Charlie straightened the sheet again before he turned to Cole. "She's going to have to get used to it. Until she starts eating and drinking like a normal human being again, she's going to get fussed over."

Cole sat next to the bed and brushed his fingers along her brow line. "Daisy said she's dehydrated. Needs to drink and—ah, hell."

"Right now rest and as much tea as we can get into her is the best we can do for her. If we don't get her better off by tomorrow evening I'll be trying a different treatment."

"What's that?"

"I'll inject fluid directly into her vein with a syringe."

Cole's stomach flipped. He looked at Charlie like the man was insane. "What the hell do you mean?"

"It is a newer treatment, one that's still in development. I learned it when I was treating cholera patients." Charlie's brow furrowed. "It does not help in every case—but I have used it before with moderate success."

"Moderate." Cole shook his head. "That don't sound real positive. You gotta give me more than that."

"If the tea doesn't work, it may be the only thing that'll save the baby."

Cole's heart stopped and his mouth went dry. He grasped Jane's hand, his head dropping. "It ain't just hurting her."

"No. Not by any means." Charlie adjusted her covers again. "She's not eating enough, and from what I can see she's lost weight instead of gaining. When you're pregnant, you're supposed to gain weight."

Cole rested his forehead against the back of her hand. Unable to speak, he took a ragged breath and tried to take in everything Charlie had said.

"She was bleeding tonight. Not a lot—but it's a warning sign. Things could get much worse if we don't get her eating and drinking again."

After several long minutes, Cole forced himself to lift his head. The weight of everything Charlie said dragged him down until he didn't know if he could be strong for her. He'd failed her once two years ago because he couldn't handle the pain and loss. Somehow this time he had to be strong enough, no matter what happened. She couldn't lose another one, she just couldn't.

"Try to get a few sips down every time she wakes. It's going to be a long night, but if you need help you know we're all here."

"Right." Cole couldn't manage more than a word in front of Charlie.

Charlie seemed to get the idea and slipped from the room without another word.

Cole didn't dare focus on his weakness, not right then. "Tom's gonna have your head. You promised him you wouldn't scare him again tonight. Then ya had to go and do this." With a sigh he rose and stretched out on the bed next to her.

He curled against her and ran his hand along her arm gently as she slept. With time he started to doze, but jumped awake every time she moved. A couple of hours later he startled when she turned toward him. When her eyes fluttered open, he propped himself up on his elbow. "Hey."

"Hey."

Concern made his stomach churn, but Cole pushed it back. He brushed his finger along her cheek. "How are you feeling?"

"Like I could get sick all over you—but I won't." She closed her eyes and sighed. A moment later she opened her eyes again and smiled sadly. "I'm not giving up. Don't you go giving up on me."

"You gotta do whatever they say."

"I know." She set her hand on his. "Including trying to keep down any liquid I can."

"Right now."

"I know. Will you help me sit?" She didn't fight when he picked her up slow and set her back down in a sitting position rather than help her sit. After a few deep breaths she managed to nod. "All right. I should try now. Then I want to sleep again."

Cole hopped off the bed and poured a fresh cup of tea, but only filled it halfway. When he returned to the bed, she took it and stared like it was filled with animal remains instead of tea. "Just a sip, please."

"I will. I need a minute." She patted the bed next to her. "Sit, talk to me, please. Distract me. Don't jostle, I'm already queasy."

He sat as slow as he could beside her. "The docs say you gotta eat more. Drink lots of tea. And you gotta stop worrying about everything."

"Easier said than done." She took a sip. Her nose wrinkled and she closed her eyes, but didn't lose control. After a few moments she opened her eyes. "There's too much to worry about."

"Tom'll help with them investors. The Inn will get fixed real soon. Alma's taken care of until she gets here. You earned some time relaxing."

"You forgot one important thing in any of that."

"We ain't talking about it right now." He knew she meant the marshal. Never mind that Tom would step in the way of any major attempt the marshal made, the threat was still there. More so, the worry over what he would try, or why he cared.

"That won't make it go away."

"Don't care."

She glanced his way and nodded. "All right."

"You should've left when I told you."

"Thought we weren't talking about it."

"Jane."

"I'm sorry."

He kissed the top of her head and sighed. "Promise me you won't go calling him a murderer again. You really weren't looking for his good side."

"I told you, I wanted them out of the room." She took another sip of tea. "It wasn't my smartest move, but I was rather focused."

"You're always focused."

A wicked smirk creased her lips before she drank another sip. "I promise to behave. As best as I know how."

He wrapped an arm around her shoulder when she nestled against him. "You do know that ain't saying much."

"It's the best I can do without lying."

"I know." He chuckled. "You'd best apologize to Tom, too. You said you wouldn't scare him again tonight."

"He'll live."

"I'd rather he be in a good mood."

"Just don't lock me in a room." Her tears were clear in her tone, and her hand shook when she took another sip. "If I don't get out I'll go stir crazy and be more stressed than I already am."

"Wouldn't dare lock you up. You'd kill me."

She lowered the tea cup to her lap. At his grunt, she sighed. "Give me a few minutes. I'll try again. There isn't much left."

He ran his fingers along her arm gently and let her rest against him for a few minutes. Another wave of fear hit him so hard he had to close his eyes. His heart beat a rapid cadence against his ribs and he pulled her close against him.

"I promise." She sniffled and nestled close. "Whatever they say. I don't want to lose our baby. Not again. It can't happen again."

When she starting sobbing into his chest, he grabbed the tea from her lap. He managed to set it aside and draw her closer. His own breathing grew ragged, and he didn't dare speak for fear his own voice would crack, or worse his words wouldn't be enough comfort.

Her breath came in short hiccups and she clung to his shirt. She shook her head against his chest. "Not again."

"Not again," he said in quiet agreement. "We ain't gonna let it."

"I love you. I meant what I said tonight. I'm fighting—for my life, and for the baby—for us."

"I love you too. And you're not fighting alone. I ain't ever letting you fight alone."

"That's what married people do."

"Damn straight, Mrs. Mitchell."

*There is in every true woman's heart, a spark
of heavenly fire, which lies dormant in the
broad daylight of prosperity, but which kindles
up in the dark hour of adversity.
—Washington Irving*

Everything hurt when Jane edged toward consciousness again. Her mouth felt as though she'd been chewing on cotton. A mix of headache and dizziness made her head swim. She groaned, setting her hand to her forehead, not that it helped with the sensation. Amidst all the aches and pains a bitter smell tickled her nose until she either wanted to sneeze or heave over a bucket again.

"Good morning," David spoke low from beside the bed.

Jane wrinkled her nose. "That would depend on how you define 'good'."

"Well, you are alive. That's good."

"That's debatable."

"What is? That you're alive? Or that it's good?"

"Yes." She turned her head toward his chuckle. A few blinks were required to clear her fuzzy view of him. "I thought Kat was here."

"She was. I came to sit for a spell, so she could go and check on the library for you." David leaned on his knees so they were eye to eye. "Plus, I brought something for you. Though you must promise to not dismiss it because of the source."

She quirked a brow in annoyance at the suggestion. However the immediate spike in her headache made her drop the gesture almost immediately. "That does not sound promising."

"I went to see Black Moon this morning."

She groaned against the mention of his native friend. A stirring in her stomach made her close her eyes to stem the nausea from flaring too strong.

"Jane. If the mix of herbs he gave me for you helps you get better, isn't that all that matters? You took the tea at your hanging."

"I was dying then."

"Don't you feel like you're dying now?"

"I suppose." She'd tried to be flippant, but her voice cracked. Try though she might to be strong, the idea of not just herself, but the baby dying as well was far too prevalent.

"I'm well aware you don't care much for my Cheyenne friend or Indians in general, but this could help you."

"This? Do you mean whatever that vile thing I smell is?"

"I'm afraid it won't be the tastiest tea you've ever had." His lip curled into a boyish grin she was sure usually melted any fair maiden's heart. "But I know you'd do anything for that baby."

"Using the child against my better senses of smell and taste does not endear me to you, Sheriff." Jane sighed deeply. "Fine. I'll try it. For the baby."

David helped her sit. Once she was, he took the extra step to plump the pillows behind her.

"You enjoy fussing too much," she protested despite her gratitude.

"You're welcome." He offered her the cup of tea.

"Did you clear this with my doctors?" The smell, now that it was right under her nose, turned her delicate stomach right on its head. She had to admit that the question had been a last-ditch effort to get out of having to taste it.

"Of course. You think I'd offer you something without checking? Cole would string me up from the nearest tree if I didn't."

"Damn. A girl could hope." She took a deep, bracing breath before allowing a sip to pass her lips. The flavor exploded the moment it hit her tongue. A hint of licorice mixed with several bitter and sweet flavors she not only couldn't place, but didn't blend well left her wincing. Even the trailing note of mint didn't ease the unpleasant mix of flavor. "Ugh."

"Sorry." He patted her hand.

"This better work. If it doesn't, the moment I am able I'm holding you down and forcing an entire pot of it down your throat." She tried to push aside the flavor because she needed to drink more to see if it helped. "Come to think of it, I might do that anyway. I think you're enjoying this."

"I'm not enjoying your pain, I promise." He grinned. "On the other hand, your reaction to the tea is a source of great amusement."

She forced herself to take another sip. While the taste was vile, she was sad to note that unlike the tea she'd been drinking through the night, this one didn't make her stomach lurch the moment it made it there. "I pray that I am able to become immune to the taste of this if it does work. It's cruel for this to be the only thing I'm able to drink. Purely cruel."

"Hopefully with enough time and tea you can counter it with real food and drink."

"I would like to be able to eat again—and not just at supper as I have been doing."

"I think your doctors would prefer that too. I overheard Daisy fretting about you downstairs."

"I do hate fretting and fussing."

David chuckled low. "We are all well aware. Think of it this way. We aren't fretting over you, we're fretting over the baby. Does that help?"

"No." She swallowed more tea with a grimace. "I'm fairly certain I haven't got any choice in the matter, though."

"You really don't."

She stuck her tongue out at him. Immature as it was, the fact he'd brought the wicked concoction didn't aid her maturity. After another large swig of the tea, she set the empty mug down. "There. A whole half cup."

"How are you feeling?"

"Still quite nauseous." She leaned her head against the wall. "However I don't feel the urge to void my stomach of the vile liquid so I suppose that is progress."

"Loathed as you are to admit it, right?"

"Most definitely." She managed a smile. "Now that you're done tormenting me."

"I think you deserved it after the stunt you pulled last night."

If Jane trusted her stomach a bit, she might have laughed. "I was busy, and you interrupted me. I am sorry I handled it poorly, but I cannot hide any longer. If Thomas must use his

Pinkerton magic and connections, then so be it. I'd rather stand on my own merits as Jane Spencer, though. I'm not a criminal. I won't hide as if I was one."

"Fair enough, but keep the Remington at home, will you?" David smiled and patted her hand. "I'm not in the mood to talk Lewis down again."

"What is he doing here anyway? Did you arrest someone I was unaware of?"

"Nothing that required the marshal. I'm not sure why he came." He shrugged. "If it eases your mind any, he's been doing as you asked. I've seen him talking to quite a few townsfolk, from Hammy to Parker Krenshaw."

"I can't only imagine what Parker had to say." She closed her eyes against a burgeoning headache from discussing the stress of the marshal yet again. So much to stress over. Parker's oddly timed arrival, the marshal, and the investors. "Oh!"

"What?"

"I need to ask Thomas to look into Cutler's partner. I don't know why, but he made me rather uneasy yesterday." She opened her eyes again, staring at the ceiling. "I also need to contact Lillian Daugherty. Between the two of us, that little library has become fairly overrun. If she is already thinking about a theater, it wouldn't hurt her to think of a larger building for the library."

"I think you're feeling better. You're talking more like yourself."

"I hate to ask for it, but I should have more of the tea. I am feeling better."

"I'm happy to oblige. Charlie will be thrilled." He poured more tea, handing it off when the cup was half full. "Just half again. You don't want to overdo it."

"I always overdo it. Just ask my family, they'll tell you." She sipped at the tea, cringing at the fresh reminder of the taste. After she'd shuddered away the revulsion, she took another sip. There was a knock at the door, to which she called, "Come in."

"Hey Lou. Well, damn if you don't look better." Tommy's nose wrinkled. "What in blazes is that stench? Is that what you're drinking?"

"Horrible, isn't it?" Jane half smirked, half grimaced. "It tastes worse than it smells, believe it or not. Courtesy of David and his Indian friend. Part of me is convinced David told him to make it vile as possible. Unfortunately for me, not only is it horrendous, it appears to be working, which means I have to drink it."

"If it helps, I guess you do." Tommy glanced at David. "Anything he can do to help with the smell?"

"I wish. Sitting next to this teapot is terrible." David laughed. "Unfortunately, in order to help her she needs a big dose of those plants. It's not pretty."

"The lesser of two evils—either I throw up until I can't function, or I drink the most vile substance known to man." Jane lifted her teacup. "So, cheers."

"Cheers," Tommy agreed. "I'll take a shift now, David. Cole is working and the investors have gone on a tour of the area courtesy of Chauncey. I'm sure Cole will be here in an hour or so."

"All right." David leaned in to kiss her forehead before he rose fully. "Keep drinking as much as you can tolerate. I know you hate being stuck in bed, and you won't get out until you drink and eat."

Jane set her hand on her stomach, a low groan erupting at the idea of food. "One thing at a time. Let me drink first. I'll worry about food later."

Tommy sat next to the bed, a smirk forming. "You're getting your attitude back. That's better than sleeping all the time or vomiting."

"Here, here." Jane toasted again before draining the cup. She set it down, unable to stop her nose from wrinkling. "Blech."

"Cole will be happy. If you need to rest before he gets here, I won't be offended."

"No. I feel like I've slept for a full week." She set her hand on his bandaged arm. "How are you healing?"

"Charlie just changed my bandages. Everything's looking real good. Before you ask, Sally's doing good, too. Her spirits are lifting now that she's able to get out some." Tommy settle back in his chair. "The Inn is coming along, as it was yesterday. I've already started checking on Underwood. He gave me a bad feeling."

"You too? Gosh, I thought I was being oversensitive, but I was going to ask you to check on him myself. She grinned at the number of questions he'd answered before she could ask. "Did I forget to ask anything?"

"Nick is suggesting pushing back his departure."

She sighed softly. "I would love for Nick to remain here longer, but he has a wife waiting back home for him. My legal matters have taken enough of his time."

Tommy leaned close. "Between you and me—he doesn't."

Jane gasped, sitting up straighter at the information. "What? How can that be? A few months ago he sent that piano that was hers."

"Exactly." He quirked a brow. "Not sure if you'd noticed, but Nick likes things particular. It can get under a person's skin something fierce. His wife had enough. Just like mine did, she went back home. I think me asking him to help Graham gave him a good excuse to get on out here."

"So maybe he'll stay?" She smiled, hoping a hesitation lingering in her soul didn't show. Though she loved all of the family that had come to stay, they inadvertently added to a deep pain she didn't dare reveal to them.

"You good?"

"Of course. I think I'd like if he stayed. He and I still have plenty to work out, and there's never enough time on a visit. Apparently I am incapable of living a quiet life, so no visit would ever be long enough."

Tommy guffawed, as she'd hoped. A good diversion from her inner sorrow had been needed. "You sure got that right. You came close for a while, but it didn't last long."

"Not nearly long enough."

Pure and complete sorrow is as impossible as pure and complete joy.
-Leo Nikolaevich Tolstoy

Jane stared at the book in her lap, unable to focus on the page it sat open to. Now that her stomach was feeling better thanks to the repugnant tea, she had little but time on her hands. Time for her mind to race over every single thing that had plagued her for months. For years, even.

She'd shooed Cole from the room so he could work. At least one of them should keep busy, after all. She certainly couldn't. Still, she now wished she had the company.

A timid knock on the door startled her from her reverie. Jane set her book aside and readjusted her seat. "Come in."

The door opened to reveal Sally, looking unsure of herself as she hovered in the doorway. "I hope I ain't disturbin' ya, Miss Jane."

"No, goodness no. I would appreciate a little company. Come on in, Sally."

Sally perched on the edge of the chair like she might bolt at any time. Her hands wrung together in her lap. "I ain't made a decision."

"I don't recall asking." Jane sat her hand on Sally's to still them. "I told you to take your time. I'm in no rush."

"I know." Sally blew out a breath. "Not that it would matter if I left. Nobody'd want a whore like this."

Jane frowned as Sally's fingers brushed over the bandage above her eye. Mild scarring could be seen around the edges. "You are a beautiful girl, and powders can hide a great many flaws, as does alcohol."

"I suppose."

"If it should come to that and you choose to run, please tell me. I will find you a safe place somewhere to work. If you run on your own, who knows what sort of establishment you'd end up in." Jane squeezed her hand before releasing it. "Thomas has been keeping you company, I hear."

Sally's features brightened immediately. "He's been telling stories of his time as a Pinkerton. It's fascinating."

"I imagine it is. I haven't been privy to too many stories of his that don't involve Clara." Jane frowned, turning her attention to her own hands.

"He's been really nice."

"He's as grateful as I am." Jane shook off the melancholy again. What was her problem?

"I just wanted to see how you are." Sally fidgeted again. "I heard you were here."

"I am feeling better, but perhaps a little tired." It wasn't entirely the truth, but she did not want to cause the girl strife by getting lost in her own melancholy. "I would like for you to visit again. Maybe I can share some of my own stories untainted by the gossip of the town. The truth tends to get mucked up as it travels from person to person."

"I think I'd like that."

"Wonderful. Come by tomorrow morning. Though I'm feeling better, I'd bet my rotten brother will force me to stay until I can tolerate solid food."

Sally smiled at the jest. "I think Dr. Young is nice."

"He's not your brother." Jane laughed softly, squeezing Sally's hand. "I'll see you in the morning, then."

"All right." Sally slipped from the still-open door, failing to close it behind her.

Jane leaned back against the pillows again, staring out the window with a deep frown.

"I thought you were feeling better." The rotten brother she'd spoken off made an appearance at her door. Charlie slipped into the seat Sally had abandoned. "Jane?"

"I am. I am." Even she wasn't convinced by her tone.

"Are you ill?"

"No."

Charlie took her hand in his. "Melancholy, then."

"Yes." She could deny it, but why bother? "It's all…"

"You have a lot going on."

"And then a lot more on top of it."

"Do you feel up to walking?" Charlie held out his hand.

"Walking?" Jane sat straighter. "But…you said…"

"You've drank an entire pot of tea today. If you feel you are up to walking, we'll go sit on the back porch where it's quiet, but you can get some fresh air."

"Fresh air? That close to your barn?"

He smirked. "I'll force you to stay in this bed for a week."

"I'll come, I'll come. Goodness, no need to be hateful."

Charlie helped her to her feet, his arm supportive under hers. "If you feel weak at all, please let me know."

"Yes, sir." She allowed him to guide her down the stairs, out the back door of the clinic. The porch was well shaded, and held a small table, a couple of rocking chairs as well as a small bench. She urged him away from the chairs to the bench where they could sit close.

Charlie's gaze was questioning, but he didn't fight her as he sat beside her. "Care to talk about what has you melancholy?"

"Isn't my life enough?"

"Can't argue your point." Charlie wrapped his arm across her shoulders.

She soaked in the comfort, reveling in the silence he allowed her. For several long minutes she simply sat and watched his horse graze through the small paddock. Finally, she steeled her nerves and spoke, "Can I tell you something without judgment?"

"Of course."

"I absolutely hate that anyone Clara knew ever found me sometimes."

He sighed, but offered no argument or judgment. "How so?"

"Because it hurts." Tears welled against her wishes, but she didn't bother to cover them for once. "Every day I can't give you what you want, or hope for. You all look for her. Even when you think you aren't."

"I suppose we do." He met her gaze when she jumped back in surprise "We knew Clara for twenty years before she up and disappeared on us. She was our sister, as much as you are."

"I know you don't mean it, and I do love you all…"

He set his hand on hers. "We know."

"I feel like I can't be me, ever."

"Can I tell you something now?"

She nodded rather than trust her voice.

"I loved Clara, make no mistake about it. She was funny, smart, and on the verge of crazy some days, but she was young. Naïve. Frustratingly, infuriatingly annoying, too." He squeezed her hand. "I didn't admire her like I do you."

Jane lifted her gaze to his.

"Maybe I do look for her in you, I can't deny it—but it's because I miss her, and seeing glimpses of her make me happy." Charlie sighed. "Maybe it isn't fair to you, but I can't help it. Please know I don't do it out of malice or wishing you were not exactly who you are."

"None of us do." Nick's voice startled them both off the bench. He stepped out of the back door. "I didn't mean to eavesdrop."

Jane held her hand over her racing heart. "Nicholas Christopher Young, you about scared me right out of my skin."

In a most unusual turn, an actual smile broke on Nick's face, disappearing as quick as it had appeared. "First I've had the honor of having you shout my full name at me."

"Didn't realize it was an honor," Jane muttered. Hand still to her chest, she sank back on the bench. "You aren't supposed to scare invalids."

"You are not an invalid," Charlie objected. A smile bright on his features led to laughter.

"Perhaps a lunatic, but not an invalid," Nick supplied.

"You are lucky I'm too weak to hit you." Jane couldn't stop her smile, even as she scolded him. "Both of you are terrible."

"It runs in the family," Charlie said drolly.

Jane sighed, leaning back against the wall.

Nick crouched down in front of her, his ever-serious expression leveled at her. "Like Charles, I admit to my own guilt in the matter. As he stated, I also mean no malice. I do not believe any of us wish to cause you pain."

"I know you don't. I know it isn't anything any of you can help." She buried her hands between her knees. "Sometimes I just wish I were where no one knew Clara. I know that isn't fair to you, either. It's actually rather selfish."

"None of us have been where you are. We all remember." Charlie pulled her hand free to grasp it in his. "We cannot imagine the burden of not remembering."

"We are learning to forgive Clara still. Perhaps you need to as well." Nick freed her other hand. "Your continued antagonistic nature toward her cannot be aiding in your attempt to live a life as yourself."

"Everywhere I go, there she is." Jane blew out a gust of air in frustration.

"You do know that she is a part of you." Nick squeezed her hand. "Always will be."

"I do."

Charlie pulled her into a one armed hug best as he could with Nick still holding her hand. "Every one of us needs to forgive her, I think. Nick is right, that includes you, Jane."

"Sounds easier than it is." Jane hugged him back, kissing his cheek. "Sorry I've left my melancholy on your laps."

"What are brothers for?" Nick rose, tugging her into a hug of his own. It was as surprisingly fierce and strong as his smile had been. He held on for several minutes before he released her. He spoke low. "We can forgive her together."

"Yes, please." Jane held out a hand to Charlie, dragging him into the hug as well. Holding them tight, she sighed. "I still hate you, Charles."

Charlie laughed outright, and Nick joined with his own hearty laugh. "It's the curse of being the family doctor. Everyone hates me."

"What's this?" Tommy bellowed. "Why wasn't I invited?

All of them grunted when he all but tackled them in a hug as well.

Jane, Nick, and Charles all complained in unison, "Thomas!"

The laughter resumed in full as all four of them broke into a far-less melancholy conversation filled jokes and barbs enough to lighten any mood—even Jane's lingering melancholy lessened in the bright light of her family's laughter.

*The real fault is to have faults and
not amend them.
-Confucius*

Cole took the last bottle out of the crate to set on the shelf in the newly completed storeroom. Against his better judgment, they'd used credit to restock themselves in liquor and glassware. Jane was sure they'd make up for it in no time, but he was still on edge.

The one upside was that business had picked up again soon as the bar had reopened. If their luck finally managed to turn, they might be able to pay off the credit before the end of the year.

Then again, luck wasn't much on their side lately.

For the moment things were calm. He'd stopped by the clinic to see Jane who, despite the obnoxiously bad smell of her tea, was looking better than she had in weeks. Even her mood had improved over the course of yesterday.

Charlie was optimistic that she might even be able to keep food down at supper for the first time in days. If that happened, she could be allowed to come home the next day.

"Excuse me." An unfamiliar, and oddly polite, crisp voice spoke nearby. "I was looking for Miss Spencer."

"She ain't here," Cuddy replied. As per orders, the man didn't divulge any information to her actual whereabouts.

Those that knew and were friendly with Jane knew she was ill, but if you didn't already know, not a soul in the Inn would tell you.

"Oh, that is a shame. I could not locate her at the library either. I was so hoping to catch her." The stranger sighed. "Perhaps Mr. Mitchell is in?"

"What do ya want?" Cole stepped out of the storeroom, his frown deepening when he realized who the stranger was. None other than Parker Krenshaw. Cole curled his lip at the man. "You're not welcome here."

"I am aware of that fact. I do have something that I believe will be of interest to Miss Spencer, though." Parker wiped his hands nervously on his trousers. "I'm afraid nothing I do can make amends for my uncle's actions."

"Ya got that right."

Parker cleared his throat. "Yes. Yes. I do wish to offer up the contents of his library. Uncle Jackson was not an avid reader, but he found it necessary to fill the library full of books."

"Books? You wanna give Jane books?" Cole narrowed his eyes. He didn't trust the man, and offering Jane books wasn't helping anything. "What's your game?"

"You misunderstand. I have heard that Miss Spencer enjoys reading, as well as her position as the town librarian. I thought she could use the books for the library, or to restore her own shelves after the fire you suffered." Sweat beaded his forehead. "I am not one for confrontation, Mr. Mitchell. I do not wish to cause trouble."

"Well then, you could leave." Cole smirked when Cuddy snorted behind the bar. "Leave here. Leave town. We ain't picky."

"I have considered it, believe me." Parker frowned. "However, I still have to finish closing out my uncle's business ventures and settling his debts. No one else in the family wished to go near his holdings. It fell to me."

"Hear that Cuddy? Even Jack's own family didn't like him." Cole chuckled, his attention going back to Parker. "I'll tell Jane you offered. Don't figure she'll want anything to do with Jack's things. Even if they are books."

"I thought as much. However, there is one book I believe she will be most interested in. I brought it with me." Parker reached into his coat, startling when both Cole and Cuddy set their hands on their weapons. When he slowly withdrew his hand, it held a book. "It's a journal. There were plenty that were horrifying in and of themselves, this particular one I thought would be of great interest to Miss Spencer."

Cole eyed the book as Parker held it out to him, unsure whether to touch it or not. After a moment's debate, he grabbed it.

"The entries begin in July of 1871 and end right before Uncle Jackson's death. You do remember when that happened, I'm sure." Parker dabbed his forehead with his handkerchief. "I know the marshal is in town. He might be interested as well."

"Why didn't they find this when he was killed?" Cole glared at Parker. It didn't add up that these would be found so long after Jackson kicked it. "Schaffer had to go through all the rooms 'cause of the bodies everywhere."

"My uncle had a hidden safe in his bedroom. It was likely overlooked. The safe in his office was shipped directly to me months ago." Parker pocketed his handkerchief. He offered Cole a nod. "I shall leave you to your day. The offer remains if Miss Spencer is interested."

Cole stared at the book in his hands while Parker left. If there was a trick to it, he couldn't see it. Maybe Jane would when he told her.

"Cole!" Tommy called from upstairs. "I need you to come look at this. You gotta make sure they're doing it right."

"Just a minute." Cole shook off his shock best he could. He turned his attention toward Tommy. "What are they messing up now?"

"Just come look." Tom disappeared back behind the door where Jane and Cole's room was being rebuilt. They'd put up the wall leading into the saloon first to help cover the noise of construction. Didn't help much, but it was something.

Cole grumbled in annoyance. He'd rather talk to Jane about the journal first. Still, making sure the room was right and ready to go for her soon as possible was important. He took the stairs two at a time. The list of things that could be wrong ran through his head as he stormed down the hall to the room. He threw open the door, prepared to yell. Instead, he stopped short. "Damn."

Tommy laughed. "Surprise."

"What did ya do?" Cole scanned the room. Something was off, he could tell. It felt bigger.

"We got the walls up, and I wanted to see what I had them do here." He gestured to the wall between their rooms.

"You didn't put the wall back where it was," Cole said in way of acknowledging it, and recognizing that was why the room felt bigger. Now that he focused on it, he could tell that the wall was at least three feet further back than it had been.

"I don't need that much room. I don't entertain whores, and I sure don't have a woman." Tommy shrugged. "Unlike Jane I don't keep my books in my room and I sure don't have the amount of clothes she does. I figured this space could act as a closet. Things were getting out of hand with them nails you were using before the fire."

Cole chuckled, thinking of the wall overstuffed with fabric and lace from before the fire. "That's no joke."

"I think she'll like it. Hopefully she'll be well soon to begin charming the pants off some new investors and she'll get a real closet." Tommy set his hands on his hips. "It's got a ways to go yet."

"We'll need new furniture, and so do you." Cole fronwed at the bare walls. "And shelves. She's got some books Graham saved."

"Speaking of. What's that?"

"Huh? Oh, right." Cole flipped the book in his hand. "Krenshaw stopped by. Said he wanted to offer all the books from Jack's library."

"Well that will stymie her. Chance for all those books, but they were Jackson's?"

"She'll hem and haw for days," Cole agreed.

"Wanna place bets on whether or not she'll take 'em?" Tommy grinned slyly. "I'll give ya ten to one odds."

"Not fool enough to take that bet." Cole chuckled. "Anyhow, Krenshaw said if she didn't want the library, she'd at least want this."

"That so?"

"Says it's a journal. One of a few, I guess. He said this one would be of most interest to Jane."

"Krenshaw's journal, eh? Ought to be as interesting as Jane's were." Tommy frowned around the room at the reminder that Jane's journals had burned in the fire.

"She could rewrite them word for word if she wanted."

"Does she want to, though? What with Lewis sniffing around?"

"More like do any of us want her to with him sniffing around?" Cole didn't need to hear the answer to that, he knew without a doubt they didn't want her to create the rope to hang herself with.

Tommy reached for the book. "I'd be more interested in his ledger. Still, this dates from July of '71. That's only a few months before her hanging."

"And his death."

"Which means, it might have whatever he and Alan did in those last months in here. Hate to say it, but Parker might be right. Jane might be plenty interested in this. So would Lewis."

"Jane gets first dibs." Cole held out his hand. "Then you can have a gander, and then maybe we'll let the marshal see."

"Works for me." Tommy slapped the book back in Cole's hands.

"I'm gonna head to the general store and order that furniture. Sooner we can get Jane in her own place, the better."

"Agreed. Just a bed for me. Dresser survived the fire with nothing but a few char marks."

"Will do."

"And don't drop that book in your room," Tommy called after him. "If you don't take it to Jane straight away, she'll have your hide."

"Think I don't know that?" Cole scoffed. "I'm not an idiot."

"Well, sometimes you are."

"Takes one to know one."

Tommy laughed. "Touché."

"What?" Cole let Tom laugh at him all the way to the door. Outside, he thought he'd take Tom's suggestion to heart. Besides, Jane would want to have a voice in what they ordered for furniture. So instead of heading to Turner's, he cut across the street toward the clinic.

Nobody was at the desk when he went inside, which was unusual. Normally either Daisy or Charlie could be found there. Figuring they had a patient, Cole made for the stairs. Halfway up he heard laughter and lively talk from the direction of Jane's room.

None of the laughter was Jane's, but she was happily chatting. Considering laughter tended to roil her stomach, he wasn't too concerned to not hear her laughter join the others. Kathy was one of them, without a doubt. One of the men was probably Charlie, but the other laughter he couldn't place.

He paused at the doorway of the room, startled at the scene inside. Gathered around the small table sat Jane with Charlie and Kathy as he'd suspected. Also with them was Sally and Nick. Most of them were laughing, and Jane wore a bright expression, her hand on her stomach as though trying to keep from laughing or getting sick.

Even Nick was grinning, which really took Cole by surprise. He'd only ever seen one expression on the man, and even when he talked there was not a change. However, at this point he was laughing with the others.

Jane tapped the paper in front of Charlie. "Keep going. You must finish."

Cole leaned on the doorframe, not willing to interrupt yet as the Charlie returned his pencil to the paper.

"You'd better not let him see," Charlie said between chuckles. "I may be good in a fight, but I wouldn't want to get up against him."

"But he has a sense of humor under that thick skull," Jane protested.

"I don't know," Kathy objected. "I think even Graham's humor could be tested by this."

Sally's laughter continued until she spotted Cole. "Oh."

Jane's head lifted at that, her gaze falling on the door where Cole leaned. "Hello there. I wasn't expecting you back so soon."

"Brung you something. What are you doing?" Cole immediately went to Jane's side, winking at her. "Ain't seen you in such good spirits for a while."

"Charles is amusing us with his skilled artwork." Jane shuffled a few papers, withdrawing a drawing of what was unmistakably Hammy. More of a caricature, the image showed Hammy tilting on a bar stool, a large beer balanced in each hand.

The next she lifted was of herself, nose buried in a book, a scolding finger extended toward him. "He started with a real portrait, but Katherine got him leaning more toward the funnies."

Cole grinned at the images she continued to pass at him.

"Look at Graham," Kathy shrieked the second Charlie stopped drawing.

This time Jane actually laughed, though she groaned when she was actually able to stop. "All right, maybe we shouldn't show that to him."

The image in question was definitely Graham, steaming mad. Literally. The body was puffed up and even thicker than the man himself, and his brow set in deep furrows, mouth in a grimacing snarl. Charlie'd shaded his head like perhaps he'd wanted to make it red, and steam bellowed from the man's ears.

Cole laughed along with the others. "That sure looks like him when he'd madder than hell."

"I've seen it enough to concur," Jane muttered. Still, her smile remained in place, but her eyes drifted to the book still in Cole's hand. "What's that?"

Cole gestured with his head toward the hall so the others could enjoy their fun.

Jane didn't argue, slipping ahead of him to get to the hall first. "Did you bring me something?"

"It was brought to the Inn for you." Cole held it out to her. "A gift from Parker Krenshaw."

All humor left her face, and she even took a step back. "Krenshaw?"

"He came by, wanted to offer you the contents of Jack's library."

A wild excitement crossed her features before it disappeared behind another frown. "Oh. Dear. What a conundrum."

"Tom and I figured you'd have trouble with that."

"The library is so full already."

"But you lost a lot of books."

"Having books in my room that have been in Jackson's, though." She shuddered. "I'll have to think about that."

Cole offered the journal to her. "Parker thought you'd be interested in this. It's Jack's."

She took it delicately between two fingers, her nose wrinkled. After a moment's debate, she flipped it open. Her eyes scanned the page, and then the next so quick he doubted she could have read it that fast.

Still, she flipped from page to page, until nearly halfway through. "Oh."

He grabbed her elbows when she swayed on the spot. "Jane?"

"The judge. The jury. His Pinkerton and the information he had on Clara was…extensive. Too extensive to be mere coincidence. And…"

Cole waited her out several minutes before he lost patience. "And what?"

"I believe he called Alan by the name of Elmer. The references to him start at the beginning of the journal. Alan was spying on me far longer than I realized. He was here, in camp." Another shudder coursed through her.

"Let's get ya sitting. You read it that fast?"

"Not entirely. I skimmed past the references of his whores and business dealings. I'm honestly surprised he got away with writing anything about Alan. Perhaps he hid it every time he wrote." She followed him into an empty room, sinking onto the chair he guided her into.

"It ain't happening anymore," he tried to soothe her. "They're both gone."

"It's like I returned the second I read any of this." Jane turned her gaze on him. "I'm all right, it was just a surprise."

"If you're sure."

"I am."

"Good."

She closed the book carefully. "I will read it more carefully later when things have quieted. What else did Parker have to say?"

"There were more of those." Cole pointed to the journal. "He just thought this one would be most interesting to you. That and the library is all. He's a nervous Nellie."

"If he's been reading his uncle's journals, I imagine he is. Then again, face to face with you in a snit could add to it as well."

"I don't like him. It weren't a snit."

"Of course it wasn't." A genuine smile crossed her lips.

He couldn't help himself, he leaned in and kissed her deep and slow.

She pouted when he pulled away. "That was not fair. I am not well enough to play."

"Wasn't fair to me either, then." He chuckled low. "Couldn't resist. Ain't seen a real smile in days. Had to catch it while I could."

"Caught it, you did." Her smile faltered for the briefest flicker before settling back in place.

"Need your tea again?"

"No, please, no. I'm trying to go as long as I can between cups. I dream of the day I no longer have to drink it in order to survive."

"Had any luck with food today?"

"I kept down some soup. Charles is insisting I try something more solid after a turn. We are starting with some bread."

"Think you can manage a walk with me?"

"I'd need more tea first, but perhaps we can get an agreement from my brother."

"He seems in an agreeable mood." Cole glanced toward the door when more laughter reached them from next door. "And Nick smiles?"

"I know, it's odd isn't it? I thought his ever-stoic expression was disturbing. It may be more disturbing to learn he can truly smile. The talk we had yesterday seemed to help greatly. For all of us, I think."

"You're getting along with Charlie better."

"I am." She set her hand on his. "Telling them how I felt about always being searched for Clara bothered me seemed to help us both. Nick as well."

"Good."

"Now what is it you wish to make me walk for?"

"Thought we'd pick some furniture for our room. They got the walls back up today."

"That's wonderful. I'm looking forward to moving back into our room."

"That all you're looking forward to?"

"No. Not even a little bit." A sly smile curved her lips. "If I continue to feel better, I do look forward to enjoying you as often as our child will allow me to."

"That kid better be real accommodating. I didn't agree to celibacy."

"Neither of us did." She laughed a soft husky laugh that didn't falter once.

"Now you're the one not playing fair."

"Turnabout is fair play, Mr. Mitchell."

"I'll remember that."

"I pray you do."

*With the past I have nothing to do;
nor with the future.
I live now.
-Ralph Waldo Emerson*

Jane sipped her vile tea as the restaurant hummed with activity around her. To avoid conversation that might weaken her resolve to keep her food down, she'd taken a table near the back. So far the plan had worked and she'd been blissfully alone for nearly five minutes.

In front of her sat the journal Parker Krenshaw had left for her. She'd read it twice already, and therefore had no further use for it. Still, she stared at the cover.

On the on hand, she no longer cared. The past had happened, it was gone. All that mattered now was her life as it stood. Then again, some of the entries still nagged at her thoughts.

Jackson appeared quite disturbed based on his writing. At one time she'd believed the worst thing about him was a bloated ego, but the man had delusions of grandeur. There was also the matter of the whores he'd had brought in to abuse quite often. Once a month when they'd been reached by stage only, once a week upon arrival of the train.

She shuddered at the descriptions of his acts toward those women. Though she'd tried to skim over them fast, her mind had retained them anyhow. No wonder Parker had hinted to Cole that the rest of the journals were quite disturbing. If this one book that spanned only six months was any indication, she could only imagine. All along she'd believed Alan was the only crazy one. Turned out two crazy men had met, and the end result was the destruction of three lives.

The notes on the bribery of the judge in her case were no surprise to Jane. She, and everyone close to her, had figured out the judge had been bribed early on. Still, she would hand off the book to Marshal Lewis, as he now approached her table.

Lewis leaned on the back of the chair opposite her. "I know the truth."

Jane stared at the plate of food she'd been pecking at. Any hint of appetite she'd thought she might possess flittered away. When she lifted her head, she noted several heads had turned their way. She cleared her throat. "Marshal Lewis."

"Mind if I join you?"

She gestured to the chair he'd been leaning on. All too aware of every stare and some murmured conversations, she sighed. After several rough nights in the clinic, and far too much time locked away, she'd been released with a large box of the tea Black Moon had made for her, and she'd been drinking it religiously in order to function.

At least she was managing to keep small amounts of food down and her nausea only reared its head a few times a day, so long as she kept drinking. Cole had 'allowed' her to come to Turner's for the simple reason that he knew there'd be several watchful eyes on her.

She pushed away the plate of food, her appetite securely dissipated.

"I've done a bit of research on you. Several interesting facts arose."

"Such as?"

"The most interesting bit of news is that your name isn't exactly Miss Jane Spencer."

"Marshal."

He leaned forward, his voice dropping low. "The legal owners of The Hangman's Inn are Cole Mitchell and Jane Mitchell."

"Shh." Even though he'd been quiet, Jane held up her hand. Tension raced through her in the worry that someone had overheard. "That is a private matter."

"Why? To what end would that need to be a secret?"

"As I said, it is a private matter. We prefer to leave it that way."

"Couldn't find much else about you legally. Seems before you came to Dominion Falls, you didn't exist."

"Many people didn't exist before if you really care to look into matters. Small families on claims, fires or storms claiming entire towns; there are so many reasons for there to be no legal records." Jane swallowed down the last of her tea to stop the fresh churning of her stomach. As it settled, she leaned back in her chair.

"Do you have an answer for everything?"

"I try to."

He studied her intently for several long seconds. A flicker of what she dared to call concern flew across his brow before it smoothed back out. "Are you well?"

"Truth be told, not very, but it is tolerable for the moment. If I happen to excuse myself, do not think it is your presence or your questions. While you have been trying to tear me down, I have been in the clinic dealing with illness."

"You believe I wish to tear you down?"

"If you do not, what is it that you wish?"

"I wish to know the truth."

"To what end?" Jane held his gaze, trying to determine his motive. "Do you want to put me in a noose and pull the lever yourself? Do you want to know what that feels like? Putting to death someone that has not committed a crime? You hardly seem the type. You aren't the type to take a bribe, or to hang an innocent man. I would hope what you did to Clara was circumstance and a bribed judge, not a cold man."

"To Clara? Or to you?"

"What do you want?"

He adjusted his hat and frowned. "I want justice."

"For whom? A man long dead? A man for whom not a soul mourned or became worse off for his death?"

"I want to know justice was dealt."

"'Justice is a temporary thing that must at last come to an end; but the conscious is eternal and will never die'. Martin Luther." She folded her arms across her chest. "My conscience is clear. I would ask if yours is."

"I'd like it to be."

"Has justice not been dealt already? Is this search you are on nothing more than a witch-hunt with no purpose but to assuage your ego?"

"Justice has only been dealt if Clara Young's sentence was truly carried out."

"You were there when it was."

"Yet you are here."

"Clara Young died. She died long before you watched her swing and looked over her cold body to ensure her end."

Lewis narrowed his eyes. Lips pursed, he held his silence.

"Walk with me, Marshal." Jane broke the silence without worry. She rose to leave.

"You said you were ill."

"And we have a dozen pairs of eyes staring at us, and several of the people connected to them have moved within earshot." She glanced pointedly at Hammy, who flushed and turned back to his plate. "Unless you enjoy having our conversation eavesdropped on, we walk."

Lewis stood. "As you wish."

Jane grabbed the book from the table. On her way to the door she paused by Hammy. She set her hand on the old man's shoulder. "You are as subtle as a bull in a china shop, Mr. Hamm. You need to work on that."

Lewis didn't speak as Hammy mumbled his apology. The apology complete, Lewis gestured for Jane to lead the way. She led him from Turner's and down the steps. Rather than head down the main thoroughfare, she led him on the slower, undeveloped, Second Street toward the depot.

Once they'd passed the depot and approached the meadow, Jane finally spoke, "I'm assuming you've reread the letters Clara sent her brother." She set her hand on her stomach in hopes it would stem the burgeoning nausea brought on by the walk and her own nerves.

"In truth, this is the first I have read most of them. I was only shown a few key letters when I came to town for

Bingham, most likely by design. This time Sheriff Schaffer gave me the entire trunk that once belonged to Clara."

"She was painfully obtuse. Ignorant. Selfish. Prideful. Deeply wounded. She specialized in quite a few of the deadliest sins—pride, avarice, envy, wrath, and she even managed to touch on sloth through the ignorance of her own mind."

"Harsh judgments."

"I've had time to consider her in detail," Jane admitted. "And I might be harsher than others considering, like you, many have judged me using her as a yardstick."

"Are you none of those things?"

"I struggle with pride, I admit—and I'm quite attached to lust, but I try to avoid the others with varying levels of success. I see no reason for envy or greed. Wrath has its place, and I might have faltered once or twice there. Sloth, in and of itself, is a pointless pursuit—I could never remain still in body, mind, or soul to let myself waste away. And gluttony? Well, there is one appetite I would be considered gluttonous with, and it ties in with lust—but in truth only talk makes me as gluttonous as you might believe."

He glanced sideways at her. "You say Clara died long before her hanging. Do you mean when she fell off the train and became—you?"

"Where to begin?" She slowed her pace to sit on a bench at the end of the meadow. With the journal in her lap, she stared into the wildflowers as they'd clue her in on how to address the matter.

"It's often been said that the beginning is a good place to start."

"If you insist. She died when she was raped at fifteen by one of her own students. She died when she left home rather than embrace her brothers help in such matters, and every unwelcome advance of a male killed her a little more." She sighed deeply at the idea of all the transgressions against Clara. "I believe her relationship with David restored her to life again. She released those past pains and embraced his love completely, but she had unreasonable expectations."

"Such as?"

"That his love would protect her from any and all harm. And so, when that Indian raped her again in her own marriage bed, she died more deeply than she ever had before. It changed her in a way nothing had before. You can see it in her letters. There was a physical transformation in the way the letters were written, their tone, their depth. The secrets began then, the code she used to pour out her grief, to hide who she really was."

He turned to face her more fully. "It was when she first began to lie."

"Goodness, no. She'd lied before then, but this time it was different." Her fingers fidgeted on top of the journal, unable to conceal all the pain she felt still facing Clara's past. "Clara died when her child was born. When he was born and she barely lived through it. When she didn't know if the child lived, or what he looked like, or even if it was a boy or a girl—that's when the questions began. Still, she couldn't see past her own ignorance to learn the truth."

Jane shook her head, unable to stop her eyes from closing at a fresh well of tears. She blinked them away so she could continue. "She died when she realized the depth of the lies she'd been living, and again when she learned the truth about her son and how she'd taken him from his father. And once again when he tried to drive the final nail in her coffin by throwing her off that train."

"And then she became you."

"No." She finally met his gaze. "Who am I?"

"You tell me."

"I have. Numerous times. Numerous ways. It's your turn. You have all of the facts. You've spoken to just about everyone in this town. Word gets around, and even in the clinic I heard of your questions. You have the truth."

He scratched his chin, his gaze drifting to the wildflowers. "Are you trying to weasel out of a proper confession?"

"Confession? Of what? I have nothing to confess. I told you, my conscience is clear. I am who I am. Who I have always been as long as I can remember."

"That's a handy way to word it."

She set her jaw in determination against the rising anger and turning of her stomach. "I will say it again. Who am I? What have you learned of me in this time of searching and questioning?"

"You're a woman everyone seems to know."

"I'm friendly."

He quirked a brow. "That might be a stretch."

Unable to stop the corners of her mouth from twitching, she chose to allow the smile rather than fight it. "I run the library and the brothel. I get saints and sinners in each of those doors. All kinds, and I accept them all. I would hope they do the same for me, whether they see me as a saint or a sinner."

"Reverend Green sees you as a sinning saint."

"Sounds about right." Jane laughed, her hand flying to her stomach when it churned in response to her mirth. "We have many discussions on our drives out to the settlement. He finds my honesty both refreshing and disturbing. I find him an exceedingly good man."

"You contracted scarlet fever trying to help a family stay on its feet when the mines slowed earlier this year. When they perished and left a child, you apparently had designs on adopting the young girl yourself." He paused when she found herself wiping at tear at the mention of Lizzie. "Not everyone appreciates the way you live your life—and yet even those that don't still stand by your claim."

"You still have not answered my question. Who am I?"

"Jane Mitchell."

"Spencer," She corrected with a smile. "Only two people are allowed to call me by my married name, and you are not one of them."

"I'll keep that in mind."

"Thank you. Are you done with me?"

"It would appear that I am, for the time being. I still feel as though I don't have the whole truth. However, there's no legal proof of any crime, and I'm not looking for any. All I've seen that Jane Spencer is guilty of is occasionally poor judgment."

"Thank goodness. You were really getting on my nerves."

His brow furrowed in frustration. "All of this, all I've done the past week, and this was never anything more than an inconvenience to you, was it?"

"It really wasn't. I knew who I was—I was simply waiting for you to realize it as well. Men are usually more thick-skulled but knowing that does not make it less annoying."

"Do you even realize who you're speaking to? I could change my stance and insist on that last bit of truth, and make this more difficult than a simple annoyance."

"You probably could, although I have a feeling you've received threats and assurances from Thomas Young that you would not win." His silence to her statement spoke volumes. She shrugged. "Even without those, I don't think you would anyway."

"You aren't afraid of anything, are you?"

"On the contrary." Jane bit the inside of her cheeks when the question stimulated to life the multitude of fears in her head. There was a great pregnant pause as she collected herself. Once she did that, she continued, "I'm afraid of everything. I try to not let my fear run me. I use it for strength. Without it I would not have anything that I have now."

"It's a good mind-set to have, if you can keep it."

"Not always—but I do as I can most days, and some days I handle it very well." She pursed her lips, focused on the town a short distance away. The question she'd had since his arrival nagged at her, and had yet to be answered. "I must ask to sate my curiosity. What brought you to Dominion Falls? There was no criminal in jail for you to take to another location, no crime with a manhunt within the immediate vicinity."

"It was suggested that if I made a surprise visit, I might find something interesting. And I did."

"I see." Another 'suggested' complication to her life. She was truly getting rather tired of people nudging trouble into her path.

"Was there anything else?"

"Two things. First, this. I have no need for it any longer and it makes me quite ill to have read it and remember as I do. This alone makes me wish I had the capacity to forget some of the things I have read." She handed him Krenshaw's journal. "It was suggested to me that I would be interested in the entries, and also that you might. Parker Krenshaw found his uncle's journals in a secret safe on the property."

Lewis turned the journal over in his hands. "You've read it. Will I find it interesting?"

"There is a good probability that you will. I believe Parker has more with even more interesting tidbits that I have no care to know. I'd prefer to be done with the past."

"I'm sure you would."

"One other thing. As I said, I have two." Jane sidestepped the statement as her stomach performed a sickening flop. Without a doubt she would need more tea very soon. "How long will you remain in town?"

"I hadn't decided." He tapped the book with his thumb before he turned his attention back to her. "I had no real business here otherwise, although now I'm curious about the journals. I do have other regions to visit."

"I would like to ask that you remain in Dominion Falls a few more days. Use the excuse of Jackson's journals if you must." She smiled brightly to ease the jibe in her next words. "Or you could consider it a favor to me to make up for the annoyance and disruption you have caused in my life."

He laughed. "That is the most absurd reason—I can't turn it down."

"It is not absurd."

"Would you give me the real reason?"

"In the interest of honesty, and necessity, I will. You do, after all, need to know the reason so you know what I'm looking for." She flinched, unable to stop her nose from wrinkling as bile rose in her stomach. "But I must ask you to walk with me again. If I may, I shall require your arm for support. I need to return home to acquire more tea, until then my steps could falter at any time."

"Certainly." Lewis rose, offering her his arm.

Jane leaned into his arm for support as her stomach took a turn for the worse the moment she was on the move again. On the way back toward town she described all that had been occurring at the inn. She filled him in on every detail, including the surprise visits of the investors and himself.

Up to and including Tommy's efforts to locate Warren, the whores' use of opium and the pregnancy and, of course, the fire. As she concluded, she suggested that they could use his assistance gaining more information. "I hope you and Tom can find a way to work together on this," She said as they arrived at the Inn where Cole stood on the porch, his jaw hanging open.

"I'll see what I can do." Lewis patted her hand. "Get on with your day, Miss Spencer."

"Thank you, Marshal." Jane reached for Cole's hand and squeezed it to draw his attention. "Would you help me upstairs? I'm not feeling well."

Cole shook his head and turned his gaze on her. "What?"

"I asked if you'd help me. I've made it almost thirty minutes without tea, but I'll need some very soon." Jane stepped onto the porch and leaned against the post.

"Oh. Yeah." His arm went around her waist. He guided her inside, not saying another word.

When he slowed to a stop inside, she furrowed her brow and looked up. All around the saloon, from Tommy to Iris, and every single customer, all eyes were on her with a mixture of fear and blatant curiosity.

She smiled and squeezed Cole's hand. "He won't be asking any further questions about Clara, or me. I believe it's over. A round of drinks on the house, Tom."

As a small cheer went up and Tom started pouring, Cole shook his head. "How in hell did you do it?"

"This time I did nothing. I've been violently ill, remember? This was all of them, the people in this town. Now please, take me upstairs." For once she didn't protest when he scooped her into his arms. She wrapped his arms around his neck and leaned against him.

He got her to their room and set her on the bed with gentle care. "Want your tea?"

"Want? No." She grimaced. "Need? Yes."

He smirked and winked. "That's what I meant."

Before he had managed to get up to start the water, a knock came on the door. Iris stood at the threshold with a teacup in her hand.

"Thanks, Iris." Cole crossed the room to grab it.

Jane smiled at the woman. "Thank you, Iris. I appreciate it."

Iris shrugged, and for a fleeting moment Jane thought the woman glared at her. Then a smile graced the older whore's features and Jane brushed it off as her imagination. "Congratulations, Janey. Glad you'll be stickin' around. He ain't tolerable without ya."

Jane chuckled when Cole did. "I know. Thank you."

Cole gave her the tea and sat on the edge of the bed. Once the door had closed and Iris' footsteps faded away he set his hand on her leg. "You sure it's over."

"He says I'm Jane Mitchell."

"What?"

"Well, he was searching legal channels. I guess when you search hard enough, you're going to find it. Nick did change it for us legally." She took another sip of tea, managing to not wince at the flavor. "He's no longer looking to harm me. In fact, I've asked him to stay in town for a few days to help us."

"How so?"

"Someone did set fire to this place. We have the investors, and Tommy and I both agree—Cutler seems earnest, but there's something off about Underwood. I've asked Marshal Lewis to do some digging for me and assist Tom how he can in finding answers. Maybe they'll find a connection between Underwood and Warren."

He shook his head. "How do ya do it?"

"I'm honest."

"To a fault."

"Most definitely."

Hope is the companion of power, and mother of success; for who so hopes strongly has within him the gift of miracles.
-Samuel Smiles

Jane's toes beat and impatient cadence on the floor. Cole made her sit on the bed and wait while he worked next door. Anxiety crawled through her already uneasy belly and up the length of her spine. For three days Cole and Thomas had been bustling about in secretive meetings and exchanges she hadn't been privy to.

While she understood they were trying to ensure she wasn't upset by anything, or stressed, or bustling about when she was supposed to be resting—they were driving her to the brink of insanity with curiosity.

The worst thing they'd done yet had been to tell her to remain in her room for the past hour, after making her stay out of the Inn and under the watchful eye of Kat all morning. She had no idea what they were doing, but the banging and racket in the next room did nothing to sate her rampant interest in the events of the nearby rooms.

The door flew open, revealing Cole sporting a giant grin. "You ready?"

"Damn it, Cole. I've been ready for three whole days. What in heavens name are you and Thomas up to? I swear, you are the worst at being secretive ever."

He chuckled. "Says you, but you still don't know what's going on. You're about to get the first surprise anyhow. The rest will have to wait until after lunch."

"Oh my word, you are going to be the death of me."

"You bet. Now close your eyes."

"What?"

"You heard me. Do it." His hand slipped under her elbow to help her stand. "Don't you worry none, I ain't gonna push you off the balcony or nothing."

"How reassuring. Must I really close my eyes?"

"If you want your surprise, yeah."

"Oh, for goodness sakes." After a long-suffering sigh, she obliged him. "There."

"See? It isn't so hard. You just gotta trust me."

"Says the man making me do this ridiculous exercise."

He led her from the room. While there's been plenty of banging and yelling minutes ago, now a silence hung in the air around them.

A few steps down the hall, a door creaked open. He pushed her forward two more steps. "All right. Now you can open your eyes."

"Are you sure?"

"Open your damn eyes."

After a chuckle of her own, she did just that. The moment her eyes opened, she gasped out loud. "Oh. My."

Along the opposite wall sat a large, heavy bed. The walls above it were lined with shelves that held her books, as well as many from Jackson's library displayed among them, with room for even more if she desired.

She drew close to the bed. On the wall above the headboard was a framed picture. Taken the day of their wedding in Denver, it had been framed and now sat displayed prominently. Under the shelves at the foot of their bed stood a dresser with Cole's box of mementos set in the corner. Across from the dresser a large sheet draped across the wall.

"What's this?" She lifted the sheet. Underneath the full expanse of the wall had been dotted with nails. The width was enough for their trunks. "My goodness. Space for our trunks, and all of those nails for clothes."

"That was Tom's idea." Cole leaned on the dresser between the sheet and the door. "He figured you liked clothes so much, and it was a mess before. He gave up part of his room to make it happen."

"He didn't need to do that, but I am so pleased he did. The mess in here always did bother me, I just had no room to put it all." She dropped the sheet to turn her attention back to the room. Many personal touches were missing, now gone in the fire, or a few in the room they'd been using. The room was lovely, though, and far more open than it had been before.

Most notably, the wall that she now realized she'd blindly thought was part of the room was gone. No longer was their bed blocked from view when you opened the door. The room felt so much larger than it had been. "Where did that wall go?"

"It was empty space. I put it in soon as I bought the place. Didn't like anyone in here, ya know. Plus, like your brother said, I didn't need it. No one came in here before with or without it."

"You're saying that all this time I could have had a closet there and didn't know it?"

"Closets are frivolous."

She laughed, unable to stop her gesture toward the sheet. "And yet, you've made a pseudo-closet here, and before that my clothes were taking up half the room, as were the trunks."

"Yeah."

She shook her head at him, grinning through her annoyance. Turning her attention back to the room, she noticed the elegant table sitting under the window with a pitcher and basin on top. A small vanity wth a mirror sat between it and the closet space. The dresser Cole leaned on was nice and tall, and had a mirror on it as well.

"It's all so lovely." Jane sighed, beginning to feel overwhelmed by it all. "How did you manage it?"

"Some of it was your brother for a wedding present."

"No. Thomas gave us the bar. He'd better not have."

"Not that brother. Nick."

Jane gasped, tears filling her eyes. "Nick? You aren't serious?"

"The dresser and that vanity and the basin are from his house in New York. I woulda never picked nothing this fancy. He bought the desk to match." Cole shrugged. "I woulda argued because you helped pick furniture, but he insisted. The bed, well you know we needed that."

She set her hand on the footboard. "Solid oak. This isn't the one we picked out. It was far too expensive."

"Put it on credit at Turner's. Didn't want to go breaking another bed."

"No, we certainly didn't." Her heart swelled at all he'd done, and how he'd worked so hard to surprise her with it. "Oh, Cole. I would have been happy with a mattress on the floor and a nail on the wall."

"I know."

"No wonder you haven't let me in here for days and days."

He wrapped his arm around her waist the second she swayed. She was guided to the bed quietly. He sat beside her. "Wanted to surprise you. You're the one that made it a home. I wanted to give that back to you."

"It's perfect. Just in time, too. Alma will be here tomorrow."

"Tom said he'd have the girls working on the room we were in soon as I brung you in here. They're packing your dresses, perfume, and stuff. The room'll be ready for Alma in no time."

"And Leanne?"

"Mike said she could stay at his hotel, no charge. Said it was only fair since we lost guest rooms in all this. Tom moves back to his room today, so we gotta look for a few new guests."

Everything was done, all without her now-useless assistance. What was more, it was all perfect. Everything she could have hoped for. The emotions became untamable, spilling onto her cheeks in a salty mixture of frustration and gratitude. She buried her face in her hands to try to get a hold of herself, but a deep sob wrenched out of her.

"Jane?" Cole rubbed his hand on her back. "I thought you'd be happy."

"I am," She tried to say, but her words got muffled by her hands. With another sob, she shook her head.

He knelt on the floor in front of her and peeled her hands away from her face. "What the hell did I do wrong?"

"Nothing." She wiped at her tears in frustration. Happiness and uselessness took away any self-control she might normally have. "I'm just so useless. Totally useless now. You did all of this, without me—and it's perfect. It's all…"

He stuttered an apology when she began bawling again.

"Iris dragged me in to help—my goodness, what's wrong?" Kat dropped the armful of dresses she'd carried in to rush to Jane's side. "Cole? What happened?"

"I dunno! I thought she was happy." Cole kept a hand clasped on Jane's knee.

Kat wrapped her arm around Jane's shoulders. "Jane?"

"It's so—so perfect." Jane moaned, burying her face in her hands at the refreshed well of tears. "I'm so useless. So—utterly useless."

Kat laughed when she started blubbering again.

Cole sighed. "I couldn't-a done any of it without your brothers helping."

Kat patted Cole's hand where it sat on Jane's knee. "Don't worry so much, Cole. She loves the room. She loves what you did for her. She merely hates being sick and weak."

Jane flew at Cole, throwing her arms around his neck as she sobbed against his shoulder.

He grunted at the impact, his arms going around her immediately. "Is this what you meant when ya said you'd get crazy emotional?"

Jane nodded against his shoulder.

Kat's laughter grew louder. Cole chuckled as he held her. "Kathy, you're not helping."

"No." Kat clapped. "I'm enjoying watching you deal with this. I need to remember it perfectly so Jane and I can both laugh at you later."

"You're laughing at me now," he protested.

Jane hiccupped, a hint of a giggle slipping out under her tears.

"Sure. That you find funny," Cole grumbled in her ear.

She managed to gather some restraint. Jane pulled away from his embrace, sniffling still as she wiped at her tears. "Thank you. For doing all of this."

Kat smirked when Jane began to tear up again. "Do you want to feel useful, Jane? Help me move your clothes in here. I think you can manage that—then you can cease making Cole look like he's stuck in a bear trap."

Cole grimaced at Kat. When Jane began to move, he turned his attention back to her. "I'll let the two of you ladies handle that. I'll get back to work down in the saloon. Where the men are."

Jane tugged him into a deep kiss, letting it linger until she pulled back. Her nerves tingled, and the sexy smirk he offered her only stimulated her more. "Thank you."

Kat tugged Jane out of Cole's arms. "All right, let's go. Put your useless self to work doing something constructive and helpful. For someone that lost so many clothes in the fire, you have a surprising number piled in that room. Plus, I really want to ask you about the more—unusual—pieces I've discovered."

"What?" Jane blinked to clear her head. A smile broke through her tears when she realized what outfits Kat had to be talking about. "Oh! Oh, right. I told you about the items Leanne gave me."

Cole cleared his throat. "I'm gonna head downstairs before the two of you get into details."

Jane chuckled low, catching his hand before he got too far. "It's probably best you do. I would hate to make you blush with the details I share."

"I don't blush," Cole protested.

"Oh, but you would." Jane stepped closer to him.

"It is truly amazing," Kat began with a solid tug to Jane's other hand. She succeeded in keeping Jane out of Cole's grasping arms. "How fast you both go from one mood to the next, but you need to behave yourselves."

Jane actually pouted. "But Katherine, it's so rare I feel well enough to contemplate such a thing any longer."

"I know." Kat chuckled, still tugging Jane further from Cole. "Is this truly one of those times?"

"No," Jane admitted. "The illness still lingers."

Kat continued dragging Jane further from Cole, toward the room they'd been staying in. "Then let us get to work. If at any time you feel well enough, I'll set you free to feast upon your man."

"That a promise?" Cole grinned wickedly at Jane. "Because I sure don't mind."

"I'd swear it on a bible." Kat snorted. "Now get. Leave her be until she feels well enough to act upon those looks the two of you are sharing."

Jane winked at Cole when he passed, but allowed Kat to pull her into the room with her things. As they gathered the clothes together, Jane regaled her with the story from the whorehouse in Denver again, only leaving out the part about Leanne being Cole's sister.

Piece by piece they moved the dresses, petticoats, and all of her things into her and Cole's rebuilt room. Cheerful conversation and organizing all of her and Cole's things filled the time until Jane was near exhausted.

Jane and Kat sat at the table to share some tea, which once again eased the burgeoning illness that threatened to ruin a good, if exhausted, mood. After Jane begged off lunch in favor of a nap—with the promise that she'd eat once she woke. Within minutes of Katherine leaving her be, Jane dropped onto the bed fully clothed and gave into fatigue.

"Jane!" Cole's shout startled her awake.

She yawned against the continuing tug of sleep, a low groan escaping when she tried to move her tired body. She could not have been asleep all that long. Why on earth did that man have to disturb her so soon?

"*Jane!*"

A glance at the clock told her she'd been wrong. In truth, almost two hours had passed since she'd laid down. That couldn't be. She shook off the lingering fatigue.

"*Jane!*"

She curled her lip at the door. If it was so important to him, he could make the journey upstairs rather than disturb every soul in the building.

"If you want your other surprise, you'd best get out here, woman."

Damn him, he knew how to get to her. She sighed her way out of bed. Pouring her tea so she could tolerate whatever might be coming. Rather than have him shout again, she headed for the door, teacup still in hand. She grabbed her reticule as she passed, as lately it often had pieces of candy inside to counteract the taste of the tea when she'd finished.

Tea in hand, she stormed from the room to glare over the railing. "What? Is it truly necessary for you to shout? We have a saloon full of people, and you choose to shout instead of simply walking up the sta—"

"Get your ass down here."

"Don't want to with the way you're behaving."

"Then no surprise for you."

She narrowed her eyes, muttering a curse under her breath. After an angry huff, she took a large swig of tea. She spun on her heel to head toward the stairs. Her good mood of earlier dissipated with each step. The man was intentionally being infuriating.

"Hasn't anyone ever told you it's not wise to annoy a woman in my condition?" Halfway down the steps she stopped short when he turned his back on her and walked outside. "Cole!"

She narrowed her eyes at his back. It might be worth annoying him back by walking right back upstairs to their room.

"Don't even think about it," he called back as though he'd read her mind.

Her jaw dropped, unsure whether to laugh or cry over his behavior. What on earth was he thinking?

Wills leaned back in his chair. His jovial features twisted with a hint of wickedness. "Trying to catch flies?"

She clamped her mouth shut. Though amused by him, she cast him a glare. Anything to hold onto her annoyance with Cole. "What was that, Wills?"

"That's better. Missed ya, Janey."

"Oh, you." She smacked him gently on the back of his head on her way past. Outside she found Cole leaning against a post casually, a satisfied grin on his features. He had his thumbs tucked in his holster. She could swear he was even laughing, the cocky bastard.

She stepped off the porch to stand before him. Hand on her hip, she glared her best glare. "What in blazes is the big idea? Are you trying to make your pregnant woman insane?"

"No."

The calm answer, the way he stared off down the road behind her only served to rile her temper. She set her tea on the hitching post. "Cole."

"Yeah?"

"*Cole.*"

"Don't shout."

She smacked him hard in the stomach. "You are about to send me right into a—"

"Look."

"Cole Mitchell. You had best start using words, or so help me…"

"Look, Janey." He nodded behind her.

She took several deep breaths through her nose to keep from blowing her stack. Once she felt calm enough to think straight, she'd done as he'd asked—no, ordered.

A small group of men that included their investor Cutler were huddled around Tommy as they stood in the middle of the street next to Kat's. While Tommy talked to them, he held the large papers of drawings they'd made of possible fronts for the building up in display. Everything he said involved a gesture in the direction of the Inn.

All of the men, save for one or two, were very well dressed. The two that weren't appeared to be acting in the capacity of a servant. Everyone was either listening intently to Tom, or focused on The Hangman's Inn itself.

Jane took a step backward onto the porch beside Cole. "Would you mind explaining what in hell is going on?"

"Your second surprise for today. Cutler liked your ideas, Tommy helped make some of them more focused. He worked with Cutler while you were in the clinic." Cole's hand rested on her shoulder. "His partner objected, but Cutler said you had good vision."

"Then what is with the group of high-falutin' shucks over there?"

"They aren't shucks." Cole offered her a crooked smile. "They're 'sociates of Cutler's. They're looking to learn our plans themselves."

"New investors? Are you serious?"

"They're gonna need some finessing. Tom may have your smarts, but he sure don't got your style."

"No. He certainly doesn't." Jane set her hand on his, matching his smile.

"We were thinking you'd wanna talk to them yourself since you got a way with people and all. If anyone can talk money out of a miser, it's you."

"Does that mean you're actually going to let me in on this?"

"You're partner, ain't ya?"

"Yes." She chuckled softly, turning to face him full on. "However, you have not let me do anything at all since I got sick."

"I wouldn't let ya miss out on nothing big." His fingers trailed along the back of her arm until he reached her hand, which he clasped in his own. "How're you feeling since you slept?"

"Much better."

"Feel like fishing?"

"I think I do."

"Look at him." Cole nodded toward Tommy. He chuckled low in her ear. "You'd think he was talking about a nice big ham the way he's practically drooling."

She smacked his arm but couldn't stop her own laughter. "Be nice to Thomas. He's helped save us both this week. Now it's time to show our good sides. I'm assuming you have the saloon floor covered?"

"Sure do. Are ya ready?"

"Oh yes."

Motherhood:
All love begins and ends there.
-Robert Browning

Mr. Cutler pulled Jane aside from the group. "I'm glad you were well enough to join us this afternoon, Miss Spencer."

"As am I, Mr. Cutler." Jane shook his offered hand. The warm smile she offered was as close to real as she could make it. Truthfully, she was well-pleased with the afternoon's events. However, the entire thing had lasted several hours, and thus she hadn't had her tea since before she'd first said hello. "I must thank you for inviting your associates to Dominion Falls."

"When Mr.'s Mitchell and Young explained your illness and how it would hamper your ability to travel to the investors you were seeking, I thought perhaps I knew a few colleagues that would be willing to travel." He leaned in conspiratorially, "I often think it's better to see things in person anyhow."

"That is a valid point," Jane agreed.

"Your proposal warrants merit. I was pleased with the way you constructed all of your plans and their variables. I wouldn't mind seeing more back from my initial investment."

"I do hope you aren't the only one that feels the same." She set her hand back on her stomach, twisting her kerchief in her other hand. Every moment now was a struggle to keep from embarrassing herself in front of the whole group of men she'd tried to impress. "You've been more helpful than I had hoped. I cannot begin to tell you how much we appreciate it."

"I don't like to see my investments fail. I almost always only invest in something I'm certain will succeed. Not all men mind so much."

Confusion filtered over the distraction of her nausea. "If you don't mind me asking—why did you invest in the saloon well before it became The Hangman's Inn? You've given the impression that you were not so impressed with Mr. Cooke, and while you agree with the income from the brothel, you preferred my non-brothel proposals."

"Truthfully, I wasn't overly impressed with Mr. Cooke, or the saloon. The development he spoke of was small in focus and still held on tight to the saloon and brothel over all else. Daniel was the one that ultimately convinced me to go with it sight-unseen."

Jane took a deep breath against the rapid uptake in the churning of her stomach which matched her swirling thoughts. Already certain of the answer, she asked anyway, "What did convince you?"

"Dominion Falls is a rapidly growing town. You pointed out as much yourself in your own proposals. There are plans to pave the streets and begin installing a sewer system, which almost makes the town progressive and a hot commodity. If the business did fail, I would have a good possibility of recouping my investment thanks to the prime piece of land offering me the options of sale or building on my own."

"Of course." She nodded even as she tried to process his reasoning and lay it against all she knew of their recent troubles. "Makes sense. It's rather obvious, really."

"Personally, I'd rather see it succeed and earn much more money rather than to simply break even. I have no interest in turning it into what I want—I leave the vision to others." Cutler smiled, gesturing toward the Inn. "Such as you and Mr. Mitchell."

Jane returned his smile. Once again, she offered him her hand. "Thank you for your candor, Mr. Cutler. We won't take up any more of your precious time this afternoon."

"Thank you." Cutler shook her hand before moving to join the others. There, he shook Cole's hand as well. The group talked for another minute in lively tones. They then turned to head down the street toward Turner's.

Cole waited until they were out of hearing range, then wrapped his arm tight around her waist. "You did good."

"Thank you."

"You need to get sick, don't you?"

"Very much so."

He half-lifted her to get her inside quick as possible. They crossed right through the customers, into the storeroom where a bucket sat in the corner. He kept one hand secure on her back until she'd relieved herself of the majority of the discomfort.

Once she felt she could stop heaving, she lifted her head. A soft groan slipped out as her stomach still roiled and churned.

"You need the doc?"

"Tea. It's been hours."

Without another word, he went to the small stove in the room. For the next several minutes he worked silently, and she tried to compose herself before she ended up over the bucket unable to drink the tea he made for her.

She wiped her mouth with her kerchief, silently willing him to move faster. Eyes closed, she leaned against the wall.

The warm cup pressed in her hands. By then she was somewhat accustomed to the smell, but her nose wrinkled anyway when she drew the cup to her lips. At first, she could only manage a small sip. After a shaky breath she took another longer sip. Silence lingered in the room. Neither of them spoke until she'd managed to get the whole drink down.

"Better?"

"A little," she whispered. It wasn't entirely untrue. At least she no longer felt as though her stomach would revolt.

"I'll take you upstairs."

"No." She set her hand on his to stop them. "I'd rather not. I'll have some more tea down here. If I'm feeling better in a while, I'd like to go to Cora's with you. I don't much feel like being cooped up in the room."

"You sure?"

"No."

He laughed heartily. With a firm grasp on her elbow he helped her to her feet. He led her to a bar stool. "Finish that tea. I brought some down to keep in the storeroom so's we can make more without having to go upstairs. You'll finish this, have another, and then we'll figure if you wanna go."

"Are you telling me what to do again? That's twice today. Seems to me like you're looking for trouble."

"I'm always looking for trouble."

"True."

He leaned on the bar across from her, hovering close. "Make sure you drink plenty of that tea. I want you feeling good."

"Don't I always?"

"To me ya do."

"Just good?"

"Damn good." He leaned in ever closer. "First time I picked you up, you felt good."

"Even half dead? Hmmm, that's good to know—because that is how I feel most days any longer." She lifted her cup to her lips when he tried to steal a kiss. Her attempt at an innocent expression only brought a grumble out of him. She reached out to grab his hand. "Are you ready for tomorrow?"

"She ain't ever been here before. Not sure how she'll react."

"You're here. That's all Alma needs."

"Nah. That ain't all." His entire body tensed until he jerked away. A dark frown settled on his features.

Jane's brow furrowed in confusion at the extreme reaction. When she followed his gaze to the door where the marshal stook, she sighed. "Relax."

"Not a chance." Cole braced his hands on the bar. "Don't care what he told ya. He's still got power over you."

"Then don't piss him off."

"I should tell you the same."

Jane took another sip of tea to hide her smirk. When Lewis sat beside her, she turned toward him. "Marshal Lewis. How is your stay in Dominion Falls?"

"Almost over. I've been making the rounds trying to get proof of your arsonist for you. Nothing Sheriff Schaffer or I can find to pin it on anyone. Of course, it doesn't help that

Mr. Warren has disappeared and stunningly, there's no record of him either, Miss Spencer."

She pursed her lips, but relaxed them immediately to get another sip of tea. "I told you, Jane is fine. I'm not surprised that you can find no sign of Warren. Thomas did say he was a Pinkerton. Apparently when they don't wish to be found, they aren't. I wish we could learn his real name—and tie him to Underwood. Any luck there?"

Lewis shook his head. "Underwood has been a virtual non-entity by all accounts. Tom is looking into the financial aspect of—"

"*Jane! David! Ma!*"

All action in the saloon stilled at the familiar voice of Isaac shrieked through town.

Jane leaped from her chair.

"I'll get a horse." Cole raced for the back door.

Jane tore toward the front. She burst from the slaoon to find Isaac racing up and down the street. "Isaac! What happened?"

"He was tryin' to climb." Isaac had tears on his cheeks as he pulled to a stop in front of the Inn. "I told him not to."

Jesse. Jane didn't need him to say the name to know. Her knees buckled beneath her. To her surprise, her downward progress was halted by a supportive hand at her elbow.

Marshal Lewis spoke firmly, but quietly. "Where?"

"We were fishing by the creek, out near the settlement. Lizzie and Cindy are still there with him." Isaac's horse spun as he kept looking for others. "I'm sorry. I tried."

"Get your ma, get Daisy or Charlie, and find David." Jane came to her senses as adrenaline coursed through her. She spun at Cole's shout, pulling away from Lewis. Cole's hand reached for her. She leapt the moment their hands clasped and swung up behind him.

The second she gave him a direction, he took off at a breakneck pace. He didn't slow Faro until they got close, and when he did he helped her down so she could continue on foot.

Jane tore along the path by the creek until she saw a shock of white-blonde hair, and Lizzie's cries reached her ears. A sob burst from her chest as she raced forward to drop to her knees beside Jesse. "Jesse! Sweetie"

"I'm sorry, Ma." Tears shone in Jesse's hazel eyes. His hand clasped in Lizzie's, he whimpered. "You told me not to."

"Shh. It's all right. I'm not mad. It's all right." She smoothed her hand over his forehead gentle as she could. "What did you hurt?"

Lizzie grabbed Jane's hand, gesturing toward the tree behind her. While sobbing, she tried to explain what had happened.

Cindy sat a few feet away, head buried in her hands. She rocked back and forth. "It's my fault. I dared him."

Cole knelt next to Jane as she tried to comfort all three children in one fell sweep. With negligible results. In a heartbeat, he moved to the other side of Jesse. Now in between the two girls, he pulled them both close. "Ain't no one's fault. It happens. He's gonna be fine."

Jane offered Cole a brief smile of gratitude before she turned her attention back to her son. "Climbing the tree?"

"The branch broke." Jesse whimpered.

Jane kissed his forehead. "What did you hurt?"

"My arm hurts real bad." His teeth chattered on his intake of breath. "My foot."

"Anything else? Your head? Did you hit your head?" She brushed some stray curls off his forehead.

Jesse shook his head. "I'm sorry, Ma."

"Shhh. Don't be silly. It was an accident." Jane pulled his head on her lap when his teeth chattered again, smoothing his curls. "It's all right, baby. Dr. Daisy will be here soon, and we'll get you back to town."

*He who does not trust enough,
will not be trusted.
-Lao Tzu*

Approaching footsteps and Isaac's instructions interrupted Jesse's reply. Cole rose with the girls, guiding them a step back to make room for Daisy. His brow furrowed when Marshal Lewis followed behind Daisy. Concerned though he was, Cole turned his attention back to Jane.

"Young Mr. Turner says the child fell." Lewis stayed back from the scene.

Cole's lip curled, anger rising to cover the concern he felt over Jesse and Jane at this point. Who knew why Lewis had tagged along. "Can't stop that kid climbing for nothing."

Lewis' brows rose. "Interesting."

"No it ain't," Cole snapped. "Kids do it all the time."

"No, not that." Lewis folded his arms across his chest. "The boy keeps calling her Ma. She doesn't seem to mind, considering it isn't supposed to be her boy. Plus, her worry seems more than concern for another's child."

Cole held the girls tight against his side. It wouldn't do Jane any good to lose his temper now. "Thought you were going to leave her alone."

"I'm merely commenting on the interesting tableau before me."

"Ain't sure what you mean, but leave her alone." Cole fought tooth and nail to remain calm as the man spoke. At the same time, he didn't dare take his eyes off Jane, Daisy, and Jesse. Jane's entire focus remained on her boy.

Once Daisy had set Jesse's arm in a sling and moved to his foot, Jane called the girls over. Cole let them go without argument, ready to lay into the marshal.

Lewis didn't give him the chance. "She's with child, isn't he?"

Cole clenched and unclenched his fists. He wouldn't outright admit such a thing, although he figured half the town suspected by now. The fact that Jane had called the girls over to comfort Jesse while she went to get sick behind a tree didn't help matters. "Why do ya say that?"

"I have six children. I've come to recognize the signs of a woman might be in a delicate condition, Mr. Mitchell."

"Does it make a difference to you?"

"Depends."

Jane approached, a kerchief to her mouth, effectively ending the conversation. "I'm going back in the wagon. Daisy says his arm is broken, and his foot might be as well. Would you please assist in getting him in the wagon? I'll walk with Lizzie and Cindy."

Cole nodded his agreement, but moved only after a warning glare toward Lewis. He grabbed Jesse to carry him to the wagon, relieved to see Lewis not confront Jane right then. Hopefully the man would leave her be at least for the ride back when he couldn't be in the wagon to keep an eye on things.

Just in case, Cole rode close to the wagon. The whole way back the conversation between the four kids kept any option of more risky talk at bay. Once back at the clinic, Cole stuck close to Jane the whole time.

After Jesse's arm and foot were set and wrapped, Jane sat with him until Kathy showed up with the girls, who asked for a turn. When she emerged from Jesse's room, Jane collapsed against him. Her soft sigh felt heavy. "David was off with Arthur helping put up fences at the new ranch south of town. I imagine he'll be along soon."

Cole held her close as they waited. Within ten minutes the front door burst open. David raced in, disheveled and filthy with dust.

David stopped short at the sight of Jane. "What happened? Isaac just kept saying he was sorry."

"Cindy dared him to climb a tree." Jane wiped a tear from her cheek. "A branch gave out and fell. His arm and foot are broken."

David's brow furrowed. "Is he all right?"

"He feels guilty for climbing after I've told him not to, and for scaring Lizzie and Cindy." Jane smiled, chuckling softly. "Katherine is in his room with the girls at the moment."

"With Lizzie in there, he's probably plenty happy I'm guessing?" David relaxed into a smile at Jane's laughter.

"Yes." Jane relaxed back against Cole. "She makes everything better."

"I'm going to see him." David glanced at Cole, then Lewis, before his gaze returned to Jane. "Are you all right?"

"I will be, now that I know he will live." Jane waved him toward the door. "Go see him. It'll ease your mind."

Cole squeezed her shoulders when David disappeared into the room. "Let's get you home, Jane. You need some tea."

Jane patted his hand. "I do need tea, but first."

"Jane," Cole warned. "I think we should get you home."

"Marshal Lewis." She turned toward the man in question as if Cole's warning meant nothing. "Go ahead. I'm waiting."

Cole blew his frustration out in a big gust of air. He turned to face the marshal as well, eying the man with a dark appraising look. Under Cole's careful study, the marshal didn't balk, but Cole also didn't see any indication of malice.

Jane took a deep breath. "I thought you were satisfied. I took you as a man of honor and accepted your word."

"I was satisfied. I also had no proof." While his words were strong, Lewis' tone remained gentle and calm.

"The mind of a child—" Jane began.

Lewis interrupted, "The love of a mother."

Jane's head dropped; her shoulders slumped. "What is it you wish me to say?"

"I told you. I want the truth." Still, the man didn't give off an aggressive vibe. Cole might not be great at reading people, but he knew aggression when he saw it. Lewis had none. In fact, he was more relaxed than he had been earlier.

"To what end? There is only blood on the path you tread." She sighed. "I have tried to avoid such a path—I've seen where it leads. You've seen where it leads. Must we walk that route now? When there are less dark ends to reach?"

"Trust must be earned; truth is the sure path to that."

"You have not gained my good faith either, Marshal." She pinched the bridge of her nose. After a moment, her back straightened. "I do not respond well to threats and ultimatums. Your quest for truth is admirable, but as Thoreau points out, 'it takes two to speak the truth; one to speak and another to hear'."

Lewis frowned. "I cannot take action and be prepared for the possibility of future attempts to make me alert that a dead woman is walking around without the truth. For the sake of your child don't you—"

"Do not threaten me." Jane's hand clenched on Cole's hand so tight he thought he might need Daisy himself. He set his free hand on her shoulder in hopes to calm her. "I asked you to what end. If I'm satisfied with the answer, perhaps you'll get more from me than a door slammed in your face."

"Is it fair to ask someone to make a decision without all the facts?" Lewis' brow furrowed in clear frustration. "I thought you preferred honesty."

"Such honesty could be used by you to construct my own noose." Even though she remained ramrod straight, Jane's hand relaxed its grip on his. "Shall we continue in circles?"

Cole squeezed her shoulder. Though he might not be great at reading people like Jane in most cases, for the first time since Lewis had arrived in town, Cole wasn't worried about what he'd do. There seemed to be not a lick of malice in the man. "He don't wanna hang you."

Jane and Lewis both startled at his proclamation. Wide-eyed, Jane turned toward him. "What?"

"He don't." Cole focused on Lewis. "Do you?"

"No. I told you I was done looking for a crime." Lewis nodded to Cole in acknowledgment. "I meant it. I only want the truth."

"You don't?" Jane's body grew rigid, several small gasps escaping her lips.

"Miss Spencer?" Lewis took a step forward when Jane crumbled.

"Son of a—" Cole barely managed to catch her before she hit the ground. She groaned when he lifted her. "Jane."

She blinked lazily until a sharpness returned to her gaze. A weak smile graced her lips. "I believe it was the shock of you reading him better than I did."

Cole chuckled. "Not funny."

"Then stop laughing." Her smile grew broader.

Lewis walked closer. "Shall I get Dr. Pearson?"

"No. I'm all right. Set me down, Cole." Though he did as she asked, he was relieved she leaned against him. "It was shock on top of a very long day. I'd like you to tell me, Marshal—to what end?"

Lewis held her gaze. "For my own conscience."

"No law," She all but ordered.

"No law," Lewis agreed.

Jane nodded. "All right. Then I'll tell you."

"Not right now," Cole objected.

"No. I need rest. We will meet soon, Marshal Lewis."

"Soon," Lewis concurred.

No matter what you've done for yourself or for humanity, if you can't look back on having given love and attention to your own family, what have you accomplished?
—Elbert Hubbard

Jane's leg hooked around Cole's. Her arm draped across his chest, her soft sighed slipped across his chest.

He chuckled low and deep. "So that's what that look was all about."

"What look would that be?"

"This morning." He tapped her nose when her attempt to look innocent met with spectacular failure. "I couldn't tell what you was after. You looked annoyed."

"I was." She propped herself on her elbow to meet his gaze. Though she tried to appear stern, a soft smile lingered on her delicious lips. "You were tense as all get-out and I was feeling poorly. In the interest of our sanity, I did what I had to in order to remedy the dilemma so that you might be calm when Alma arrived."

"You saying this was all about me?"

"Hell no. I was tense as well."

Laughing, he pulled her close to brush his lips across hers. "If you were feeling so poorly, how'd ya manage it?"

"Two full cups of tea, a bite of breakfast, and then more tea. After that was done, I popped in a candy to get rid of the vile taste and ran right back here."

"And dragged me from the saloon, ripping half my clothes off before we got all the way to our room."

"Exactly."

"You really are my kind of woman."

She shifted to straddle his hips, her moist heat positioned perfectly to get a renewed rise out of him. Delicate fingers danced across his chest, teasing him further along. "I guess it's a good thing I stumbled into your saloon, then, instead of any number of the buildings in this town."

"Good thing I checked to see if you were alive after Graham said you was dead."

"Somehow I have a feeling you didn't double-check so Daisy might be able to display her superior doctoring skills."

He gripped her waist to flip them. At her squeal, he crushed his lips to hers. She curved into him without argument until he began to pull back. He nibbled on her bottom lip before he released her. "Had to have been. You weren't much to see lying on the floor all dirty and bloody."

She hummed in what could have been argument or agreement. He didn't much care as her fingers played along the muscles of his back, her body still arched eagerly into his. "I think I might need to make this a morning ritual—doing whatever is necessary so I might feel well enough to enjoy you. I feel much more focused now."

"That so?" He nipped at her neck. Her salty sweetness filled his senses as he moved closer to her ear. "What're you focused on?"

"The marshal."

He froze where he was, crossed between annoyance and desire when her giggles made her tremble against him. With a bit of effort, he straightened his arms to peer down at her. "You're kidding, right?"

She tugged him back toward her. He obliged without much of a fight. Her legs wrapped around his waist as he resumed his nibbling along her neck. She sighed. "Leanne."

"Interesting, but no."

Her nails dug into back until he hissed. "You."

"Better."

"Your big—"

"Janey!" Tom pounded on the door.

"Get the hell outta here, Tom." Cole snarled toward the door. "We're busy!"

"Twenty-minute warning." Tom pounded again. "Train'll be here in thirty minutes."

Jane pouted, her hold on him lapsing. "Damn."

"Plenty of time," Cole murmured against her chest.

"You really think so?"

In place of a verbal response, he proceeded to show her just how much they could accomplish in twenty minutes. By the time Tom pounded on the door again they were both breathless, wrapped tight in around each other.

Jane laughed at Tom's impatient pounding. "Thank you, Thomas."

"Just shut up and get your asses ready," Tom yelled with one last hit to the door.

Cole chuckled as Tommy's laughter boomed through the door before his footsteps faded away. "We'd better move."

"Yes. We must be there when Alma arrives." Her hands lingered on his skin as they slowly separated. She sat, her kiss landing on his shoulder before she slipped out of the bed. He threw on his clothes quick as possible. Jane did the same in between sips of tea. When she was fully dressed, she stood there, frowning at the corset that she held instead of wearing.

"You're supposed to gain weight, remember? Doc said it was wrong that you didn't."

"I know." She tugged at her bodice, glaring at herself in the mirror. Turning side to side, she released a frustrated sigh. "I don't mind, except I have few enough clothes as it is—and now those are not going to fit much longer."

"Shoulda known you'd be worried about clothes."

She winked at him in the mirror, a bright grin on her features. "Speaking of which, get your shirt on. We don't have much time."

He did as ordered, throwing on the last of his clothes, well aware that her gaze never left him once. Much as he appreciated the attention, his own thoughts wandered to recent events. Even worried as he was about Alma's arrival, the idea of Jane's meeting with Lewis bothered him more. He grabbed the tie she held out to him, throwing it around his neck as she began to button his shirt.

Halfway up his shirt, she froze. Her gaze drifted to his curiously. "And you talk about my mind the minute things get quiet. What's the matter now?"

"I'm wondering if it's smart for you to meet Lewis alone like you're planning."

She finished the buttons, her easy smile long gone. Her lips pursed taught as she grabbed her reticule to tie to her belt. The night before they hadn't had a chance to get much further in their talk with Lewis before Jesse had called out and asked Jane to stay with him.

In the ensuing quiet discussion, Jane and Lewis had agreed to meet privately in another couple of days. With Alma coming to town and Jesse's injuries, Jane wouldn't have much time.

When he didn't move despite them both being ready, she sighed deeply. Hand on her hip, she confronted his statement. "It's the smartest choice. Without a corroborating witness to whatever I tell him, it's less likely he could use my words against me. He's not going to harm me. You said yourself he doesn't want to hang me, he only wants the truth."

"More than one way to skin a cat."

"'The greatest way to live with honor in this world is to be what we pretend to be'."

He lifted a brow, not moving from his spot.

"Socrates."

"You're gonna say that to him, aren't you?"

"Of course. Now come on. We're going to be late." She straightened his tie a last time. Her wink carried her out the door. When they got downstairs, she pointed at Tommy in warning when he opened his mouth.

"Was just going to say you look relaxed." Tommy held his hands up in surrender. "I'll be here keeping an eye. Figure you don't want a huge crowd to welcome the girl."

Cole nodded to him, appreciative of the man's continued silence if he knew the truth about Alma or Leanne. Something told Cole that with as many secrets as Tom seemed to keep under his hat, he knew a hell of a lot more than any of them could imagine.

Jane led him from the Inn quickly, and they both picked up the pace on the way to the depot as the train whistle sounded in the not-too-far off distance.

Cole set his hand on the small of her back, his free hand clenched at his side.

"Relax. You're already tensing up."

"Sorry."

"She's going to be fine. Leanne said Alma seemed excited."

"How would she know?"

"Be nice. She'd know same as you would."

He frowned, a sudden worry hitting him like a raging bull. "You told anyone? Kat?"

"All anyone knows is that Alma is a distant relation you're helping out because she has no other family." Jane offered him a sideways glare for his accusation. "That's a task I leave to you if you decide to own up to it. In the meantime, Leanne is an old friend. Graham and Norman, plus half the men in this town knew her once upon a time, they simply don't know who she is in relation to you beyond one of your former whores."

Guilt nagged him for his allegation. "Sorry."

"Uh-huh." She gathered her skirts to climb onto the platform. The train drew ever closer in the distance. When he stopped beside her, she sighed. "Stop fidgeting."

"Now who's ordering who around?"

"Me, of course." She clasped her hands behind her back. A hint of a grin teased her lips back into a kissable smile. "Oh, that's right. I almost forgot. You don't like demanding women."

"You ain't funny."

"Then why in heavens are you laughing?"

Mike hopped up the steps near him. "Aren't you in a good mood?" He nodded to Cole, then leaned in to give Jane a kiss on the cheek.

"You're running behind this morning. Aren't you usually here at least five minutes before the train?" Jane smiled at her brother. "Thank you again for offering Leanne a room. It's nice have two rooms earning money instead of one."

"No problem. Happy to help you get back on your feet." Mike glanced from Jane to Cole. "Any luck with the investors?"

Cole shook his head. "Not yet. We're still waiting on word."

"We only met with them yesterday," Jane added. "They're all still in town, even. I expect at least another meeting, maybe two before they leave. Then we have to wait for their final decisions."

"I'm certain you charmed them all into handing over their entire fortunes, Jane." Mike winked, laughing when Cole started to chuckle.

Jane's cheeks took on a delicious pink hue. "I highly doubt that. After all, I was only aiming for a small portion."

"More like a large portion," Cole muttered under the screech of brakes. The passengers began to disembark, and tension ratcheted back through Cole. He didn't have to search long to find them, as Leanne and Alma were among the first off the train. "There they are."

"*That* is Cole's 'old friend'?" Mike stared agape.

Jane winked Cole's way. "Yes. She is."

Mike's mouth opened and closed a few times before he furrowed his brow. "Her?"

"Yes, Michael."

Alma moved quick across the platform to a secluded corner, Leanne hot on her heels. Alma's gaze focused on the roof of the platform, her fingers tapping on her skirts. Leanne spotted them, guiding Alma along inner edge of the platform where there were less people.

Mike shook his head. "And you aren't jealous?"

"Not in the least." Jane snorted at her brother, then pushed her fingers under his chin to shut his mouth. "Now close your mouth before you become infested with flies. Ingrate."

Cole laughed out loud, but the laughter faded when Leanne rushed toward him to throw her arms around him. She kissed him soundly on the cheek, drawing even more attention to their group. "Damn it, Leanne."

"Oh, there's no harm." Leanne kissed his cheek again before hugging Jane tight "It is wonderful to see you again. My goodness, you are looking well."

Cole took the chance to escape another embrace from Leanne and turned his attention to Alma. Dressed in her finest, her hair curled so intricately he suspected Leanne's handiwork.

Her ice blue eyes remained fixed on a corner of the roof, but a soft smile settled on her lips. She tapped her fingers on her leg still, but she spoke low, "Cole."

"Alma." Cole moved closer, pausing to glare at a passerby that was staring at Alma with disdain. When they turned away, he focused back on his sister. "Did you like the train ride?"

"Swoop! Swoop!" She lifted her hand, dipping it at each swoop.

Leanne's laughter filtered over. "Alma was fascinated with the telegraph wires the whole trip. I couldn't pry this girl from the window for a minute."

Cole chuckled. "Is that so?"

Jane appeared at Cole's side. She laced her hand with his, adding a reassuring squeeze. "Considering it's that or staring at people on the train, I can't say as I blame her. There are very few activities that satisfy boredom on a long train ride."

"Alma. I'm going with Mike here to see my room. I'll meet you all for supper at six." Leanne stood beside the flustered, pink-faced Mike. He held a suitcase in his hand, Leanne held her carpetbag in front of her. "Is that all right?"

"All right, all right." Alma nodded, still tapping her hand on her leg.

"I have an idea." Jane waved the pair off, her focus still on Alma. "I know all of this is new and strange for you, Alma. I know one thing that isn't, though. We have a piano."

Alma stopped tapping. Her gaze twitched to Jane before returning to the ceiling.

Cole kissed the top of Jane's head. He'd find a way to thank her for her thinking later. Every time he got locked up, he knew she'd step in. "Good idea. You can come play for a while. When you're ready, we'll show you the room we set up for you. Jane got it fixed up real nice. Even gave you a few books."

Jane had already ducked under Cole's arm on her way off the platform. "Norman will send your bags over, so first things first. Let's see the piano, shall we?"

Alma grinned as she approached Cole's side. Her nerves, and perhaps excitement, showed in the way she gripped his arm. Still, she allowed him to lead her down the street with no outbursts. Inside the saloon, Tom had already moved the patrons near the bar, farthest from the piano. Cole's curious gaze at Jane only got a shrug in response.

A few feet from the piano Alma released her vicelike grip on his arm. She dropped into the seat, her fingers on the keys before her butt hit the chair.

The music filled the bar quickly. Soon as it did, a low murmur filled the silence as the patrons began chatting again.

Jane leaned into Cole, a soft smile on her features. "She's home."

Cole wrapped his arm around her shoulder. "We all are."

*He that raises a large family does, indeed,
while he lives to observe them, stand a
broader mark for sorrow; but then he stands
a broader mark for pleasure, too.
-Benjamin Franklin*

"Jane," Cole whispered in her ear. The light touch of his finger brushed along her temple.

Her body relaxed further at his touch. She sighed softly.

"Wake up, you dunderhead."

She groaned deeply. Blinking her eyes open, she glanced at him askance. Her wits came slowly to her. "Dunderhead?"

"Figured if you weren't really asleep, you'd be smacking me for it." He winked, a low chuckle carrying through the room. "It's about suppertime."

"Already? Wait—when did I fall asleep?"

"Right after we brought Alma home."

She sat so fast the world spun. Luckily his arm was there to brace her. "Oh. My. I wanted to show Alma her room."

"Already done. We've been in there reading." He cupped her cheek. "You fell asleep standing up about five minutes after you started leaning on me. Alma followed me upstairs when I brung you up. We've been reading and talking since."

"I fell asleep?"

"Standing up. Guess you was tired."

"Guess so."

"We gotta go soon for supper."

"Of course. Of course. I—first." She flew across the room to the bucket. Over her own sick she heard him call for tea. A soothing hand ran along her back. The towel he offered was more than welcome to clean up and dab the cold sweat. "Sorry."

"You all right?"

"I will be." She held the towel over her mouth when her stomach churned again. "Go with Alma, she shouldn't be alone so long. Give me a few minutes to gather myself."

"You sure?"

"I'm certain. Go. I won't be far behind. After a little tea I'll be right as rain." She squeezed his hand to reassure him. When Lark appeared with her tea, she smiled. "See? My tea is already here. Go ahead."

Jane sipped the tea Larkspur left for her while Cole slipped from the room. The entire cup was drained before she began to feel in control of her stomach again. She grabbed the box of tea they kept in their room and steeped another cup while she straightened her hair. If she wanted to eat, she would need at least two more cups to tolerate food.

She gulped down the second cup, pouring the third quick as she'd finished. After she'd locked the door behind her and paused to smooth her skirts, something caught her attention. Cole's rich voice reading the familiar's words of Gulliver's Travels echoed out of the room next door. She peeked into the room to find him reading at the table near the window. Beside him sat Alma, her fingers tapping on the table as Cole spoke.

"Passes under the general name of…" Cole's brow furrowed as he studied the book. Alma's finger stopped tapping. He seemed to notice with a glance in the girl's direction. "Of…"

"Balnibarbi," Jane spoke to save him further consternation. "And the metropolis, as I said before, is called Lagado."

Cole gave her a smile of relief, well-tempered with a concerned furrow of his brow. "This is why you do the reading. I ain't learned enough."

"You are learned enough. You learned to read over a year ago, and you know numbers, and you have become quite a skilled negotiator," Jane objected.

"Words like…" The page fluttered in his hand.

"Balnibarbi."

"That. Them words aren't fair. You read from now on."

"Oh, heavens no. Your voice and cadence are far more intriguing and well-suited for the listening. Am I right, Alma?" Jane smiled when Alma nodded in agreement. "Because you are focused on your reading, you follow a far more clear-cut rhythm than I do. I change with the emotions I feel—and thus my reading is more chaotic."

"I ain't ever found your reading chaotic," He protested.

"I read you stories of a different nature where chaos is welcomes. Alma likes stories of adventure and love, but she prefers a metronome of a pace. Hence, why she taps." Jane took a deep breath to push back a brief flash of nausea. "If you would like to carry the book, Alma, I can continue reading as we go to Cora's. We'll see Leanne there."

Alma brightened, rising to her feet. She took the book from Cole.

Cole crossed the room and wrapped his arm around her waist. Jane leaned into him without argument. She smiled at Alma. "Let's go."

On their way out, Cole leaned in to mutter, "Guess the morning relaxing wasn't so good for you?"

"It was worth it," Jane said with a smile. "I thought I told you to go on ahead without me. I didn't expect to find you reading."

"Alma asked to wait for you."

"There you are." Tom grinned at their group. "You're running a little behind your time."

"I fell asleep and then had to…" Jane pursed her lips to block the unseemly crass description. "Well, I was indisposed for a few minutes. We're going to be a little late meeting Mike and Leanne for supper. Are you still planning on joining us?"

"Of course. Hello again, Alma. What's that you've got? Gulliver's Travels? That's a good one." Tom didn't force himself too close to the girl, and she didn't shy away from him. "How far along are you?"

Jane slowed their progress as Alma showed the book to Tom. He took over the reading without missing a beat. The pair fell into step together on their way out the door. Jane sighed happily. She fell into step when Cole moved them forward again. "I think Alma's going to do just fine here."

"I hope so."

"I watched you with her. I don't know why you're so nervous—when it's the two of you alone, you are as amazing with her as you are with me. You don't give yourself enough credit."

"I ain't…"

"What? You've been more family to her than your father ever was. Hell, you protected her when your pa wanted to literally destroy her; and you protected Leanne all of these years as well."

He didn't respond, only slowed to a stop.

She turned toward him and pressed her finger into his chest. Considering the bustle of people, she kept her tone low. "When her ma died you made sure she was cared for. You claimed her as your daughter to get her into that school where she and her talent could thrive. Thanks to all of those measures you took, she has grown into a fine young woman."

"I sent her away 'cause I was…"

"What? Embarrassed? Afraid? Natural reactions to the idea of a child that is different, and not your own, especially after what you went through with a healthy infant. At least you didn't send her to an asylum."

"Worse than what pa wanted to do," he muttered.

"Exactly. She would have suffered, if not died. You did what was right. You've tried to grow beyond your initial reactions. Stop worrying *when* you're going to mess up again. Accept the fact that you will. We both will. All you need to do is love her. She adores you and trusts you like no other, even Leanne."

"You done?"

"Are you?"

He held her gaze for a long minute. Without warning he tugged her close and kissed her deeply until her knees buckles. When he released her, he grinned. "I am now."

"Vile."

"I know."

"Let's get to supper. Alma will be waiting for us." She slipped her art around his waist. At the door to Cora's, she paused. "On second thought, maybe she isn't waiting for us."

In the corner, apart from the crowded group of adults, Alma sat with Cindy and Arthur. The rest of the kids were close by at the next table. Conversation wasn't vibrant, but it definitely carried on both with and around her.

"Them kids." Cole shook his head.

"Yes. I think Alma will be all right here if she has Arthur and Cindy on her side. Don't you?"

"Probably."

She continued her perusal of the restaurant. The scene she found left her laughter bubbling free. "Oh dear. Your 'old friend' is going to cause quite a stir."

Leanne sat between Tommy and Mike, with Nick across the way. Her main focus appeared to be on Tommy, but all three men were leaning in close. Whatever story she was telling them had her in near tears, and Mike turning bright red. Tommy boomed with laughter. Daisy, sitting next to Mike, appeared none-too-pleased with the conversation.

Cole chuckled. "Thought you liked that about her."

"True." At the table Tommy and Nick leaned even closer. "Oh dear. This could get ugly."

"It could get fun."

"Cole." Jane barely managed to get the word out.

"Yeah?"

She let out a shaky breath to try to control the rise of bile. "Go sit with them. I'll be there in a few minutes."

"Again?"

Rather than answer, she bolted down the steps and raced around the building. Once she'd relieved herself of the scant contents of her stomach, she pressed a kerchief to her lips. She took several deep breaths to be sure she was finished before making her way back up the steps. Thankfully she found a cup of tea already waiting, and offered a wan attempt of a smile.

Daisy frowned her way. "Cole suggested that you two—relaxed—this morning?"

Cole snorted loud enough to temporarily grab the attention of the others at the table. "She was feeling fine at the time. Are you saying we can't enjoy ourselves when she does?"

"Don't you dare. If you say that, you might as well put me in the ground." Jane picked up her tea to take a healthy gulp. Cole's hand laced with hers. "Because when I feel well enough, I will be making time with Cole. Otherwise the next six months or so will be the most wretched you will ever spend in my presence, I promise."

Tommy's laughter boomed through the restaurant again. "She's not kidding."

"For the risk of feeling ill, I will manage." Jane shrugged. "As long as the baby is—"

"Baby?" Leanne interrupted. "You failed to mention that little nugget, Jane! Cole is going to have a child? Oh, goodness. No wonder he is hovering over you so much. I wish you'd told me when you were in Denver."

"It was still new to us in Denver." Jane laughed. "We were going to enjoy it for a while in private, but my brothers have astonishingly big mouths. I was planning on telling you in a less…"

"Uncouth," Tommy suggested.

"Thank you, Tom. Yes. A less uncouth manner." Jane kicked him with the toe of her boot. "You are the uncouth one. Shut your trap and stop monopolizing the conversation."

Tom closed his mouth, glaring darkly at his sister. Jane glared right back, though she couldn't stop the hint of a smile.

Cole turned away from the glare contest to face Daisy. "Is the baby at risk?

"Always if she gets too sick," Daisy said quietly. "It's best to avoid any activity that makes you ill, Jane."

"Some days simply laughing makes me ill. Or walking. Or sitting reading a book. Usually it's sleeping alone that does it because I go so long without tea." Jane still hadn't broken the staring contest with her brother.

"Still…"

"The activity itself did not make me ill. It made me more relaxed than I've been in days," Jane assured Daisy. "It was the failure to not acquire enough tea immediately after, or for several hours after that. We went to get Alma and then I made the mistake of falling asleep before I had more tea because I was apparently exhausted after all the excitement."

Tommy snorted, breaking contact.

Jane straightened in triumph. "Anyhow, I had two cups before I came here, but it clearly wasn't quite enough. Either way, the tea helps, but nothing stops me from getting ill if my stomach decides it's going to."

Mike smirked. "I wouldn't doubt her, Daisy. She may be boorish and enjoy her activities a bit too much, but there's no way she'd do anything that would risk the baby. You saw her last time, you know she wouldn't."

Cole squeezed her hand at the mention of last time. Jane herself lowered her eyes when they stung with tears. A gentle kiss to her temple soothed them away.

"My appointment with you is tomorrow. You can reassure us both that everything still looks good." Jane lifted her head back up, satisfied the sting of tears was gone. "I would be most comforted by your reassurance."

Tom opened his mouth to speak, but Jane cut him off before he could utter a word. "Now with that last bit of respect to my doctor, talk of the baby is no longer allowed. There are, after all, far more interesting things to discuss. Leanne has just arrived in town for the first time in years. I'm quite certain you boys wouldn't balk at paying her little mind."

"I sure wouldn't." Tommy wagged his brows.

Mike rolled his eyes, but jumped right into the conversation. "Would you care explaining how it is you know Cole? All Jane has told us is that you're an 'old friend'."

Jane did a double take. "Wait. Leanne has been at your hotel all afternoon and you didn't bother to ask her that question?"

"Well, there was a tour of the hotel. She took time to get settled in and then…" Mike turned beet red up to his ears. After an uneasy glance toward Daisy, he cleared his throat.

Leanne twisted a lock of hair around her finger. "He spent a bit of time trying to appease some of the guests as I took a lovely, refreshing dip under the waterfall."

"Yeah." Mike grimaced, though a hint of a smile lingered on his features.

Jane's jaw dropped. Laughter bubbled up as the meaning of Leanne's sly look crept in. "Leanne! Did you get into the water without clothes?"

"Not a stitch." Leanne bit her lip, her reticent look failing when she winked.

Jane's laughter grew at the look on Tom's face. He leaned back to study Leanne from top to bottom. After another turn with the same look, he rubbed his hand over his face with a sigh.

"And to answer your question, Mike, I was once under contract at Cole's place. Wasn't I?" Leanne winked at Cole. All three brothers leaned forward at that news. "That is, I was until I left to open my own establishment in Denver—one of a more high-class variety than Cole's."

"You run a whorehouse?" Nick's brow rose. "And before that you worked for Cole?"

"No wonder Graham keeps looking over here," Mike muttered. "Tell me you didn't…"

"Hell no," Cole snapped. He cleared his throat at his own abrupt cutoff at the suggestion. "Who'd ya leave in charge while you're gone?"

"Tammy. She's been with me the longest." Leanne leaned back in her chair, stretching luxuriously. "She knows how I like things—handled."

Tommy eyed her. "So—how *do* you like things handled?"

"Why." Leanne leaned toward him. "With a *firm hand* of course."

Jane burst into laughter when all three of her brothers shifted in their chairs. Daisy's look had darkened, but Jane couldn't contain her laughter anyway. This was going to be a long, and rather interesting, visit.

Leanne leaned over toward Jane when the food arrived. "Is it cruel, Jane?"

"Perhaps." Jane shrugged. "Then again, a little cruel can be fun."

"Depends on the payoff."

*Time wasted is existence;
used is life.
-Edward Young*

Daisy had been subdued most of Jane's appointment. She wrapped up the exam with a pat to Jane's knee. "How often are you still getting sick?"

Jane hopped off the table to gather her petticoats. "Every morning, of course. That's always when I've gone hours without drinking any tea. Otherwise, as long as I have some tea about every hour I do fairly well."

"Define 'fairly well'."

"Maybe once more during the day depending on what I'm doing, but that isn't every day." Jane straightened her skirt over the petticoats. "If I do happen to get sick, I always immediately drink two cups of tea as quick as I'm able."

Daisy perched on the edge of the exam table beside Jane. "I'm glad you're following the instructions I gave you. I have to say you're looking much better, and have even put some weight on. How much are you eating now?"

"I stopped wearing the corset as you'd suggested, and all of my clothes are starting to feel tight. I believe I am definitely gaining weight." Jane pondered her eating habits of late. "I still manage one fairly good meal during the day. I do try to get at least some food at least three other times during the day. It's never much, only whatever I can stomach—but none of Cora's greens. I can't even go near the restaurant if she's cooking greens."

Daisy chuckled. "Every pregnant woman I've treated has had one thing at least that she couldn't stomach, even without your issues."

"So I've heard. Was there anything else?"

"Any further bleeding?"

"No, thank goodness. None that I've seen. Nothing aside from my constantly turning stomach and exhaustion."

"Exhaustion?"

"I fell asleep standing up yesterday." Jane laughed when Daisy did. "Granted it was after I'd spent my morning relaxing with Cole, but to fall asleep standing upright is definitely not something I ever imagined. I must admit, happy as I am to be pregnant, I'm not happy with what it's doing to me. I don't care for feeling weak and tired—unable to do everything I want to. Excuse me for sounding every bit a petulant child."

"You don't have to apologize to me. You're not the first pregnant woman with these same complaints."

"As long as I do not end up restricted to lying in bed all day, I might escape this pregnancy with a measure of sanity. So, are you going to keep me sane today?"

Daisy squeezed her hand briefly. Before she spoke, she opened the door. "Come on in, Cole. I was about to let Jane out of here, and I'm sure you'd like to hear what I have to say."

Cole didn't hesitate. In moments he stood at Jane's side. The warmth of his hand immediately settled on the small of her back. "There a problem?"

"Not at all." Daisy smiled between them. "Everything looks like it's progressing well. Outside of the constant nausea she feels, Jane appears healthy. Now that she's gaining weight, I'm quite pleased."

Jane's sigh of relief was echoed by Cole. "You still wanna see her every week?"

"Yes. Until you are able to make it through a full week without getting sick I would like to continue keeping an eye on things. Especially given your history. How far along do you think you were last time, Jane?"

As always, a lump lodged firm in Jane's throat at the mention of her last pregnancy. She lowered her gaze, gathering comfort from Cole's proximity. "I'm not entirely certain."

"You remember everything," Cole muttered.

He wasn't wrong. She did remember, and knew she had to have become pregnant their first time, for she'd obtained protection after that. "You're right, I do. I got pregnant in June, lost the baby in October. So three and a half, maybe four months. It was so different back then. I'd had no signs at all. No illness, no…"

"You're much sicker this time." Daisy studied her, but her tone remained gentle. "And though your life is chaotic, you haven't been in a train accident nor are you and Cole…"

"Doing what we do second best," Cole chuckled.

At Daisy's quizzical look, Jane laughed outright. "He means fighting. What we do best is—well—not fighting."

Daisy shook her head. "Impossible. Either way, you're doing everything you can to help move this one along healthy. You're further along now. You are improving, and that is a good sign. Call me over-cautious."

"No. I won't do that. I appreciate it. We both do."

"You're free to go. I'll see you next week."

"Thank you." Jane wrapped her arm around Cole's waist as they left the exam room.

Cole leaned closer. "Feel better?"

"Do you?"

"Yeah."

"God, because I do as well." She peeked at him through her lashes. "And I still have half an hour before I am to meet Kat and Leanne for tea."

"Half an hour, eh?"

"A whole thirty minutes. Eighteen hundred seconds. Considering it only takes two hundred and seventy-eight for both of us to be happy, that adds up to six times the happy."

"I like those numbers."

"Oh, so do I."

"You're feeling all right?"

"For the moment, and you're wasting precious seconds." She squealed when he scooped her up and ran into the saloon fast enough she had to hold on tight. With every step, she pulled at his tie, his buttons, anything to move them along faster.

He kicked the door to their room closed behind him and wasted no time joining her in removing the layers of clothes between them. They collapsed into bed together, enjoying every remaining sixteen hundred and twenty seconds.

Jane buried her fingers in his hair as the clock chimed on the wall. She giggled. "We went well over our time. I'm now officially late."

"Do ya care?"

"Goodness, no." She whispered as his lips trailed along her neck. "But I am going to need more tea soon."

"Soon." He nipped her ear, his warm chuckle trembling along her body. "Not now?"

Humming, she pulled him into a deep kiss. Her body arched into his eagerly.

"How many seconds?"

"Two hundred seventy-eight."

"One…two…three…"

Counting quietly, they were lost in moments, enjoying the peace in the way they knew best until they lost count again.

Reality edged its way into their bliss with murmurs of discontent from downstairs. An angry bellow from Tom pulled them both out of their embrace. They turned their gazes toward the door almost in synch.

Tommy's next yell was undeniably clear. "What do you mean, *missing*?"

"Damn," the muttered simultaneously.

She sighed deep. "Hopefully tonight I'll feel well enough to continue this. We'd better find out what he's going on about."

"And you better get your tea."

"Yes, sir."

"I'll deal with Tom. You get your tea and go see Kathy and Leanne before they stir up trouble without you. I know you'd hate to miss out."

"You're not wrong." She slipped from the bed to get dressed. "I would hate to miss out on stirring up a little trouble."

He pinched her ass before she could finish throwing her chemise on.

"You behave! Tom is still ranting—it must be something important."

"Yes ma'am."

Without the complication of the corset, she dressed quicker than usual. She kept an eye on the clock as she buttoned the shoes fast as she dared lest she rip off a button. With a small sigh she stood, only to find herself swept up in his arms.

"*Iris!*" Tommy's shout delated the gratification of their kiss.

She patted Cole's chest. After a bad attempt to keep her pout hidden. "Go. Figure it out. I promise to remain uninvolved even if I am dying of curiosity. I know you will tell me if it's serious enough to warrant some stress on my part."

"I get to decide?"

"Colton James."

"Yeah, yeah. I'll tell you if it's big." He swiped a kiss on his way to the door.

Jane took a deep breath as if it would help tamp down the high level of curiosity on her part. Eye on the clock, she waited a full minute before following him. She took care to avoid anyone that might tell her what was going on. Even so, on her way through the saloon she heard hints of the heavy discussion happening in the storeroom.

It took all of her effort to push aside her concern and head to the depot as promised. Laughter hit her ears through the open window of the depot before she pushed open the door to the back room.

"There you are." Kat waved to a chair. "We've been waiting on you. I have your tea ready for you and everything—where *have* you been?"

"Getting a good report from Daisy." Jane poured herself some tea. "And then we were celebrating the good report."

"I must say I'm surprised to see you at all if that's the case." Leanne winked.

"Cole can be quite thorough in a short amount of time." Jane sipped her tea, the past hour enough to keep her grin in place. "Believe me—you'd be surprised how little time we both need to walk away satisfied."

"Would the lot of ya keep it down?" Norman popped his head in the doorway. "I do got customers that don't like hearin' your kind of talk."

"Don't you worry yourself, Norman. Kat only talks about you when we don't have an audience. I don't have the same level of decorum, however. Besides, Cole likes being bragged about. It bolsters his reputation."

Kat smirked. "He doesn't need any help with that."

"He certainly doesn't," agreed Leanne. "But he likes it anyway. Now you've left me curious. Just how much time do you need, Jane?"

"Two hundred and seventy-eight seconds—he's very, very good, and thorough." Jane pinched her lips together when Norman grumbled. The door between the depot office and back room slammed shut. "Then again, that is only leaving us merely satisfied. Completely satiated takes much more time."

"The two of you could lock yourselves in a room for a week and not be satiated." Kat snorted. "I know—you've tried."

"All that time in Denver locked in our room didn't do much to help." Jane released an overdramatic sigh. "It's a real problem, believe me."

"You poor baby." Leanne patted her arm. A fake pout puffed her lips.

"I know, I know. It's a tragedy. Fortunately, I don't mind working to correct it as often as possible."

"That little game you played on him at the Bonne Nuit didn't help, either." Leanne wagged a finger at Jane. "I swear I've never seen Cole's head spin quite so much as he did when you were teasing. It was so much fun to watch."

"I really wish I could have seen that." Kat's gaze drifted off. "Jane showed me the outfit she wore, but refused to put it on."

Leanne's brow rose. "Was Cole close by?"

"Yes, he was," Kat admitted.

"Then I'm sure that's why." Leanne chuckled. "It wouldn't have stayed on long."

Jane sipped her tea, making a vital attempt to appear innocent. "That isn't entirely true. I do possess a modicum of self-control when it's required."

Leanne whispered a loud aside to Kat, "Does she?"

"Not a bit," Kat asserted.

"Katherine!"

Leanne burst into laughter until they all burst into giggles. The end result of which was Norman popping his head through the door to glare at them again. Leanne cleared her throat and straightened, a small attempt to appear properly behaved again. "Would you mind telling me the story on those drooling boys, Jane?"

Kat's brow furrowed. "Drooling boys?"

"Thomas, Michael, and Nick." Jane sighed. "You were late to supper last night so you missed the show. Leanne had all their attention—yes, even Mike."

"What about Daisy?"

"She was right there." Jane shook her head. Men were so obtuse sometimes. "What's there to know? All three of them were Clara's brothers. They're good men. Tom is like me in male form—so even less tact. Nick is—particular and wounded, but all over a good man. Michael…"

Leanne leaned back, biting her lip in thought. "He and Daisy taking advantage of their feelings?"

"They're in denial of their feelings." Jane twirled her empty cup on the saucer. "They've been making eyes at each other practically since Mike got to town. For some reason Mike isn't making his move to officially court her, or bed her, or anything."

"And Daisy, because of almost four years as a whore, is exceptionally careful about how she behaves these days." Kat swept her arm with a sweet cake still in hand toward the direction of town. "No one will ever forget what she was, but she's trying to be the opposite, so she won't make the advance either."

"In other words, they need a little push. I might be willing to help with that. The other two, though." Leanne eyed Jane. "Free game?"

"If you'd care to play, I suppose." Jane chuckled. "I don't have the heart to tell them myself you aren't…"

Leanne snorted. "You haven't told them? I'm guessing you've told Kat?"

"Yes. Katherine knows the nickname I gave you." Jane grabbed a sweet cake of her own. "Other than her and Cole,

I've kept certain secrets very well. Despite the common belief that I cannot keep a secret, I'm quite good at it."

"Sure you are." Kat rolled her eyes. "You're terrible at it."

Jane could hardly contain her laughter. So many people still had no idea of her marriage to Cole, Kat included. Jane knew she'd feel awful guilty about it eventually, for the moment it remained fun.

Leanne leaned back in her chair. A spoon slid back and forth between her fingers. A wicked smirk had taken residence on her visage. "If they don't know of my high esteem as the Virgin Madam, this could be even more fun. If you don't mind, Jane."

"Please. They need to get messed with, and Mike needs a good shove toward Daisy—they all enjoy picking on me far too much. It's about time they got some back." Jane thought of a caveat to add. "As long as you aren't out to break hearts, busting a couple of egos won't bother me."

"I'll have to consider my options." Leanne tapped her chin. "I do hope you'll both help me plan a way to mess with those boys."

Katherine laughed. "Are you kidding? Of course we will!"

"Excellent." Leanne turned her attention back to Jane. "While I'm pondering options, I'm dying to hear how Jane came to the conclusion that it only takes two hundred and seventy-eight seconds."

Jane poured another glass of tea, trying desperately to cover her grin. "I'm not sure it's a story even you would be able to bear hearing, Leanne."

"Now you must tell it," Leanne protested.

Kat piped in, "I'm with her, Jane. You'd best tell."

"Well." Jane leaned in conspiratorially. "You know those clocks Cora has for sale in the store? Well, Cole and I were back in that corner…"

Truth is generally the best vindication against slander.
—Abraham Lincoln

Jane walked down the aisle between the pews with Reverend Greene. After her tea with Leanne and Kat, she still hadn't heard word from Cole or Tom. The mere knowledge that something had happened and she remained uninformed worked her already taut nerves.

"Are you certain you want to do this?" Reverend Green gestured toward the front pew. "I'm sure it can be delayed or avoided completely with very little effort."

"What? Oh, no." Jane shook the distracting thoughts from her head. "That isn't it. I'm afraid my mind is in many directions at the moment. I know this is the right thing to do. Marshal Lewis means me no harm. Though revealing the truth to him is nerve-wracking, I must trust my instincts. Based on his recent behavior toward me, this is the right thing to do."

"As well as the location you chose."

"Yes. Thank you for allowing me use of the church for this meeting. It feels safe—a proper sanctuary."

"As always, I'm happy to help." Reverend Green squeezed her shaking hands. "When you told me the purpose I couldn't deny the request."

"I can only pray it's not a mistake. I fear what will happen when I speak the truth."

"John eight, thirty-two."

"'And ye shall know the truth, and the truth shall make you free'."

"Believe the words."

"The words I believe most now are Psalms one-nineteen, verses twenty-nine and thirty," she admitted.

"Go ahead. I won't say it for you, you must say it. Believe it as you do every time you recite it to me."

"'Remove me from the way of lying; and grant me thy law graciously. I have chosen the way of truth: thy judgments have I laid before me'." She took a shaky breath to release more of the tension. "I have tried, and that's why I feel I must do this."

"And as with every step you've taken that was made with your true heart, you won't regret it."

"I know you're right." Footsteps pulled her from the conversation. She rose when Lewis stepped through the door. "Marshal Lewis."

Reverend Green rose as well. "I'll leave you to your solitude, Jane. Remember your words and your heart."

"Thank you, Reverend." Jane moved to the nearest window. Gaze on the meadow, she ran the Psalms over and over in her head like a mantra to calm her.

"I would ask you both to remember this is a sanctuary." Reverend Green lingered by the door. "You are both protected and only God will hear and know the truth."

"Thank you," Marshal Lewis said. When the door shut, his footsteps drew close to her.

Jane breathed out a long, slow breath. Before he could say a word, she blurted, "What is your name?"

"I beg your pardon?"

She turned so she might meet his gaze. The kindness and lack of judgement she found didn't fully ease her nerves. Damn Cole for passing his nerves onto her. "If I am to do this, it must be as two people talking—though I dare not call us friends. If I were to call you Marshal Lewis it would be more like an inquisition. What is your name?"

"Alfred."

"Thank you." She returned to the pew she'd abandoned on his arrival. Her gaze drifted to the window while she contemplated how to start. For all the words she had, all the things to tell, where to start? Her head screamed at her to start at the beginning, but how could she know what beginning would satisfy him.

Alfred cleared his throat in the lingering silence. "Would you prefer for me to start with a question?"

"It would probably be best."

"Are you Clara Young?"

"No."

"Were you?"

She kept her gaze focused on the heat-dried flowers bending in the breeze. These things were so difficult to explain to people that didn't understand—and she wasn't sure anyone truly could. "Maybe this was a mistake."

"How so?"

"No one who has never had amnesia can understand. No one will ever understand."

"Try."

She turned to face him. "I am not, nor have I ever been Clara Young. Not to my recollection. I suppose the correct way to explain is that this body once housed her soul, and still contains some small fragments of her mind."

"Fragments?"

"Bits and pieces that emerge into my life without me asking for them. A few scattered memories. Facts that emerge like the middles names of her brothers. Or speaking French."

"And?"

"Occasional feelings. I love the Young boys as brothers, but don't remember them, I don't remember growing up with them. I can't laugh at their shared memories. I never grew to love Daniel as she did, though he's a good man. The facts I do have came from her letters. All I do have are a few fleeting memories, pieces of a life I lay no claim to, but have affected my life more deeply than you can imagine."

"You've tried to remember."

"Yes." She looked down at her hands. "I've also feared remembering. Based on what I've learned of Clara…I like my life. It isn't perfect, but it is mine."

"I read all of the letters. You remember none of it?"

"No. I learned of her deeds in the same fashion you have learned them. Among my few memories is the memory of being pushed off a train shortly before I came to wake in Dominion Falls, meeting Clara's former husband, and riding in a stagecoach to what I assume was Clara's first traverse to Utah."

Not once did his gaze leave her. Nothing but curiosity, and she dared say concern, lingered in his expression. "What is it like to not remember?"

"Infuriating. Frightening. Lonely." She stared over his shoulder into the empty past, the gaping hole that still ached every day. "When I woke here in Dominion Falls I had a head full of thoughts and words that were not my own. I had a full sense of my faculties, I knew everything but who I was, which I suppose was appropriate considering how not even Clara was herself for seven years prior."

He remained silent, allowing her to continue without interruption.

"I could remember the words of Plato, Socrates, Hugo, Poe—but not my own. I had no home, no family, I truly had nothing but words. I was in a world completely foreign to me. I had the words and skills to navigate through it—but you would be surprised how much of life revolves around your sense of self."

She wiped a tear to gather herself. "I had to learn how to become."

In the silence, he tilted his head quizzically. "Become what?"

"Just to become." She met his eyes. "I awoke nothing. No one. Piece by piece I built a life. I learned who I was. I formed friendships, caused plenty of scandal, created—and suffered—animosity. I found love as well as pain, grief, and great joy. I found it all. I became."

"Alive."

"Yes. I suppose so." She smiled at his offered word. "I became alive. I became me. Then, David arrived."

"And recognized you."

"The first clue into a past I wasn't sure I cared to remember any longer—I was rather enjoying being who I was and had become content to leave the past where it was.

Learning her name had little effect on me, it only bolstered me further to become my own person."

"When did you begin to learn the truth of Clara?"

She turned her attention back to the flowers outside. "When Michael arrived. I learned of her rape and pregnancy, and that she had left David with the full knowledge that the child could be his. I hated her. I was disgusted by her."

"Yet you still didn't know everything."

"No," she whispered. "It wasn't until *he* returned to town."

"Mr. Bingham."

"He'd been in town on a previous occasion, dressed as a cowboy. Rough, crude, and threatening. He frightened me, but then with the Renegade attacks I forgot about him until he returned looking terribly different. He spoke French that I somehow understood—and he had Jesse. The moment that boy stepped off the stagecoach, something in my soul broke."

"Broke?"

"I knew somewhere inside me that he was Clara and David's boy, my boy. I tried to deny it, because I couldn't dream that she would keep him from David for so long. I was thrilled he was there, terrified of what it meant, and impossibly more disgusted with Clara."

Her lips billowed at the force of the breath she blew out. "I wanted to save Jesse. I had no idea who Alan was, but he frightened me something awful. I wanted the child safe, returned to his father."

"His father, not you?"

"I did not feel I deserved to be part of his life after what Clara had done. I felt I had to know exactly what she'd done so that I could make right the horrible wrongs she'd done to

David. I had no idea the depth of her horrible wrongs. I couldn't begin to know until Alan told me on the train—when he took Arthur and myself."

"What did he tell you?"

"Not much, really. He said I'd told him to kill the child. He said I'd caused Mr. Querney's death by my actions, but was careful not to say explicitly that I'd pushed him."

"You believe he pushed Mr. Querney in front of the train?"

"I believe so, but Clara's actions led to his death. I believe she tried to tell Mr. Querney the truth and Alan wouldn't allow it." She shook her head, her eyes drifting closed at the first sting of tears. "All of the suffering the day he took Arthur and I; Guy's murder, Al being shot, Arthur's kidnapping—all of it happened because of Clara. Because she was stupid and ignorant, a fool who let herself get involved with a monster"

"So you blamed yourself."

"Indirectly, yes. I did all that I could to save those children, exacerbating my own injury in the process. Risking…" She trailed off, refusing to reveal the truth of her first pregnancy. It was irrelevant to the story. "It was by chance that I remembered the trunk when I saw it in the depot's abandoned luggage cage."

She opened her eyes again to face him. "It took months for me to piece together the clues left in the trunk and the Poe book, and by the time I did and Cole went to Yankton for the letters, it was too late. I would never know the truth—because you had been alerted, as well as the judge and the Pinot's. As we now know Alan himself urged Mr. Krenshaw to alert you all."

"The trial."

"Which we also know was rigged from the start. I had no idea Alan had gotten to Jackson, I simply assumed Jackson hated me for my initial rejection of him, as well as his continued problems in the town."

"I was not bribed," he pointed out.

"I never claimed you were. You didn't need to be, the judge was the only one who needed his pockets greased since I waived my right to jury. You, you had a keen eye on justice, and that was all they needed from you."

"Your testimony."

"I told the truth as I knew it." She wiped a tear that betrayed the way her insides were shaking by bringing the events back up again. Speaking of her death always rattled her to her soul. "I meant what I said, I was ready to accept my fate."

"I must ask." His brow furrowed. "How did you live through it?"

A tricky question to answer without causing trouble for others. Rather than risk, she told the truth as she still did not fully understand how the mix of events worked to save her. "I cannot say for certain. I did not ask to be saved, make no mistake. When I walked up those stairs I was terrified, but I was prepared. Amnesia is not a defense, I never wanted it to be. I don't know how I lived—how I was spared. All I do know is when I woke up in that coffin—"

"You were in a coffin?" His eyes widened. "I thought they knew you were alive shortly after the fact."

"No. I had been nailed into a coffin inside Graham's undertaker's office. I woke in the dark—" Her voice squeaked unwillingly, a deep shudder running through her.

"No voice, nailed in, barely able to move. Unable to scream. Weak as could be. I'd been in there at least a day, I believe. I scared the dickens out of Graham by waking him pounding on the coffin."

"They would have buried you."

Her throat shut tight, emotion stuffing her nose, burning her eyes. For the first time in a while she felt the cold grasp of death as though it were yesterday. "Yes. But for the flash freeze the day before my hanging that meant they could not dig the grave. Thankfully Graham didn't embalm the dead then as he does now."

"I…"

"I was hanged, make no mistake. Do not doubt. My larynx was nearly crushed. I experienced difficulty with my vision for months after. It was every bit real. I do not know how I was spared." She tore her gaze from his to focus on the swirls in a pane of glass. She prayed the pattern would soothe the fresh upset to her soul. "I did all I could in the months before my hanging to live honestly—to a fault I remained true to who I was. I hated the deception of living after my death, but I also knew there was no other way to get Alan to pay for his crimes."

She rubbed her arms to stem the chill of death that lingered in her memory. "We came up with a foolish plan, one that Michael was smart enough to see as foolish, and thus he called in the cavalry. Thomas, Nick, and Charles saved my life and Cole's—and then saw to bringing Alan in for justice."

"Or revenge?"

"Alan was destined to die, you've received innumerable evidences of his crimes. You know that in the wilds of the west the law of the land can often win over law itself.

Colorado remains without statehood. Some men don't even recognize you as law. Alan was an escaped criminal when he was shot, so his shooting was justified."

"I thought you would be honest with me."

"That is honest." Calmer now, Jane turned to face him again. She knew the question that was coming, and not one soul but herself and Nick knew the truth of it. Who had truly killed Alan in that barn. Not even Cole knew for certain.

"Did you take the law in your own hands? Did you kill Alan?"

She smiled, her brow quirked. "You have a confession for his death."

"You came here—"

"I came here today to tell you the truth about Clara and myself. I can only tell you that I am not the person that did the crimes Clara was accused of and hanged for. I am not even the same woman you saw hanged and declared dead."

"Clara was good at deception."

"Socrates once said 'The greatest way to live with honor in this world is to be what we pretend to be'. I have done all I could to live a life of honor—to be what I have claimed to be since I first came to be. You have seen all the evidence of the life I live now. I am trying to live with honor—and even my public indecency is only in the eyes of the beholder."

"Do you feel it absolves you of the crimes?"

"I didn't commit them, but I will forever carry the memory—no, the burden—of what her mistakes and ignorance led to. I use them to guide me so that I might live a life she never could. For the rest of my life I will carry the shame of her crimes and mistakes. I will remember how cold death's grip is, and it will forever influence every thought and decision I make. There will not be a day I don't think of Clara."

"Jane!" The door burst open at Cole's yell. He rushed in with Tommy right behind him. "Marshal Lewis, good. You're still here."

"We weren't finished," Jane pointed out.

"Sorry." Panic and anger lined Cole's features in a way she'd not seen since the fire. "I told you I'd let you know if it was important."

Jane rose slow as molasses. After all the talk of her death, her emotions were too raw for too much, but she couldn't ignore it. "Cole. What is it? What's happened?"

Tommy spoke first, "It's gone Lou. I can't account for how."

Panic raced through her until she swore her heart stopped beating. "What's gone?"

Cole gripped her shoulders. "Sit."

"No." The word sounded weak to her ears. Tears threatened to spill again.

"Please."

Jane dropped back into the pew as slow as she'd stood. When he knelt before her, she couldn't tear her gaze away. "Please tell me."

"The money. All our earnings and winnings. The safe is cleaned out."

Alfred rose while Jane herself remained frozen. "How much?"

"Almost three thousand," Tommy said quietly. "We let it build all month. We're due to pay on our creditors and investors in a couple of days, that's when it's always the highest."

"W-who?" Jane found her voice, but still couldn't blink. Each word squeaked as she tried to regain her senses. "Who would do that to us? Which one was it? Who?"

Cole's grip on her arms remained tight. "We can't figure it."

Jane took several deep, ragged breaths. The oxygen supply seemed to dwindle no matter how deep she took breath in. She shook her head, ignoring Tom and Alfred's nearby conversation. "No. Not now. This isn't happening."

"I'm taking the marshal over," Tommy spoke louder again. "We'll talk to everyone."

"No," she whispered. She found her feet and began to pace. "That's it. It's over. We can't—how? Oh heavens. *How*?"

Cole pulled her close when she collapsed against him. While she sobbed, he held her tight. The door closed signaling Tommy and Alfred's departure. Cole kissed the top of her head. "We'll figure it. We always do."

"Who would do this? Why?"

"I don't know, but Tommy'll figure it out."

Tommy. Why would Tommy figure it out? She was supposed to be so damned smart, she was supposed to know their staff. All the distractions she'd allowed in the way of her own clear head in recent months had to stop. She had to take control again.

Cole stumbled back when she shoved him off. "Jane?"

She spun on her heel, storming from the church. Every step toward town she felt was step back into herself. When Cole's hand grasped her arm and spun her, she had to fight the urge to slap him.

"Jane? What the hell are you doing?"

"I'm going back to find answers."

"You're too upset. Tommy and the marshal will handle it."

"I'm tired of leaving it up to everyone else. I'm pregnant, not *dead*."

To Be

Continued...

In Book 6 of the
Dominion Falls Series

Home

Signal

About the Author

Sarah Cass, author of over twenty novels in 4 series, is devoted to giving her readers well-crafted, emotional stories, with depth to even her secondary characters—to give readers a full world to explore. Stories that explore not only the labyrinths of the heart, but the nightmares of the soul. A RONE finalist, she is also owner and creator of Redefining Perfect. By day, she's a nurse, a mother, wife and cat-mom to 4 mischievous beasts. By night she crafts stories that take her across centuries. From the old west of Dominion Falls, to the small town of Lake Point for the holidays, and even into the paranormal land of Shifters and Magic in The Tribe. She loves hearing from her readers. Visit her at www.authorsarahcass.com

Other Books in
The Dominion Falls Series

Independent Brake
Changing Tracks
Derailed
Dark Territory
Green Eye
Home Signal
Red Zone

Coming Soon in
The Dominion Falls Series

Dust Raiser
Chase the Red
Blizzard Lights
Dead Man's Switch
Bird Cage
A Highball Arrangement
Douse the Glim
Blood
Grave Digger
Bad Order

Books by Sarah Cass
The Tribe Series
The Tribe
The Wolf
The Chief
The Raven
The Lake Point Series
Santa, Maybe
Deep-Fried Sweethearts
Stalled Independence
Witch Way
A Thorough Thanksgiving
Eve's New Year
Heartstrings & Hockey Pucks
Luck of the Cowgirl
Stars, Stripes & Motorbikes
Free Falling
Love for Hire
Haunted Hearts
Stand Alone Novels
Masked Hearts
Leap